That Fateful Lightning

Lightning

A Novel of the Civil War

By

Celia Hayes

That Fateful Lightning

ISBN-13 978-0-9897824-1-8
ISBN-10 0-9897824-1-7

Printed in the United States of America.

Original cover art by Covers Girl

Geron & Associates
A Division of Watercress Press.
2023

Dedication and Appreciation

This fictional exploration of the 19th century abolitionist movement in the United States, and the nearly-forgotten effort by the volunteers of the US Sanitary Commission is dedicated with respect to that fearless body of women who formed the backbone of those dual efforts. Some of them appear as characters in these pages. Others just left written accounts, which were part of my research.

To Mary Bickerdyke, Mary Jane Safford, Mary Ashton Rice Livermore, Amy Hopper Gibbons, Rebecca Pomroy, Annie P. Erving, and others who in their post-war reminiscences wished to be anonymous. They served with patriotic and loving heroism, meeting challenges which make 21st century professional feminists look like spoiled, bitter, man-hating snowflakes in comparison.

Celia Hayes,
San Antonio, December 2023

Contents

Chapter 1 – Look Away, Dixie's Land..1

Chapter 2 – The Glory of the Morning.. 11

Chapter 3 – Not a Man Shall Be a Slave 24

Chapter 4 – Bring the Jubilee 47

Chapter 5 – And Pay the Reckoning on the Nail............................... 70

Chapter 6 – The Stars Above in Heaven 90

Chapter 7 - We Loved Each Other Then, Lorena 111

Chapter 8 – Our Hearts Will Soon Lie Low 130

Chapter 9 – His Torch is at Thy Temple Door 141

Chapter 10 – Sifting Out the Hearts of Men 157

Chapter 11 – Trampling Out the Vintage... 169

Chapter 12 – Beneath the Starry Flag 183

Chapter 13 – Rally From the Hillside, Gather From the Plain........ 202

Chapter 14 - The Watch Fires of a Hundred Circling Camps.......... 218

Chapter 15 - Our Jimmy Has Gone For to Live in a Tent................ 239

Chapter 16 - Soft Falls the Dew on the Face of the Dead 257

Chapter 17 – Say Goodbye to Goober Peas...................................... 276

Chapter 18 - Treason Fled Before Us... 295

Chapter 19 - Just Before the Battle, Mother.................................... 312

Chapter 20 – Hurrah, Hurrah, The Flag That Makes You Free...... 330

Notes.. 356

Contents

Chapter 1 – Look Away, Dixie's Land
March, 1842 – Boston, Massachusetts

A week after the reading of her last surviving brother's will, Minerva "Minnie" Templeton Vining sat in the old-fashioned parlor of her father's tall house on Beacon Street with her sister-in-law Annabelle, while an errant spring breeze stirred the curtains ... as well as the festoons of black crepe which adorned the façade of the Vining mansion. Narrow windows of the austere neo-classical design which had been the height of architectural fashion early in the century now overlooked the broad avenue and leafy avenues and meadows of the Common and the boggy marsh beyond. The room within was furnished in the old manner; chairs, tables and shelves made in the austere style of two generations past, of fine polished woods and sparingly ornamented. The late Lycurgus Agrippa Vining had resisted any change to the mansion which he had ruled as absolute dictator for half a century. The paintings and portraits, blue and white China trade porcelain, ranks of books in solid leather bindings, somber dark-red brocade upholstery, and old-fashioned crewel-embroidered curtains testified equally to the wealth and pride of the family, and their magnificent disinclination to follow mere fashion, thereby wasting any portion of that wealth on transiently popular fripperies.

"Your fathers' house and a substantial income are now yours to control absolutely!" Annabelle, Minnie's sister-in-law and dearest friend marveled, as she added sugar to the cup of tea. Minnie had poured the tea from a silver pot which was one of the family's treasured possessions, coming as it had from the workshop of the noted Boston silver artisan, Paul Revere. In one of the account books in the old Judge's study and library was preserved a bill made out in Revere's own spidery handwriting, for that very teapot and a dozen silver spoons to be adorned with acorns and oak leaves.

"Indeed," Minnie set down the teapot with a gentle clinking sound and took up her own refreshed cup. She was a confirmed spinster, early in her fourth decade. A lively and energetic woman, she appeared at least ten years younger. She was a woman of decidedly firm opinions, yet attractive to the eye for all of that, at least to those who entertained a taste for fine-boned features, and arresting blue-grey eyes, animated by a formidable and unsparing intelligence. "I knew that Cousin Peter might be named my trustee, with Virgil now gone to his own heavenly reward, and Pindar as well – but Cousin Peter is too sensible a man and of too advanced an age to attempt any thought of treating with me as if I were a silly child in need of correction and protection. Virgil was so overbearing! He meant well, but he was so contemptuous of female capabilities, in spite of my providing every evidence to the contrary!"

Four brothers Minnie had once, all named for classical scholars or statesmen: Virgil, Horace, Leander the firstborn, who had only lived to the age of seventeen and died before Minnie was born, and Pindar the scholar, who had died of a sudden fit of apoplexy in mid-lecture in his university class some five years previously. It was a family tradition, that affectation in classical names. Now Minnie had outlived all her brothers, leaving her the sole heir of her family.

"I should say not!" Annabelle Vining chuckled. She was fair, and looked younger than her age; her pale, silver-gilt hair was piled in complicated loops and curls. She was a slender woman of the same age as Minnie; like Minnie, garbed in the darkest black of mourning. "One might very well try to rope and ride one of those wild bison creatures of the plains. Horace spun me such a tale of the President of Texas shooting one of those dreadful beasts in the streets of the capitol of that benighted place!" The humor briefly departed from Annabelle's pleasant countenance. They had been friends since their earliest childhood, indulged by their parents, friends of the heart, as well as of marital and distant blood connections. Annabelle was a Saltinstall, a cousin of that family, which counted for much in Boston.

"My brother had many tales to tell of his travels," Minnie acknowledged, although she held deep in her heart the one deathbed secret which she had never revealed to anyone but her late brother Virgil and the family lawyer, who had been sworn to secrecy. She would take Horace's confession to her own grave, rather than distress Annabelle by revealing it. Annabelle was his wife in the eyes of the law and of Boston. *Telling the absolute truth can often be a brutal cruelty,*" her father, Judge Vining was wont to say. "*Consider well the costs of relieving your own conscience, Minerva, if that cost comes at the expense of another's peace of mind and happiness.*"

Minnie never said a word to her sister-in-law, about that low-bred woman in farthest Texas, the one who had cohabitated with her youngest brother and bred four nasty brats with him, or perhaps with some other man, no matter what her brother claimed was a proper marriage in that benighted place. Consumption took Horace painfully, on his final return to the place of his birth. Minnie did not like to think of that even now, or the embarrassing situation which had brought him home for that one last time.

That woman in Texas was a nobody and of no character at all. Annabelle – dear, innocent Annabelle – deserved a measure of peace of mind, if not happiness, in the wake of a marriage-not-marriage to a husband who was never present in Boston but always gone on interminable ocean voyages and travels in a vain attempt to recover his health.

The marriage, at first so promising and encouraged by both families, shriveled up and blew away in the wind after the baby Sophia was born; sweet-tempered, fair Sophia, with the Vining grey eyes and Annabelle's silver-gilt hair. She was called Sophia among the family, and 'Little Wisdom' when she was small. Minnie had been painfully aware of the days of agony that Annabelle endured in giving birth; strangled screams, the hurried visits by the eminent physicians, concerned faces of the midwives, and hours of waiting on the arrival of a living child ... all imprinted on Minnie's memory in colors as vivid as that of the blood on the sheets consigned to the care of the laundresses. Another vivid memory of Annabelle's face, pale and bloodless, when Minnie was finally permitted to visit her dearest friend as a new mother, holding the tiny bundle of the baby Sophia to her breast. *I won't do this again, Minnie, endure that unbearable pain. I will never share his bed again. I care nothing for a woman's duty, not if it means the death of me, and it surely will, the next time.* Minnie agreed; she feared a death in childbed as well. Her own mother, briefly the Judge's second wife, had died so in giving birth to herself, and the Judge's first wife perished of childbed fever after bearing Leander, the first-born.

4

True to her word, Annabelle refused to share a chamber or the marital bed within it, ever again. Horace, frustrated and unwell himself, finally abandoned Boston and took himself off, first to the Caribbean, seeking health in a mild climate, and then to Texas. He found a fleeting restoration of health and spirits there, as well as a degree of social status, and some kind of relief with the company of That Woman, who had already borne him four bastard sons without any more trouble than a sow dropping piglets in a byre.

Good women had such trouble with bearing children ... whereas the other sort seemed to have no trouble at all. That unvoiced fear and the memory of Annabelle's agony haunted Minnie. She had often wondered privately if she would also fare badly in what was supposed to be the main duty of a woman.

"So many tales, indeed," Annabelle smiled, ruefully now, and Minnie wrenched her attention back from those dark alleys of memory and imagination. "I could hardly credit some of those adventures in Texas! You were such an angel, Minnie – nursing Horace through those last awful days. Need I say again how grateful I was for that? It was all such a tangle – our darling Little Wisdom in such difficulty with that baby that she lost. It was all that I could do to nurse Sophia, night and day! I feared so much for her, recalling what I had endured at her birth! Richard was a treasure in her travails, of course, but a husband is not so attentive as a mother would be!"

"It is what we do, my dear – for those whom we love," Minnie replied with some mild resentment. She had served devotedly as a nurse for years; Papa-the-Judge in his last years, Horace upon his final return from Texas, and Virgil in his protracted decline. In her heart of hearts, she was quite thoroughly tired of such duties. Her sister-in-law sighed.

"We do, Minnie," and her expression brightened with genuine curiosity. "And such you did for your dear brothers, as well as your father. Now that you are a spinster of completely independent means what will you do with yourself, and this establishment?"

Minnie set down her teacup and regarded the parlor; hers and hers alone, to do with as she thought fit. This was a heady feeling, and Minnie longed to stretch her wings and soar, soar on the pleasant updraft of a generous income and control over it, after two decades of being bound by obligation to family, to the needs of father and brothers. Papa-the-Judge had held absolute rule over the household in his long lifetime. He was a magnate in the China trade, a minor hero in the Revolution (*a very reluctant one, to hear him tell it in unguarded moments with Cousin Peter*), as well as a respected jurist. If Papa-the-Judge had been stern and exacting as a father, he also wanted and expected the best from his children. She had quietly resented Papa-the-Judge's adamantine control, even as a girl, but never to the point of rebellion. She and the cleverest of her schoolfellows, Mary Ashton Rice had plotted to attend the female seminary in Charleston together. But Papa-the-Judge (*for so she always thought of him*) firmly rejected that notion, as unsuitable for a daughter of his. '*A flock of bluestockings, chattering and flittering – no, my girl, you will remain in this house, and I will see that you are better-educated than any of them,*' he told her when she broached the subject to him.

"A clever woman, your mother," Papa-the-Judge had often said, on those rare occasions when he had been moved to speak of such personal things. "Bold as brass, fearless – she was a spy in our war, Minnie – did I tell you of that?"

"Yes, you did, Papa – often," Minnie had replied.

During his last days on this earth, Papa-the-Judge had often patted her hand, at the conclusion of maundering about in his reminiscences, and promised, "Well, then, Minnie – you are to be well-provided for, my girl, since you aren't inclined to matrimony. Your brother Virgil will be your guardian, then – only fitting as your brother. A sensible man. Have seen too it, y'see. The only intelligent female child of my blood ... the image of your mother. She was a spy, you know. Carried messages for Doctor Warren's network, back in the day when the bloody Lobsterbacks. Bold as brass, although she was only a bit of a child when I first lay eyes on her ... she would want to see you holding to your own independency."

"I know, Papa," Minnie would answer. She knew very well that she was the image of her mother. There was a small, framed portrait painted on ivory in Papa-the-Judge's monumental desk, secreted in one of the small drawers, which Minnie knew the secret to opening. When she was younger, she had often compared the painted features to her own, reflected in the small elaborate glass mirror which hung opposite the window in Papa-the-Judge's study. In any case, Cousin Peter, and others who had known her mother had often commented on the likeness.

No, she would not change the parlor, or the library which had been Papa-the-Judge's and then Virgil's, or even all that much about the house. All too dear and familiar, and now it was all to be hers, to order as she liked, but Minnie felt a restlessness in her. *Perhaps she should change herself now that she was free!* She felt like one of Sophia's cherished pet songbirds, looking out from an elaborate silver cage, to which the door was open, wanting to spread her wings ... yet wondering if she yet dared. *Yes. She did.* Minnie sipped from her own teacup, and then set it down again with a tiny, decisive clink against the saucer.

"I have decided to go traveling," she announced. "Not terribly far, Annabelle! First, a visit to Richmond; Cousin Peter's daughter Susan has invited me. You remember her husband, Ambrose Edmonds? He is in holy orders to a very respectable parish there. They have both written, extending their hospitality, in celebrating the wedding of their oldest daughter to a worthy young man this summer. Lydia, if I recollect. I am of a mind to accept. Would you like to accompany me? I would welcome your companionship and you do recall how we attended Susan on her own wedding."

"How long would you remain away from Boston?" Annabelle regarded Minnie with an anxious expression, and Minnie smiled in a manner calculated to reassure.

"Not terribly long; the length of summer and the wedding festivities and return before winter makes travel even more miserable. It is ..." Minnie sighed. "My dear, I long to escape these walls for a time, and refresh my soul by gazing on new vistas. I beg you to accompany me, for the sake of respectability. And ..." she shot her sister-in-law a severe glance. "It would be energizing for the both of us. We are both allowed considerable freedom as widow and spinster? Why not explore, as far as we are permitted by the strictures of a decent society? Why should we be kept mewed up in our little, tiny parlors, like falcons wearing blinding hoods, when we might soar?"

"Because ..." Annabelle began, irresolutely, and Minnie couldn't keep herself from snorting.

"Because, fiddlesticks! I have a purse and the inclination, and I want to do something other than sit in my parlor, see that Bertha and Jerusha dust the furniture properly and take calls on my at-home day. I want to travel, Annabelle! I want to see the Holy Land, the castles of Germany and the marvels of Spain, as Mr. Irving wrote about them in his *Tales from the Alhambra*! There is a larger world out there, Annabelle! Shouldn't we go and see them, rather than just live as silly simpering angels in the house?" She fixed her sister-in-law with her most ferociously determined expression. As Minnie hoped that she would, Annabelle crumbled.

"Of course, I will accompany you," her sister-in-law yielded with a sigh. "It isn't respectable for you to travel all that way alone. And I will think about the Holy Land and those other foreign places. At least we shall be visiting kin, there in Richmond. But ... have you set a date for traveling? Will I need to pack any winter things in my trunks?"

"Next month, I think," Minnie replied, in secret relief. "I shall have to see to the arrangements, and consult with Cousin Peter, of course. But oh!" she smiled and clasped Annabelle's hand. "It will be such fun! We can make plans over supper. Will you send a message to Richard and Sophia to come and dine with me tonight? I will tell Mrs. Norris, and have Jerusha set three more places."

"But you are still in mourning," Annabelle protested, and Minnie made an unladylike face.

9

"Oh, stuff and nonsense – you are family."

Chapter 2 – The Glory of the Morning

"I'm afraid Cousin Peter is delayed," Annabelle fussed nervously, as she and Minnie waited on the platform of the Lowell Street Station, that magnificent modern temple of commerce on Causeway and Lowell. "If he has fallen ill, or forgotten the day ... I will never forgive myself."

The clamor of the busy station echoed around them; the shriek of steel wheels on rails, the gasp of steam escaping, newsboys shouting their wares. They were to travel to Richmond by gradual stages. They would go all the way by train, escorted by Cousin Peter and Annabelle's son-in-law, Richard Brewer – Sophia's husband. Minnie had impatiently thrown back the black veil that draped her bonnet. A slight breeze from the harbor, wandering tentatively between the pillars which upheld the station roof, and the clattering engines with their burden of railcars, blew the ends of that veil to and fro. She and Annabelle still wore the deep black of mourning, although not the unrelieved shrouds suitable for widows, to Minnie's great relief. She hated looking through a black fog of veil.

"Mother Annabelle, I don't think Mr. Vining would have forgotten something of importance such as this," Richard Brewer patted his mother-in-law's hand. He was brown-haired, square, and solid. Minnie considered him to be a sensible young man, sober beyond his years, yet graced with a puckish sense of humor which somewhat alleviated the solidity of his bearing and his burdens of wealth and privilege.

Minnie's gaze now fell with relief upon a trio of familiar figures, coming along the platform towards their party.

"Look, it is the Reverend Doctor Slocomb and Lolly Bard, accompanying Cousin Peter! Dare I think that the Reverend has come to bid us farewell, or a safe journey? Or is he perhaps bound on a journey likewise? I would relish his company, if so – for his opinions and discourse are always so diverting!"

"I doubt that he can be parted so long from his adoring flock! Especially Mrs. Bard and the other ladies of the parish," Annabelle observed, with a mischievous smile in Minnie's direction. "Perhaps he is making an exception in your case, Minnie! You are, after all, an heiress to no small estate, and the good reverend is yet unwed..."

"Ridiculous!" Minnie snorted. Annabelle would gently tease her about the handsome reverend, a half-decade Minnie's junior, but his waving locks of dark hair already touched with gray, making him look as if he was her equal in years. He was not unpleasing to look upon, nor was Minnie quite without susceptibility to male charms.

The Reverend Slocomb was a man fully in command of those charms; a rugged physique, tall and broad of shoulder, a countenance in which the features of a classic Greek statue mingled appealingly with lively intelligence and charm. A passionate orator and of abolitionist sympathy, his sermons in the pulpit of Beacon Street Congregationalist Church riveted the attention of all listeners, packed closely in the private pews and in the galleries. He had even had a collection of them published, and Minnie had purchased a copy from her allowance, although Virgil waspishly described him as a producer of pretentious windbaggery sufficient to raise a Montgolfier balloon.

Lolly – or Eulalia – Bard, on the other hand, was one of the silliest women of Minnie's acquaintance. Lolly was Minnie's age; short, plump, and still pretty, with round blue eyes in a girlish face, and soft tendrils of light brown hair curling between her cheeks and the brim of her bonnet. She had several children, all grown, and was the widow of a man who had been, as Lolly often insisted, very important in railways. She had settled in Boston after the death of her husband, to be near the home of her oldest son. Over the previous three or four years, Minnie and Annabelle had listened to Lolly Bard chatter about her husband and her boys' every excellence, to the point of tedium. The other ladies in the Congregationalist parish tolerated her with mixed fondness and exasperation; feather-headed in the extreme, her heart and sympathy were in the right place. She never had a bad word to say to or of anyone, save those who owned slaves. Lolly Bard, silly and charming, was at least as adamant as Virgil Vining had been, regarding the Abolition cause. Minnie often wondered if Lolly had set her cap at Virgil as a potential suitor, but Virgil's feelings towards her had been one of waspish exasperation, even before his health declined.

Now the Reverend Slocomb had spotted them – the party of two black-clad women and a man, with a towering mountain of trunks and carpetbags piled next to them on a pair of luggage barrows.

"My dearest Miss Vining!" he exclaimed, advancing and abeam with smiles, deftly evading a newsboy with his basket of fruit and sheaf of newspapers. The Reverend bowed over her hand, all honest and friendly affection. "Mrs. Vining, Mr. Brewer – good day to you all! My dear old friend Mr. Peter Vining tells me that you are departing with him on a journey of some time!"

"To visit kin," Minnie couldn't help but smile, and hoped that she was not pinkening. Annabelle would tease her privately over that, if she even noticed, which she likely didn't. Lolly Bard had her bonneted head bent close to Annabelle's and seemed to be giving advice concerning long journeys on the train carriages. "We will be in Richmond for almost four months – the length of summer. We felt the need of a change of scenery, and I am ..."

"Tired of Boston?" Reverend Slocomb kept her gloved hand still imprisoned within his. Minnie felt the warmth of his regard, the appeal of his consideration and resisted the impulse to simper like a schoolgirl. Meanwhile, Cousin Peter Vining, advancing at a somewhat slower pace, leaning as he did on his trusty cane, flashed a boyish grin at the party.

"Belle, dear – Minnie! Richard, you young scamp! Here I am, better late than never. They were afraid I would be late for the train, a pestiferous invention, yet better than marching all the way! Had you despaired of my arrival?"

Minnie flashed a brief smile at the Reverend Slocomb, sliding her hand out of his with a grace that obliviated any lack of manners. Cousin Peter Vining was over the allotted age of fourscore and ten and increasingly lame from toes lost to frostbite in the bitter cold of a winter encampment when he was a mere lad in the Revolution, although otherwise wiry and spry. In defiance of those years, and unlike the Reverend Slocomb, Cousin Peter still contrived to appear younger than his calendar age. It was in his eyes; Minnie had always thought – the lively interest and energy of her father's younger cousin.

Cousin Peter had been raised in Milford in Delaware. At the age of seventeen he had followed Washington with stubborn devotion, marched south with the Delaware regiments and fought at Cowpens. The spirit of independence burned with a white-hot fervor in Cousin Peter. Perhaps that kept him still young, after all those travails in his youth. It was his oldest daughter Susan and her husband who had invited them all for a long visit, and Cousin Peter to make his home with them from now on, as his long-time housekeeper had died around the same time as Minnie's brother Virgil. Minnie privately hoped that Cousin Peter was yet strong enough to endure the journey without damage to his health, for all that they had planned to do it in leisurely stages, and rest for a day or so between.

"An adventure!" Cousin Peter kissed Minnie's hand, and then Annabelle's, before explaining to the good Reverend. "I have never outgrown a taste for adventure! And Susan is my dearest child, and I long to see her again, one more time. She has three beautiful daughters – we are to attend on Lydia's wedding. Susan sent me the loveliest letter some weeks ago – her youngest, Amy, is collecting a button-string; a button from each of her relations! We can indulge Amy with the very finest and most personal buttons, I daresay."

"We can, indeed," Minnie pushed back her bonnet sufficiently so that she could also kiss Cousin Peter on his age-withered cheek. "And we can present them personally, of course. I am anticipating this visit with such longing! It is not that I am tired of Boston," Minnie added, with a sideways smile at the Reverend Slocomb and Lolly Bard. "But one longs, sometimes, for other vistas ... other sights! I decline to rusticate away, to the point where I do not dare set foot outside my own doorstep, lest I encounter some unfamiliar sight and swoon out of fright at the strangeness of it all."

"You were the perfect dutiful daughter, ministering to Cousin Lycurgus, and then to your brothers in these last years," Cousin Peter murmured, his voice husky with suppressed emotion. "Eh – and you are well-deserving of a holiday, my dear Minnie."

"A perfect saint," the Reverend Slocomb added. "The very model of daughterly and sisterly devotion! We shall miss your presence at our services, and in the good work performed by the good ladies of the congregation, Miss Vining. Hurry back to Boston, as soon as you may ... your return will be an event much longed-for ... I speak personally, of course. Although I am certain that the other ladies will welcome you home ..."

"I am certain that they will," Annabelle pursed her lips, just barely amending the knowing smile in which they had originally arranged themselves. "We well know the degree of respect in which Miss Vining is held by the good ladies of the Beacon Street Church."

Minnie just barely held herself back from sticking out her tongue at Annabelle, who knew well where to jab the sharp needle of her teasing. An affectionate tease, for the most part – but Annabelle's aim was unerring.

"I have no apprehension when it comes to telling ladies when they are being silly geese," Minnie retorted. "That appears to be the source of the intelligence that I am respected among them,"

"Touché, Aunt Minnie," Richard Brewer grinned. "A hit, a very palpable hit ... I believe that is now our carriage, and now is the time to mount it – that is, if we wish to gain favorable seats for our party."

"Lead the way," They made their farewells to the Reverend Slocomb and Lolly Bard, who was still pouring out advice, admonitions, and warnings to Annabelle.

In a spirit of rebellion, Minnie left the black veil hanging back over her shoulders, as Richard offered her his arm, and Cousin Peter did the same with Annabelle. Richard snapped his fingers at the porter with his barrow, already taking up the long handles, as another porter lingered, asking if he could be of service. Now was the moment of departure.

"Have we remembered everything?" Richard asked.

"Oh, yes certainly," Minnie replied, catching the second hovering porter with her eye. "I made a list, of course. It's in my reticule, along with our tickets. Bring along those pillows and shawls. We wish that the older gentleman be comfortable for the days' journey. He is a veteran of the Revolution, you should know." She lowered her voice, adding, "It may be the very last long journey that he shall make – to make a home with his daughter, near where he was in one of the very last battles and watched the surrender of Cornwallis to our army. We wish that he will be comfortable on the journey..."

"Oh, yes, ma'am!" the porter breathed – reverently, Minnie thought. He was a gangly lad with the unfortunate spots of adolescence on his face. The accent of Ireland was thick in his speech. "I would be honored, indade! With Gen'ral Washington, he was?"

"Yes," Minnie replied, thinking of the many stories that Cousin Peter had told over the years. "Through the winter camp at Valley Forge. He has always said that Lady Washington herself brought a bowl of hearty beef broth to him, when he lay ill and ailing with camp fever; that and a slice of fine wheaten bread, fresh from the ovens. He was heartened to think that the General himself so cared for his soldiers that his lady wife might come to the camp to minister to them."

The young porter armored himself with a pile of cushions and traveling robes. "It would be an honor indade, y'r ladyship!" He went ahead of their party, shouting their importance to all within hearing. "Make way, make way – for one of General Washington's soldiers – aye, 'tis true, ye rascals, for the lady has told me so..."

Minnie breathed out a small sigh, as she followed, holding onto Richard's extended elbow. "Irish, and a fabulist!" she murmured. Richard grinned.

"You did tell him true," he replied in the same low tones. "Cousin Peter was one of Washington's loyal soldiers and one of the few surviving into this modern age. It is only his right that such respect and consideration should be extended to him!"

"Yes, but I did not mean for our party to take such advantage!" Minnie answered, as Richard courteously stood aside to allow her to mount up into the First-Class passenger carriage at the end of the train, to escape smoke and soot from the engine. Such a cloud almost hid the engine from sight. Once underway, that smoke would plague passengers at every turn of the breeze, especially when comfort demanded that windows in the coach be kept open for air.

"Allow the porter-lad this moment of glory," Richard advised, his hand on Minnie's waist, guiding her towards their pair of seats – into which Cousin Peter was being settled by Annabelle once the porter-lad had made the seats more comfortable with cushions and robes. "And tip him generously. He may not be so grasping as to demand such renumeration, but I judge that he deserves it. Cousin Peter looks to be as comfortable as a man can ever be, setting out on such a journey."

"As you suggest," Minnie sighed, and reached into the reticule, dangling from her wrist. "Give him this, and thank him for his service to us…" She withdrew several coins, giving them to Richard, as she settled into the seat closest to the window on the side of the carriage opposite to where Cousin Peter and Annabelle sat. She thought that Richard added some more coins from his own purse when he handed them all to the Irish lad, who touched the brim of his cap and breathed in tones of awed respect,

"Thank you sor – and ladies – pleased to have been of service, I am. A safe journey now!"

Richard nodded; if he said anything in reply, Minnie did not hear it, for just then, the rail car jolted, just once, without moving again, although the noise from the engine ahead of them intensified.

The porter took his leave of them expeditiously, as someone outside on the platform shouted, "All abooooord!" She smiled towards Annabelle, now fussing over Cousin Peter's lap-robe, but the other woman did not see her. Cousin Peter looked content enough, though. They should be in Worchester before the day was out; a day of journeying not long enough to exhaust them all. Minnie settled back into her seat, comfortable enough since it was padded with horsehair-stiffened upholstery. She had a book of poetry by Tennyson, an unread novel by Sir Walter Scott and her cherished copy of *Tales from The Alhambra* packed into the small carpetbag full of comforts, now stowed under the seat, so she should not lack for diversion during the day's journey.

"What will you do with yourself, Aunt Minnie, now that you no longer have the daily care of the Judge-your-father and Brother Virgil to fill your days?" Richard asked, most unexpectedly, as the carriage jolted again. Outside of the train windows, the columns which held up the roof over the platform jerked, and began to slide past, faster and faster. The Reverend Slocomb, briefly appeared, and then vanished, as the train trundled past, out into the rail yard, where polished steel tracks met and diverted, and diverted again, as if some gargantuan comb had swept and then separated them all. It was already raining – for which Minnie was grateful, for it kept the smoke from blowing overmuch into their car.

"I have not thought overmuch about that," Minnie replied, although she had. "I have put aside such consideration until after our return from this diversion. There are some matters best considered at leisure, Richard."

"True," Richard agreed. Minnie thought again of how much she liked Richard – the husband of Annabelle's cherished daughter, Sophia. She liked him for his incisive mind, his willingness to consider the unconventional with detachment, and not least, for his respect for her own intellect. What a pity she had not encountered a man of his like, when she was of an age to consider marriage. Marital contract with such as he would have been bearable; indeed, even agreeable to her.

Now he ventured, "Upon what track do your thoughts run, Aunt Minnie? Towards more active leadership in the ladies' committees? Your unencumbered inheritance allows you a degree of freedom unknown to most spinsters, and without the daily cares of familial responsibilities ... you may indulge most whims – even if it is only sitting in the parlor, perfecting your needlework and knitting stockings for orphans."

Minnie laughed outright. "I should perish from the tedium! Although I will say that I find such a diversion – working with my hands, while partaking in a stimulating discussion! I confess, that is what I regret the most, now that my father and Virgil are gone. Before his final illness, Papa-the-Judge was the most stimulating conversationalist. He set me to study *Blackstone's Commentaries* when I was yet a girl, and we would often review those old cases, once brought before him – for amusement and to exercise the intellect, which he believed was most necessary..."

"You have a fine legal mind, Aunt Minnie," Richard acknowledged, solemnly. "If you had been born a man, you would have been one of the finest practitioners of the art in Boston, if not in the State."

"No," Minnie replied. "The study of law was a mere small interest; a diversion, not a ruling passion. Virgil was a passionate abolitionist, almost to the point of tedium. He and Mr. Garrison were the best of friends, until they fell out over disagreeing whether our Constitution supported the institution of slavery. My brother agreed with Mr. Spooner on the matter." She sighed and added. "There are so very few outlets for respectable women of a certain class, Richard. I have too rational an intellect to find excessive religiosity appealing. I would never become a Millerite or a Mormon, or even devote myself to a ridiculous fraud such as Swedenborg's spiritualism – my father instilled too much skepticism in me to ever fall into something so foolish or illogical. I daresay that I will find something to divert myself ... but in the meantime, let us devote ourselves to the pleasure of travel and sightseeing! They tell me in the travel books that the splendors and curiosities one encounters quite make up for the inconvenience and discomforts. I am determined to travel to Europe, and England next summer!" Minnie's spirits rose. "I want to see the castles and cathedrals of France! And imagine – to walk through the Palace of Versailles, and to see the Seven Hills of Rome! And most of all, the Alhambra of Granada! I have dreamed of that enchanted palace for years! Would that not be a sufficient reward for the discomforts of travel ... you must have read Mr. Irving's account of the Moorish pleasure-palace? The only reason that I might hesitate, though – such a place in reality could never equal my imaginings of it." Minnie sighed again, a rather wistful sigh.

Richard laughed and patted her gloved hand. "Never mind, Aunt Minnie! If the spirit moves you in that direction, then Sophia and I will accompany you! I would like to see the Old World myself, and I trust that my French and Latin is good enough that we should rub along without any difficulty ... we have friends who have spent summers in Italy, and aside from the dirt and thievery in the less disreputable parts of towns, they speak very well of their experiences. It is only a week's journey across the Atlantic pond in one of the steamer packets, if the impulse takes you to go a pilgrimaging, then we should be happy to accompany you!"

Richard's square and deceptively bland countenance was alight with enthusiasm and interest; Minnie considered the diversion of a voyage abroad accompanied by her closest family and found the prospect a most pleasing one. Annabelle might be reluctant to be pried loose from Boston and her accustomed haunts again, after this journey, but Richard would be able to persuade Sophia of the benefits of foreign travel – foreign travel to farther fields than just Richmond in Virginia.

"I like that plan!" Minnie said, finally, seeing from the window at her elbow that they were traveling out through the new outskirts of Boston, and hearing Cousin Peter lament that all was so changed from his youthful days that he hardly recognized the city at all. "I think – that when we return from Richmond at the end of summer – that I will consider the benefits of an excursion abroad and begin planning my – our itinerary. For I have money, and we have the time and inclination, certainly!"

"We do that," Richard replied.

Chapter 3 – Not a Man Shall Be a Slave

Summer, 1842 - Richmond, Virginia

"Oh, welcome to Richmond!" Cousin Susan exclaimed, upon welcoming the party of weary travelers, some three weeks later. Minnie, Annabelle, and Richard arrived in good spirits, Cousin Peter in an excellent mood, walking with hardly any reliance on his two canes. "I told Sampson to wait outside with the carriage ... and to come for your trunks and bags as soon – Papa, you look absolutely splendid!" Susan Edmonds embraced her father, the skirts of her impossibly wide crinoline swaying gracefully as she did so; a matronly twelve years older than Minnie, Susan was still the very picture of the latest fashion. Minnie felt quite dowdy in comparison, in her mourning black and narrow skirts. "I was afraid that such a journey ..."

"Nothing to fear, Sue-sue," Peter returned the embrace, with affection, and sneezed as the feathers on her bonnet tickled his nose. "Pardon – dearest girl, no need for worry at all. Minnie, Annabelle, and Richard took admirable care of this old soldier! It was the easiest of journeys, I assure you – and all the way along, we had leisure to take in the sights! The new capitol building will be a marvel when completed! They say that it may rival the dome of St. Peters' in Rome! As for the monument to General Washington ... did we write about how we visited the General's estate on the Potomac? It is much decayed, I fear, for want of income on the part of the General's heirs. There is a plan afoot, I hear, for a consortium of ladies who honor his memory to purchase the place, and preserve it as a temple to the General and to Lady Washington ..."

"That's very good, Papa," Susan replied, absentmindedly, "I know that you thought the best of them both! But modern times, modern times!" Susan's distracted gaze went from her father to Minnie and the others. "My dear cousins! Welcome to Richmond – we shall have so much fun, introducing you to our friends here, and preparing for Lydia's wedding! There are so many amusing excursions ... do you ride, Minnie? Belle? We have the sweetest pair of saddle horses in our stable, for the use of the girls, of course! And Preston Devereaux has returned from business in China! He returned through the southern trail from Santa Fe, all the way through the desert wilderness He tells the most thrilling stories, about his adventures among the heathen Indians and Orientals! He is staying with his cousin Captain Levi Chaffin! You wouldn't know them, of course. He married the loveliest young lady from Rochester upon his return from duty on the frontier! They have three children now, can you imagine. Captain Chaffin is on leave from the Army, of course. His family own Marylebone Hill – a noble property near Claremont on the James, but they keep a fine house in Richmond as well. They are coming for tea tomorrow with Mrs. Van Lew and Miss Van Lew; I do so hope you will be recovered from your journey ...."

"I am certain that we shall be, Sue," Minnie broke into the exuberant torrent of words with some difficulty. "It has not been a journey of such length or difficulty as to render us incapable of participating in a merry social round, but I do think that your father may need a lengthy period of rest before attempting anything especially strenuous ..."

"Minnie, my dear, I may be old, but not yet dead," Cousin Peter returned. "And I have been taken the most tender care of, throughout this journey..."

"Still," Richard Brewer collected his valise, and a couple of the traveling rugs which had made their situation in the rail car ever so much more comfortable, "It is the end of a tolerable journey. The ladies and I and your father are gratified to arrive safely at last. If you would lead the way to your carriage, my dear Mrs. Edmonds ..."

"Oh, of course!" Susan fluttered. She took her fathers' arm, Richard the other, and they walked along the platform and out past the ticketing office, where Susan imperiously ordered the station master to see to their baggage, telling him that it would be come for presently. Outside the station a brake hitched to a matched pair of fine bay horses stood waiting for them, under the care of a Negro coachman in elegant livery every bit as fine as Richard's dark suit.

"Sampson, take us home directly and return for the luggage," Susan commanded, with barely a glance in the coachman's direction, even as she accepted the man's aid in assisting her to step up into the brake.

It was, Minnie thought, as if Sampson was not an actual human being, but an automaton, put on earth to do the chores, without any thought to whatever automaton-thoughts they might have. *They must have thoughts, desires, ambitions,* Minnie thought to herself in a brief moment of reflection as she in turn accepted Sampson's strong hand in assisting her to set one foot into the metal step and another into the brake. It was not as if she had never seen Negroes before – so dark, so alien!

– but this was the first time she had ever encountered one held indisputably as a slave.

The Edmonds town mansion sat behind an ornate iron fence on Broad Street, a noble avenue which climbed from the heart of Richmond to the heights above. The house was a noble brick structure on a high foundation, which housed the domestic offices. It was surrounded by splendid trees and a bright and well-tended garden. Susan had told them that many of the finest families in Richmond lived nearby.

A wide whitewashed staircase mounted to a door surmounted by a beveled glass fanlight. Daisies, iris, roses, white-flowered jasmine, and azaleas nodded heavy and well-flowered branches, around the margins of a velvet-green sward set with croquet hoops, inviting benches and a rustic summerhouse made from unpeeled branches. The neighborhood was called Church Hill, for the venerable towering white steeple of St. John's which crowned it; a pleasant district of generous streets edged with brick sidewalks and shaded by towering green trees in full summer leaf. Similar establishments rambled down the hill in every direction, adorned by equally fragrant gardens and shaded by well-grown, thick-trunked trees. Minnie would have been loath to admit – it was at least the equal of Boston, and perhaps even better, as far as the climate went. She and Annabelle were given to understand, through Cousin Susan's breathlessly disjointed narrative as the brake traveled those elegant avenues of Church Hill, that the female seminary overseen by Susan's husband, Ambrose Edmonds, was not terribly far away. Susan referred incessantly to her husband as My Dearest Ambrose.

"Susan has done very well for herself in marriage to a man in orders," Annabelle whispered to Minnie, as Susan and Richard, with Cousin Peter between them, climbed the front stairs. "And here I thought a divine was to live in genteel poverty!"

"Shush! You are being a terrible cat," Minnie whispered back. She recollected when the newly ordained Reverend Ambrose Edmunds had appeared in their social circle in Boston; a gawky young man with a prominent Adams' apple, some ten years older than the school-room aged Minnie and Annabelle, and Minnie's even younger brother, Horace. Ambrose Edmonds was a remote connection, Minnie recollected. When Cousin Peter's oldest daughter accepted his proposal of marriage, both she and Annabelle attended Susan, in her fashionable wedding ensemble ordered from Paris. She and Annabelle had worn Parisian dresses as well, with circlets of rosebuds in their hair; whispering and giggling together at how Ambrose had fumbled with the wedding ring, and when he and Susan had knelt before the altar, everyone had seen how he had a patch on the sole of his shoes.

Twenty years older now, Ambrose was still lanky and diffident, with an affected cough, clerical collar and a narrow countenance adorned with sweeping side-whiskers. He appeared shortly before suppertime; somewhat of a crowded affair in what would ordinarily have been a generously apportioned dining room, with the presence of Cousin Peter, Richard, Minnie, and Annabelle, as well as the Edmonds' daughters. All three girls had places at the table; Lydia, Charlotte, and Amy the youngest, who was sufficiently mature to attend supper with their parents and guests.

"Such pretty children," Annabelle confessed later, as she and Minnie prepared to retire for the night, in one of the second-floor chambers set aside for guests. "An excellent thing that they take after Susan, rather than their father... But oh, the trial which awaits Lydia upon marriage. I worry about her, recalling my own troubles! And Charlotte will be married soon, I suppose. They are of the age where that fate is inescapable." Annabelle was already in bed, pleading weariness from the days' journey as a means of retiring early. Minnie was also tired, but she sat before the vanity, brushing out her long hair: a hundred strokes, without fail. She studied her reflection in the mirror, under the mellow light of the small oil-lamp: she did not feel old, Minnie thought, even though her light-brown hair was developing paler patches at her temples. She could not be old; not when she had so much energy, so much more than Annabelle, who often claimed exhaustion, even back in Boston.

"I do not think marriage would be such a dire sentence as all that," Minnie protested. "It is just that a few of our sex have no interest in limiting ourselves to a domestic sphere. Most girls long for such a connection and are very happy in it. You should not speak of Susan's girls as if they are to be sentenced to a prison or the workhouse. Besides, My-Dear-Ambrose seems to be an indulgent father.

Annabelle giggled. "You are a wicked thing, Minnie, to make such a jest of Susan's husband, after he was so kind as to host us for such a long visit!"

"I cannot help it," Minnie stroked the brush through her hair one last time and commenced braiding it up for the night. "And you have also made fun of Ambrose as well! I could never see him as the answer to a maiden's prayer, although he seems to suit Susan well enough, and they are long-wed and happy in that state. I will be the perfect guest and not make a jest of him under his own roof ... still," Minnie tied her nightcap over her head. Lifting the glass chimney from the lamp, she blew out the flame, and found her questing way to her side of the bed in the dark. "I did not think that he would be a slave-owning man, now. I thought it possible that one might live among such, without partaking of the dish, such as it is. It vexes me, 'Belle. Virgil was one so sternly in favor of abolition – an original member of the Anti-Slavery Society! I read the weekly issues of the *Liberator* to him, when he could no longer read them himself."

"Myself as well," Annabelle sighed in the dark, as Minnie lifted the covers and slid into bed. "But tomorrow is Susan's 'at home' day, and we must stiffen our resolve to be courteous to her friends, no matter how we feel about the peculiar institution. I hope the matter does not arise, in polite conversation! I cannot think why you chose to visit Richmond, knowing it to be such a nest of pro-slavery sentiment!"

"Because it is Susan, and her family," Minnie settled the light covers over herself, and reached out to Annabelle's hand in the dark. "She is our kin, and beloved by us for many years. And Cousin Peter even more beloved! No, we could not permit him to travel on his own, not at his age. He is the last of his generation, 'Belle, and Susan is his dearest child. I cannot – will not – believe that the matter of slavery, as vile as the institution is, could sunder cousins, brother from brother."

As Minnie half-apprehended, Annabelle continued to plead exhaustion after the previous day's journey, as did Cousin

Peter. They remained upstairs in the rooms allocated for them. She and Richard breakfasted with the Reverend Edmonds, Susan, and her daughters in the pleasant dining room of the Edmonds house, which looked out upon the extensive kitchen garden at the back of the house. They were served there by a pair of Negro maids, silent and unsmiling, mere girls and supervised by a stern-faced older woman; Hepzibah, whom they were given to understand was Susan's housekeeper. Under Hepzibah's authority, the household ran with the exquisite and measured motions of a fine clock.

Minnie did have to admit that the house on Church Hill was beautifully kept, the rooms immaculate, the linen fresh, the silver polished, and the lamps tended with care. Vases of new-picked flowers adorned every room. Yes, the Edmonds slave servants were efficient and attentive, under the stern hand of Hepzibah, who appeared to exercise considerable authority over the household, even to Susan's daughters. Minnie had yet to hear Susan raise her voice to any of her household, issue an order in any but the most gracious manner. Nor did she observe Sampson, or any of the maids demonstrate anything but cheerful obedience. Susan and Hepzibah appeared to be on terms of comfortable familiarity, which Minnie found to be most curious. Face to face with the reality of the institution was far removed from contemplating cruelties in abstraction and at a comfortable distance.

On the day after the morrow, Richard would return North; his law practice would not admit of an absence from his office for two or three months at a stretch. In the fall, he would return to escort Annabelle and Minnie on their return.

"Alas," Richard admitted cheerfully, "I am not a gentleman of leisure, and I might be flogged by my partners, if I do not return to bear up my portion of labors."

"Alas; indeed, neither am I," My-Dear-Ambrose agreed, sanctimonious in his clerical collar, hardly taking notice of the silent maid in her white apron and plain dark dress replenishing the platters of sausage, toast, and biscuits. "Labor, and not leisure is our common condition!"

Minnie did notice a flicker of emotion crossing the maid's dark impassive face at the mention of corporal punishment, a flicker quickly gone. The tall clock in the hallway chimed a melodious quarter hour.

"A quarter past already? I must be off, then, my dears." The Reverend Edmonds hastily downed the last of his coffee as he rose from the table. He bent to kiss his wife's uplifted cheek, saying, "Amy, child – it is time for school. Gather up your books and bonnet and let us be off." He bid them all a hasty farewell and departed with his youngest daughter.

"What plans have you for the morning, Minnie?" Susan asked, after the front door opened and closed again. "Do remember that my at-home is this afternoon. I so hope that Annabelle and Father will be able to come downstairs. I expect that Pres Devereaux will have so many amusing stories to tell of his experiences among in China and India. I have a mind to match him with Charlotte, he is a most excellent catch as a husband! Levi Chaffin has been soldiering on the frontier, so I expect that he and Father will have so much in common!"

"This morning, I think that I shall go for a long walk, and enjoy the fresh air," Minnie replied, taking note of the giggle and blush from sixteen-year-old Charlotte at the mention of a possible suitor. "I have spent so many days, sitting in a train car, or waiting on a station platform that I would relish a turn in the fresh air at leisure, and the enjoyment of the many lovely gardens which we passed yesterday. In Boston, there is talk of constructing a public garden adjacent to the Common, but nothing has come of it yet..."

"The grounds at St. John's are planted with so many wonderful trees and ornamental flowers," Susan nodded, rather absently. "If you like, My-Dear-Ambrose may conduct a private tour of the building for you and Father, as his duties at the school allow. The Virginia burgesses met there, and that was where Patrick Henry gave his immortal speech, urging the cause of freedom over death..."

"Indeed," Minnie replied. "Your father would certainly relish the prospect of a private visit to that place. A pilgrimage, as it were."

She, Susan, and Richard chatted idly over the remainder of their breakfast, Richard allowing that he would also be delighted to examine the interior of such a storied building before he departed for Boston. Minnie contemplated the leisure of a morning spent as her own whims directed, with neither the care of a household or the demands of an invalid to be considered. She wished for the company of Annabelle on this morning but conceded the hours would be perfectly enjoyable in a solitary condition. It seemed ... almost unnatural. The only obligation in her day was to be in the parlor in the afternoon, to help Susan receive her visitors, several hours hence.

She set off as soon as she changed into a plain black walking costume from the light cotton dress she had worn for breakfast. Cotton calico from England, she thought again.

Woven from the king of crops in the South, woven in English mills by free workmen ... or were they, really? It was a conundrum, Minnie thought, having read much of the dire conditions in English mills. Not so much in American mills, though – and she had thought much on this. It was one of the Reverend Slocomb's obsessions; the morals and condition of the mill girls, although Minnie often thought to herself that any labor which allowed the support of a free woman in a comfortable condition should be honorable enough. Better that, than that of a common ... no, Minnie wrenched her mind from that consideration. Any honest and useful work within the capability of a woman to perform; that was her perfect condition.

Minnie made it a leisurely walk, often stopping to admire certain gardens, especially those which were at their springtime best. The mansions and townhouses on the slopes of Church Hill commanded views of the distant James River, and the wooded islets beyond the chimneys and towers of what Minnie assumed to be the Tredegar iron works, from the wisps of grey smoke which hung over them. It appeared that such of the prosperity of the Edmonds household derived from the good reverend having prudently invested in the workings. Minnie could not wholly disapprove of such perspicuity when it came to trade. A good portion of the Vining fortune had been made in the China trade, on tea, porcelain, and silks shipped on fast clipper ships. Papa-the-Judge had often been scathing in his estimation of aristocrats, both would-be and actual, who looked down their noses at participating in 'trade' and commerce. *"Material wealth does not descend like the rain upon the* worthy," he was fond of saying. *"It must be worked for and tended like a garden."*

Like the gardens of the houses on Church Hill. Although, as near as Minnie could see, the hands tending those well-kept gardens were all black. She climbed to the very top of the hill, to where the shadow of the tower of St. John's lay across the carefully scythed grass. If it weren't for the wedding and her fondness for Cousin Peter and Susan, Minnie now thought that she would have preferred an extensive excursion to France and Italy, as a means of celebrating her independence – if only she had been able to persuade Annabelle to accompany her! It was so exasperating of Annabelle, to be so reluctant, Minnie thought as she walked down from the hill where St. Johns' raised a tall white tower into a faultlessly blue sky. *Without her private circle in Boston, she has all the backbone and constitution of a well-boiled stalk of celery*, Minnie thought – and not for the first time. *It is your duty to see to installing something of a spine in Annabelle*, she recollected Papa-the-Judge observing on numerous private occasions. *An organ which doubtless will serve her well in life and marriage – assuming she ever has sufficient spirit to appreciate the utility of it*. Annabelle clung to the tight circle of her Boston friends, worried over Sophia even after her daughter married Richard. On the whole, Minnie reflected, getting Annabelle to accompany her to Richmond may have been the most that she would ever be able to do.

On her return to the Edmonds house, Hepzibah opened the door for her saying, "Miz Susan is in de parlor with Ma'am Vining an' de girls, Miss Minerva."

Susan called from the parlor, obviously having heard the bell, and the door open and shut. "Minnie, is that you, dear? You must join us! Mrs. Van Lew just sent a boy with a note saying that she and Miss Elizabeth would be here momentarily."

"Allow me to change my dress, Sue," Minnie replied, and hastened up the stairs to the room that she and Annabelle shared, to discover that someone, Annabelle or one of Susan's housemaids had already laid out one of her afternoon dresses; a simple gown in the pale violent of half-morning, with a lacy fichu, the creases from having been packed in a trunk all neatly pressed out by the unseen hands of Cousin Susan's Negro maids. Minnie hastily unbuttoned the skirt and bodice of her walking costume and exchanged her stockings and high-buttoned boots for clean white stockings and plain dainty slippers. By the time she had effected this change, and hurried downstairs, the maid was already opening the front door to admit two ladies. Minnie fairly scampered into the parlor, and settled onto the divan next to Annabelle, who whispered,

"You're late! We were beginning to despair! Did you lose track of the time?"

"The gardens of Church Hill are so splendid," Minnie gasped. "I confess that I did, and I am sorry, Susan. I was admiring certain of the trees; those with white flowers, of four or five petals."

"Dogwood trees," Charlotte piped up, and Susan chided her.

"Dear, speak when you are spoken to. Yes, the dogwood trees are particularly splendid this spring, although you have missed the jonquils at their best. But the magnolias are soon to bloom...Yes, Sadie?" That last was addressed to the maid, deferential in her dark dress, white apron, and turban, lingering in the doorway.

"Mrs. Eliza Van Lew, Miss Elizabeth, Ma'am," she murmured, and stepped aside from the doorway as Susan rose from her chair.

"Eliza, my dear!" she exclaimed to the older lady; a pleasant-faced matron with pink cheeks and very white hair, dressed as modestly as a Quaker in a grey walking dress bereft of any additional adornments. "And Lizzie – we are so pleased to see you today! Come in, come in! I must introduce you to my cousins, visiting from Boston: Mrs. Annabelle Vining, and Miss Minerva Vining. They have come to celebrate Lydia's marriage with us and then to stay the summer over ... the gentlemen will join us shortly." Susan and the Van Lew ladies exchanged brief social embraces – the older lady with more open affection than the younger. "They traveled by train, all of the way," Susan added, and the Van Lew ladies chorused their wonder and approval.

"From Boston!" Exclaimed Eliza Van Lew, as she turned her attention towards Minnie and Annabelle. "By train – what a marvel the railway has become. Now, I was brought up in Philadelphia, and my daughter attended school there, and now the matter of travel has become so much less onerous than it once was ... how welcome you are to Richmond!"

"We have been received with every fondness and courtesy," Annabelle replied. Minnie regarded Miss Lizzie Van Lew, recognizing as if with a secret Masonic handshake, another stubborn spinster of her own ilk. Miss Elizabeth was pleasing in her aspect and person, and fashionably clad; a perfect fair rose of the South, with flaxen hair, unearthly blue eyes, and that fine complexion lauded by every sentimental novelist and fashion paper. Yet, Miss Van Lew defied convention, for her nose was a perfect beak and those eyes reflected a piercing and unsettling intelligence.

"Miss Vining," she said, and her voice was pleasant and cultured. "May I sit with you and converse? I would adore to hear of how the abolitionist cause is progressing in the North. We hear so very little of the matter here in Richmond, you see – only fulminations against such wicked persuaders such as your Mr. Garrison, and the Reverend Slocomb. Since he is of Boston, may I presume that you are acquainted?"

"But certainly," Minnie answered, heartened at encountering a kindred spirit among Susan's circle of friends. "Mr. Garrison was a particular friend of my late brother, although they had fallen out over some aspect of campaigning for the cause of abolition. I cannot recall the specific issue as Mr. Garrison is a passionate advocate and not easily brought to compromise. But he and my brother eventually reconciled. Reverend Slocomb ministers to the congregation which I attend – and I have the privilege of a personal acquaintance with him, as well as a personally-inscribed volume of his sermons ..."

"Indeed, I have a copy of that very same book!" Miss Lizzie beamed, radiantly.

Minnie laughed. "I am reassured in making your acquaintance, Miss Van Lew. I had become convinced that such abolitionist sentiments are most rare in the South,"

"Alas, they are," Lizzie Van Lew agreed, without rancor. "But I care little, nor does Mama, or my brother John. Among our circle of friends, it is considered merely an eccentricity peculiar to the Quakers of the northern States, and thus tolerated. My late father left us so considerable an estate as to shelter us well against that public opprobrium which might fall upon those of lesser means, otherwise!"

At that moment in their conversation, Richard and Cousin Peter joined what had become a most pleasant gathering: Susan fussed over settling her father into the most comfortable chair, and Richard took a seat on one of the spindly parlor chairs opposite the divan where Annabelle sat with Minnie and Miss Van Lew. No sooner was the introduction made, than Susan's maid announced the arrival of another party.

"Captain and Mrs. Chaffin, and Mr. Devereaux, with Mr. James Chaffin, Ma'am," the girl said, and suddenly it seemed that Susan's parlor was very full, although a large portion of that came from Mrs. Chaffin's fashionable crinoline as she leaned on her husbands' arm, and the breadth of shoulder of the man who followed the pair into the parlor. Minnie couldn't help that her eyes were drawn to him, as if by a magnet; tall and fair-haired, with rugged sun-bronzed features and eyes of a particular pale blue hue, a specimen of vigorous maturity, whom she judged to be about the age of her own. He possessed the same arresting quality as the Reverend Slocomb; of an actor commanding the attention of an audience as he strode the boards. Captain Chaffin, and the younger James Chaffin were practically invisible, by comparison.

"Why, Miss Elizabeth!" Preston Devereaux exclaimed, in a gentle drawl which Minnie had begun to identify as that trait of those from the deeper south. "You mus' do me the honor of acquainting me with your charming friends!"

Elizabeth appeared entirely unmoved by his courteous regard, even though it drew the interest of the other women in the room as a sunflower follows the sun. "These ladies are Mrs. Edmonds' Boston relations," she replied, in a voice devoid of the least scrap of flirtatious interest. "Miss Minerva and Mrs. Annabelle Vining – may I make you acquainted with this gentleman, Preston Devereaux? Mr. Devereaux is lately returned from ... where was it? I heard that it was traveling abroad; I cared little for where, although I prayed that it be far, far from Richmond!"

"My dear lady Tongue," Preston Devereaux returned, seemingly much amused. "I thank you for the courtesy of your introduction, Miss Elizabeth of Kate Hall. Ladies ..." he kissed Annabelle's raised hand, and then Minnie's. "Consider me to be at your most devoted service!"

Minnie and Annabelle briefly met each other's eyes.

A rogue, indeed, was Annabelle's unvoiced comment.

Yes, but an amusing one, Minnie signaled.

"I deduce from your manner of speech that you are from another place than this," Minnie ventured, for yes, Preston Devereaux's accent was the most deeply marked in Southern inflection that she had heard thus far.

"Charleston, Miss Vining," he replied, with a smile which drew her, although not as deeply as it would have, if she had been as young as Charlotte Edmonds. "My family there is said to be descended from a latter sprout on the family tree of that Robert Deveraux, once the Earl of Essex and favorite of Good Queen Bess."

"Charleston," remarked Captain Chaffin, from across the parlor where he had taken a seat next to Cousin Peter. Captain

Chaffin possessed a shock of hair so dark as to be nearly black and yet had the same pale blue eyes as his cousin. His young wife was deep in conversation with Eliza Van Lew, and the younger Chaffin held a cake of plate from which he and Lydia were sharing alternate bites. "Where it is often said that the inhabitants most resemble the heathen Chinee – in that all eat rice and worship their ancestors."

That *bon mot* earned a ripple of amused laughter from the ladies within hearing, and a chuckle from Preston Devereaux, who appeared to take no offense, as he regarded the three ladies – Miss Elizabeth, Annabelle, and Minnie.

"I trust that you are finding your visit to Richmond enjoyable?" Preston Devereaux inquired, as if he really were interested.

Minnie replied, "We have only been here for a day, Mr. Devereaux, but we have been warmly welcomed by our kin, and friends such as Miss Van Lew..."

"Richmond is so very different from Boston," Annabelle echoed.

Miss Elizabeth set aside her teacup. "We were having the most interesting talk," she remarked, as every word were a razor-sharp little dagger. "Regarding mutual friends, and an interest in abolition."

Minnie exchanged a glance with Annabelle; for all the care taken in leaving certain topics of conversation unexplored in the interests of civility among friends and kin, Miss Elizabeth was treading heavily among the conversational caltrops.

"Indeed," Preston Devereaux raised an eyebrow. "A fascinating topic, Miss Elizabeth. Alas, not one of interest to me: I may truly boast of having not a single drop of abolition blood in me."

"A pity," Miss Elizabeth observed, acidly "I daresay that a single drop would make you into a man, rather than your present nonentity."

Minnie drew in her breath with a horrified gasp, fully expecting Preston Devereaux to react as any ordinary man who had been insulted by a lady in the confines of another lady's parlor, but instead, he merely chuckled appreciatively.

"Touché, Miss Elizabeth, my very dearest shrew. I did invite that hit! Miss Vining pray do not look as if you meant to take offense on my part. Miss Van Lew and I have been in the habit of verbal jousts such as this for years. Such bouts sharpen our relative wits and amuse our friends no end."

"Be warned concerning Mr. Devereaux's conversation," Miss Elizabeth returned, with an air of stark warning. "He assumes attitudes not from any deep conviction, but merely from a desire to provoke and tease. He is a veritable whirligig, turning as the conversational wind blows."

"I have heard that Mr. Devereaux was abroad on foreign travels," Annabelle interjected, in a manner intended to be placating. That gentleman smiled as if he divined her motivation and was prepared to be indulgent of it. "I would like so very much to hear of his adventures. Our cousin Susan says that you traveled to China, and then returned through the Mexican territories! So very exciting! What was it like? One hears the most fascinating tales of adventures and riches to be had in trade with China and India."

"I was in China, on an errand of some import for a relative of mine, and on my return, the ship on which I was traveling was disabled in a sudden storm and must make port for repairs in a grimy little place called San Diego," Mr. Devereaux accepted a cup of tea and a plate of cake from Susan's silent housemaids. Minnie made a private memorandum to herself; make sufficient conversation with Susan's household slaves to learn their names. It seemed rude to her, not to know the names of servants, other than Hepzibah and Sampson, or not even to be able to tell them apart, so alike they all appeared, in their anonymous dark dresses and dark faces, below snowy-white turbans, as if interchangeable human automatons, given into service. Mr. Devereaux continued.

"From there, I traveled through to Santa Fe, and then to Mexico..."

"Did you find your fortune in those places?" Miss Elizabeth sounded most skeptical; Minnie and Annabelle hung on every word. "The Devereaux family has long possessed a talent for acquiring a fortune, and then almost immediately losing it again."

Minnie noted that Mrs. Eliza was deep in conversation with the young Mrs. Chaffin – ah, from Rochester, in Western New York, she recollected. They must have interests, if not kin in common. Minnie understood that Rochester, like Boston and Philadelphia were all very public-spirited places. Richard and Cousin Peter were likewise deep in conversation with Captain Chaffin on matters of military interest, both recent and of a historic nature, Minnie assumed. Charlotte and Lydia appeared likewise engaged in an intense conversation with the younger Mr. Chaffin. Minnie gathered that he was Lydia's intended, from the fond manner in which Susan made him welcome to the parlor. She would have been more interested in the lad, but for being fascinated in the tale which Pres Devereaux had to tell.

"I did come away with a great quantity of silver," that gentleman responded. "Since I had purchased a quantity of Chinese silk and other rare commodities, all of which I traded for silver coin in Mexico..."

Minnie, Annabelle, and Miss Elizabeth listened to his tale with intense interest, Miss Elizabeth even refraining from a further exercise of witty repartee with Mr. Devereaux, as he related his adventures in India and China, of visiting towering palaces set with carven precious stones, strange gods in their temples, and of Indian princes whose clothing was sewn thick with jewels and gold lace. Pres Devereaux even claimed to have been favored by a fabulously wealthy raja, who presented him with an emerald the size of a small hen's egg set in gold for his daring in killing a tiger with a single shot, after having been invited on a royal hunt.

"This would truly seem to be out of a fairy tale!" Annabelle exclaimed, and Preston Deveraux chuckled.

"By way of proof, I had that jewel made into a fob for my watch-chain when I returned home, as a memento of that excursion..." and he brought out his massy gold pocket watch, a timepiece with a fob of a single dark green gem – which was indeed the size of a small egg.

Minnie and Annabelle murmured their awe and admiration over this marvel. Miss Elizabeth only sniffed. Minnie wondered idly if Pres Devereaux's watch chain and fob were something which she had seen before.

"The value of a slave or two, from the Main Street auctions," was her only comment.

"Indeed," purred Pres Devereaux in reply. "And I would purchase one for you, Miss Elizabeth! Two, if that is what you would wish. Only not with my royal emerald – merely to it's current value."

"Would you, indeed?" Miss Elizabeth's gaze sharpened. "And I so do wish it!"

"Your wish is my command, my dear queen of shrews. Tomorrow, I have some leisure time, if you would accompany me to the Shockoe Bottom slave pens … these are," he added for Minnie and Annabelle's benefit, "the retail and wholesale markets for wares of the human sort. I daresay, that if you are of proper abolitionist sympathies, you ladies might be interested in seeing for yourself those pits of hell so limned with such glorious detail in your Northern newspapers."

"I … would find that a most appalling prospect!" Annabelle exclaimed in horror. "No, I would not wish to be party to such awful scenes … if by my presence, I would seem to be approving of the awful business of slavery!"

"You have not the … innards for it, although it is an institution condemned all throughout Massachusetts," Pres Devereaux's lips thinned, and his countenance seemed suddenly harsh.

"My sister may not, but I do," Minnie replied, crisply. "I would wish with my own eyes – and unflinching – to observe the cruel barbarism of the peculiar institution. I would, Mr. Devereaux! My father was particular with regard to evidence. He was a judge, and a rigorous practitioner of the law."

"Very well," Pres Deveraux replied, and it seemed to Minnie that he looked upon her with respect – not the respect accorded to a woman in that courtly manner peculiar to gentlemen, but one who saw her as an equal in intellect. "Then tomorrow, I shall call for you at ... say, nine? And I will show you ladies the slave markets of Richmond."

Chapter 4 – Bring the Jubilee

"You cannot be serious!" Susan gasped when Minnie informed her of Preston Devereaux's invitation, at breakfast the following morning. "The Shockoe Bottom is the very worst, lowest part of town, a very sink of depravity and vice ... no respectable lady ought to go anywhere near the Negro jails! Minnie, I can't allow that – what would My-Dear-Ambrose say? People will talk!"

"I cannot imagine that he can have very much to say at all, since I am not in his guardianship and am well-beyond legal age," Minnie answered, crisply. "But if it should comfort you and Ambrose, I will go heavily veiled, and not speak a word to anyone save Mr. Devereaux, as Miss Elizabeth has also promised. In any case, Captain Chaffin will also accompany us. He is providing a closed coach, so there will be even less for the censorious to take notice."

Susan still looked perturbed. "I am not happy regarding this excursion, Minnie, not happy at all. The Van Lews are notoriously eccentric, but My-Dear-Ambrose and I have our position in Richmond society to think of..."

Minnie sighed: what Papa-the-Judge called the Moloch of Society must always be appeased, or at least seem to be appeased, in Boston and now apparently everywhere else. "Sue, dear – I promise that I will not behave in a manner which will cause you and the Reverend Edmonds the slightest moment of embarrassment. I am no longer ten years old, giggling at your back because your husband kneeling before the minister has a hole in his shoe and all in the front pews can see it!"

By the dint of much persuasive and soothing talk, Minnie managed to allay both Susan and Annabelle's apprehensions, although Susan did appeal to her father, in a last-ditch effort, demanding that he forbid Minnie's expedition. Cousin Peter only grunted. He was never at his best until at least late afternoon, and the summer heat in Richmond had begun to tell on him – it seemed to be very much warmer at night than in Boston. Tall windows, which invited every stray night breeze inside to cool the inhabitants, did not alleviate the miseries of Cousin Peter's venerable years. Richard Brewer had already departed on the earliest train for the North.

"Filthy business, slavery," he said. "Blight on our republic, if you ask me. Not what we fought and died for, selling humans as if they were cattle or horses." He shot a shrewd look towards his daughter and Minnie. "I'll not forbid it, Sue-Sue. Minerva knows her own mind. All I'll ask, my girl – is that you keep your sympathies for abolition in check. They're a bad lot, the slave-jailers, and brokers. They're men with a lot of money at stake, and if there is anything that I have learned in life, it's that such men turn vicious when their livelihood is at stake."

"I will be most circumspect," Minnie promised.

Susan still looked worried. "I don't know why you insist on seeing such awful things for yourself," she protested.

Minnie replied, firmly, "Because I must – and because then I can freely bear witness to what I have seen with mine own eyes, and not rely on the breathless tales of those with a partisan interest in the unfortunate institution."

"I still can't understand ..." Susan began, and Annabelle regarded Minnie with reproach in her eyes.

"Neither do I," she quavered, and Minnie got up from the breakfast table.

"I concede to it being a mystery to you all then," she said, rolling up her napkin and inserting it in the ring which lay beside her plate. "Please excuse me, Susan. I believe I shall go for a walk before I change. Mr. Devereaux and Captain Chaffin promised to arrive on the dot of 9."

Minnie walked the length of the block on which the Edmonds house stood, after changing into her plain black walking dress, and assuming the plain untrimmed dark bonnet which went with it – although she tossed the mourning veil back over her shoulders. She hated looking at the world – especially on a beautiful summer day – through a black fog. She was also disappointed that Annabelle did not support her in this excursion, even if she did not wish to join in it herself.

A spine of well-boiled celery, Minnie concluded, yet once and again. Although they were the same age, Annabelle now appeared so much older than Minnie; a thing for which Minnie had no explanation – she herself felt as energetic as a girl, still. *Where had that spark of zestful energy gone, in her dear friend? Had marriage and motherhood extinguished it entirely?*

The carriage arrived before the Edmonds' door just before the hour of nine. Annabelle, waiting with Minnie in the front parlor, made one last attempt to dissuade her from the excursion.

"It might be dangerous!" she insisted. "You heard what Cousin Peter said about being recognized as being of abolitionist sympathies, among those whose livelihood depends on perpetuating the peculiar institution."

"I have no apprehensions, 'Belle," Minnie replied. "We will be accompanied by a gallant soldier, and a gentleman who recently returned from hunting tigers with rajahs in India; I am certain that both Captain Chaffin and Mr. Devereaux have faced such dangers as would make a set of slave-driving ruffians a mere annoyance in comparison." Outside in the street, the sound of carriage wheels carried to her ears. "I believe that will be the coach ... if we do not return for dinner at midday, make my excuses to Susan, dear."

"Is there nothing I can say?" Annabelle dropped her embroidery hoop into her lap and clasped her hands together. "Nothing to make you consider turning aside from this course?"

"No, nothing," Minnie gathered up her reticule and tied the strings of her mantle at her throat, as she heard voices at the door – Susan's housemaid, and that of Captain Chaffin. "Not once my mind is set on a course which I have determined."

"Be most careful," Annabelle whispered or that was what Minnie thought she heard, as she left the parlor. Outside, an elegant dark grey berline carriage awaited, drawn by a pair of matched, dapple-grey horses, whose reins lay in the hands of a coachman – another black slave, in a fine dark grey coat and starched white stock, the elegance of whose attire rivaled that of Captain Chaffin himself.

"Miss Vining! Good morning!" Captain Chaffin took her arm, going down the steps. "You know, this is not considered an acceptable outing for a lady, But Pres insisted, and he's a hard man to gainsay."

"I have been assured of this, solo and in chorus," Minnie replied, with some asperity. "But I will not be deterred!"

"No, I was afraid not," Captain Chaffin sighed, as he assisted her to step from the ground, onto the narrow carriage step. "You and Miss Van Lew are of a kind, I perceive. I should warn you, though – ladies do not generally attend slave auctions. You see ... umm ... it is the practice among prospective buyers, to assure themselves of the health and fitness of a male slave they are interested in ... that they remove their garments, in order that their bodies may be closely inspected."

"Good heavens!" Minnie exclaimed. "Surely, they do not require that of females in public! Why, that is barbaric!"

Preston Devereaux took her other hand, with a mocking grin, and settled her onto the seat next to Miss Van Lew, observing, "Barbarism is in the eye of the beholder, Miss Vining – as I have good reason to know."

"Not in that portion of the auction," Captain Chaffin replied, and Minnie could have sworn that the man's countenance reddened – but that was in the relative dimness of the carriage interior. She and Miss Van Lew had already pulled heavy veils over their bonnets, as if the carriage wasn't dim enough. Captain Chaffin tapped on the glass of the window nearest the driver's perch, and the berline lurched away from the Edmonds' front door. "It is my understanding that such is required now and again, in ... a private viewing of the ... um... merchandise. Well before the auction and bidding begins."

"Of a high-yellow fancy, most usually," Mr. Devereaux, suave as ever. Minnie would be willing to swear that the gentlemen were as determined to discourage herself and Miss Van Lew from the proposed excursion, only that they had chosen a more subtle means of going about it. The carriage rocked gently, as the black coachman in elegant livery clucked to the horses.

From the corner of the closed carriage, Miss Van Lew remarked, as if making a note of the weather, "That would be a woman with a bare minimum of African blood, Miss Vining. Such is the tendency for owners of female slaves to engage in congress upon their bodies. After generations of such conduct ... one cannot really tell free from slave at sight. It requires the judgement of a veritable Solomon, a patent scrying-glass, and a notarized affidavit sworn before witnesses, to tell the difference between a free white woman and a black slave."

"I see," Minnie retorted, although she didn't ... not entirely. But untried waters were to be ventured upon, and hopefully without fear or favor. "I perceive that you gentleman both have experience with the matter of holding Negroes in the condition of bondage. I suppose that you both hold slaves."

"We do," Captain Chaffin admitted, through suddenly thinned lips. "But I can assure you that we treat our people well and fairly. None of Marylebone Hill's people have ever been sold down the river, not in my lifetime or that of my father."

"My own family, alas, does not own as many slaves as formerly," Pres Deveraux admitted, with an exaggeratedly tragic sigh. "The reversals of the cotton trade made it necessary that we dispense of the excess in recent years; they will multiply naturally, you know. Conditions over the last few years were desperately unfavorable for Deveraux crops; insufficient income to support the family and our dependents at the current market price of cotton and tobacco. Do not look so horrified, Miss Van Lew, Miss Vining. Our agent arranged private sales, and specified stringently that families would be sold entire and only to purchasers of whom he approved. Otherwise, what are we to do? In the North, one may merely fire workers superfluous to momentary needs, and one is relieved of all further responsibility for their welfare. Is that not a cruelty, according to your Christian lights? Are we not our brothers' keeper, after all?"

"But free men possess the inalienable right to order their own lives," Minnie retorted. "To work at whatever they chose, to travel where they will without hindrance, to contract marriage to a woman of their own choosing ..."

"To starve in a gutter, if that is their choice," Pres Devereaux agreed, smoothly. "Without any notice being taken of their situation. Is it not kinder, Miss Minerva, in the situation of a lesser breed, when sick or old, no longer able to work — to be taken care of? Housed, clothed, fed, to have the attention of a doctor when ill? It is a great responsibility, even greater than that of being a father with children. Children grow up and take charge of their own lives, eventually, but the responsibility for your field hands and house slaves never, ever ends."

"I admit of no fair comparison," Minnie was indignant. "Between a slave, subject to the whims of an owner, and the condition of a free man or woman. We are God's creatures, of His creation, every one of us! No matter what our native capabilities may be, all deserve that freedom!"

"The African race are like children," Pres Devereaux spoke with infinite patience, nearly as irritating to Minnie as open condescension would have been. "Would you allow a small child do as they wish, in every respect? That would be careless, irresponsible, unfitting..."

"Mr. Devereaux is provoking you deliberately, Miss Vining," Miss Van Lew interjected. "Did I not warn you yesterday of his habit of being a dancing whirligig, assuming attitudes merely to tease and provoke?"

"You did, indeed, Miss Van Lew," Minnie replied, and scowled at Mr. Devereaux, unseen through her veil. The berline, meanwhile, had left behind the relatively smooth streets of Church Hill, and descended into more crowded – and therefore more rutted and potholed thoroughfares closer to the river. Minnie craned her neck, at the familiar shriek of a locomotive steam whistle. They were passing very close to the railway lines which threaded Richmond like a ragged spider-web. Here was the hubble-bubble of commerce, of loud voices, the grinding of cartwheels and cracking whips. Over it all floated a distant vision of the white-pillared state capitol building, a classic Roman temple set in a grove of young trees, floating above it all like a white-sails of a distant ship, above a vista of common warehouses, narrow side lanes and a tumbled wasteland piled with trash threaded through by a muddy stream.

"I told Rufus to take us past Lumpkin's, first," Captain Chaffin murmured to Mr. Devereaux, who absently stroked his narrow mustache, as he nodded in agreement with this itinerary.

"Ah, yes," he continued pleasantly to Minnie. "Robert Lumpkin. Keeper of the most notorious slave-jail in Richmond, familiarly called 'The Devils' Half-Acre.' A man equally notorious for his riches accumulated in his chosen trade as for the brutality he exercises in the conduct of it. Low breeding always shows. Although, he has made his slave concubine his legal wife, for what that might be worth, socially."

54

"On occasion, the peculiar institution encompasses curious complications," Captain Chaffin murmured.

There was an uncomfortable silence in the berline as the coach continued down a rough and rutted alley; Miss Van Lew behind her veil, and Captain Chaffin looking out from his side as if he wished to be anywhere else but here. Only Pres Devereaux appeared to relish the company and the occasion. *Really, what an appalling man!* Minnie thought to herself. *And Susan wishes to match hers' and My-Dear- Ambrose's Charlotte with him as a husband!*

"Ah, yes, there it is; that fortress with a stout wall all the way around." Pres Devereaux announced, cheery as a cricket with a happy song. "Not as scenic as the Tower of London, or as romantic as the prison of Chillon in Lord Byron's cheery ditty, is it, ladies?"

Minnie could hardly bear to look upon such a scene of misery: yes, a stout plank wall, encompassing a foot-trampled yard with a rambling brick building farther down the sloping hillside. Iron bars set into every window made it plain that it housed prisoners. Three other buildings stood somewhat closer to the rutted lane in which the berline had paused; buildings which had a look of domesticity about them, especially since there were no bars in the windows.

"It is a mystery to all good sons of the South, how those of Abolition sympathies continue to defy the law," Pres Devereaux mused. "And it is the law, enacted by Congress some fifty years ago that such property as escaping slaves must rightfully be returned to their proper owner."

"There is the law which is written by men, who are not perfect, and those higher laws instituted by our creator,"

Minnie stated, for she was truly rankled by Pres Devereaux's bland self-assurance. "That law was created by such imperfect men – who compound the insult to freedom-loving citizens of the North by insisting that we endorse the brutality of slavery by cooperating against our moral sense. It's not enough that slave power confines itself to those places which have willingly chosen to endorse the practice – that we could endure and have for decades! But to demand that we in the North who object to fellow human beings as objects to be bought and sold in the marketplace go against our own conscience, and cooperate with slave-takers on free soil? Is it not as the great Luther himself advised – to go against one's conscience is neither right nor safe!"

"Bravo, Miss Vining," Pres Devereaux applauded. "A fine piece of oratory, I must say! You might almost convince a man such as myself to the cause of abolition – almost; but that I am a Southerner, and our fortunes here depend upon exercise of the peculiar institution."

"Ah, your fortunes," Minnie nodded. Yes, a momentary concession. That would disarm an opponent in the legal hustings, Papa-the-Judge advised, when he had guided Minnie in her studies of his old trials and in his volumes of Blackstone's Commentaries. "Fortunes which are based primarily on agriculture and the export of cotton. But what of industry? Where are your armories, your factories? Why must the raw materials produced in your plantations be shipped wholesale to the mills of England? Why must your fortunes depend on forced labor of Africans, who were originally imported to these shores under conditions of great hardship and cruelty? It is said that a sound tree will bear sound fruit, but a tree with roots in poisoned soil will bear naught but poisoned fruit. I would hold that slavery is the most poisoned soil of all!"

"We do have industry in the South," Captain Chaffin spoke vigorously for nearly the first time in this exchange. "Behold the chimneys of the Tredegar Iron and Locomotive Works! That must count for something, Miss Vining!"

"And that would be your only example?" Minnie tempered her exasperation, did her best to sound conciliatory. "Has the South nothing to equal the fabric mills of Lowell and Fall River, a long-ranging transport project such as the Erie Canal, the iron works of Pennsylvania, New York, and New Jersey? The Tredegar works is a fine one, indeed. The canal and basin for river commerce here in Richmond again are very fine, but when the North has five or ten such enterprises for every single one in the South, you will forgive me, Captain Chaffin, for not being entirely convinced of the advantages of the peculiar institution."

"Miss Vining's mind is made up," Pres Devereaux interjected. "And will only admit such facts as those which confirm her existing prejudice. We should drive on. I had it in mind to see the auction at the Old Fellows' Hall on the hour of eleven."

Minnie opened her mouth to object to this accusation. She was perfectly capable of exercising reason, when a sensible reason applied for admission, but at that moment, she recalled Miss Van Lew's warning; that Pres Devereaux lived to be provoking.

"I would not want to miss it," She brought herself to say, with something of Miss Van Lew's tone of cool disinterest. As the berline rolled on, threading through several narrow alleys, she added, "Besides notice in the newspaper, I would suppose – how else does one discover such auctions?"

"There are auctions almost every day save Sunday in the Old Fellows Hall basement," Pres Devereaux answered. "As well as in other places. You will note the red flags hung out here and there, before places of business? That will signify an auction of slaves. The time and particulars of those to be auctioned are listed on pieces of paper pinned to the flag. Most usually it is a lot of half a dozen, maybe twenty. It is only upon the liquidation of an estate because of bankruptcy that there might be more."

As the berline emerged from a narrow defile between the high walls of warehouses into a wider street, the Negro coachman on the box stayed the horses. A faint thread of discordant music assailed their ears, just as the smell of horse dung, smoke and ripe privies assailed their noses. Minnie pressed a handkerchief damp with *eau de cologne* against her nose.

"Why are we halted?" Miss Van Lew demanded. Pres Devereaux craned his neck to peer out of the coach door.

"A coffle from the country," he replied, after a moment. "Or so I assume. There are a great many of them, heading towards Lumpkin's from the direction of the Mayo bridge. Did you wish to observe, Miss Vining? We are admirably situated to appreciate the parade."

"Yes, of course," Minnie gasped, as a melody badly played on an out-of-tune fiddle became louder without making the tune any more recognizable. A tall, bearded ruffian on horseback approached the berline, tipping his hat to Minnie and Miss Van Lew, although they must have appeared to him as nothing more than a pair of veiled bonnets. The rider, a man in dusty and travel-worn clothing, wore a brace of revolvers at his waist, and a long rifle slung over the saddle-horn and dangling by his horses' withers. The fiddler marched next to him, at the head of a long double file of Negroes – all men, all barefoot and hatless in ragged clothing, chained together at the wrists to a long chain which went the length of the file. Minnie lost count after thirty pairs of the ragged marchers had passed, attended watchfully by four or five well-armed white men on horseback – all heavily armed. The slaves chanted as they marched, a song or work-chanty in a patois so thick that she could not understand it, or even if they were words at all in a civilized tongue.

"They chain those male slaves, day and night, for the march through the country for the security of the agents accompanying the coffle," Pres Devereaux remarked, with the air of a schoolmaster, enlightening a slow pupil. "As you will observe, Miss Vining – there is only a handful of white men accompanying ten times that number. Ah, here come the women. Observe that they are not chained."

A dozen women, some of them carrying or leading children, followed in the wake of the chained coffle and in the wake of their footsteps, three wagons. The first was an open one, seemingly crammed to bursting with more women and small children. Minnie noted that some held an infant to breast. The second and third wagons were heavy freight vans, presumably carrying supplies and shelter. Surely the slaves were not expected to sleep on the ground and forage for food, chained as they were? She looked sideways to Miss Van Lew. Even if she had been able to discern Miss Van Lew's expression through the veil cast over her bonnet, Minnie did not know what the other woman might think of the scene. A woman of clear abolitionist sympathies, and yet living in a city where the horrors of slavery were a familiar and oppressive presence. This was courage, or perhaps cowardice in making no more effective protest against the vile institution ... Minnie, confused, sought out Miss Van Lew's gloved hand.

"I have seen enough of the coffle," she said, proud that her voice did not tremble with outrage. "Please tell your coachman – Rufus, is it? – to move on."

"We must get on towards the auction," Pres Devereaux rapped with his knuckles on the glass coach window. "I had my eye on two suitable slaves to purchase for Miss Van Lew; I believe that I can get them at a price equal to or less than the value of the India gem on my watch chain. The first is a sturdy woman of twenty years or so, with a child of three; accounted to be an excellent seamstress, never been whipped, and certified by the broker to be in good health, save for a clubfoot from birth, a condition which doubtless will account for less enthusiastic bidding. Two for the price of one is my expectation."

"I would not see a child grow up under the condition of slavery," Miss Van Lew commented, dryly. "I approve of your judgement in this matter, Mr. Devereaux. And the other?"

"A musteefino girl of ten or eleven; one of those high-yellow fancies," Pres Devereaux seemed to purr like a satisfied cat. "The natural daughter of a dealer in cotton who most unfortunately went bankrupt, and his estate had to be liquidated to pay off his creditors. I expect the bidding for her to be intense. But because I can economize on the first, I may spree on the other without exceeding the agreed-upon budget."

"Spree as you will," Miss Van Lew did not seem to be the least as shocked as Minnie was. "You know as well as I do that the poor child will otherwise become a concubine or put into a life of the vilest degradation imaginable."

"I could not let such a thing stand!" Minnie exclaimed; she couldn't help herself. "Mr. Devereaux, let me add whatever may become necessary for success to your bid for that child! I command a generous income of my own, and I can make a bank draft available to you in whatever quantity required! I would just need ... the time to arrange it."

"Ah, Miss Vining," Pres Devereaux stroked his narrow mustache. "Then you would become a slave owner, at least in part ... I note that you are most particularly passionate when it is in the matter of a person all but white, as if such a condition is somehow more outrageous when imposed on a woman who most nearly resembles your own race. You were not so impassioned regarding the plight of a crippled African with a child in arms."

"I am not such a shallow intellect as to feel the plight of a white person enslaved is somehow more deplorable than that of an African!" Minnie snapped, although secretly acknowledging that Mr. Deveraux's jibe contained an element of truth. Knowing that the daughter of a debtor could be sold as property merely on the account of possessing a single drop of African blood ... What if such an accusation could be made against Papa-the-Judge; that his long-deceased wife, Minnie's mother, had an ancestor held in a slave condition? She herself would be in danger of being in the same plight as the girl in question, save that Papa-the-Judge had been a shrewd and canny administrator of his inherited estate. And that she, at her age, was in no danger of being purchased by anyone as a potential concubine, even if her mother had been found to be descended from an African slave, instead of from an English bondservant. "Indeed, the whole matter of slavery – of any color or condition is abhorrent to any thinking person. Do you not know, Mr. Devereaux, of those persons, who were American of every color – who were taken as slaves and put to brutal labor by Algerine pirates, within living memory?"

"I do indeed," Pres Devereaux replied, warmly, and Captain Chaffin added,

"And we eventually took Derna and made the Bey of the Tripoli coast yield up all American captives, so strong were our feelings regarding enslavement of our own citizens."

"As was our perfect right to do so, seeing that those poor chaps were taken on the high seas, when going about their own mercantile affairs," Pres Devereaux stroked his narrow mustache again. Minnie was beginning to see that gesture as a clash of foils preparatory to a duel – a duel of wits rather than blades.

"But for those poor Africans in bondage, you have no such tender feelings of concern?" Minnie pressed her advantage, ruthlessly, and Pres Devereaux laughed.

"Of course, not! They are not of my kin and nationality, so why should I care?"

"Because it is the matter of slavery, that being the thread that binds the two matters," Minnie argued. "If it is wrong to seize formerly free white men going about their own business, clap them into chains and condemn them to forced labor in an alien country in one instance, then logic would suggest that it is equally wrong to do the very same to Africans. And the happenstance that such has been going on for ... how many generations does not mitigate in the least. I would rest my case, Mr. Devereaux, Captain Chaffin. If slavery is an injustice and an offense in one, then it is wrong in all!"

Pres Devereaux vented a deep sigh. "Miss Vining, I grant to you that the institution itself – although one which has existed since the dawn of time, ever since it was thought more economical to press the losers of a tribal conflict into servitude than to slaughter them root and branch – presents somewhat of a burdensome embarrassment to us, that in this present day, the engine of our Southern economy is based on slavery. You and your Northern abolitionists do not care for its continuance; Miss Van Lew is unapologetically opposed; my dear Cousin Chaffin has the reservations that any man of tender sensibilities might have – but there it is. Instant abolition is not a solution, I would assure you. What might be done for the thousands in bondage without damage to all? To both those owners of slaves who will be deprived of a considerable investment, as well as labor in a myriad of enterprises, and for those slaves themselves, suddenly cast adrift into a hostile world? Transporting them willy-nilly back to Africa? After being removed for decades from the continent of their ancestors, their customs, and ways: how will this be resolved, Miss Vining? Conundrums in the real world often remain surprisingly resistant to facile solutions."

"I have no answer to that specific challenge," Minnie fixed Pres Devereaux with a glare which was doubtless diminished by being filtered through her veil. "Perhaps transport to the

Liberia colony is a solution, although from all reports, conditions there are not promising in the least! But the institution of slavery cannot be tolerated by right-thinking people, in the North as well as elsewhere. There will be no good coming from an insistence on its perpetuation, for whatever reason, however it might be veiled in the guise of spurious legality and long accustoming to the practice!"

"And there the matter must rest for the moment," Pres Devereaux appeared smugly oblivious to Minnie's ire. The berline halted before a long clapboard building, built into the side of a hill with a gentle slope to it, so that the basement level, Minnie observed upon looking out of the window, opened at the street level on the lowest side. The coach rocked gently as both the gentlemen arose from their seats. "We are just in time. The bidding will begin in ten minutes. Ladies – if you will permit... we will enquire of the broker and auctioneer if we may bring the selected candidates out of the hall for your perusal."

"I would ..." Minnie began, but then Miss Van Lew gently squeezed her hand, warning her to tactful silence. When the gentlemen had departed the berline, Miss Van Lew remarked softly,

"How brave you are, Miss Vining; to make the cause so direct and in such words, words of logic and fire! I wish sometimes that I could be as direct. Alas, I can only bring my own native wit to bear in the parlor, and with old acquaintances such as Mr. Devereaux. I cannot bear the direct regard and fire," and Miss Van Lew sounded so distressed, behind her veil and the lady-like demeanor required of a Southern woman of the upper classes. "I would so wish that I had your confident disregard of proper convention, but I do not ... and otherwise, I have the care of Mama, and our household. I wish that I could go out with a slashing blade but all that I may manage are these small gestures of defiance."

"You do very well with them, dear Miss Van Lew," Minnie reassured her. How curious that the redoubtable Van Lew girl thought so little of her own courage. "It must be so difficult, so different for you, in the heart of the wicked system, whereas I live among friends who wholeheartedly support the abolition cause and do not fear to say so. I have not had to guard my tongue so stringently! I have always been in the habit of speaking freely, even when younger. I was a confirmed spinster from my earliest schooldays, I suppose..."

"I envy you, most wholeheartedly," Miss Van Lew uttered in the tones of one making a confession, and Minnie sought to comfort the younger woman.

"Each and every one of us has their own life, their own secret fears and apprehensions, which are really known only to ourselves and our Savior; who are we to judge another, when all we have is our own imperfect sight!" she said; they sat in silence together for some minutes, until Miss Van Lew turned her head to look out of the berline's window.

"I believe that we are to survey the merchandise, Miss Vining. Endeavour not to encourage their hopes. At these horrible auctions, the slaves of course are pinning their hopes upon being purchased by someone who seems kind and generous. I do not wish to raise such hopes, only to see them dashed. That is just another cruelty, you see ... upon the endless menu available under the slave system."

Outside the coach, an interesting cortege had assembled on the cobblestone sidewalk, supervised by a very elegantly clad youth of race so mixed that he was not that far off from the colors of his two charges, and observed with interest by the usual kind of loafers and ner-do-wells who attended every kind of public spectacle, hoping for diversion from hum-drum lives. The mulatto youth held the elbow of a woman ... no, two girls, one a little older than the other in each hand. Both girls were clad alike in shabby grey calico dresses, with starched white fichus and aprons. Minnie's heart was wrung for sympathy. The darker and older of the pair – the clubfooted girl, who limped painfully – held a toddler clad in a baby dress and wrapped in a cheap cotton coverlet to her breast. That girl's face was carefully blank, and yet Minnie detected some flickers of hope in it, mostly for the way that she looked from the coachman on the berline to Miss Van Lew. The other – a mere child in Minnie's estimation – merely looked down at her feet in abject humiliation and despair. Captain Chaffin, his countenance sent in so fixed an expression that Minnie surmised that his inner feelings were one of equal dejection, rapped smartly on the berline's door.

"We have been permitted to bring the two ... the prospects briefly before you, Miss Van Lew, Miss Vining." he said, as Pres Devereaux handed Minnie down over the metal step. "This is Lizetta with baby Cipio, and Josephine."

Josephine barely raised her eyes from the cobbled sidewalk at her feet as she bobbed a brief curtsy. She looked even younger than eleven, swathed those too-large clothes. The dress boasted a cheery red ribbon bow at the neckline, and another length of red ribbon bound her hair – wavy hair of a dark auburn hue, growing back from a decided widow's peak which lent her countenance a perfect heart-shape. *I would not think she was African at all,* Minnie thought in horror, *but wholly white.* She recollected what Miss Van Lew had said, about requiring the wisdom of a Solomon. Meanwhile, Miss Van Lew was addressing the older girl.

"Well, Lizetta, have you anything to say for yourself? I do not want to waste Mr. Devereaux's funds. You are accounted to be an excellent seamstress – is this true."

Lizetta raised her eyes to meet Miss Van Lew's gaze.

"I be that," she answered, with a demeanor in which honest pride warred with apprehension. "My mam, she taught me plain sewing. Old Miss – she showed me how to do fancy 'broidery ... and 'bubbin lace, too, 'afore she passed on. I k'n do fancy millinery, too. My lil' Cipio, he's a fine healthy boy, his feet be sound – an' he already minds good. You won' have any regrets over bidding on me, ma'am. Just 'cause I can't walk good, don't mean I can't work good."

"I'm sure you do," Miss Van Lew assured the girl, and perhaps only Minnie apprehended the tension in the younger woman's voice. "Mr. Devereaux is going to bid for you and your son. I cannot make any assurances of success, Lizetta..."

Lizetta's gaze sharpened. "Ma'am, if you buy me ... they say that de Van Lews, dey do good by their nigras ... dey free dem on the instant. Be that true?"

"Yes, that is true," Miss Van Lew replied. "But do not pin your hopes to our feeble efforts, Lizetta. There is nothing certain in this world – only in the next."

The mulatto youth gave the younger girl a sharp shake. "Say hidee to the ladies, Josie! Dey gonna bid for you!"

The girl raised her eyes, hazel and swimming with unshed tears, and her lip trembled. She was only a child, Minnie sensed. She must have been sheltered for all her brief life so far; sheltered and cherished. And now she was thrown in among the cannibals, without any of the mental armory possessed by the older girl, who had known only of slavery since birth.

"Ma'am..." the child whispered, and it seemed as if the tears were about to spill over. "P-p-p-please, ma'am..." her voice broke on a sob, and the mulatto youth shook her elbow again, while hissing in an undertone,

"You stop that cryin', Josie! You gwine smile, look happy, now! Ain't no one gonna pay nuthin' for a wet dishrag!"

Miss Van Lew opened her reticule and took out a lace-trimmed handkerchief. She put it in Josie's hand, saying, "It's all right, child – and he's right; most everyone wants to see a smiling face. Dry your tears, now; Mr. Devereaux is acting as my agent, and he has every intention of success in bidding on you today." Josie sniffed, dabbed at her eyes with the handkerchief, and almost looked as if she might be daring to hope. She made as if to return it to Miss Van Lew. "No, you keep it, Josie. And we will all pray for Mr. Devereaux's success in the bidding for you and Lizetta both."

"It's time," the youth said. "Gotta go back inside – you done lookin', ma'am?"

"I am," Miss Van Lew replied, and the mulatto youth directed his charges back into the doorway from whence they had come. Captain Chaffin followed, but Miss Van Lew stayed Mr. Devereaux with a brief gesture. "For both the girls," she said. "Go as high as necessary. I will procure additional funds from my brother."

"And I from my own account," Minnie promised, and Mr. Devereaux tipped his hat to them.

"Your wish is my command, dear ladies." But then he ruined the pose of chivalry by adding, "Save my soul, I have no sympathy at all for this most quixotic passion of yours, purchasing slaves by ones and twos, only to turn around and manumit them. You could never begin to purchase every slave in the south, Miss Van Lew – your actions barely make a dent in the supply."

"This is true, no doubt," Miss Van Lew agreed. "And it is little enough, in the face of the numbers, but this little means everything in the world to Lizetta and Josephine!"

Chapter 5 – And Pay the Reckoning on the Nail

"And did Mr. Devereaux truly make the highest bid?" Annabelle inquired breathlessly upon Minnie's return to Susan's house in mid-afternoon, with the news that Pres Deveraux had successfully bid on three slaves, on behalf of Miss Van Lew. After the grubby commercial squalor of the Shockoe Bottom district, Church Hill seemed a veritable paradise, floating serenely above the mud and misery of the auction houses, the slave jails, and the crowded streets, over which the miasma of smoke from the Tredegar Works, from steamboats on the waterfront and every passing locomotive hung like a shroud.

"He did, indeed," Minnie replied, sinking gratefully onto the softest chair in Susan's parlor. They were alone for the moment; Susan and her older daughters had gone to the dressmakers for a fitting of dresses for the wedding, which was to be the following week. Amy the youngest and My-Dear-Ambrose had not yet returned from school. "And to our very great relief! That poor child! It would have broken all of our hearts if Mr. Devereaux had not been successful! Although it might very well be so that the heart of the hardest among the gathering for that horrible auction might have been moved to pity ... Captain Chaffin thought it might be so, for she was the very picture of woe, when the bidding for her opened! Mr. Devereaux described the scene to us in the most vivid terms. All those poor creatures appeared so very apprehensive, under a pretense of stoicism, never knowing if they were to be sold to a brutal or indulgent master, although he said that the one prime field hand appeared almost jubilant when the bidding for him reached over seventeen hundred dollars."

"So like a man!" Annabelle's lips pursed. "Assured now of his value in the eyes of the world! I suppose there is an odd sort of pride in that!"

"He may as well take pride in his value," Minnie observed. "Such pride is likely the only thing that a slave can truly own."

"And what of Miss Van Lew's new acquisitions? How do they fare?" Annabelle took up her piecework; a wool-work pair of slippers she was working as a gift for Cousin Peter.

"I believe they were most happy and relieved to be thought worthy of Miss Van Lew's regard, especially the younger girl. She thanked us very prettily, and the elder swore that her loyalty and affection for Miss Van Lew would be undying in a most touching and earnest manner … or at least, I think that is what she meant, in her rough language. Miss Van Lew was so embarrassed by such effusions of gratitude. That was the last that I saw of her purchases; such are the vagaries of the practice that once the sale was completed, the broker made all the arrangements to have them transported directly to the Van Lews' residence. John Van Lew, her brother – he is the head of the family – will legally register the manumission of Lizetta and her little son."

"What kind of accommodation will be made for them, being free Negroes now?" Annabelle frowned over a tangle in her wool thread. "I suppose it would be like one of Sophia's little songbirds suddenly discovering that the cage door is open. Overjoyed to be free but realizing that very freedom has unexpected perils."

"Miss Van Lew considered that matter. She and her family are very well-connected throughout Richmond. Mrs. Van Lew is acquainted with a dressmaker who is also a Quaker and of sympathy to the abolition cause, and doubtless will look kindly upon hiring a skilled seamstress. As for Josephine – a child, still. Being so nearly white, she presents something of a difficulty; the possibility of being kidnapped in the street and sold again by an unscrupulous agent, unless she is sent away to the North to a careful guardian – and that is Miss Van Lew's intention. Josephine will be sent to Philadelphia under the protection of the Van Lew connections, placed in a boarding school in that city for an education, and then manumitted when she is 18. Ironic, is it not? That a slave might have more security in being well-known to be the property of another, than merely being free in her own right. The peculiar institution – never was it more rightly named in common discourse!"

"You are impassioned by this visit to the Shockoe markets, I perceive," Annabelle had finally untangled the knot in her wool-work. Now she looked at Minnie, with a most grave expression, and Minnie felt a clutch at her throat – for Annabelle had aged before her very eyes in the last months. Where and how long ago had the mischievous schoolgirl fled? Annabelle now appeared so weathered and aged, her hair gone almost entirely white – and she had been of fair hair in youth, so that transformation had appeared almost without notice or remark.

"I am!" Minnie sprang up from the chair, as if she could not sit comfortably through this tumult of emotion. As if she must be pacing up and down, to give space and allowance to her raging thoughts. "It is one thing, Annabelle – to know of the

72

pernicious institution of slavery though broadsides, lectures, and sermons. Of that I know very well, to an almost tiresome length ... so tiresome that I would think I have become immune through constant exposure. But entirely another to see it in the faces of those held captive under that vile institution ... nay, to see it in practice! In the streets of this very city ... Virginia, which was the home of so many of our founding heroes of this, our dear republic! How art thou have fallen, this place which was the lynchpin of our revolt against tyrannical royalty! Now come to be the marketplace of human souls! I cannot bear it, Annabelle – to be voiceless in the face of such an awful injustice as slavery!"

"And what are you planning to do about it, Minnie, dear?" Annabelle, having untangled the knot in her yarn, bent her head again over her wool-work, and Minnie paused, in her pacing across Susan's fine Turkey parlor carpet.

"I do not know, dear sister – but I shall be moved to a more active part, upon our return to Boston in the fall. You may depend upon it!"

"I hope also that you may also be depended upon to consider our duties as guests, in the time that we have remaining in Richmond," Annabelle stabbed the needle into her work, and her eyes met Minnie's in honest apprehension. "We have always been fond of Susan; she and My-Dear-Ambrose have been so generous to host us for this summer. I do not want their relations with friends here to have been marred by some perceived insult on our part."

"I will be as silent as a tomb!" Minnie promised. "For the remainder of our visit and with regard to the odious institution of slavery! You know me ..."

"I do," Annabelle interrupted. "All too well, and of your temper when righteously provoked, not to mention your impulse to rush straight into an encounter before considering. Promise that you will unburden yourself of your opinions on that matter to no one but me!"

"Or Miss Van Lew, who is even more adamant on the topic than I am," Minnie temporized. "Poor girl, I think she feels terribly constrained. And Mr. Devereaux, who does not seem capable of taking offense at anything at all. I will promise, Annabelle." Minnie sought out her own workbasket and took out the so-far-completed roll of white tatting, regarding it with marked disinterest.

"Speaking of Mr. Devereaux," Annabelle sounded as if she were making a determined effort to change the subject, "Susan thinks that he really remains here in Richmond to pay court to Charlotte; his talk of conducting business here is merely a pretense."

"He is considerably older than Charlotte," Minnie remarked. "And she is barely out of the schoolroom! I cannot imagine that he would see much to appeal in the dear child besides youthful charm and a pretty manner, but of course we will oblige."

Charlotte, the middle child of Susan and My-dear-Ambrose's daughters, possessed a neat figure, guileless blue-grey eyes, the fair-and tight-curled hair which marked the Vining kin, and a fine creamy complexion marred only by a sprinkling of pale freckles across her nose and cheeks. If she possessed any deep intellectual gifts, Minnie had yet to discover them. Although Minnie had not the opportunity for any but the lightest and most conventional parlor conversation with the child; she hoped for the sake of the parties concerned that Charlotte did possess some deeper capacity.

"Susan says he is a man of substance, from a good family, and well-able to support a wife, now that he has gotten over his lamentable taste for adventurous travel. He is quite the most eligible bachelor among their friends; he will be quite a catch for Charlotte." Annabelle, whose marriage between herself and Minnie's brother Horace had been arranged almost before either one was out of small clothes, spoke as if this was a naturally foregone conclusion and one of which she approved wholly.

"If she can land him," Minnie took out her crochet hook, and reviewed the flimsy paper copy of directions for a tatted-lace collar, before commencing work on the intricacies required; Knot after tiny knot, in fine hard-twisted silk thread. Really, she wondered why she should spend her time and days doing fiddling little parlor needlework things like this, merely because such spun out the time and the days of a woman's life? It was different when in attendance on a sickbed – a diversion which she could take up or put down, as needs required. "I wonder," Minnie added, irrelevantly, "If once Charlotte has landed her prize matrimonial fish – will she decide if she really wants it, after all?"

"Of course, she will," Annabelle was entirely serene. "He is well-established in society and life, pleasing to look upon; all will approve, so why should she not accept his proposal of marriage?"

"When he makes it," Minnie looped a series of knots around the shaft of her crochet hook. "Ah, well – a relief to me that I am well-beyond this kind of nerve-wracking nonsense, and have no need of such anyway, to secure a position and a suitable income. Still, I shall do my best for little Charlotte. She will look upon him with worship in her eyes and agree with his every word on every matter imaginable under the sun. I shouldn't wonder that Mr. Devereaux will begin to die of boredom before a month of matrimony, or within the time that it takes ..." Minnie brought herself sharply up. Instead of what she was thinking to say *'until she bears an heir to him'* for that was exactly what had happened between Annabelle and Horace. She hastily amended, "To discover that girlish prettiness and charm may not endure for very long. It has been my observation that a forthright character and honest friendship between the parties to a marriage is a better harbinger for a happy and enduring marriage than all the romantic moonshine ever written."

"He is a very eligible man," Annabelle insisted. "I am certain that Charlotte will be a most suitable wife. I would be most happy to oversee their courtship."

"We shall dress all in black, like a Spanish duenna, and sit in the corner, mumbling over our beads and needlework," Minnie predicted. "If will assist Susan in any degree, I will perform this duty with a cheerful countenance masking considerable boredom ... but honestly, 'Belle, I will be glad to return to Boston in the autumn. Perhaps next summer I will travel to Europe! Wouldn't you like to come with me, 'Belle? Think of seeing Paris! And Rome! All the artists and antiquities. Germany, too – for the science and letters. And castles! Wouldn't you like to visit a real castle, then?"

"You would expect me to accompany you?" Annabelle sounded apprehensive. "I do not really relish the prospect! Of course, I will go if you insist on ... but so far! And everything foreign! Their incomprehensible ways, the fleas, the miseries of an ocean passage ... "

"Only if you would truly relish such a program," Minnie replied, realizing with a suddenly discouraged heart, that Annabelle would not. It would be better, asking Richard and Sophia to accompany her on a trip to Europe and the Holy land. How much more appealing was the prospect of their young enthusiastic interest than Annabelle's dutiful and unhappy presence. Honestly, travel to foreign parts would be a chancy adventure. Annabelle would not be happy ... *Ah, sufficient unto the day*, Minnie told herself, taking up another series of knots in her tatting.

The garden invited the household every morning. In the lazy afternoons, Susan's friends gathered, often with children – children who were polite, well-tempered and utterly adorable, especially Captain Chaffin's two small sons and their little sister when they romped at their childish games on the velvet-smooth grass. Those days of leisure were forever preserved in Minnie's memories like the petal of a fair flower, forever embedded in golden amber; the Chaffin children playing at bowls, or catch, or in hoop-races in the garden with their father and Pres Devereaux – their happy confiding trust in all around them, and the little girl, toddling in her brief skirts after her brothers, brave in their newly-acquired breeches. Seeing the darling children at play almost made Minnie regret her own fears about the bearing of children – fears long laid to rest.

So many friends and neighbors of Susan and My-Dear-Ambrose gathered on those afternoons on Church Hill! Their daughters and their pretty school-girlfriends looked like flowers themselves in their swaying bell-like crinoline skirts, while their mothers sat with Susan, Minnie, and Annabelle in the summerhouse or on the verandah with their needlework, gossiped among themselves and watched their children and marriageable daughters. Sometimes their lazy days were varied with an extended picnic excursion out in the countryside, or on one of the wooded islands in the river – all laid out for the party by silent Negro servants who saw to every convenience and need. Minnie almost had made herself forget the awfulness of the slave system, on those occasions – until she looked at the impassive face of those silent servitors, and wondered what they were thinking of it all.

"Today, Mr. Devereaux is coming to call," Susan announced one morning at the breakfast table. She had an anxious look on her otherwise serene countenance. "I am certain that he intends to ask My-dear-Ambrose for permission to court our dear little Charlotte ... and it is about time! She is perfect for him, and he ... well, he is the catch of Richmond ... but this very day and at the same hour, we have the final fitting for Lydia's wedding gown! And I must be there – can you be darlings, and play chaperone in my stead? It would be in Charlotte's best interest, and after all, he is such a good catch!"

"Of course," Annabelle agreed, even before Minnie could reply. Susan beamed.

"Oh, perfect – I knew that you would!"

For Mr. Devereaux's first call as a suitor, Minnie and Annabelle presumed that Pres Devereaux and Charlotte Edmonds would likely sit together on the small divan in Susan's parlor and make uncomfortable conversation. Meanwhile, she and Annabelle would sit at a small distance in the corner, pretending to attend to their needlework, knowing that their mere black-crow presence would put a severe damper on any but the most respectful overtures and expressions of affectionate regard. Instead, Pres Devereaux arrived with a wooden case under his arm. Upon being shown into the parlor, where Charlotte, Minnie and Annabelle waited – he greeted each with a courtly kiss of the hand, and announced,

"Dear little Miss Charlotte – do you play chess? I saw that there is a proper chessboard inlaid into the top of that very fine little gaming table, and I would relish the opportunity to school you in that marvelously intriguing game..."

"Chess, Mr. Devereaux? Papa tried to teach me once – but it was all so complicated, remembering all the different moves that pieces could do. Papa became exasperated and quite out of temper, but if you wish me to learn to play," Charlotte cast a despairing glance towards Minnie and Annabelle, "And it amuses you. But please, don't shout at me when I forget!"

"I would never lose patience with so charming a young lady," Pres Devereaux assured her, but that did not seem to reassure Charlotte the slightest bit. Minnie suppressed an interior sigh and set aside her tatting.

"If you would like me to do so, dear girl, I will come sit next to you and advise you on the best move. My father was a most expert player, but through the long experience of matching against him, eventually I could check-mate Papa's king at least half of the time."

"Would you, Cousin Minnie? Charlotte's expression of gratitude turned her countenance from woeful to sunny in an instant, and Pres Devereaux's continence likewise brightened. Minnie's heart sank a little; she regretted now having intruded on the couple, and with such a boast, even if Charlotte seemed touchingly grateful.

"I would welcome your entry into the lists of the chessboard, Miss Vining! Now I have brought my own set, purchased in China! Let me set them out on the top of that most splendid table, and we shall commence!"

The game table to which he referred sat in a corner of the parlor; a small inlaid table-top, set on a single pedestal and three legs. "If you would allow me, ladies," Pres Devereaux added, setting aside the case, and picking up the small table. It was not a heavy table, although it was made of the finest mahogany, burnished a dark golden-red, and the top inlaid with alternating squares of ebony and a pale honey-colored wood which Minnie could not name. Pres Devereaux set the table a convenient distance before the settee and brought up a single chair for himself. Minnie took a seat beside Charlotte on the settee and began tutoring the girl on the protocols of the pieces, even as Pres Devereaux set them out. Charlotte's pale, lightly freckled countenance reflected the near despair of a person close to drowning.

"I can hardly remember all that!" she whispered. "You will promise to advise me, Aunt Minnie; every move! I must..." Charlotte left the rest of that sentence unfinished.

"You will remember readily enough, as you become accustomed to the game," Minnie replied, also in a whisper. "You are not unintelligent: It is only a game, a thing to occupy the time in the parlor of an afternoon or an evening. And you wish to charm and engage Mr. Devereaux. As this is one of his passionate amusements, you should learn sufficient skill at it. As for my advice in the game of courtship, my dear – as unskilled and unready as I am to apply it in my own instance – I am rather more skilled in chess, as that provided so much diversion and amusement to my dear Papa…"

"It is a game of war, of strategy," Pres Devereaux enthused. "From ancient India, and into Persia, and then brought to Europe during the crusades. It is an amusement practically universal, as you may see from my set – all carved in the decorative idiom of China…"

"Quite ornate," Minnie agreed, tamping down her delight at the sheer artistry and detail of Pres Devereaux's exotic chess set. The white pieces were the pure pale ivory, in the likeness of emperors, empresses and a pair of grand mandarin noble dressed in their Oriental finery, the rooks being two-tiered towers of a peculiar architecture, and the knights in segmented armor and mounted on stocky ponies and brandishing curved blades. The pawns were individual, each distinguished by the hand of the artist, by different weapons and position. The dark pieces had been dyed a pale brown by some artifice, which curiously brought out rather more vivid detail – the pen and fan held by the queens, the elaborate headpiece worn by the kings. "But my father always said it was the plainer sets which lent one to focus more strictly on the game."

"I cannot wait to begin," Pres Devereaux's vivid blue eyes were sparkling with anticipatory delight. Your move, my dear – in tradition, white makes the first move."

Charlotte's left hand sought out Minnie's, even as her other hand hovered over her two rows of pieces. "Your kings' pawn, advance two spaces – it may, on the first move, you see,"

Minnie murmured encouragingly, and Charlotte obediently moved her first pawn."

"Ah," Pres Devereaux considered the board and the serried pieces with the liveliest interest. "The Spanish gambit, I daresay." He moved the black king's pawn forward two spaces and then awaited Charlotte's response at Minnie's whispered urging.

"Now your queen's knight – two ahead and one over. This lets you command the center, dear – and on the next move, advance your bishop diagonally four squares ahead."

All through that sultry afternoon in Cousin Susan's parlor, the chess pieces advanced, retreated, feigned an attack, dodged a threat, mounted a new attack ... Minnie relished the whole contest enormously. Pres Devereaux was at least the equal of Papa-the-Judge when it came to mastery of the board – but Minnie had been schooled by her parent in the most severe discipline. Although merely a game, it was a most entrancing one to her, several degrees more interesting to her than knotting silk threads, even if at the end of one exercise she possessed a dainty tatted-lace collar, and at the conclusion of the other, only the satisfaction of check-mating Pres Devereaux's king and observing the dawning respect in his countenance.

"Miss Minnie, you are an unsung prodigy! We must match again, at the earliest opportunity, for our mutual enjoyment ... and for the schooling of Miss Charlotte in the diversion of kings!"

"I shall await your visit to this house with the greatest anticipation," Minnie replied, with a demure manner – a manner which came so awkwardly to her usually straightforward character. She allowed Pres Devereaux to respectfully kiss her hand, to nod towards Annabelle, and then to take both of Charlotte's small hands in his, in a manner to be expected of a serious and approved suitor, "Miss Edmonds, this has been the most diverting afternoon. Truly, are you interested in the intricacies of this most noble game?"

"I am indeed, since it is of most overpowering interest to you!" Charlotte replied, with a degree of aplomb which spoke well of her determination to please this most promising of her suitors. "I really am," she added, in a small voice, more fitting to the schoolgirl that she was in truth. "I will take counsel with Aunt Minnie, and endeavor to become a most fitting opponent to you. With time and practice, I am certain that I can become her equal ... at least, as far as chess is concerned. Of those other qualities..." and Charlotte sent a perfectly worshipful glance in Minnie's direction. "I can only dream of such!"

"On the next Tuesday, then," Pres Devereaux tucked the padded case containing the marvelous Chinese chess set under his arm. "I will inform your parents of the time. A carriage ride, perhaps – and then a game?"

"If that is your pleasure," Charlotte bobbed a brief curtsy, and the black housemaid appeared with his hat and cane, to show him out of the Edmonds household. When the door closed on him, Charlotte giggled, and sank onto the divan. "Oh, Aunt Minnie – that went so wonderfully well! Will you really teach me? It would be ... well, Mama says that Mr. Devereaux is such a good catch ... and it is perfect that I should marry him, but I should know so little regarding his peculiar enthusiasms. Mama says that I should endeavor to learn ..."

"I am certain that she does," Minnie replied, and immediately regretted her asperity. "And your mother is most certainly correct. A husband and wife most certainly should share the same tastes and diversions, even if only to have an amusing conversation over the supper-table. Yes, I will try to teach you to play chess well ... well enough to give Mr. Devereaux a diverting match."

"Oh, thank you, Aunt Minnie!" Charlotte embraced Minnie, in a fit of exuberant affection. "I will be so grateful! Mama tells me that I must fix his affections on me, but she never offers up a word about exactly how I should go about doing that! And I ... I would want him to love me," Charlotte confessed, in a very small voice. "He is perfect. And I wish to be worthy of him. Will you be a darling, Aunt Minnie – and help me?"

"I will," Minnie replied, feeling something of resignation. Such a dear girl, and so committed to win the loving regard of such a man as Pres Devereaux! Charlotte kissed her on the cheek, just as the outside door opened again, and Susan's voice echoed in the hallway outside the parlor. "Oh, there is Mama! I suppose they have Lydia's wedding dress, at last! Such a trouble over the final fitting, because Lydia is all nerves, and her corset has to be tightened another two whole inches! I promise that I shall not make such a fuss when I wed Mr. Deveraux! I must go and tell Mama that he has been such a darling! Thank you again, Aunt Minnie!"

Minnie and Annabelle were once again and briefly alone in the parlor, as Minnie sighed. Annabelle quirked a skeptical eyebrow over her embroidery pattern, an expression which

Minnie read as easily as if her sister-in-law had expressed her doubts in words.

"Charlotte is a dear," Minnie said in low tones. "And this is what she most desires – to make a good marriage. It is the fate of most of our sex, is it not? To be joined in the holy bonds to a man of good sense and character..."

"Your Mr. Devereaux is all of that?" Annabelle murmured, and Minnie's temper took flame, or at least, a mild flicker.

"He is not my Mr. Devereaux," Minnie replied. "He is Charlotte's good suitor. How can you say anything to the contrary? His attentions are not anything that I desire! He is the most aggravating man in Richmond!"

"But you like him!" Annabelle replied, with a tiny smile. "He plays an excellent game of chess, and you strike a spark from him, like flint and steel upon tinder."

"Stuff and nonsense!" Minnie took up her neglected crochet hook and the silk thread upon it, wondering where she had left off in contriving knot after knot. But she did wonder if Annabelle might be right. For Pres Devereaux was such a handsome figure of a man, with his weather-tanned face and pale blue eyes ... and he lost at chess that very day with such good grace. Were Minnie any younger, she might be ... Minnie resolutely shoved that thought aside and resolutely counted loops of silk thread. No, it would never do. He was Charlotte's intended.

On the following Tuesday, Susan's last 'at home' day before the wedding on Sunday afternoon, Pres Devereaux arrived before the Edmonds residence, at the reins of a light Tilbury gig, drawn by a single fine horse.

"Ladies, I believe that there will be sufficient room if we squeeze together on the seat, since you ladies are passingly slender," he announced, jovially, as he handed up first Minnie and then Charlotte with an especially fond regard. "I have a mind to drive out to the countryside around Stony Run and regard the lovely aspects of the meadows and rivulets with the flowers all in summer bloom. Our household cook has provided a picnic basket of edible delights. Shall we venture forth to relish nature in all her splendor?"

"Oh, yes! Charlotte replied with enthusiasm, as she tied the bows of a wide-brimmed hat under her chin and took up her reticule and parasol. Minnie had already donned her own plain bonnet. She had the crochet hook and spool of silk thread already, expecting that she would have need of work to busy her hands as she preserved the amenities appropriate to a courting couple. How very boring, she thought to herself – but still far more pleasant than dutiful attendance on a sickbed.

It was a pleasant ride; the gig was well-sprung, and there were hardly any unpleasing jolts to the passengers, even when the road raveled out into a series of ruts and ridges. She did enjoy the passage through the fringes of the Church Hill neighborhoods, out into the wooded and rolling country beyond, a pure azure sky arching overhead, a sky hardly marred by any passing cloud.

"This is now Henrico County," Mr. Devereaux announced. "A very pleasant tract of land, is it not? I have heard tell that the city is considering purchase, for an expanded city burial ground."

"Ohh, let's not talk of such things." Charlotte exclaimed. "When it is such a lovely day! Cousin Minnie, is this not the most glorious countryside in the world that you have ever yet laid eye upon?"

Appealed to, Minnie merely resettled her bonnet on her head, and replied, "Why yes, my dear – it is very pleasing to the eye. Although I have not yet laid eyes on the gardens of Kent, the pastures of daffodils in the Lake Country, the many picturesque castles on the banks of the Rhine, or the marvels of the Alhambra, so I may not honestly make a comparison ... but yes, it is a veritable garden. In future years, I hope to see those other places," she added, noting that Mr. Devereaux looked across Charlotte to meet Minnie's eyes with an expression of approval on his countenance.

"Will you indeed, Miss Vining? A most ambitious undertaking, I must say."

"Having read much of such scenes, I long more than anything in the world to see them with my own eyes," Minnie replied, wistfully. "I am certain that even the most accomplished artist cannot convey even a portion of such splendors – even an artist in words such as Mr. Irving ... You spoke of China, and of those marvelous tropical islands ... Mr. Devereaux, were they not even more beautiful in reality than in any vision called in words or paint?"

"Pale simulacrums, all," Mr. Devereaux agreed. "But now ... is this not a lovelier prospect than anything from the hand of an artist!"

At that very moment, the gig reached the top of a low hill, and from that eminence, a brilliantly yellow field of blossoms spread out on that sun-kissed slope – a meadow so thickly grown with them, and with the white spires of Queen Anne's Lace that the green of their stems and leaves could barely be seen. A fair of colorful butterflies roamed unceasingly from blossom to blossom.

"Sundrops," Charlotte exclaimed. "Yellow primroses! I should like to pick some for Mama – yellow is her very favorite color."

"Your wish is my command Miss Edmonds," Mr. Devereaux reined in the single horse which drew the gig, drawing to a stop on the grassy verge a little apart from the roadway. He tied the leathers over the metal railing above the dash, climbed down and turned to assist Charlotte down from the conveyance.

"I think that I shall wait for you here," Minnie confessed. "I have no wish to muddy my shoes or the hem of my dress – and besides, I believe that I see bees at work among the flowers and have no wish to be stung."

"You may sit chaperone upon us from the carriage then, Cousin Minnie!" Charlotte replied, merrily, over her shoulder, as she waded into the near-to-waist high ocean of flowers. Mr. Devereaux patted the nose of his carriage horse, bade him to be a good boy and to stand fast and followed after Charlotte, with somewhat of the same air of resignation that Minnie had oft noted in indulgent spouses and suitors when presented with a whim or flight of fancy on the part of the women that they loved. It spoke well of Mr. Devereaux that he was so kindly disposed towards Charlotte's impulse, she thought, as she opened her reticule and took out the spool of silk thread and her crochet hook.

At least – this was so very much more pleasing than Susan and Dear-Ambroses' parlor – so overcrowded with furniture ... so purely yellow. As if no other color existed in the whole of the universe. She made several knots onto the hook and looked up. Yes, Charlotte and Mr. Deveraux were now well-out into the meadow of flowers. The sun beat down up on the meadow and on the meagre shade cast by the Tilbury's folded hood.

Minnie bent her head down over the finicky business of her tatting, now and again looking up to assure herself that Charlotte and her suitor were conducting themselves in a manner most circumspect. Yes – they were some distance apart. The proprieties were ensured. Minnie threaded another series of loops and heard the sounds of another horse on the road behind them. A horse at speed, the rattle of a wagon. Nothing to do with them, the Tilbury was well off the beaten road, Mr. Devereaux's horse placidly standing where he had been bidden by his master, the gig rocking only slightly back and forth as it shifted under harness.

The other wagon and team sounded closer – they were on the same road. Someone shouted hoarsely; Minnie looked up in sudden alarm, Mr. Devereaux's Tilbury gig was struck by a sudden sharp, overwhelming force. A horse – it made a sudden scream, like a woman in sharpest pain, and Minnie was launched into the air, to land with a sudden agonizing jolt onto the hard ground of the road. She knew nothing more, other than a sudden crashing blow to her head, and a crack to the arm that she flung out – too late – that sounded like a tree branch breaking. And then – she knew nothing but dizzy darkness and an inability to breathe.

Chapter 6 – The Stars Above in Heaven

She couldn't breathe. All the air was sent from her lungs by the force of that fall. A constellation of exploding stars blotted out the sky overhead, and Minnie felt herself suspended between not being able to draw a breath and a white-hot agony exploding up to her shoulder and down to her hand, and from her head, which had struck the road with cruel force. Somewhere, a woman was crying out in alarm. She sounded very young, panicky – Minnie felt herself lifted, as limp and powerless as a rag doll in the grip of something. She couldn't think, only felt – and what she felt was pain, pain, and more pain.

"Miss Minnie! Wake up, open your eyes – speak to me!" a voice begged – a somehow familiar voice. A man. Authoritative ... and for some curious reason, frantic in concern.

Minnie obeyed the command to open her eyes, although her sight was somewhat baffled by ... oh, yes, the brim of her bonnet, now crushed and disarranged, and a flood of something sticky and warm on her face, wetting the collar of her dress. And this was the countenance of ... oh, yes – she fished in her dis-jangled memory for a name. Mr. Devereaux, the handsome and raffish adventurer ... presently courting the very young Charlotte Edmonds.

Yes. She was supposed to have been their watchful chaperone.

Minnie struggled to recall – yes, an aggravating and contrary man, a whirligig of opinions posed for nothing more than to harass and torment ... but he ... he was a man ... and

Minnie fished for knowledge and insight in her present torment. A man who waged a war on a chessboard and was the most gallant when losing to a mere woman.

"She's bleeding so awfully!" the younger voice exclaimed in horror. Charlotte; yes, that was Charlotte, daubing ineffectually at Minnie's forehead with a dainty handkerchief smeared horribly red. Mr. Devereaux replied,

"Her head struck a large rock on the ground, I believe – and it is well known that such injuries always bleed out of all proportion ... Miss Minnie, please speak to us!"

"Wha ... h'ppened?" Minnie stumbled over the words. It hurt to speak.

"A runaway team, on the road!" Charlotte exclaimed. "The driver could not control them – he had fallen from the wagon, and the wagon struck Mr. Devereaux's gig ... they kept on going! And now the wheel is utterly smashed! What are we to do, Mr. Devereaux? What are we to do, all this way from town? Surely, Cousin Minnie needs a doctor at once!"

"Miss Edmonds, calm yourself, I beg you." Mr. Devereaux sounded as if he barely maintained control of his emotions, Minnie thought through the pain in her head and shooting up her arm like bolts of white-hot lightning. "Take your shawl and spread it out on the grass over there ... good. Miss Minnie – forgive me if this causes you pain..."

"Hurts," Minnie gasped, but with recovering her breath and voice. "My arm. The left. I ... cannot move my fingers without pain ... I fell with it under me..."

Mr. Devereaux's strong fingers palpated Minnie's arm, and the burst of white-hot lightning intensified, almost to the point of Minnie losing awareness entirely.

"I fear that one of the bones in your arm may be broken, my dear Miss Minnie!" he exclaimed in a whisper. "But I beg you – do not be stoic on my behalf. If you would cry out, or faint … I cannot bear that you would suffer in silence to spare my – our feelings. I would … Yes, Miss Edmonds – is Minnie's shawl still in the gig? You must fetch it, girl – she must be wrapped closely, against the bodily cold that attends upon sudden injuries such as this. And find me … find me a straight stick, a length or branch sufficiently strong to construct a splint…"

Minnie felt a new warmth on her face as Charlotte bent over her. The girl was crying, and her tears splashed upon her own face. *Useless!* Minnie's own intellect raged. *Don't be such a silly-billy, child! Do as Mr. Devereaux asked and be quick about it!*

Now she felt herself to be lifted – Mr. Devereaux's strong and steady arms underneath her shoulders and be knees both. He stood, lifting her from the dusty road as easily as she would herself have borne up a small child … He must be very strong, Minnie's disjointed intellect observed, over the searing pain in her skull, and the white-hot agony in her arm.

Charlotte had gone away. Gone… gone somewhere. Minnie neither knew or cared. When she was aware again, and strictly enjoining her scattered thoughts to obey, she lay on her back, on something softer and more yielding than the hard and dusty road. Within her vision, Mr. Devereaux was tearing strips from a handkerchief – a large man's handkerchief, of a rather more useful size and material than Charlotte's wispy bit of lace. Or maybe it was a cloth napkin… Minnie's thoughts went wandering again.

"Cold," Minnie whispered, for she found herself shivering, in spite of the warmth of the day. Charlotte appeared, her face pale against the bright sky.

"I found your shawl, Auntie Minnie," she said, sounding as if she were trying to be brave and not succeeding very well at it, as she tucked the folds of it around Minnie. "Mr. Devereaux has unhitched his horse from the gig. The poor thing was frightened to death, nearly – but unharmed. Which is good, as Mr. Devereaux paid a goodly sum for him. Once he has splinted your poor arm ... we are going to walk back towards town, with him carrying you and I leading the horse. He says there should be someone along this road with a wagon, once we are closer..."

Minnie tried to thank the child. She still shivered, even after Mr. Devereaux removed his coat and added that to the shawl. He knelt next to her, with a small flask silver in his hand.

"Miss Minnie," he ventured, with the gravest of expressions on his face. "I am prepared now to splint your arm, but I fear that it will briefly prove to be agonizing in the extreme ... if you are not of committed temperance principles, might I persuade you to drink a little of this brandy? It's for medicinal purposes, after all. While it will not abolish pain entirely, it will take a little of the edge from it."

Minnie brought herself to nod in acquiescence; he uncapped the flask and held it to her lips while she sipped. It tasted ...warm, warm and fiery. After some minutes, it seemed that the pain ebbed a little in her head, leaving her feeling a little as if she were floating, floating up into the sky like the little tufts of cotton-white cloud.

"I'm going to bind up your arm now," Mr. Devereaux warned her. "So that the broken ends of bone will not grind against each other. Ready?"

Minnie nodded acknowledgment and set her teeth as Mr. Devereaux laid gentle fingers on her arm, murmuring instructions to young Charlotte.

Think of the clouds, she commanded herself. Look at the clouds, and think of nothing ... no, think of the chess pieces, obedient and passive on the board. There was no pain. Chess pieces felt no pain. Breathe deep, look at the clouds and think of Mr. Devereaux's marvelous chess pieces.

Oddly enough, this method of mental diversion proved effective; she did not banish the pain of a broken bone so much as she succeeded in setting it aside, in removing it from her immediate attention, although a sharp movement as Mr. Devereaux secured the last knot – perhaps that of the broken bone ends settling into place – nearly broke that adamantine concentration on the floating clouds overhead and figures of ivory. Upon the final knots being tied, securing her arm to a length of scrap wood – was it a broken bit from the Tilbury gig's hood? She rather thought so – Mr. Devereaux cleared his throat.

"Are you ready, Miss Minnie? We should not have to walk very far before encountering help. This is not a well-traveled road, but in about half a mile, it runs into one."

"You might take the horse," Minnie suggested, faintly. "And leaving us, ride ahead and beg for assistance..."

"I will not think of abandoning you, or Miss Edmonds," Mr. Devereaux insisted. "Not under any circumstances would I leave you alone ... you two ladies alone. No – we return together, no matter how slow our progress! Not another word, Miss Minnie; I will not hear any argument."

Saying so, he stooped and lifted her into his arms once more, swathed in shawls and coat. Curiously, Minnie found this of considerable comfort. She hurt in every limb and sinew – but Mr. Devereaux would not abandon them all and take the horse. It felt as if she were part-floating, carried in tireless arms, until she floated away entirely into the sky and was aware of nothing more.

That blissful state of nothingness lasted for a breath of time to Minnie, and yet that state seemed to be disjointed, with the reality of Susan's guest room mingled alternately with curious dreams. There was sometimes a woman singing, in a soft and nearly tuneless chant: *Oh! let my people go. Oh! go down, Moses, Away down to Egypt's land, And tell King Pharaoh To let my people go!* Minnie often felt moved to wake up and tell the woman that Pharaoh was just the ancient Egyptian term for king, or ruler, and so the song didn't make sense at all.

She might have tried that, but the woman just replied, 'Oh, now hush yourself, Miz Minnie, it don' matter none at all.' When next she opened her eyes, it was to the sight of Annabelle, as pale bleached muslin. There was a doctor there, sometimes, an older gentleman whose frowning countenance was framed by an amazing set of chin-whiskers, who consulted with Susan in whispers.

"Rest and recuperation, my dear Mrs. Edmonds! Your cousin is amazingly fortunate to survive such an unfortunate accident! Why, last month, I was called to the bedside of an unlucky gentleman who was thrown from the seat of his wagon with the team at a full gallop! Such a sad case, and he left a widow and three small children..."

On several occasions, she dreamed of floating through the sky among the clouds, with no fear of falling, and of eccentric conversations with the regal ivory queen of Mr. Devereaux's Chinese chess set. The queen sat next to Minnie's bed, fanning herself slowly with a long-handled fan of curious design, having set aside her inkpot and feathered quill pen aside, near to the spirit-lamp, which sent up a pale wavering flame, the only point of light in the room. An evening breeze stirred the pale curtains at the long windows. There were flowers in the room, and more outside, the fragrance of night-blooming jasmine heavy on the night air.

"We have all the power, you know," the Queen observed, in that last dream-conversation. "All the power there is in the world. Life, birth, death ... men willingly seek out death, if we command them so. Oh, the king is the king, for all that victory in the game depends upon him, but only the queen commands all other power in the game."

"My father often said something of the same," Minnie replied, and the Queen laughed, indulgently.

"Very wise ... for a man! That power must be wielded carefully, of course. With as much care as if it were a thing made of glass. Women are made for that kind of power, you see, with our delicate hands and soft voices. We must wield it, and wield it wisely and well, or else ..."

"Or else, what?" Minnie was fascinated by this conversation, for the ivory Queen had red hair, streaming down over the shoulders of her robe, and she spoke with the accents of England, the great Elizabeth herself, Minnie did not doubt.

"Because in their ignorance and haste, if not cunningly guided, uncaring men will do great harm ... but they must never know that we have such power. They must be brought to think that they act of their own volition ..."

"It all sounds dreadfully complicated," Minnie ventured, and as the Queen laughed again, the dream thinned and vanished.

At that moment, Minnie came to full awareness; it was not night, but mid-morning, and that was Annabelle sitting with her needlework in the chair at Minnie's bedside.

"Oh, no it is not," Annabelle replied, cheerfully. "It is a very simple geometric pattern. I can work it in my sleep. Are you truly awake and rational now, dear Minnie?"

"Yes," Minnie answered. "And almost sorry to be so, as I was having a most curious and interesting dream ... Oh, my – where did all these flowers come from?"

"From a well-wisher," Annabelle giggled. "From Charlotte's intended, Mr. Devereaux! He has sent them every day or so since that dreadful accident – a bouquet each, for you and for Charlotte both. How are you feeling – does your arm still pain you dreadfully? You were insensible for many days, of course – which worried us all, especially Mr. Deveraux and Cousin Susan although Doctor Marcus was most sanguine. Do you remember anything at all?"

"Curious," Minnie shook her head – quite carefully, as the last thing she could recall was how much it ached. "I remember falling from the gig, and of Mr. Devereaux binding up my arm, and then carrying me ... then of being in this room, and a great fuss of people coming and going ... how long has it been?"

"Nearly a fortnight," Annabelle replied, comfortably. "And you have missed the wedding, of course. Susan and Cousin Peter were most distraught, but My-Dear-Ambrose said that as long as you did not seem to be on your deathbed, that they should carry on, although dear Cousin Peter was all for delaying the nuptials in any case."

"I am glad that they carried on with their plans," Minnie attempted to sit up in the bed, and Annabelle hastened to set aside her needlework, to assist her and set another pillow behind her back. "Although I am sorry to have missed the wedding. Did it all go well? I so hope that my bad fortune did not place too much of an additional burden on Susan. After all, she and My-Dear-Ambrose have been so very hospitable ..."

"Lydia was beautiful as a dream," Annabelle resettled the covers over Minnie's legs. "And Charlotte with the other girls – like a garden of pretty pink roses. The reception after the wedding was in the gardens here, with cake and lemonade... The newlyweds traveled to Louisiana for their wedding journey, as Captain Chaffin has connections there, and called on them to offer hospitality to his brother. Did you know of Mr. Jefferson Davis who is in politics? – Mr. Davis is the son-in-law of General Taylor! He is excellent friends with Captain Chaffin, since they were at the Military Academy together, and served together with Colonel Henry Dodge, out in the Arkansas Territory! Sylvie Chaffin was good friends with Mrs. Davis ... Mrs. Jefferson Davis, that is ..."

"I am so sorry that I missed such a glorious occasion," Minnie allowed, with real regret. The wedding was the main reason that she and Annabelle had accompanied Cousin Peter to Richmond. She had even had a new dress made for herself to wear for the occasion, and a bonnet trimmed with a deep ruffle of French lace and a cluster of silk violets.

"Everyone asked after you," Annabelle assured her, as she took up her needlework again. "Asked with such tender concern – Miss Van Lew, and Mr. Devereaux, especially." Annabelle pursed her lips, attempting to hide a smile. "Mr. Devereaux called every day, asking after your condition and Charlotte's. And when he did not call, he sent flowers, and other tokens of his regard and concern. Charlotte is now so very much in love with him, saying that he is the dearest and most gallant gentleman of her acquaintance, and of course she will accept his proposal the minute that he offers it, never mind that Susan says about affecting a becoming and lady-like reluctance..."

"I am likewise sorry to have put everyone through such a bother over myself," Minnie admitted with a sigh. "I am not accustomed to be such a bother,"

"No, dear; you are most often the one making a great bother and fuss over someone else," Annabelle didn't even try to hide the smile. "But at least in Susan's house, her servants are equal to the tasks at hand." She reached out and picked up a small bell, which sat on the bedside table. She rang it, saying, "Are you the least bit hungry? Susan will wish to know that you are awake and rational. She will be ever so reassured to know that you have at least a little appetite. We had breakfast some hours ago, but I am certain ... Yes, Hepzibah," she added, as Susan's housekeeper opened the door to the guest bedroom. "You may tell Mrs. Edmonds that Miss Minnie is awake and in her right mind ... Are you hungry, dear? I am certain that

99

Hepzibah will see that you have whatever dainty you would wish. She has been helping me attend to you, in addition to her other household chores – she has a remarkable command of simple remedies, for which we are all so very grateful."

"Yes, ma'am, Miz Annabelle," Hepzibah beamed proudly. "My mama taught me, just has her mama taught her – an' she was born in the house of a doctor, back in the English colony times, an' the doctor knew remedies for anything which ailed man or beast."

"I am certain that your mother taught you well," Annabelle replied, but Minnie wondered if her sister-in-law was being absolutely sincere. Someone who knew remedies also knew poisons and ... Minnie wrenched her mind from that horrid possibility. There would be no honesty within the slave system as it was practiced in the South, Minnie acknowledged to herself and not for the first time. There were always these sentimental anecdotes about how loyal were to their owners – but Minnie could not see anything in it but a helpless prisoner tamed by long custom and powerless dependency into a hollow semblance of such an emotion as a means of surviving that captivity – not when a slave might be cast into the markets willy-nilly, and led away as livestock by another buyer. *How old was Hepzibah, exactly?* Minnie wondered – hardly older than Minnie herself, but then it was so hard to judge the age of Negroes. Minnie had already gathered from Miss Van Lew that those enslaved and consigned to the slave markets often found it expedient to disguise their age, to appear younger and fitter for the work to which their owners or prospective owners assigned them.

"I'll ask cook for a boiled egg and some toast, Miz Annabelle," Hepzibah didn't sound the least bit servile, though. She clicked her tongue in mild annoyance at the slightly disarrayed collection of flower vases crowding the mantel, the windowsill and the chest of drawers. "An' some o' dat willow-bark tea. Thass good for pains in de head... You don't mind, Miss Minnie, Miz Annabelle – I take these ol' flowers away, they half-dead anyhow."

"I'd like a little bite of fried ham with the toast," Minnie announced, for she had suddenly recalled her appetite.

"I don't think you should," Annabelle sounded uncertain, "...a light invalid diet is what Dr. Marcus advised..."

"Miz Minnie, you shouldn't overtax yourself!" Hepzibah chided her, in a most overbearing manner. "You ain't had any but beef tea or warm milk an' water since you been brought back by Mistah Deveraux! Just 'cause you is better now, don't mean you is all the way better!"

"I still would like ..." Minnie insisted, and Annabelle murmured,

"Dear, I think you had best do as Doctor Marcus advised..." just as Hepzibah put her hands on her substantial hips.

"I'll go downstairs now, Miz Minnie, and fetch yore tray ... mebbe Cook has a li'l bit o' poached chicken from dey stockpot. She been stewin' dat ol' rooster since yestidday," Hepzibah added, as she took up the two vases containing the two most-wilted flower bouquets. The door closed on her back, and Annabelle giggled; a most girlish giggle.

"Honestly, there are times when I wonder who owns whom? And I thought Sophia's Irish domestic was the most prickly and commanding female in the household..."

"It's different," Minnie sighed, and laid back against the pillows. "Different, in the South, with the peculiar institution. Honestly, I wish with all my heart that there could be a fair resolution to it all, Annabelle..."

"Are you tired, dear?" Annabelle, in sudden alarm. "You look so pale..."

"No, I insist – that I am perfectly recovered," Minnie retorted. "Although my arm does ache, a little. Broken bones heal, do they not? I have missed too much of life. I will rise from this sickbed as soon as I am able, as I have inconvenienced Cousin Susan for as long as I might in good conscience trouble her as a good hostess..."

Within a week, Minnie was able to leave the bed and sickroom and dress herself with the aid of Annabelle, for her broken arm was still splinted and bound. It was Tuesday, Susan's customary at-home day. Hepzibah fussed at her to rest and not overexert; which attention Minnie found at once endearing and exasperating.

"I'm not a child, Hepzibah – and not entirely incapable of caring for myself!" Minnie complained. She was seated at the dressing table, having combed out her long hair, but it was Annabelle weaving her hair into a long braid and pinning it up into a bun. Hepzibah had remade the bed with clean linen, and was folding up Minnie's nightgown and wrapper, laying them in readiness on the smooth coverlet. For some curious reason Hepzibah had begun to treat Minnie, and to a lesser degree,

Annabelle, in the same proprietary manner that she treated Susan's daughters.

"I done doubt that, Miz Minnie – it's only been a week since you wuz feelin' better. An' if you have a relapse, don't you go on blamin' anyone but yourself." Annabelle's eyes met Minnies' in the mirror, a shared look of amused resignation in them.

"I will ensure that our dear invalid doesn't overexert herself, Hepzibah," Annabelle inserted the last of several hairpins into Minnie's coiffure and regarded her handiwork with an air of satisfaction. "There! Are you ready to go downstairs? Mr. Devereaux presented his card this morning – along with the usual tokens of his regard for you and dear little Charlotte. My own suspicion is that he wished to observe and confirm for himself that you are well-recovered from your little adventure with the smashed carriage ..."

"Carried you in his arms all de way from out Stony Creek ways," Hepzibah interjected, with a shake of her head and with tones which combined awe and disapproval. "Even do' a waggoneer brought y'all back the last couple mile! Miz Minnie, dat is a devotion mos' powerful. You take care, you hear me? Marse Devereaux, he a man to be reckoned with – an' careful, like. Like a flame in a powder-mill!"

With that dire prophetic statement, Hepzibah collected the most aged flower bouquets from the room and absented herself, her petticoats swishing with emphasis. Minnie looked into the mirror again, as Annabelle pinned a lace and linen house-cap over Minnie's hair.

"Honestly, Minnie – she is so forward!" Annabelle lamented. "A woman of that color and station! I wonder how Susan endures such presumption!"

"I wonder also," Minnie confessed, after a moment. "But it comes to me that women of determination and ability, no matter of what color, or station in life, can exercise power, in any way that they can. It's the power of the queen on the chessboard, you see. Hepzibah may be a slave, owned as certainly as Mr. Devereaux owns his prized carriage horse. But she is skilled in household management. Dear Susan depends on that skill and that is Hepzibah's entrée into power." Minnie laughed a little, as the certainty of this realization came to her. "Subtle power within the household, you see. Cousin Susan desires her household to run smoothly and well, for the love of My-Dear-Ambrose and Hepzibah manages all that very well. Being a privileged house slave, she is afforded a certain degree of authority. Being a woman, she demonstrates that to other women. As well that she has probably supervised Susan's girls from the time they were in the cradle. Still ... her position is perilous."

"How so, dear," Annabelle ventured. "As near as I may see, there is much affection between Susan and Hepzibah – and not misplaced in the least."

"Because as dear as Hepzibah may be to Susan and her daughters, as skilled as she might be in managing a domestic establishment," Minnie adjusted the set of the lace fichu at her throat, and yielded up her seat at the dressing table for Annabelle to make adjustments to her own afternoon attire, "Her comfortable existence in this house hangs on chance..."

"As does the existence of every woman not blessed with a secure and independent income," Annabelle settled herself before the mirror and began taking the pins out of her own hair. Minnie, feeling suddenly tired – although she would never admit this to Annabelle or to Hepzibah save under the tortures of the Spanish Inquisition – sat on the side of the bed and waited for Annabelle to finish with her own toilette. She continued, feeling as if she had been given the answer to a small puzzle. "Suppose that My-Dear-Ambrose fell into debt, through some mischance. Although honestly, I do not think he has ever felt the least bit reckless in his life, unlike some gentlemen of the South that I might mention. But suppose that he did, for the purposes of my argument. And by some further mischance, he died, leaving Susan in debt to creditors. She would have no choice. She must sell all those assets of value, just to keep herself from poverty and starvation. It is a wicked choice presented to her, but a household of slaves present the most substantial block of value to an estate, as such it stands under the slave system."

"That would be wicked!" Annabelle considered that prospective event, outlined by Minnie, who continued, remorselessly.

"Yes, it would be. But it would be a solution to a temporary market reversal. That quadroon child whom Miss Van Lew purchased during our excursion into the Shockoe Bottom? She was a natural daughter of man dealing in ... what was it? Rice, I think. She was a child, indulged and loved, or so Miss Van Lew informed me – but when all was reversed upon the death of her father, her value was all in the marketplace. I am certain that Susan feels the most tender regard for

Hepzibah; but what Hepzibah must know, although she might be able to tell herself otherwise – is that she can be sent to the Shockoe Bottom slave markets and sold. Perhaps with regret on the part of the family that are all but blood her own. But she can be sold. And that ... that is a cruelty. A cruelty which must weigh heavily upon those who have the intellect to think on it, overmuch."

"I see," Annabelle set down her hairbrush, and met Minnie's eyes in the mirror. "Malignant, is it not? The whole of slavery in the South ... and elsewhere? I vow that we shall be more dedicated abolitionists after this visit than we ever were before."

"There is much to be said for observing the monster with your own eyes, rather than at a comfortable distance and in a church pew, listening to the Reverend Slocomb," Minnie ventured. "Perhaps I might do lectures on that subject ... oh, to groups of ladies," she added hastily, upon seeing Annabelle's expression of utter horror, reflected in the mirror.

"Public talks?" Annabelle pushed in the final pin to her own coiffure and settled the brief lace and lawn widow's house-bonnet over it. "Really, Minnie, that just won't do! You have a social position to uphold! You can't just go about giving public talks! Why, anyone might attend! What would everyone think? What would the Judge have said about that?"

"That the cause, my conscience and the occasion demand it," Minnie replied. "I imagine that the same was said to Papa-the-Judge and to Cousin Peter in their youth when the matter of revolution against King George first came about. '*Oh, think of your social position! Rebel against our King? Why, we'd never*!'"

"I suppose that you are right," Annabelle admitted with a sigh. "Still, I consider what social cost we may have to pay amongst those whom we think of as friends and kinfolk, should we come out foursquare in public for abolition of the noxious practice."

"There is always a cost for doing right, 'Belle," Minnie replied, feeling quite comfortable in that statement of which – to her – was obvious. "And if they should think the worst of us, in opposing slavery, and putting all the energies and resources that we have to bear against it ... then, such persons were no true friends of ours!"

"Would you cast off dear kin from your regard," Annabelle still appeared troubled in her mind, as she stood from before the dressing-table mirror. "Those who have tendered us hospitality and their fond regard – their deepest affections, their care for you, for us both. Especially after your unfortunate accident..."

"I admit, my dear, Susan may feel that I have betrayed her hospitality," Minnie took up her light shawl, a woolen thing from India, woven as finely as the flimsiest lawn fabric and colored in bright and exotic patterns. "But the vileness of slavery itself! I cannot remain silent when silence implies approval."

"Courtesy demands a tactful silence under this roof," Annabelle reminded her. "There; are you ready for Susan's callers? When you tire, dear, you can easily make your excuses."

"I am not the least bit tired," Minnie insisted. "Only of being confined to a bed in this chamber. Otherwise, I hunger for social diversion; thirst for it, like a man on a deserted island!"

Annabelle tilted her head, hearing some slight noise from downstairs; a door opening and closing, distant voices in the entry hall.

"Your diversion has arrived, I think!" she replied, and she and Minnie went downstairs to Susan's parlor – there to see Pres Devereaux, with his hat and gloves beside him on the divan. He was alone, sitting bolt upright on the divan. He stood up with eagerness, as Minnie and Annabelle entered the parlor. His eyes seemed to burn a more vivid blue in his tanned face, as he clasped Minnie's hands with tenderness in his.

"My dear Miss Vining!" he exclaimed. "I am lost for words, in telling you how happy I am to see you recovered! I ... and your friends here were ... that is, we were ... I called every day hoping for good news of your condition."

"As you can see," Minnie replied, unaccountably warmed by his obvious regard and relief. "I am well enough to take part in Susan's social whirl, and I have such pleasant memories of our chess match!"

"I will call on you for a match as soon as it may be arranged," Mr. Devereaux enthused – and Minnie noted that he only released her hands with reluctance. "In the meantime, if you are sufficiently recovered, would you take a turn around the garden with me? I have ... well there is a question to ask of you, a question that I feel would be best asked in private..." for some unfathomable reason, Mr. Devereaux seemed nervous, uncertain. Minnie couldn't begin to fathom why.

"The sunshine will be most welcome to me," Minnie replied, "And the sight of Susan's roses ...although," she added hastily. "The flowers that you have been sending to us are ...

they are most welcome, but poor substitute for a garden in summer."

The tall French doors opening from the parlor onto the front verandah stood open, admitting that slight breeze which stirred the window hangings, and brought the faint scent of jasmine and honeysuckle. After weeks indoors, confined to bed, the garden drew Minnie irresistibly. Everything seemed impossibly large, lush, colorful. Mr. Devereaux offered her his elbow, and she leaned on it with good grace, feeling something of the same feeling of being sheltered and protected, as she had felt when he carried her away from the scene of that ghastly carriage accident. The garden, even a little wilted in the heat of late summer, still reflected the anxious care which Susan's outdoor slaves took of it. Spent blossoms were dead-headed and removed, leaves and twigs swept from the greensward, the rambling jasmine and roses pruned and trained to arches and trellises. Minnie felt her spirits reviving, as her strength returned.

"I have not been able to thank you properly for your care," she ventured finally. "Looking after us on that day. I think that I shall not be able to ride with confidence in a carriage again for some time, knowing that you are not present."

"Would you, Miss Vining?" This appeared to cheer Mr. Devereaux. "Indeed, I am honored by your trust and regard. It makes the question that I mean to ask of you an easier one to venture, knowing that you think of me in that degree."

"And what question might that be?" Minnie looked at him sideways; he was so much taller than she, all she might see of his countenance was his profile against the sky above, the sky which in summer was so very like the color of his eyes.

"Come. Let us sit under this trellis," He led her towards the pergola at the bottom of the garden, heavily hung with pale pink roses, which had shed tender velvety petals underneath, like gentle confetti on the benches set underneath. He took out a handkerchief and swept some invisible dust off the bench before the two of them sat down upon it, side by side. "Mrs. Edmonds' garden is a treasure, is it not? I have found it to be so very restful. Of all the gardens on Church Hill ... hers is the most accomplished in design. Every aspect rewards the eye and the senses..." his words meandered off into thought, and Minnie wondered where they had gone, with some impatience. Charlotte and her mother would be in the parlor soon.

"You had a question which you wished to ask of me?" she chose in favor of asking directly; Minnie had no gift for social subterfuge, especially when it came to the male of the breed.

"Yes... of course." Pres Devereaux appeared to hesitate, and then to plunge ahead, like a horse to a race. "Minnie ... Miss Vining. Would you do me the honor of consenting to marry me?"

"What?" Minnie gazed at him, in mixed shock and sheer disbelief.

Chapter 7 - We Loved Each Other Then, Lorena

"I do beg your pardon," Minnie wished that she had remembered to bring her fan out with her on this excursion into Susan's garden. Deploying it would have given her some additional moments to consider this wholly unexpected development. "Mr. Devereaux – did I hear you correctly? That you are proposing marriage? To me?"

"Yes, indeed," Pres Devereaux appeared slightly crest fallen. "I thought that you might welcome such. I confess that I … well, I hold you in considerable honor and affection. Which is, or so I have been informed, is a sound basis for the marital state. You play chess extraordinarily well; your conversation is diverting and original …"

"And I am too old, as these things are accounted," Minnie replied, laying out her metaphorical cards with a flat snap on the table. "I will confess that you are a gallant and superior gentleman; among the most diverting of my meagre acquaintance … but I am disinclined to marriage."

"To me as a person, or to the institution itself?" Pres Devereaux … no, Minnie did not know him well enough to judge if his expression was one of hurt, or not. His question was another shot as if an arrow into her self-knowledge.

"Honestly…" she began. Pres Devereaux sought her hand, which she did not attempt to elude; warm and strong, sheltering, and protective.

"Honesty, Minnie. Miss Vining. Speak honestly, we should never endure a lack of that quality between us."

"Then I shall speak as plainly as my wont shall be, Mr. Devereaux. I find you to be most pleasing, in your character and person. And I will not forget how tenderly you cared for me, following upon that dreadful accident with the carriage! A lifetime ago, as a girl – I would have welcomed and accepted your proposal without reserve. But I am no longer such an innocent. My life for these many years has been devoted to the care of others, to putting their needs and desires ahead of my own inclinations. I am reluctant to take on another round of such obligations..." she floundered, helplessly tangled in her own reluctance to admit, baldly, that now she had become her own woman she was disinclined to take up another such round of duties. She was even more reluctant to admit to her fear of bearing children. Her own mother had died in childbed, as did Papa-the-Judges' first wife, and Annabelle had suffered agonies in bearing Sophia. "I could not be that kind of wife which a man of your quality deserves. I believe I am enough of a good friend to judge what would best make you happy in marriage ..."

"Starting as the dearest of friends would be an excellent foundation for a marriage," Pres Devereaux insisted. "I do not see that as an impediment, my dear Miss Vining."

"But I do," Minnie admitted, sorrowfully. "There is also the matter of ... the peculiar institution. I could not endure life in the South, where I would be reminded every moment of every day, of the cruelty of slavery."

"We could live elsewhere," Pres Devereaux offered. "In a place which ..."

"No, my dear friend," Minnie clasped his hand in both of hers. "That is no solution. You are a man of the South; your fortune and family, your home and your connections all lie here, or among your Charleston kin. How long would you remain content with me under that kind of estrangement from all you know and love so very well? Cut away, root and branch from your native soil? You would begin to resent my uncompromising determination to have nothing to do with slavery and I believe that would break both of our hearts. And …" Minnie steadied herself with a deep breath. "You would want children; a family. No, don't deny this; you have spoken so fondly of your own younger brothers and sisters, and I have seen you with Captain Chaffin's little ones, on so many pleasant afternoons! You would want children from a marriage; it is the reason that the Almighty has instituted that sacrament among us! I am nearly past the age where I might safely bear them. I love children also – but I also love life, and I very greatly fear that in giving you even a single child, I would risk giving up the other! My dear Mr. Devereaux – could you ever forgive yourself for being the instrument of exchanging my life for that of an heir to carry on your name?"

"I do not believe that I could," Pres Devereaux's countenance was ashen. Plainly, he had never considered that eventuality. "There are means of governing marital congress…"

"No, dearest Pres. Separate bedchambers are not a solution; man and wife are meant to be to be two halves creating a whole." Minnie's heart was wrung; he cared so much for her, and she for him, but not nearly in the same degree. With an effort, she made her voice calm, steady, as if directing the places on the chessboard. "We are not meant for each other. The stars themselves militate against it. Accept that in good heart. Besides," she added, in a voice wholly practical. "Charlotte adores you. The Reverend Ambrose and Mrs. Susan wholly approve you as a suitor for her hand. She is a much more suitable candidate for your wife than I!"

"She is a child," Pres Devereaux's voice cracked with the deep emotion which freighted his words. "A mere and charming child. Miss Vining, I beg you to reconsider your answer!"

"No, Mr. Devereaux – it becomes you not to beg, least of all to me." Minnie secretly rejoiced at the calm resolve in her voice – for she was mightily tempted to yield to the impulse of her baser impulses, accept his fond embraces and consent to be his wife. *But the mere fact of having mental reservations ... no. Deep and abiding love admitted of no doubts.* If it was meant to be, she would have accepted instantly, without a second thought. "Consider us to be dear, and affectionate friends, nothing more. Charlotte may indeed be a child, but I have a measure of her character; she has such determination to make herself equal of the honor that you have offered me! She is already giving herself to the study of chess, in order that she might be a fit opponent. Do not break her heart by spurning her affections."

"There is nothing that I might say to change your mind, then?" Pres Devereaux did not readily yield up her hands; Minnie eased hers from his grasp, and replied,

"No. You have honored me with your respect and friendship; I am grateful indeed – and honored beyond measure, for you thinking me worthy of your name. I think that we should return to the parlor – before people begin to think there is something amiss."

Minnie, on rising from the garden bench, felt Susan's sun-drenched garden sway just a little around her. She took Mr. Devereaux's proffered elbow with a feeling of regret and gratitude for his strength and innate chivalry. They retraced their steps, returning in silence to the parlor; now somewhat more filled with callers than it had been when Minnie and Pres Devereaux had absented themselves; Susan, resplendent in a crimson and white striped confection, exclaimed her pleasure at seeing them both,

"Especially as you are so recovered, my dear cuz!" she gestured towards the chess table, now drawn to a corner, and set out with a plain collection of pieces. Minnie supposed that Susan or perhaps Charlotte might have found them in a drawer somewhere. "Will you be up to assisting Charlotte in a match with Mr. Devereaux this afternoon?"

"I think not," Minnie replied, feeling as drained as if she had just returned from a long journey. "In fact, I will only sit with you all for a short time – I am exhausted. I confess that I am not as well as I felt myself to be earlier in the afternoon."

"Do you wish to withdraw from the parlor?" Annabelle set aside her needlework, with a sharp glance of concern at Minnie's face. "I will see you upstairs then ... I think you have overestimated your strength, my dear."

"No, I will sit downstairs for a while," Minnie replied. Mr. Devereaux showed her to the most comfortable of the unoccupied chairs, with every evidence of tender concern, although they did not speak again, save in remarks suitable to the impersonal and civil restraints of Susan's parlor. Minnie took up her workbag from Annabelle. *Was she still doing that tatted lace collar?* She supposed that she was, the silk knotwork laid aside all these weeks ago. She took the spool of silk thread and her crochet-hook into her hands, convinced that she should, at least, make a good pretense of recovery from the carriage accident.

In the corner of Susan's parlor, Charlotte and Mr. Devereaux bent their heads over the inlaid chessboard. Minnie regarded this with mixed feelings. Yes – Pres Devereaux was compliant to her suggestion that he consider honoring Charlotte with his name and devotion ... and yet, Minnie couldn't help feeling regret, among the burble of insipid conversation between Susan and her stream of callers. Finally, she laid aside her crochet-hook, and murmured to Annabelle,

"I think I am tired. I should withdraw now, 'Belle. No one should notice our passing, I think."

Following on their withdrawal from Susan's parlor and retreat upstairs to the guest bedroom, Minnie cast herself onto the bed. Yes, she was exhausted, even feeling slightly faint; not from just the physical exhaustion, but the foray out into the garden and Mr. Devereaux's unexpected proposal. How taxing that had been to her emotions. She could not quite bring herself to confide in Annabelle about that proposal of marriage. Instead, she said,

"'Belle, can we send a telegram tomorrow to Richard? I think that it is time that we return home. Within the week, if possible. I feel that our social usefulness to Susan is at an end."

"Are you certain, dear?" Annabelle ventured. "I am still enjoying myself, and Susan has talked of asking us to manage a booth at the school's autumn bazaar."

"Yes, I am," Minnie replied, even as a tentative knock at the door announced the hovering presence of Hepzibah, or one of the junior maids. "I am done with Richmond and the South. We have done our duty by Cousin Peter, and Susan's social obligations. I want to go home to Boston, and never lay my eyes on a slave again. I will work to hasten the day when every single Negro in the North and South breathes the air as free men and women!"

It was another fortnight, and the first cool temperatures of fall had begun to trim the leaves of certain trees on Church Hill with autumnal tints, before Richard Brewer appeared at the front door, dapper and self-contained as always. He was ushered into the hallway of Susan's house by an attentive household staff one late afternoon. Hepzibah appeared in the parlor to announce his arrival. Such was the efficiency of Susan and My-Dear-Ambroses' household staff that his meagre luggage was already being conveyed upstairs, if Minnie correctly interpreted the hasty patter of footsteps in the hall.

"Cousin Brewer!" Susan sprang up from her chair. "Fortunate your arrival in time for supper! I am desolate that Annabelle and Minnie wish to depart! The bazaar is next month!"

"We had always intended to return by late summer, Susan," Minnie protested. "As much as we have enjoyed a leisurely visit, I have my own household and social circle to consider, and I know that your hospitality cannot be prolonged indefinitely!"

"I wish that you would stay at least a little longer!" Susan insisted, but Minnie sensed that such protests were only social and half-hearted at best. She did not hold that against Susan; it was sufficient that she had made a comfortable home for her venerable father in what must inevitably be his declining years, as fit and hale as Cousin Peter still appeared.

"No, my dear – indeed, we must go from Richmond and your pleasant household," *Annabelle could be depended upon to play her social best*, Minnie reflected. She had still not told Annabelle of Pres Devereaux's proposal of marriage; a curious kind of discretion held her back from that, as if it was a precious gem that she must keep to herself, lest it be sullied and fractured by common knowledge. "The wedding was most memorable – all our Boston kin will know of it – but our dear and sweet Minnie must take up her social duties among the ladies at the Beacon Street Church. The Judge's estate must be ministered to, and Minnie is the best-equipped to see to it."

"Indeed," Richard Brewer agreed, settling into a comfortable chair, and accepting a cup of tea from the hovering maid. *This one was named Persy, short for Persephone. Minnie had divined her name, and the names of half a dozen other house servants by many searching questions directed at Hepzibah during her convalescence. Minnie was hampered in this as they were all dressed much alike and were much of an age and coloring.* "I have already purchased tickets for departure on the day after tomorrow. Mama-in-Law and Aunt Minnie seemed desirous of returning in all haste, so I took that liberty, seeing it in their best interests!" His eyes sparkled mischievously. Minnie wondered if there was something Richard left unsaid about the Reverend Slocomb's congregation.

"I am agreeable," Minnie replied; she was although the return journey might very well prove exhausting beyond her strength after the carriage accident. "Thank you, Richard – I am ready to return home. I want to see how the garden has fared. It has been in my mind that I have been remiss in all that

I am responsible for in Boston, while I have been lazing myself away all this summer."

"Your garden does well," Richard replied, in the same humor. "Your peerless Mrs. Norris and her family have seen to that. Alas, I cannot say the same of the larger garden – that is, the Beacon Street congregation." His mien sobered. "All is not entirely well with the Reverend Slocomb's circle. There is a scandal brewing, perhaps about to come to a full frothing boil..." Richard looked sideways at Susan. "A small tempest in a local tea pot, and of interest only to those in the near vicinity; I will not bore you all with the particulars. I had the most interesting fifteen minutes on the train between Fredericksburg and Richmond; a party of extremely belligerent men who represented themselves to be slavecatchers. Upon hearing that I was from Boston, they were convinced that I was a ringleader of abolitionists engaged in smuggling slaves to the North. I invited them to search my luggage; if I had any Negro dwarfs packed among my shirts, they were perfectly welcome to confiscate them. And if I was smuggling them to freedom in the North, then why on earth was I traveling in the opposite direction? I showed them my ticket, of course. Logic," Richard added, with a sigh. "It is the most marvelous concept. Almost capable of defeating the most obdurate stupidity. They did not find any dwarves, of color or otherwise, in my trunk, but it did not prevent them from emptying out all my clean things onto a filthy-dirty railway platform."

"I will have Hepzibah take your things to be laundered," Susan exclaimed. "I am so sorry, Cousin Richard! It's just that feelings are running so high..."

"Understood, and thank you for the considerate hospitality," Richard replied, with a wry smile. "I promise on my gentlemanly honor that I will not preach abolition to any of your friends or household during the remainder of our visit. I am here merely to escort my dear Mother Vining and Aunt Minnie back home, and that is the long and short of it."

"I will be so glad to be home," Annabelle confessed, as she and Minnie prepared for bed that evening. Minnie agreed; she was still feeling the aches and pains from the carriage accident. "And to feel something other than this relentless Southern heat!"

"It will be cold soon enough," Minnie had already retreated to bed, her nightcap covering knotted rags with which she was determined to try for a fashionable set of curl-tendrils in her last days in Richmond. "I think that we will soon look back upon Southern warmth with nostalgic fondness. Think of the dreary damp, the soot and smoke, and the slush melting in the gutters – and remember Susan's garden!"

"I don't care," Annabelle returned, as she turned down the flame in the single oil-lamp which lit the room, and then blew it out. "I want to be home. I want to be home in Boston. I do not ever want to leave home again."

"That might be best," Minnie said, with a sense of sorrow. So much for her dream of visiting England, Germany, and fabled Italy, in company with Annabelle; all gone glimmering down into the well of dead dreams. Annabelle took no joy from imagining visiting faraway places. Increasingly, that exasperated Minnie, although she knew that Richard and Sophia were agreeable to that venture. It just wouldn't be the same. Minnie fell into sleep, considering that long-thwarted longing, and dreamed of the enchanted towers of the Alhambra, under the vivid blue skies of Spain.

Minnie, Annabelle, Richard, and a quantity of luggage, were delivered to the pillared splendors of Broad Street's Union Station in good time by the efficient good offices of Sampson the coachman, and a muscular young male slave who Minnie did not recognize, to her mild regret. She had tried to learn the names of all Susan's household slaves, but could only claim familiarity with the girls who worked within the house, not the male slaves who worked outside of it – all but Sampson, the coachman! To know their names and a little of their lives, even though there was otherwise such an unfathomably deep gap between her own existence and theirs. It was the very least that Minnie could do in striking a blow – even one so light as to be a feather-stroke against the awfulness of the slave system. Even as she, with Annabelle and Richard entered the Broad Street Depot, they could look up at the hill on which the State Capitol floated, serene and classical against a pure blue sky. Farther down in the mud of Broad Street, a coffle of chained slaves shuffled by, ebony dark or the color of coffee. It was as if their presence mocked every civilized ideal written into the laws of the United States, represented by that stately columned façade etched against that sky.

Someday, Minnie silently promised herself, as Richard offered his elbow. *Someday – I pray that we will all live to see the stain of the slave abomination cleansed from the garments of our republic!*

The daily Richmond, Fredericksburg & Potomac train was already waiting; the immense iron engine which drew it seeming to leak steam from every pore and sending up a vast pillar of coalsmoke; the very air about the locomotive seemed to shiver with repressed energy, energy impatient of being released. Minnie sighed and brushed several small black cinders from the breast of her dark grey travel costume. There was a considerable line of respectable passengers to board the First-Class coach, handed up the steps into the coach one by one.

"Susan's boy has seen that our trunks were loaded into the baggage car," Minnie tore her thoughts away from the stain of slavery represented by the coffle they had passed. "Shall we stay the night in Fredericksburg?"

"I have made a reservation at the Milford Inn" Richard replied. "When I passed through – I was certain of the date, and the Milford has a well-deserved reputation for being the most comfortable of all the establishments in Fredericksburg."

"Comfortable it may be, but it is not home – where I most long to be!" Annabelle sighed, and Richard patted her gloved hand consolingly.

"A week or two, Mother," he said. Meanwhile, Minnie's attention was drawn by the young lady ahead of them; a slender young woman, most fashionably dressed in the bell-shaped full skirts that were the highest of fashion; a heavy rich brown materiel which had the sheen of silk, and over it a mantle, striped in brown, dark orange, and gold, trimmed lavishly with festoons of bullion fringe. Minnie frankly envied the colors, wishing she had the presence to wear the same. Alas, she had another year and more, until she could put on lighter mourning colors; insipid shades of lavender and grey, never such a confection of rich colors worn by a young Southern miss of fashion. The young lady had on a bonnet trimmed in knots of matching ribbon, with a brim so deep as to hide her face, save when she turned her head slightly to speak to the slave woman in attendance upon her.

Does she procure her clothes from France, Minnie wondered? So very on-point with the imported fashion papers that Susan's daughters cooed over, so much more *a la mode* than a Richmond modiste could have created.

The train porters were helping the passengers to ascend into the First-Class Coach. So the line of passengers inched steadily towards the door. All the while, the engine belched black smoke, and porters scurried to and fro, wheeling barrows of trunks and carpetbags piled high upon them. Between one moment and the next, Pres Devereaux appeared, a parcel wrapped in brown paper tucked under his arm and looking up and down the platform. Even at a distance, she could see his somber expression lighten as his questing gaze fell upon them. He shouldered his way through the throng of passengers, the porters with their barrows empty and full, and friends and family come to the station to bid farewell.

"My dear Miss Vining," he exclaimed, as he approached. He sounded short of breath. "I am desolate at the thought of your departure from Richmond – so charming and worthy an opponent is a rare thing!"

"Mr. Devereaux," Minnie replied. "I … I thought we had already said our farewells some days ago."

"I know," Pres Devereaux acknowledged. "But in consideration of that private conversation between us, I determined that I should ask one final time if you had cause to change your mind."

"No," Minnie averred, seeing that Richard and Annabelle were looking at them with expressions of curious and puzzled interest. Even the fashionable young woman in the embellished mantle had turned her head. *Temptation ... take this cup from me*, Minnie begged silently. "No, Mr. Devereaux. I have not changed my mind. I am neither fickle nor persuadable in my affections."

"I expected as much," Indefinably, Minnie sensed the slump of defeat in his shoulders, an expression of desolation in his eyes. "Although I entertained a fond hope ..."

"Boo-o-o-oed!" came the call from the train conductor, and the shriek of a steam whistle split the smoky air. "All aboard for Ashland, Milford, Fredericksburg, and steamboat connection at Aquia Creek to the National City of Washington and the north!"

Minnie lost the next of Pres Devereaux's words; his lips were moving, but she could not make them out. "... A token of my deep affection," he said, as he put the package into her hands. "Adieu, my dearest Miss Vining. Until we meet again."

She had no choice but to accept the package, for the conductor was handing up Annabelle into the coach, as Pres Devereaux yielded to Richard, those pale blue eyes of his over Richard's shoulder, before he donned his hat and turned away from her gaze. Minnie climbed into the coach, following Annabelle and the fashionable young lady, whose Negro maid was carrying her valise and a heavy carpetbag with apparent ease. Minnie was stayed in the aisle by the maid, who blocked her own way, while she stowed her mistresses' valise and carpetbag in the overhead rack for small luggage. Richard and Annabelle had already claimed the pair of seats opposite. The coach looked to be crowded this morning.

"Miz Bonnie," the maid addressed her mistress respectfully. "Will you be wantin' anything else, afore I go to the nigra coach?"

"No, Ben ... Beneatha," Miss Bonnie replied, and her eyes flicked up to Minnie, standing in the aisle with her reticule and that brown-paper wrapped package in her hands. She had put her bonnet back, and Minnie could clearly see her face. "Best go now and let the lady past."

Minnie's interest was piqued and then alarmed. The fashionable young lady, Miss Bonnie, if that was her name, was as beautiful as her maid was not. The mistress had a complexion a goddess would have envied, huge dark eyes set in a face that would have graced an ancient Greek sculpture, and black hair combed back under the lace frill and ribbon festoons which edged her bonnet. She spoke with the drawling accent of the deepest South; charming in a woman, even more charming in a man like Pres Devereaux. The maid, Beneatha, was a tall, gangling creature, with knobby and work-worn hands, and a complexion upon which African blood and blinding sun had not done any favors. She towered over Minnie, who thanked her stars for her own unfashionably modest crinoline, as Beneatha squeezed past in the narrow train aisle. Even though the weather was mild, Minnie noticed the shawl wrapped tight around Beneatha's shoulders and neck. *I suppose the poor thing feels the fall chill most awfully*, Minnie told herself, a*fter being accustomed to the heat of Africa.*

125

Aloud she ventured, "May I presume to introduce myself, since it appears that we must share the seat? Minerva Vining. My sister-in-law and I are returning North after a long visit to family in Richmond. Are you from Richmond? I thought that I had met every person of note among their Church Hill neighbors during our visit."

"Miss Bonnie Beauchamp," the younger woman replied, and scooped enough of her silken skirts and lavish petticoats aside to make room for Minnie. She smiled, revealing even white teeth. "No, my family resides in Charleston. I am traveling North ... traveling for my health, as far as Newport. For the cool ocean breeze, you see."

"I understand that the summers in the more distant South are so very unendurably hot," Minnie sat down, the package still in her arms. "Richmond seemed beautifully temperate, to me – and our cousin's garden was a veritable Eden. You travel alone, Miss Beauchamp? All that way? My family ... at least my sister, Annabelle – refuses to venture anywhere without a male escort, so we have the assurance of protection from her son-in-law. He is a lawyer in Boston, you see – and of no small repute."

"From Boston, you say?" Bonnie Beauchamp tilted her head to one side and regarded Minnie with mild curiosity. "Might I inquire if you are of abolitionist sympathies? I have heard that many of that locality are."

"I..." Minnie hesitated. Since the rail car was so crowded, she would be sitting next to this young woman until the next station, and likely farther. "I hold certain opinions regarding the peculiar institution, but I would not be so ill-mannered as to make a raree-show of them while amongst those who are of the opposite inclination. That would be ... rude. And tactless. But most of all, rude."

"Ah." Bonnie Beauchamp smiled again. "Manners. That which lubricates society. I travel with Beneatha, who is all the protection that I require, being a Beauchamp of Rival Plantation – whether in the North or the South or in the nigra coach. She is the most ferocious of watchdogs, Miss Vining. I need fear no interference when Beneatha is with me."

"Rival Plantation," Minnie mused, as the train car gave a sudden jerk. The pillars of the station outside the train windows seemed to move, at first halting, and then with increasing smoothness as the train rumbled along Broad Street, the facades of businesses, a scramble of houses in their ramshackle gardens and the distant chimneys of the Tredegar Works. Over the noise of the engine, and the rumble of iron wheels on shining rails, she must raise her voice. "Might that be near to the property of the Devereaux family? They are from Charleston, I believe. Mr. Preston Devereaux was the gentleman seeing us away at the Broad Street Depot ... who pressed upon me this most awkward last-minute gift!"

"I ... do not have the pleasure," Miss Beauchamp appeared to hesitate. "Of knowing that gentleman socially. I ... my family has been mos' circumspect with my upbringing."

"I do hope that your visit to the North may bring you a wider set of acquaintances," Minnie remarked, as Annabelle looked across the aisle. "And that your ... that is, Beneatha will permit the most gentlemanly of your admirers to extend their regards!"

"What did Mr. Devereaux bring you?" Annabelle also had to raise her voice, to be heard over the train noise. "So awkward, that he would present it at the last moment, when it could not be packed away with our trunks!"

She sounded cross; Minnie hoped that the journey to Fredericksburg would prove smooth, and without tedious interruption. She divested the parcel which Pres Devereaux had so hastily thrust into her arms, of the string and brown paper which had swathed it, revealing a wooden case of dark red mahogany cunningly inlaid with mother-of-pearl inlays in intricate patterns, set so deeply in the wood and lacquered so well that the lightest of touch could not detect any join between wood and inlay. Minnie gasped – she knew that case very well. Hardly daring to breathe, she found the catch, and opened it, balancing the case most carefully on her lap. Inside, each piece nested in a separate niche, lined with faded crimson velvet, was Pres Devereaux's carved ivory Chinese chess set. It was a gift of such personal and generous magnitude that Minnie could only stare at it for some moments, quite overcome. There was a small envelope tucked into the niche which contained the White Queen. Minnie took out the envelope and read the brief note enclosed.

To the Queen of my heart, the most admirable woman of my acquaintance. Think of me, when you indulge in the Game of Kings – Now and forever, your most devoted opponent – PD.

She folded the note, replacing it in the envelope. As she placed it in her reticule and closed the case, she met Miss Bonnie Beauchamp's curious gaze.

"The gentleman was ... is a friend of mine," she remarked, keeping her voice level with an effort. "He was fond of matching me at chess. I can only think that he found me a worthy opponent, in rendering me this gift!"

From across the aisle and beyond Richard Brewer, Annabelle remarked,

"My dear, he has gifted you with his set of chess pieces! Such very generous a gift! How well it will look in your parlor! I might believe that he was fond of you, and your matches in Susan's parlor! What a souvenir of our stay in Richmond!"

"It is, isn't it," Minnie answered. She closed the case and regarded the diminishing view of the hills of Richmond, turning gold and russet from the turning of the season, and wondered if there wasn't some small part of her woman's heart that she was leaving behind, in spurning the adoration of a man like Pres Devereaux.

Chapter 8 – Our Hearts Will Soon Lie Low

Arriving in Fredericksburg in the early evening, after a more than tiring journey, Minnie wished for nothing more than a soft bed and a night of comfortable sleep. It did not escape her notice that both Annabelle and Richard covertly regarded her with concern, especially as she did not wish to entrust the case with the Chinese ivory chess set to the care of the railway porters, or to the driver of the brake which arrived to convey passengers to the Milford establishment.

"No, I treasure Mr. Devereaux's gift too highly to entrust it to anyone else but myself," Minnie insisted, although her broken arm ached like a sore tooth. She carried the chess set close to her chest, still marveling at Pres Devereaux's generosity. They were to spend the night at the Milford, although Richard had conceded that they might spend an additional day and night there, if Minnie and Annabelle required additional rest before another day of travel. Their trunks would be sent on to the landing at Aquila Creek, for the steamboat journey up the Potomac to Washington. All they would take for a night or two in Fredericksburg was contained in a carpetbag or two, and Richard's valise of clean shirts and male necessities. It was a short journey to the Milford from the railway station, perched as it was on a low rise above the river, and the railway bridge which crossed it.

"I think that we shall order supper to be served to us in our rooms," Annabelle declared as they alighted at the Milford – a comfortable place which Minnie recalled from their journey earlier in the summer, where the windows of their rooms looked out onto the gentle Virginia hills. Now they would be clothed in the colors of early fall … but Minnie was too tired to relish that view.

"I could envy our companion of the journey," Annabelle remarked again. "That Miss Beauchamp, Minnie, who shared a seat with you? Her maidservant; I vow that woman was a veritable packhorse. I observed her lifting the heaviest trunk without any effort! I suppose that physical strength is a recompense for her being the very plainest example of our sex that I have ever laid eyes upon."

"Indeed," Richard chuckled. "My first thought upon regarding Miss Beauchamp's attendant was that her servant was a man dressed in female garb, and that this was a kind of cosmic jest upon us all! Aunt Minnie, are you well?"

"I am," Minnie insisted, for it had occurred to her that Miss Beauchamp's servant Beneatha would have made a credible man, indeed. However, that was none of her business; she was indeed exhausted from the journey and the emotional turmoil launched from Pres Deveraux's final gift to her.

"You don't look it at all, dear," Annabelle fussed, and even Richard cast a critical eye upon her. "I think that we should rest here tomorrow and continue the following day. We may catch the afternoon train, and then retire to our stateroom on the steamboat for the overnight journey along the Potomac."

"I would rather continue to Boston without delay," Minnie protested, but she was overruled, not by Annabelle and Richard so much as her own exhaustion, and the renewed aches from barely healed bones. A day of leisure in Fredericksburg, and another good night's sleep in the comfortable beds provided by the Milford would do her a world of good.

A comfortable supper provided on trays to their room revived Minnie no end. Richard came from his own room to join them for it, set out by a silent Negro woman servant on the small table which sat before the large window in the best room available at the Milford.

"I shall be glad to be at home in Boston again," Minnie confessed. "Although, we did enjoy ourselves. But Susan and her dear Ambrose do have a perfectly hectic social schedule, what with his school obligations, and all her friends. I so enjoyed the company of Miss Van Lew, and of Mrs. Chaffin. I hope that both those ladies will come to visit, since they have friends and kin in the north. Mrs. Chaffin and the children will be living with her family for the next few years, while Captain Chaffin takes up duties on the Frontier. How awful to be separated from a family for that period of years!"

"And of Mr. Devereaux?" Annabelle inquired, with a hastily concealed smile. "Will you entertain any social calls from him? He appeared to hold you in considerable esteem!"

Minnie briefly wished that she was ten or eleven again, so that she could stick out a mocking tongue in Annabelle's direction. Annabelle always knew precisely where to stab the affectionate and teasing needle.

"I think not," Minnie replied, with every appearance of equanimity. "He was a most interesting and courteous gentleman, with a talent for chess, and the intention of courting Susan's daughter Charlotte. He accompanied me and Miss Van Lew to the notorious slave markets, you know..." she added, as an explanatory aside to Richard. "Miss Van Lew had challenged him to purchase slaves to the value of his Indian jewel. Slaves which she had every intention of freeing or making arrangements, which she did. It was an interesting experience," She added. "But one that I do not particularly wish to dwell upon. What now is the talk of Boston, Richard? You hinted at some scandal perhaps affecting the Reverend Slocomb..."

"Not a scandal, per se," Richard crumbled a few oyster crackers into the very acceptable fish stew which the Milford's kitchen had provided, along with a light collation of salad and cold meats. He sounded most lawyerly precise. "Not so far, as nearly as I can ascertain, not having the advantage of tea-table gossip. But Sophia tells me that there is concern among the certain ladies of the congregation, that the Reverend Slocomb may have been untowardly affectionate to a certain lady in particular."

"Jealousy; I am certain that there would be nothing to it," Annabelle declared. "He is a handsome gentleman with a good living and an excellent reputation! Of course, he should marry, upon finding a young lady to his taste and affection ..."

"Alas, dear Mother," Richard replied, and Minnie could swear that he had a twinkle of affectionate and mildly malicious amusement in his eye. "It seems that the lady who is the subject of tea-table gossip among Sophia's friends as the object of the good reverend's affections is already married. And her husband is not indulgent; rather infuriated, to put the matter bluntly."

"I am certain that such talk is only gossip of the most spiteful kind," Annabelle declared, while Minnie murmured,

"In defense of the Reverend Slocomb as a man of the cloth, I cannot believe that he would be silly enough to respond with love-talk, even if a woman did make protestation of her affection for him. And is he not soon to begin a series of lectures on the cruelty of the slave system? He was to publish another book of his sermons on the subject, I know..."

"Silly? Perhaps," Richard finished the last few spoons of stew in his bowl and helped himself to more from the covered tureen in the middle of the table. "But a man and a well-spoken devil at that might yet be susceptible to flattery."

"I cannot think so ill of so noble a man as the Reverend Slocomb," Annabelle insisted, and Minnie opened her mouth, and then closed it, deciding to hold her peace on that subject. Both her brother and father had been acidulous in their judgement of the good reverend, and she had never in her life known either to be wrong in judgement.

Finally, she ventured, "We will be home soon enough to see the truth of whatever story is making the rounds of the parlors and chop-houses. Shall we remain in Washington to break our journey for another day or so? I might wish to see if there is any progress on the public buildings. My brother Virgil," she added, with a slight catch in her voice, "Had an interest in matters architectural."

"They have not even begun the new works," Richard answered, comfortably. "I think that we should make that decision when we arrive. I am likewise eager to return, Aunt Minnie." Richard regaled them with a few more recollections of the summer in Boston, while Annabelle and Minnie finished their own meal, then he excused himself from their room. The silent maid came for the dishes. Minnie and Annabelle prepared for bed, drawing the curtains over the tall window on a darkening indigo sky, split with clouds which the last rays of the sun gilded with red, bronze, and molten gold.

"I shall be glad to be home," Annabelle remarked yet again, as she blew out the last flame which lit the room.

"As will I," Minnie agreed. The narrow, old-fashioned house on Beacon Hill, which in spring had seemed to her a veritable cage, was now a refuge to her, or at least an easy rest for a while. Or so she thought.

***

Richard, Sophia, and Annabelle, solo and in chorus, all urged Minnie to remain at the Brewer house, once they returned to Boston on the afternoon train from Worchester. Minnie demurred, saying that she had long been a guest in other places for long enough.

"Richard was kind enough to send a telegram to Mrs. Norris that we were on the way home, and that she should make the house ready for my return. If you would just have your coachman detour a little out of your way." With a look at the bustling platform, and the arching roof of the Lowell Street Station, Minnie added, "I have also spent time enough in railway stations, and in hotels. Honestly, Mrs. Norris will prepare a simple supper for me. It is enough to set my feet under my own table tonight, and then sleep in my own bed."

"I am certain that you will have visitors enough, Aunt Minnie, as soon as your friends learn that you have returned from a long visit to the South," Sophia agreed, although Annabelle still looked concerned.

"Are you certain that you will be well, dear Minnie?" she murmured, as they took their seats in the Brewer coach, waiting for them in the station forecourt.

135

Minnie sighed. "I am certain, Belle. I long to be home again, in my own rooms, among my own books and concerns."

Yes – in her father's narrow and dark old house, which for all it's shortcomings, at least overlooked the Common from the front windows; that house where Minnie had lived with her brothers since birth. Now returning to an empty house, Minnie felt the absence of Papa-the-Judge and her brother Virgil keenly. Of her four brothers, three older and one younger, all were gone, leaving Minnie feeling rather alone in an empty house. Leander died as a youth, even before Minnie was born, Pindar, Virgil, and Horace were also gone, although Minnie couldn't help feeling some slight resentment over how the three between them had all grasped more interesting lives than hers to the present. Horace had played a bold part in fomenting a revolution in Texas, carried messages for General Houston, and had fought in a great battle there. Pindar, ensconced among his manuscripts and lectures at Princeton like an old badger in his comfortable burrow, had an interesting intellectual life. Even as a semi-invalid Virgil had managed through dint of copious letter-writing, to be a considerable voice among the movement to abolish slavery. Considering that circumstance, and her recent visit, perhaps there would be something to be built upon in her experience of the visit to the Shockoe Bottom slave market and her stay in Richmond.

Too much to think about, when she was wearied from the long journey, and distress from ... never mind. Perhaps a time in the comfortable old house was what she needed, tended by Mrs. Norris and the other servants; Jerusha who was Mrs. Norris' widowed daughter and cook, Bertha, her younger daughter, and Bertha's husband Jeremiah Daley, respectively maid and gardener/man-of-all-work. *(Sensibly, Mrs. Norris sent out the laundry, which spared them all the most grinding household labor.)*. Minnie needed time to think and plan an independent future, one unburdened by the duty of care for aged or ailing relatives. She welcomed the thought of a night of comfortable sleep in the familiar shabby bedroom which had been hers since girlhood. The house was truly her own domain now … although Minnie could not help but feel the familiar and familial shades whispering to her, of duties and obligations.

What would she do with herself, now that the diversion of travel to the South was done and the European excursion wouldn't be undertaken for months. What would she do to fill the hours and days until then? She had been raised since childhood with the dictate of being useful, to her family and to society at large. Now at leisure and fancy-free? What would she do with herself?

Minnie knew, as she knew everything else with clarity and purpose – the life of a lady of materiel substance and leisure was not for her. She possessed a substantial income, an education the equal of any male among her peers; she could do as she liked, a privilege not afforded to many women of her class and standing. She was not meant to frivol away those fortunate gifts on a trivial social life; social calls, a round of vicious and tedious gossip over the teacups, an obsessive concern with doings among neighbors, and the Beacon Street Congregationalist ladies.

"Perhaps I might still interest Annabelle in a pilgrimage to the Holy Land, on the grounds of religious devotion," Minnie remarked to the walls of the parlor, and most particularly, the portrait of Papa-the-Judge, painted in his youth by Copley. He had been handsome, mischievous; Copley had even hinted at Papa-the-Judge's daring aspect, in that portrait.

Pure flummery and nonsense, she seemed to hear her father reply; *A mental crutch for weak-minded simpletons.* Papa-the-Judge had little respect in private for organized religion. He claimed to be a Deist, but Minnie thought at heart he was a pagan of the stern old Roman sort, making private sacrifice to his gods on the family altar, and as Pres Devereaux had jested – worshipping his ancestors. Whom Minnie knew very well, were mostly worthy of honor and respect. But Papa-the-Judge ... as she considered that thought, Mrs. Norris tapped politely on the parlor doorjamb.

"Miss Minnie, supper is prepared. Would you prefer it served in the dining room, or on a tray?"

"A tray, please," Minnie replied. She felt a mild pang of guilt at not having taken more than mild interest in Mrs. Norris over the last few years. How long had she served in this household? Minnie had been at dame school when Papa-the-Judge had hired her – a widow of good character with her daughters. Mrs. Norris and her family had the little apartment over the coach house in back, and Minnie did not grudge them in the least. Now Mrs. Norris was of a good age, but still hale and vigorous. Jerusha ruled in the kitchen, while her sister Bertha and Mrs. Norris managed the housekeeping. Mrs. Norris and her family were just part of the household fittings, ever-present in the background, as much as the wallpaper, or the woodwork in Papa-the-Judges' old study, which had been Virgil's bedroom when he became too ill to go up the stairs. Pres Devereaux's gibe about disposing of paid workers when their utility was completed, as opposed to that of slaves, who must be cared for in old age, still stung in Minnie's memory. What was to be done for Mrs. Norris when she became too old to work? Ah – Minnie's good memory served her well, despite her exhaustion from the long journey. Mrs. Norris had a bequest in Papa-the-Judge's will, and another in Virgil's. Besides that, she had her daughters Jerusha and Bertha. Still, Minnie contemplated the memory of Pres Devereaux's comment and knew that there was some justice to it. But she was just too tired to contemplate all of this now.

Time enough tomorrow. Mrs. Norris opened the door for Bertha, carrying a heavy tray.

"We fixed you some light soup, Miss Minnie," Mrs. Norris announced. "You should eat it all, every bite. You do look most awfully tired, if you don't mind me saying so."

Minnie supposed that she must obey Mrs. Norris, just as her daughters obeyed her, without question.

"I am not all that wearied," she replied. "In truth, dear Mrs. Norris – I must now consider what I should do next, now that the social obligation of my visit to Richmond is done, and Cousin Peter is comfortably settled with Susan and her dearest Ambrose..."

"They were such a handsome couple when they wed," Mrs. Norris fussed over setting up the folding stand at Minnie's knee. "I remember thinking so. Such a good catch for Susan, I said so to Norris – he was still alive at the time. Norris thought he wouldn't amount to much, but then Norris didn't hold much with clergy an' those men who didn't work with their hands. Not manly, in the proper way, Norris held, god bless him. Glad to hear from you and Miss Annabelle, that Miss Susan is happy, and her girls are settling, or about to settle with good husbands."

She stood aside, while Bertha set the tray on the stand, and uncovered the bowl of soup, and some slices of warm brown bread, wrapped in a pristine napkin.

"Now, you eat that all, Miss Minnie! I have some good apple duff kept warm for you, with cream, for a sweet. You can't have a pudding until you eat your supper," Mrs. Norris added, and Minnie was brought to laugh. Yes, it was good to be home, being chided in the familiar accents of Mrs. Norris, as she did when she and Annabelle were playmates and schoolfellows.

"Nothing is as good as your apple duff," Minnie promised. "Save your excellent soup, and I promise to eat every bite. It is so good to be home, Mrs. Norris – Bertha. Susan maintained a superb household, and an excellent cook but all of them were slaves. I am glad to be home, where the air is free."

"Enjoy your supper, then, Miss Minnie," Mrs. Norris beamed. "For Mrs. Bard left her card today. She told Jerusha that she would call upon you tomorrow, as she had a matter of import to speak to about."

Oh, merciful Lord, Minnie thought.

But tomorrow was tomorrow.

Chapter 9 – His Torch is at Thy Temple Door

Minnie, exhausted and bone-weary from several days of uninterrupted travel on the cars, retired early, and slept soundly that first night upon returning home to Boston, although she did experience a particularly vivid dream, of being carried in Pres Devereaux's arms, while he protested his love for her. In that odd, unsettling manner of dreams, she found herself arrayed in a white dress and a veil over her hair, standing in a church, protesting that she didn't want to be married.

Miss Beauchamp from the Richmond train stood next to her, saying, "But he is your husband now, so of course you must obey him."

"No!" Minnie exclaimed, and threw her bouquet on the floor, and tore the veil from her head. "No, I detest veils, and I will never obey!"

"You'll be sorry," Miss Beauchamp promised as she turned into Susan's domineering housekeeper, black Hepzibah. "You shouldn't overtax yourself!"

"I won't!" Minnie replied, defiantly, and somewhere a clatter of horse hoofs on the cobbles resounded like a thunderclap and she woke, sitting straight up in bed. The light of a pale dawn leaked around the edges of the window curtains. Minnie regarded the familiar walls of her own bedroom with relief and wondered what had led to that particular dream.

She had no intention of obeying – obeying anyone – as if she were a being with no thoughts or desires of her own. From downstairs came the faint rattle of iron potlids on the great cookstove in the basement of the tall old house, and the indistinct voices of Mrs. Norris and Jerusha; the reassuring tenor of life as it had always been in Papa-the-Judges' house. Minnie slid out from the covers and dressed; a plain toilette, and her hair in a simple and heavy knot at the back of her neck. The tall clock in the hallway struck the hour of eight as she hurried down the stairs, through the parlor and into the dining room, where the double-rank of elegant chairs flanked the dining table on either side.

"I'll have breakfast in the parlor," she called into the stairwell, reconsidering the lonely dignity of sitting in the dining room by herself. She supposed that she should sit at the head of the table now that she now owned that portion of Papa-the-Judge's estate; a bleak honor, indeed. When she was a girl, the dining room had often been a crowded, lively place, with Papa-the-Judge at the head chair, her brothers and their friends, Annabelle, Cousin Peter, and his family ... no, the dining room was the refuge of shades and memories. Best to close the doors between the parlor and the dining room, crowded as the latter was with the ghosts of brothers and friends.

Perhaps she might invite Annabelle, Sophia and Richard to dine on some later occasion.

"Very well, Miss Minnie," Mrs. Norris called in return. A moment later, Bertha came up the steps from the cellar kitchen, slightly out of breath between the hurry up the narrow utility stair and the weight of the tray with a teapot, a rack of newly toasted bread, and a plate of scrapple and scrambled eggs upon it. Bertha set the tray on the unfolded stand, which stood before the largest window in the parlor, that which gave a view out onto the street, and into the meadows and solitary stands of lonely trees in the Common.

There was talk of building a lavish public garden adjacent to the Common, Minnie had heard through gossip with various friends.

That would be so very pleasant to look on, she thought again, as she attended her breakfast, after expressing her gratitude to Bertha. Nothing like a good breakfast and a good stout cup of the finest China tea, without having to be diplomatic over the breakfast table. "Tell Jerusha I will wish to consult about menus for the week, and the marketing. There is no need to fix supper for me this evening; I will be dining at the Brewers'. Richard has said that he will send the coach for me."

Bertha cleared her throat. "Shall I bring more tea and some cakes when Mrs. Bard arrives? She left her card yesterday, saying that she had something of importance which she wanted to discuss."

"I remember," Minnie sighed. "I will receive her visit. I have no plans for the day, other than to write letters, an account of our stay in Richmond and my visit to the slave markets for Mr. Garrison's newspaper. I hope that Mrs. Bard will be concise as to her purpose. She is otherwise the most tedious woman of my acquaintance..."

Virgil had been even more scathing; "That woman is too good for this earth," he declared on many occasions. "She deserves to be under it, inspiring the roses and daisies."

It did not escape Minnie's observation that Bertha smothered a small burst of laughter at her own observation.

"Very well, Miss Minnie. I will bring a tray of tea and cakes to the parlor when Mrs. Bard is received."

"Thank you, Bertha," Minnie answered, and consumed the remainder of her breakfast, feeling a mix of relief at being home ... and yet a small portion of boredom. Today she would write letters, begin an account of that visit to the Richmond slave markets – but what then? What should she do with herself now, besides travel? As a woman of active years, possessed of an independent income, an interest in public matters, especially regarding those victims of the peculiar institution, and no small feeling of obligation towards those others less blessed by fortune, she ought to do something! There were no feelings of guilt over being thus favored, but such a standard had been bred into her bones and encouraged since birth.

Sufficient unto the day, Minnie told herself. *And I hope that I may dissuade Lolly Bard from lingering too long*. Today she was given over to letters, words, and memories of that appalling venture into the Shockoe Bottom district – and to firmly suppress any belated feelings of love for Pres Devereaux. She would rather think of him as a guide and worthy opponent.

She had too much to do, to bother with romance.

When Minnie had finished breakfast, she didn't wait for Bertha or Mrs. Norris to come and retrieve the tray. She walked across the hallway into Papa-the-Judges' library and study, a magnificent room with tall bookshelves on every wall, save that of the front, where a deep window embrasure and built-in seat commanded a view of the Common. This apartment now was entirely her own, as was every other room. Here, her brother Virgil had chosen to spend his last days and hours, sleeping fitfully on a day-bed chaise moved into the corner. In his more alert hours, he dictated a stream of letters to Minnie, sitting with her pen in hand, and inkpot at the ready, at the elaborate slant-front desk which had been Papa-the-Judges'. The tall secretary desk was a magnificent thing, purchased from part of his fortune earned from investing in the China trade. Made from dark golden maple wood adorned with contrasting inlay, the desk was full of niches, shelves, drawers large and small, some of them secret. Minnie knew the hidden catches to all the secret spaces within the desk. Papa-the-Judge had trusted her, implicitly. She uncapped the inkbottle, dipped her trustiest pen into it, and began to write ...

My dear Miss Van Lew ... we are safely returned at last from our long visit...

Minnie had finished that letter, another to Susan, enclosing a third for Cousin Peter, and begun on her account of visiting the Shockoe Bottom, when Bertha tapped discreetly on the door to the study.

"Mrs. Bard is here, Miss Minnie. I showed her into the parlor. I'll bring up the tea directly."

"Thank you, Bertha," Minnie wiped her pen nib clean and corked the ink bottle with a sigh. "I'll be in directly."

She performed a quick assessment of her appearance in the gilt-trimmed Spanish looking glass hanging in the entryway, and set a hospitable smile on her face, before opening the parlor door.

"Mrs. Bard," she exclaimed. "How kind of you to call! Mrs. Norris told me you had left your card yesterday."

"We were expecting your return weeks ago, dear Miss Vining," Lolly Bard's bulging reticule lay next to her on the settee. As was proper for a courtesy call, she had not removed her shawl or her gloves. "And ... I had hoped that we were sufficiently close enough friends that you would call me Lolly, and I might use your first name."

"Then I suppose that we should," Minnie agreed; anything to rush Lolly Bard's visit so that she could return to her writing. "I have sent for tea to be served, if you would care to partake with me."

"I did not wish to interrupt what you might be doing," Lolly made a not very convincing protest. "And please do not trouble yourself unduly. Since you have only just returned from your journey, you must have ever so much to do in catching up."

"It is no trouble," Minnie yielded, well-resigned and knowing that Mrs. Bard – now Lolly – would take her time approaching any discussion of whatever it was which had so worried her. Five or ten more minutes of exchanging trivialities – and she really ought to get back to her writing. "I was writing letters, and an account of a visit to the slave market in Richmond, which I intend to forward to the Reverend Slocomb, and perhaps to Mr. Garrison for publication in the *Liberator*, but I need to rest my hand after so long a stint with pen and ink."

"You write with so fine a hand," Lolly replied, innocent of any artifice. "As fine as any scrivener or secretary. Your little notes are a pleasure to read, indeed. My own writing ... Dear Mr. Bard would say that he had pleasure unending from any of my letters, for it would take him months to decipher what I had written to him when he was away, overseeing the building of his railway."

At that moment, Bertha carried in the tea-tray, laden with teapot, sugar-bowl, creamer, china cups and saucers, and a three-tiered tray of small cakes and tartlets which were the pride of Jerusha's kitchen. She set it on the folding stand which had supported Minnie's dinner tray the previous evening, and tactfully withdrew. Minnie poured out the tea and wondered when Lolly would come to the point of her visit, or how much longer this process might take. She really wanted to return to her writing, but another five or ten minutes of trivial chatter must be endured.

"Here is your tea, Lolly. You told Bertha that some matter of concern to discuss?" Minnie ventured, observing the parlor clock advancing. Lolly must come to the point soon; she was punctilious about the length of calls.

Lolly accepted the china cup with a sigh and added sugar and cream. "It's the Reverend Slocomb," she confessed, after a stir and a sip. "Minnie, dear, I am most awfully concerned. I fear that in his injudicious affections, that he has let our cause down, most horribly."

Minnie repressed her impatience and replied, "I have heard talk of a lawsuit, was it? A suit for divorce. He was making protestations of love to a married woman. I cannot think that such may be true!"

"But it is," Lolly replied, in all earnest. "He has been pledging love to Mrs. Lionel Forbes for simply months, and Caroline – Mrs. Forbes – has been returning it. It is not gossip, for I have observed them on many occasions with my own eyes; their affection is not a thing about which I can be mistaken. It is most distressing – surely, she is old enough to know better than to be so flagrantly indiscreet! Mr. Lionel Forbes has now petitioned for a divorce on account of his wife being unfaithful, named the Reverend Slocomb as his wife's lover and brought forth disinterested witnesses to testify to their many meetings! The embarrassment to our congregation, to our cause! How could the Reverend be so thoughtless as to compromise his own moral standing? She will be cut off from her children, and he from the pulpit and leadership within the church! How can he be so recklessly indiscreet, Minnie? The scandal of an adulterous connection taints every word he has ever spoken. How can he take any position of moral authority with any credibility, now? Mark my words, the husband of every woman in his congregation will be wondering if he is speaking words of love to their wives, and with justification! He and Caroline will become pariahs in society, in Boston and everywhere else!"

"I am certain that the situation cannot be as public as you declare," Minnie began, feeling as if she were about to be drowned in the spate of words.

Lolly replied, "But it is already an open scandal in Boston, and soon everywhere else! It's in all the Boston newspapers, naturally – with many a coarse sniggering jest! You would not have known since you were traveling; you won't have seen the libelous speculation in the latest Southern newspapers. It is horrible, Minnie. The things that have been published regarding Reverend Slocomb; to the embarrassment of our congregation, they are mostly true! How could he have done this, to us, and to our cause?"

"A man," Minnie replied, sore to her heart with a sense of mild betrayal, as she had taken the Reverend Slocomb to be at least an honest and moral man. "Only a man, my dear Lolly. As such, prone to fits of irrationality in their affections. The stories that Papa-the-Judge related to me touched on every imaginable vice, large and small – I confess to being very disappointed in the character of the Reverend Slocomb! But I cannot divine the purpose of this visit, Lolly. Is there some action that you wish me to take, regarding his matter?"

"Yes," Lolly replied, setting down her teacup with an air of resolution. "The Reverend Slocomb was to deliver a public lecture regarding the evils of the slave system at the beginning of next month, in the African Meeting House, hired for the purpose, and hundreds of tickets already sold. For the reason of public scandal, he cannot. We were wondering if you would do the lecture instead?"

"Me ... a public lecture?" Minnie was utterly taken back. "I had considered parlor meetings, in private and only with ladies of the congregation, but to a mixed audience, and anyone at all? I couldn't begin to consider such a thing."

"Why not?" Lolly asked, in wholly reasonable tones. "The Grimke sisters did; and very well received lectures they were, too. Mr. Bard and I attended one. A most moving experience!"

"But those ladies are radicals, quite shameless and outspoken about it. They were read out of their Quaker meeting and denounced by the Congregationalists! Even the Reverend Slocomb censured them from his pulpit, saying that it was unnatural and immoral for them to speak so openly, and he is quite in sympathy with their cause!"

"And he is quite the fitting judge," Lolly pointed out, triumphantly, as her sweet pretty face reflected an unaccustomed passion. "Of what is moral and proper, now! Minnie, you must do this; there is no one better suited among us, now. You are lately returned from the South! Are you not even now writing an account of your experiences there? There is no one who may forbid you this, as an independent spinster of fortune; you speak forcefully, with the logic of a man. Duty is ours; the events are in God's hands – so said Miss Angelina Grimke in her letter to the women of the South. Say that you will do it!"

"I will think on it with careful consideration, now that you have asked," Minnie replied, as memory of those stark moments in the Shockoe Bottom renewed themselves; the dark faces of those in the slave coffle, whose singing masked dreadful misery, the gratitude of the two girls purchased by Miss Van Lew. Her resolve hardened. "Although ... I suppose that I have no real choice in the matter, only reservations and fears."

"Fears and reservations which are quite understandable, dear Minnie," Lolly Bard set down her teacup and clasped her hands together. "But as dear Mr. Bard always used to say – we must not take counsel from our fears!"

"The time, occasion and the cause demand it from me, no matter what may result," Minnie's resolved hardened, as if she took courage from her own words, thinking again of Mrs. and Miss Van Lew's utter fearlessness in challenging the dragon of slavery in it's very den. How could she not follow that shining example? "Then I will do this lecture which you propose, based on my own observations formed over this summer in that den of iniquity."

Lolly beamed rapturous approval. "You will? Oh, splendid – the other ladies were certain that I might persuade you."

"They were?" Minnie blinked. "How might they be so sure of that?"

"Because I am so very persuasive, Minnie dear." Lolly in turn appeared rather baffled. "Dear Mr. Bard used to say that I could talk St. Simon off his tall pillar. It is one of my gifts, you see. Possibly the only one, as there are many other ladies much cleverer than I. I am so glad that you are agreeable! You will make the most enlightening lecture; I am certain of it. Oh, my! Is it half past the hour already? You have been so kind, and the ladies will be so pleased!" She peered earnestly up at Minnie, as she gathered up her reticule and adjusted her shawl. "I do hope that Annabelle and Mrs. Brewer will not be unhappy with you in agreeing to do this. I would regret causing any family dissention for you!"

"I will talk them around, in that case," Minnie answered, "And if I am not successful, I will send for you to exercise your persuasive gifts on them!" She was relieved that the visit was over, and she might return to setting down her account of the slave auction. Indeed, she now felt newly inspired, even energized. Really, it now seemed like the most splendid and bold deed imaginable, like Joan of Arc taking up a sword and obeying the commands of her angels.

"I know that you will, dear Minnie," and Lolly giggled like a schoolgirl. "You are nearly my equal when it comes to persuasion!"

We'll see about that, Minnie said to herself. *We'll see.*

"Oh, you cannot!" Annabelle wrung her hands together. It was early evening, in the Brewer parlor, with the hour of suppertime drawing closer. Minnie had just taken a deep breath and announced her intention of giving a public lecture to benefit the cause of Abolition, as a last-minute replacement for the morally suspect Reverend Slocomb. "I told you, Minnie, when you spoke of this before! You simply cannot! What will Susan think! She will be horrified at how you are taking advantage of her hospitality! It's not fitting, and it's dangerous! What if the hall is attacked by a mob? You know how high feelings are running! Tell her, Richard! Tell her that this is utterly forbidden! You are the man of the family, now! Tell her that this is impossible!" Annabelle appealed to her son-in-law to exercise his male authority.

Thus appealed, Richard Brewer gave every indication of being loath to do so. Instead, he merely grinned, and made as if to drink a mock toast to Minnie.

"Hurrah, and hurrah again, Aunt Minnie!" Then Richard's demeanor turned utterly serious. "My dearest Mama Annabelle, I have no intention of ever giving orders to Aunt Minnie; which is indeed a fools' errand. And by the way, I completely approve of speaking out against the abomination of the slave system in every possible theater and pulpit. The more Northern voices from every sex and condition condemning the practice, the better, in my opinion! The Southerners demand that we overrule our own moral objections and cooperate in that iniquitous barbarity? Not enough that we tolerate the existence of the slavery system in the south, we must now tolerate – yea, uphold! – those cruel and oppressive laws, down to every jot and tittle within our own communities, upon the demand of the slaveholders? No, Aunt Minnie has my complete agreement for this proposed lecture. If she requires a bodyguard on this and other occasions," Richard looked at her very straightly, and Minnie rejoiced that she had his fearless and uncompromising support, "Then I shall provide it – myself and certain of my friends of the same sympathies. This is Boston, my dear ladies – recall our proud history in the fight against tyranny, the tyranny of a Crown, presuming to rule over free men … and free women as well!"

A ringing endorsement, indeed. Minnie took heart from Richard's unswerving support.

"But should there be violence?" Sophia quavered uncertainly, as Annabelle dissolved into tears. "What if there is danger to Aunt Minnie, or to us?"

"Then we will meet that danger, squarely," Richard replied, firmly. "There comes a time when we cannot be ruled by fears, especially in the face of what we believe is a towering injustice. But I don't believe there will be any danger to this household. Trust me on that account, Sophia, Mother Annabelle. This is Boston, after all – verily the cradle of independence. We stood proud against British injustice and so shall we against the evil of slavery." He smiled across the parlor at Minnie, "In any case, I do verily believe that Aunt Minnie is more of a danger to a pro-slavery mob than they are to her."

"Your vote of confidence is so very reassuring," Minnie admitted. "I think that much of my talk will be drawn on our stay in Richmond. Perhaps I may draw on some of your observations as well, since you have a lawyerly eye for detail …"

"Indeed," Richard sat back in the parlor armchair which he had claimed for his. "You have only to ask, Aunt Minnie … and I have been meaning to tell you and Mother Annabelle; do you recollect that lovely young lady, Miss Beauchamp from South Carolina, who shared the car with us, between Richmond and Fredericksburg."

"The girl with the very homely Negro servant!" Annabelle exclaimed. "You were seated next to Miss Beauchamp, Minnie!"

"I do recall, most vividly," Minnie replied, rather exasperated at the abrupt change of topic. "I so much admired the colors of her mantel and bonnet. She was a most charming companion. What of this, Richard?'

"Ah," Richard concealed a small smile behind his hand. "This morning, at the office, I received a copy of a weekly newspaper from Halifax, containing a very curious account of a successful escape of a slave couple from the South. The paper was the very latest edition, and the report was the first account, according to their reporter. It appears that we – that is, Aunt Minnie, you and I inadvertently assisted the efforts of that collection of affiliates known as the Underground Railway, during our journey."

"Richard!" Sophia gasped, and began to weep, and Minnie regarded her niece with mild exasperation. Really, it was as if Annabelle's daughter had no spine at all or had inherited the one of well-boiled celery from her mother. "They did not mention our names! How could you even think to involve yourself in an enterprise so dangerous to Mama and Aunt Minnie and Cousin Susan?"

"I did nothing of the sort, my dear," Richard sounded faintly exasperated. "But to relieve your apprehensions on that score, we were not mentioned by name. Indeed, my dear, we were only adjacent and mentioned in passing as a party from the North, during a portion of their escape. We merely provided an appearance of respectability at a critical juncture of their journey, in the view of prying eyes. Aunt Minnie made conversation with Miss Beauchamp; in the eyes of the conductor, and the car attendants, I assume we all appeared as one traveling party."

"What was the story in the Halifax newspaper?" Minnie demanded. "Was Miss Beauchamp assisting her servant to escape? Is that what the report in the newspaper was about?"

"Ah," Richard sat back in the armchair, and smiled. "Yes, this is the most delicious part. Miss Beauchamp was a slave herself; a natural daughter of her owner, so nearly white in blood, appearance, and demeanor that she appeared to be a free woman, to all observers, save those which may have had personal knowledge that she was a Negro in part. That maid of hers? Her husband tricked out in the garb of a servant maid! He was a skilled cabinetmaker, apprenticed to a concern in Savannah! He saved that portion of his wages that he was allowed to keep, and used those funds to purchase tickets, and her fashionable clothes! They boldly traveled together on the trains, all the way to Halifax in Canada! You must give them credit for nerve, Aunt Minnie. No one, on observing the two of them together would have assumed anything but the appearance they wished to make, unless they had good reason for suspicion."

"We did wonder about Miss Beauchamp's maid, do you recall?" Annabelle ventured. "She looked so very homely and mannish; strong, too. Stronger than a natural woman."

"But they are now safe in Canada, then?" Minnie wished most urgently to know, reflecting on how assured Miss Beauchamp had appeared, how confident, although her heart must have been about in her mouth, every time she and her supposed maid came under the regard of a conductor or a ticket agent. Minnie rejoiced at that small and almost inadvertent part which she and Richard and Annabelle had performed – assisting two more to escape the cruel bonds of chattel slavery. Her determination to speak up in public and continue the fight against that cruel institution was reinforced and redoubled, to take up the crusade which had been lifeblood to Virgil, before his health declined. She was secure in herself, in her position of riches and privilege; this was a blow that she might strike against the vile institution, without risking grievous personal harm.

Richard answered, almost casually, "Yes, they are – according to the Halifax newspaper. They are now safe, and able to live out their lives in the freedom that our Creator ordained. It is an irony," and Richard grinned, "That now escaped slaves must make their way to Canada, into the arms and governance of those very same British which we fought for our rights as free men and women."

"An irony, indeed," Minnie replied. "And it would have made Papa-the-Judge very sad, to contemplate such a situation."

Chapter 10 – Sifting Out the Hearts of Men

Minnie, having agreed with some trepidation to lecture at the tall brick-built African Meeting House on Belknap Street, set to work in earnest. The venue had been arranged previously to accommodate the Reverend Slocomb, and so was not precisely to her liking. It was a large and substantial hall, and she had often accompanied Virgil to abolitionist meetings and lectures held there. But it was one thing to take a place in the audience – quite another to speak from the lectern, to what she feared would be a large audience. She took comfort from knowing that at least a handful of other women had spoken there. Still, the thought of becoming a public figure, someone known to a larger community than merely family and friends – was a prospect to make her quail and wish that Lolly Bard had not been quite so persuasive.

"I shall draw on account of mine and Miss Van Lew's visit to the Shockoe Bottom district," She ventured to Annabelle, after she had spent a week or so thinking about it all. "But I will not mention Miss Van Lew, or the names of the gentlemen who accompanied. Nor will I mention Susan or My-Dear-Ambrose, as our hosts in Richmond. Mr. Spooner has given me some excellent suggestions. He was a very good friend of Virgil's, as they agreed most vehemently that our Constitution did not make any accommodation for the vile institution of slavery, and Mr. Garrison felt so strongly otherwise. I shall appeal to the innate chivalry of men," she added. "Since in my opinion, helpless women and children feel the brunt of their helpless condition. You and I, 'Belle – we are free women, and our condition is comfortable. Even those girls who work in the mills have a morsel of that same advantage; they earn a living wage, may marry as they wish. Such women who have no men to depend upon for support – even they are not in so ill-favored and helpless a situation as those women such as Miss Van Lew purchased! To have no choice but to submit to a master, no redress against being forced to submit to their vile lusts, or have your infants torn from your arms! That is most uniquely unjust."

"You hope to appeal to tender emotions, then?" Annabelle bent her head over her needlework – another essay in Berlin wool-work, a pair of slippers, this time for Richard, for Christmas. "Is that your theme, then? Appealing to the better angels of male nature?"

"I would appeal to the heroic chivalry of men, to protect women and the little children of <u>any</u> color. It is a natural thing, I do so believe," Minnie replied, thinking back upon how Pres Devereaux had tended her so carefully following that carriage accident. "Even the worst and lowest of men have some remnants of finer feeling; a wish to appear to be better than they are. I think, dear 'Belle, that many of those men recruited to the cause of abolition consider only the dry letter of the law. I should like to bring some of them consider the truly frightful condition of a female slave."

"I am certain, Minnie dear, that other lecturers have brought that point to them ... those Grimke ladies have certainly dwelt upon that point..."

"They have," Minnie replied. "But I intend upon bringing them to consider the full horror; to paint a picture for them in words, so that they might feel the terror and helplessness –

from what I saw with my own eyes in Richmond or heard tell of from Miss Van Lew."

"You will do as you think best," Annabelle sighed, and worked another row of her wool-work. "But Cousin Susan will be dismayed to hear of you speaking out so forcefully, and to an open gathering! I am afraid that she will count herself very hurt and consider this a betrayal of the family."

"It may be so, 'Belle. But I will do as I think best, when the cause, my conscience and the occasion demand it. Cousin Susan's disapproval of my actions is her own affair." Minnie spoke bravely enough, in part to reassure herself; Susan, her circle in Richmond, and her household had all been welcoming to Susan's Boston cousins. Save for the Van Lews, they all lived with the comforts that slavery of the Negros provided, without consideration of the basic wrong, the affront to simple humanity. Minnie would speak and damn the consequences.

She made that resolve silently. Now she was bound on a course – a course carefully considered and decided upon. The die was cast, as Virgil her brother so often observed. *Ilia jacta est*. She did experience a horrific fit of doubts, upon the moment that the Brewer family coach delivered her with Richard to the side entrance of the tall brick African Meeting House, mere blocks away from the Vining house on Beacon Street. Richard handed her down from the coach, and took her arm, as the door opened. A tall and handsome young man, mixed in race but athletic as to figure and aquiline in features, smiled tentatively at Richard and Minnie, as he closed and bolted the door after them. This floor, Minnie had been given to understand, was the ordinary meeting room, with a low ceiling – a plain and unadorned room; a school on some days, and workshop on others. The church sanctuary on the second floor, with a generous balcony around three sides of the room was lit by tall arched windows in the daylight – in the late afternoon, the place would glow like the inside of a paper lantern. She could already hear the rumble of voices from upstairs – yes, a good crowd. *Ilia jacta est,* she told herself once again, and fingered the thick stack of notes in her reticule. Not that she needed them, particularly. She had prepared as carefully as Papa-the-Judge or Virgil would have wanted.

"There's a good crowd gathered upstairs already, Miss Vining," he said, and Minnie recollected his name, from attending anti-slavery society meetings with Virgil. The young man was himself an escaped slave, who had managed against the odds to educate himself to a very high degree, even while still held in bondage. Disguising himself as a sailor to escape from his master, he had become a lay preacher in New Bedford.

"Is there indeed, Mr. Johnson?" She racked her memory and retrieved his name. "I ... do not truly know if that is frightening or reassuring."

"A great many indeed," the young man grinned. "And too many Johnsons in New Bedford – my wife and I have taken the name of Douglass, to avoid confusion."

"Richard Brewer, Esquire," Richard nodded. "Miss Minnie is my wife's aunt."

"Frederick Douglass, at your service," the two men shook hands formally. "The lecture is set to begin in ten minutes. I will make some brief introductory remarks, and then Mr. Garrison will introduce Miss Vining. Upon that moment, the audience is all yours. I understand that Mr. Garrison has been an acquaintance of your family for many years, for he said that he knew you well."

"Mr. Garrison was a good friend of my brother Virgil Vining," Minnie nodded.

"I remember him now," Frederick Douglass' handsome countenance suddenly expressed the most profound sorrow. "My sincere sympathies on your loss, Miss Vining. I may only imagine the depth of your grief for a dear brother – for he was our fearless brother in the most noble cause of all."

"Thank you," Minnie was briefly overcome; Virgil, as cross and demanding as his invalid state had made him during his last years had been a dear brother; in youth, tenderly indulgent of the much younger Minnie and Annabelle. Minnie knew now that she had been quite brattish to Virgil, when she was a girl in short petticoats and he a youth of twenty or so. "You are so very kind – I hope that I shall take his place, in some small way, and make Virgil proud of me. Our cause is a noble crusade."

"It is, indeed!" Frederick's smile lit up his face. "An' you will make your brother proud, Miss Vining! Of that I am certain. Speak from your heart ... and one bit of advice if I may be so bold. Pick that one person in the hall, and think on speaking to them, if you have the collywobbles at facing such a large gathering."

"An excellent suggestion," Richard agreed. "In pleading my own cases, I have often made the practice of directing my remarks towards the most sympathetic of the jurymen. Speak to that one person as an affectionate friend ... and it all comes clear in the verdict."

Frederick Douglass consulted his pocket watch, and then replaced it in his waistcoat pocket.

"Nearly time," he reported, with a jaunty air. "If you will be so good as to follow me to the head of the stairs. You may wait on the landing, out of sight of the audience, but from there you might see and hear Mr. Garrison and me."

Silently, Minnie took Richard's arm, and followed after Mr. Douglass. Light from the main hall, and the noise of the crowd therein intensified as they climbed the stairs. She took a deep breath, as Mr. Douglass smiled over his shoulder at her, as she and Richard paused on the top landing.

Too late to back out now. Mr. Douglass strode out, towards the platform where the railed lectern stood, two or three steps above the main floor. The crowd seemed to roar – whether in approval, welcome, or displeasure Minnie couldn't say. The noise was palpable, almost a physical thing, like a brick wall of sound. *How could she ever make herself heard over that?* The noise in the hall diminished to a rustle of whispers, as Mr. Douglass climbed the brief steps to the lectern, held up his hand for attention and began to speak. Minnie hardly took in a word of it. In turn, Mr. Garrison, lean and beak-nosed with a monk-like fringe of hair around the imposing dome of his skull, took his place. Finally, Mr. Garrison fell silent, and gestured; a grand sweeping gesture towards the stairwell where Minnie waited.

Now.

Richard pressed her hand, his expression encouraging. Minnie quelled the shaking of her knees, the thumping of her heart, lifted her chin. *She was a Vining, a Vining of Boston, the Judge's daughter, her mother had spied for George Washington when she was just a child herself. She should fear nothing.*

Her footsteps sounded loud on the polished wooden floor of the Meeting House, even louder than the low rustle of the audience, shifting and whispering. She reached the steps to the lectern where Mr. Douglass waited to assist her up those steps if she required it. Up the steps, and to the lectern itself, where Mr. Garrison beamed his approval and encouragement. Someone had thoughtfully arranged for a sturdy wooden box for her to stand upon. Without it, she might have been dwarfed by the tall lectern. Mr. Garrisons' lips moved, but what he said was lost in a roar of acclamation, and then she stood alone, looking out over the packed pews on the main floor, the crowded balcony above.

All those eyes, she thought irreverently. *Like a box of salt fish looking back at me. Good heavens, was that her old schoolfellow Mary Ashton Rice, come from teaching school in Charleston, standing at the back?* Her eyes fell on a familiar face, almost in the front pew; Lolly Bard, who smiled as if they were chance met in a parlor, on a mutual friend's 'at home' day. Ah, yes; Pick that one person in the hall, and think on speaking to them...

She would speak to Lolly Bard, as if Lolly represented all who had come to the lecture, in her pretty and addle-pated person. That one thought was as if a magic spell had descended on Minnie, instantly dissolving her fears, just as a warm spring day melted the last of the ragged and dirty winter drifts of snow. She was utterly at ease, confident and in command of herself, command of the thick little clutch of notes in her reticule, and command of that audience. She squared her shoulders, reminded herself that she should speak clearly and through Lolly, that such of the audience in the back row would hear her.

"Good day, my friends! For I shall indeed speak to all who are in this place as friends and sympathizers to the cause of abolishing the dreadful scourge of slavery from this nation, a nation founded on freedom and equality among all nations! I am Minerva Templeton Vining, of this city. In the spring of this year, I visited kinfolk and friends in Richmond, Virginia ... and took the opportunity to visit the preeminent slave market in that city..."

***

"You were magnificent, Aunt Minnie!" Richard enthused, in the carriage for the brief ride back to the Vining house on Beacon Hill. "I should think that you will be asked to speak again, and often! Were you in the practice of law ... well, best not think on that, since I hardly need the competition!"

"I am just glad that it is over," Minnie replied, sinking back against the carriage cushions, wishing for the moment when she might take off her shoes and loosen her corset lacings. "But it did go well, Richard. I should thank you for assisting with preparing my remarks. I did thank you, didn't I?"

"You did," Richard replied. "And most generously. In faith, I am now moved to support abolition myself, although my sympathies were always in that direction. I now think that Mr. Garrison and young Mr. Douglass might wish to confer with you about continuing to lecture on that topic, since this venture reached such an appreciative audience."

"I will consider it, should I be offered such an invitation," Minnie considered the prospect, and found it an agreeable one. The carriage horse turned the corner from Walnut Street, and after a block, drew to a stop before the tall, old-fashioned façade of the Vining house. The coachman climbed down from his perch and unfolded the metal step. "It was invigorating, Richard. It made me feel as if I was striking a good blow against the iniquitous system, as if I had a good cause to fight for, as Virgil did. As Mr. Garrison, Mr. Spooner and Mr. Douglass now do. If I wish to take up a sword in that fight, would you and Sophia think any less of me?"

"We wouldn't dare," Richard answered, as he scrambled out of the coach, and standing on the stone sidewalk, held up his hand to assist Minnie down. "Good night, dear Aunt Minnie. Make certain that you have the shutters tightly latched tonight, and the doors locked. If there is any trouble with a pro-slavery mob arising from your talk tonight, do not hesitate to send a messenger to me. But I do not believe that such would dare, in Boston of all places!"

"Don't worry about me, Richard." Minnie replied, as she searched in her reticule for the massive key which would unlock the front door. Papa the Judge had been adamant regarding securing the house after dark, as he had sat in judgement over so many miscreants and their kinfolk who might well hold long grudges. "You do remember that Jerusha's husband Jeremiah Daley lives here as well. And I have Papa-the-Judges' old blunderbuss and I'm not afraid to use it. Have no fear that this house is full of frightened and unprotected women!"

"Good," Richard answered, although he bade his coachman to linger long enough to watch Minnie climb the stairs unlock the massive door and pass within.

There were no untoward local repercussions from Minnie's talk at the African Meeting House. As Richard predicted, she was invited by Mr. Garrison and Mr. Douglass to participate in an expanded series of abolitionist lectures throughout Massachusetts. This breathtakingly bold proposal required all of three minutes of consideration before she agreed to it. She happily revised her lecture notes, finished the written article for Mr. Garrison.

Barely a month after the lecture, she received a letter from Cousin Susan in Richmond, whose outrage at what Susan termed, *'an unforgivable abuse of our hospitality and the respectful affection due to kin, our church and our race'* fairly blistered the pages it was written on, even rendering Susan's handwriting almost illegible in places. The letter concluded with a declaration that the Edmonds family no longer considered Minnie to be kin, but instead, a stranger whose every thought and word were poisonous. Any future communication from her would be returned unopened and unread. Minnie was shocked and grieved. This would cut her off entirely from Cousin Peter, who had served almost as a second father.

"I did warn you," Annabelle observed sadly when Minnie showed her the letter. "I suppose that news of your talk was communicated to them in a Southern newspaper, and the very worst construction put on your honest feelings."

"I am afraid that she will not allow me to correspond with Cousin Peter, now," Minnie sighed. "Which is what I regret the most. That this dreadful matter of slavery should so estrange us from the dearest of our relatives!"

"Would you have held back from speaking at the African Meeting House, if you had been certain that Susan would consider you a traitor to the family?" Annabelle ventured, and Minnie shook her head.

"No. I could not keep silent, 'Belle. To do so in the face of such a hideous injustice is to become complicit. Perhaps I should have written to her privately and let her know what I was about to do, rather than leave her to learn about it from the newssheets. It's too late now, though."

"Perhaps she will reconsider when she meditates on the principles of Christian forgiveness," Annabelle suggested. "Fortunately, Susan made no such mention of refusing communication with me, at least. I may write to Cousin Peter on your behalf, then. Still, it is very distressing; Minnie, I think I must go lie down for a bit. I have not been feeling very well, of late."

"Should I ask Sophia to send for the doctor?" Minnie was shaken from her own worries, noting that Annabelle did indeed appear very pale about the lips – indeed, almost frail.

"No, dear. I have had these spells off and on since returning from Richmond. They always pass after a good rest. I shall think about what I will write to Susan and Cousin Peter, without sounding as if I am apologizing for you speaking your mind." Annabelle rose from the chair in the Brewer parlor and steadied herself on the tall back. "Do not fret ... I'll see to it that our affection and respect for Cousin Peter is not interdicted by Susan's anger with you."

"Thank you, 'Belle," Minnie replied, feeling some relief – tempered with momentary worry for her sister-in-law and oldest friend. "That must suffice for now ... are you certain you don't want Sophia to send around for the doctor?"

"No, dear – I'll be feeling better as soon as I lie down," Annabelle replied. Reassured, Minnie made her own way out of the Brewer townhouse and walked the leisurely way through the new Back Bay neighborhood and up Beacon Hill, to where the Vining mansion stood tall and proud, overlooking the Common, not two blocks from the golden dome of the statehouse.

I am in the right, Minnie thought, looking out over the old heart of Boston, thinking of all that history, the history of freedom and the natural rights of citizens, citizens of all colors and degree. *I am in the right, and I will go on speaking out. No matter what the cost.*

Chapter 11 – Trampling Out the Vintage
November, 1853 – Rochester, New York

"Minnie dear, there is a telegram just this last hour delivered for you," Lolly Bard hovered in the ladies' parlor of the rooming house in Rochester on the lake. "I haven't opened it, I assure you. Things like this are private!" Lolly handed Minnie the envelope and fussed with the sleeve of her wrap – it was cold, now that it was winter where the wind blew off Lake Ontario, even colder than Boston where the wind came from the Atlantic. Minnie and Lolly had just returned from a lively lecture and discussion upon the topic of the necessity for good citizens of abolition sympathies to continue to resist and nullify the Fugitive Slave Acts, which commanded that citizens of the North cooperate in the capture and detention of escaping slaves. This ruling had aroused furious protest across the North over the last three years. It was bad enough, Minnie had said often enough, that slavery existed and was legal in the South; let folk who could square it with their own consciences make accommodation, but then to demand that everyone else collude in the wretched practice, aiding and abetting the vile trade? That was going too far.

"I pray that it is not bad news although it is my sad experience that sudden telegrams usually are..." Lolly's voice trailed off as Minnie ripped open the telegram envelope and read the brief contents.

Mother A dying stop. Return home soonest stop. Richard sends.

"We have to return to Boston," Minnie felt the world around her suddenly jolt, and then return to its customary place. "This is from Richard Brewer. Annabelle is ... she is desperately unwell. Never mind – we must return to Boston at once."

"Oh, my dear Minnie!" Lolly looked as if about to burst into useless tears, but then recovered herself. She had been traveling with Minnie as companion, adjutant, and secretary for nearly ten years, as the second-most-dedicated woman of abolitionist sympathies in the Beacon Street Congregationalist Church. Against all expectation, the Reverend Slocomb still presided over his flock, having lived down the scandal of being named in the Forbes divorce suit. It was Mr. Lionel Forbes and his wife who had to leave Boston over the matter, which Minnie thought terribly unfair, when it was the Reverend Slocomb who appeared to be the most guilty in the matter. Minnie had to admit, against considerable prejudice, that Lolly had an unparalleled gift for organizing church bazaars in support of female suffrage and the abolition of slavery, and more importantly considerable skill at making railroad connections and finding friends and sympathizers to offer hospitality, in all their travels across the North in support of the cause. Minnie had never been able to work out how Lolly accomplished such miracles of connection and courteous compliance; mild-speaking, silly, fluttery Lolly, who blinked apologetically when asked to explain such successes.

"I am just persuasive, Minnie dear."

Over those years, Minnie warmed to Lolly as a traveling companion, although the other woman was and would never be as close and dear as Annabelle was. Now Minnie's heart turned over again. *Not Annabelle, dear sweet Lord, do not take my sister in all but blood from me,* she pled silently. She sank into the nearest chair, the telegram crumpled in her hand. She sensed Lolly's hovering presence, the quiet rustle of her petticoats and day dress, as Lolly put a handkerchief into her other hand, saying,

"I will arrange it all, for our journey home. Miss Anthony will understand perfectly that you cannot appear tomorrow. She and Mrs. Stanton and their friends will understand perfectly that you need to be at home with your dearest ones. As for the train arrangements, do not fear. I have many connections among my husbands' friends, and I will call upon them and request their favor and courtesy. I will even go to the State Street Depot this very moment and see what I might arrange through an interview with Mr. Corning's agent; he is the major shareholder of the New York Central, you know. He and Mr. Bard were good friends. He will take the time to meet with me if he is in town. I fear that we will not be able to commence a return to Boston until tomorrow – midday at the latest."

"Do what you think best, then," Minnie replied, as Lolly quietly took her leave from their apartments; a comfortable one, Minnie had to admit. She had been a guest in many such, since embarking on a career as a lecturer in the great cause – the cause which loomed over her life, took hold of her every thought, thoughts and emotions reinforced by the fellows she associated with in that great endeavor. There were so many friends and fellow warriors for the cause which she had encountered over a decade in the lecture circuit; men and women alike, passionately devoted to the abolition crusade.

Many had become fond friends and valued correspondents; the ascetic Miss Anthony and the comfortable and matronly Mrs. Stanton, who had very kindly invited Minnie to Rochester to appear in a lecture series with others of sympathy to the cause of abolition and female suffrage. She had renewed her long friendship with Mary Ashton Rice, who had shared those long-ago schooldays in Boston, but had married a Reverend Livermore with a parish in the booming town of Chicago. The cause had drawn Minnie into fellowship with many others; Miss Dix, who was also from Boston and scribbled improving stories for children between her inscrutable concern for the indigent and insane, and the elegant and suave Mr. William Still, a man of color from Philadelphia who fearlessly organized the escape of slaves from the South and saw to their safety and welfare afterwards. Minnie had made many generous contributions to Mr. Still's crusade from her own purse over the years, feeling as Miss Van Lew had done; while many slaves still languished in the vilest of servitude, being of assistance and encouragement to those sufficiently bold and reckless to grasp at freedom by their own efforts – meant everything to that few.

At this present moment, all of that was a momentary distraction. Minnie now felt crushing guilt over having neglected her closest kin. Family, dear friends – that was all! Dearest friend, sister in all but blood – now Annabelle was dying. Richard Brewer was not a man given to pointless drama; he would not have sent the telegram worded otherwise. Annabelle, dear 'Belle, had never been blessed with the same robust constitution as Minnie. She hated to travel; in recent years she had devoted herself exclusively to hearth, home, and the care of Sophia and Richard's small son, a child produced after so many tragic disappointments.

Minnie did not know Little Richie well enough to have any established opinion of him, other that he was a handsome lad, a small version of Richard Brewer, and superficially charming. Annabelle's daughter and Richard Brewer were the younger generation whom she held dear. Richard honored her with his friendship and respect. An advantage of five decades in age, Minnie had come to see. The very boundaries of friendship expanded, once past the age of blooming youth, where one was schooled to see every untied bachelor as an object of courtship. In that arid age of spinsterhood, with the presumption of flirtation off the table, honest friendship and respect between men and women was possible. Minnie found it a rewarding prospect. Once removed from the marriage market, so many other avenues for friendship opened before a woman! And all of that had distracted her over the last decade from those first close ties!

She wanted to pace up and down, to rage against fates – yea, even to begin walking east; but that would be silly and pointless, as she very well knew upon a moment's consideration. *Would that she had wings, and to fly!*

At least, she could pack; might Lolly return, breathless within minutes, with the welcome news that she had procured tickets on the train-cars leaving this very instant! Minnie set to work; but this distraction took only a few minutes. Both she and Lolly traveled with very little but two small trunks between them. They were in the habit of wearing their heaviest and most bulky garments for travel. She accomplished that small task and took up the novel she had brought along to read, not expecting to think very much of it; Mrs. Stowe's dramatic opus *Uncle Tom's Cabin*. Minnie had first read it as a newspaper serial. Both Papa-the-Judge and Virgil would have condemned it for containing too much sentimental Christian flummery, and contrivances of plot. *Honestly, a slave-master beating a fit and useful slave to death, out of pique over defiance? With that slave being worth at least fifteen hundred dollars at auction?* Minnie had learned much about the lamentable trade over the previous years; one of those being that the owner of a valuable slave would be as likely to kill that slave as a good Boston ship-owner would be to willfully sink one of his own clippers after a profitable voyage with a fortune stowed in the hold.

But it made a touching element in the story, and the book was being read avidly across the North. Minnie had to admit that the silly and sentimental yarn had likely brought at least as many to Abolition sympathies as had ten years of herself giving lectures and writing articles. She thumbed through the chapters of Mrs. Stowe's opus in the spirit of duty and distraction. Soon she <u>would</u> have to admit honestly that she had read it and should she ever be asked, say something laudatory. She had privately concluded that the saintly Little Eva couldn't die any sooner for her taste, by the time that Lolly Bard came through the door of their rooms, announcing with an air of triumph,

"We have tickets through to Albany and beyond tomorrow, on the morning train, Minnie! Mr. Corning's agent gave me every consideration! It's all arranged! He has even promised to send a carriage for us, and for our trunks! Oh, excellent, you have already packed yours! Well, I shall pack my own things, and I think we should have a quiet supper and retire early. You have finally read *Uncle Tom's Cabin*! Is it not the most engaging account of the horrors of slavery?"

"The most sentimental tripe I have read in years!" Minnie replied. "I disliked the good characters, could not care any less for the bad, and wish they would have all drowned together. I think that *Twelve Years a Slave* was a much more truthful narrative."

"Minnie, you are so unruly!" Lolly giggled. "Really, I expect that you will encounter Mrs. Stowe sometime, and you simply <u>must</u> say something nice about her novel!"

"I would be tempted to say that the print was easy to read, and the paper was of good quality," Minnie replied, acerbically. "Which is what my brother Virgil used to say when pressed. No, don't look at me that way, Lolly! I expect that I will say something like '*Your efforts for the cause are so warmly appreciated,*' and leave it at that. Perfect literary flummery, but if it brings more sympathy to the cause … it is what it is." She closed the volume and laid it aside. Her head ached with the effort of reading in dim lamplight once that daylight had fled. She closed her eyes.

"Has there been any further news from Boston?" Lolly asked, in swift concern.

"No, no further news," Minnie replied. "But I was not expecting such."

"Mr. Turner was kind enough to send a telegram for me, to my son; that we are returning with all haste. I am certain that Arthur will send word to your family. He has always been so terribly responsible and considerate …" Lolly continued chattering as she repacked her own trunk and carpetbag, and

Minnie let it pass over her as water passes over stone; not that Lolly ever seemed to notice when she was being ignored.

Tomorrow. Nearly six hundred miles. Three days, maybe four or five — more if there were delays on the track. Anything could happen in that time.

Anything.

The carriage sent by the generous Mr. Turner arrived before sunrise; the sky in the east holding the faint flush the color of mother-of-pearl, while the stars themselves remained faint pinpricks of light in the west. It was icy cold, a brisk wind from off the lakeshore slashing like a sharp blade through Minnie's heaviest mantle, woolen traveling dress and several flannel petticoats. It was a positive relief to reach the shelter of the State Street Station, the depot for the New York Central Railroad; a stately and classically elegant building, a noble façade pierced by twin arches. There was a good fire already blazing in the iron stove which heated the passenger waiting room, a room which at this early hour was blessedly empty.

The only other occupant was a well-set gentleman in Army blue. Minnie barely spared a glance in his direction, noting with a small pang in her heart that he rather resembled Pres Devereaux. Something about the set of his shoulders, and dark hair somewhat threaded with grey. When he raised his eyes from the newspaper that he seemed to be reading with much attention, she noted that they were the same fierce pale blue.

"Miss Minnie Vining!" he exclaimed, setting aside the newspaper, and rising from the comfortless wooden bench upon which he sat. "If I might presume upon old friendship! It's been a few years, but we met in Richmond, at the house of your Cousin Edmonds! Levi Chaffin, Major, US Army," he added, with a suddenly diffident manner, and Minnie's heart turned entirely over in her chest, remembering that gilded summer at Susan's palatial home there; the comforts provided by attentive servants, the lavish, flower-filled garden, the parties, gatherings, and picnics, all embedded in her memory like the fragile wings of an insect, preserved in amber.

The place where she had come face to face with the brutality of the slavery system. And Levi Chaffin and his cousin, Pres Devereaux had been the means of that fateful meeting. It came to Minnie that she owed him courtesy in that respect.

"Major Chaffin! You are promoted! So splendid – it has been my understanding that promotions come so terribly slow in peacetime! Did our war with Mexico do you that good? They say that it is an ill wind indeed that blows no one any good; I expect that it is the same with wars. We are now laden with slave states, so I am cheered that at least some small gain has been made from that abomination of a war!"

At her side, Minnie was aware of Lolly briefly closing her eyes and taking in a small breath. But Lolly had become accustomed to Minnie's outspoken ways, after all this time.

"As war is my profession, I expect so," Levi Chaffin smiled, with a reckless expression which so recalled the countenance of Pres Devereaux to her. "A bloody encounter does have a brutal way of clearing out the deadwood. Just so does a wildfire, out on the western plains; clear out the useless and overgrown, make way for the fit and able."

"I am most astonished at finding you here in Rochester," Minnie ventured, after belatedly introducing Lolly Bard, "And then I remembered that Mrs. Chaffin is from this town! I pray that she and the children are all well; I have such pleasant memories of watching them at play in Mrs. Edmonds' garden."

"Indeed," Levi Chaffin's expression warmed at the mention of his family. "We were visiting my wife's parents. My dear wife thrives on motherhood. We have since had two more children, both girls, since that happy visit to Richmond. My boys are now grown so tall, I am certain you would not recognize them, Miss Vining. My oldest son is determined to follow in my footsteps and apply for a position at West Point."

"It has been almost ten years," Minnie agreed, with a deep sigh. "I wouldn't expect to recognize them, since so much has changed, since they were small children, frolicking in my cousin's garden! I should warn you, Major Chaffin; we have become estranged from our Richmond cousins over the matter of the peculiar institution. My cousin, Mrs. Edmonds took it so personally when I first began giving public lectures against the practice. It grieved me very much, but she was adamant and unforgiving. And when Cousin Peter – you recollect, the veteran of Washington's Continentals – he went to his heavenly reward a year or two later, there seemed to be no basis for a reconciliation." Minnie took a deep breath and ventured mention of that other person who haunted the memory of those summer months in Richmond. "I do recall that your cousin, Mr. Devereaux was courting Charlotte Edmonds, and that was considered an excellent match. We did hear that they had married – are they well and happy?"

Major Chaffin nodded, "Their wedding was quite a notable social event in Richmond; I couldn't attend, as I was off to fight in Mexico, but my younger brother James wrote to me with a full accounting. You will recollect that he married the eldest Miss Edmonds that summer? I understand that Pres and his young missus have several children now, and Pres has taken over management of the family acres."

"I recall very well; I was teaching Charlotte to play chess," Minnie allowed, stifling the brief pang of regret that she felt, upon mention of Mr. Devereaux. The carved Chinese ivory chess set held a place of honor in the study in the house in Boston, which was still her own, no matter how far and how often she ventured from it. "Your cousin Mr. Devereaux so relished the game. I thought it a fine thing that a married couple should have a common intellectual interest; since your cousin and I derived so much pleasure from a chess match." Her voice trailed off, as she recollected Pres Devereaux's sudden declaration of love for her. "I am glad to hear that they have been blessed with children. I often watched him playing with your little boys in the garden. So happy were they, and he also. I am glad to hear that domesticity agrees with him."

She detected a sudden flash of sympathy on Major Chaffin's weathered countenance and wondered if he were about to speak it aloud; and if Pres Devereaux might have confessed to his cousin anything of that bolt-out-of-the-blue love for her spinster self.

"And that your great devotion to the cause of abolition has been rewarded as well," he said. "My Dearest's friends in Rochester were agog to hear that we had met you socially – the indominable and celebrated Miss Minerva Vining! But what of your sister, Mrs. Annabelle?" He hesitated, obviously anticipating bad news from the somber expression on Lolly Bard's face.

"We received news last night that she has taken very ill, and so we are returning to Boston in haste, to be at her bedside whilst she recovers," Minnie explained. "We hope that her condition will not worsen! Oh, why did we travel all this way — we did not expect this sad news!" She was abruptly overcome with apprehension, desolate with the fear that Annabelle would already be gone from this earthly existence before she and Lolly returned to Boston! *Oh, why had she placed her devotion to the Cause over care for kin? How had she let her undying determination to see the institution of slavery made unlawful override her concern for those she held most dear?*

"That is most disheartening intelligence," Major Chaffin's expression reflected nothing but the most profound sympathy. "Allow me to extend my sympathies, Miss Vining. Our duties and obligations, even those taken on without being oath-bound, take us far ... sometimes too far to be with those whom we love in a time of crisis. Because we also have a duty to those with whom we serve, and an obligation to obey the orders of those whom we serve."

"I serve no one but the Almighty," Minnie replied, warmed by Major Chaffin's profound sympathy, and understanding. "But I see that you understand, and your sentiments are most comforting. Fortunate is our encounter, on this dreary morning. We are bound for Albany, and if Mrs. Bard has secured our connections, we may be in Boston before many days have passed. Where are you bound on this morning?"

"To Baltimore, and then to Washington," Major Chaffin answered with a sigh. "On official duties..." Outside of the waiting room, the distant rumble of iron wheels on tracks echoed through the depot. Lolly cocked her head to one side, listening carefully.

"Minnie, dear, I think that will be our train arriving. On time! Such an achievement! Regularity in arrival and departure is the standard which Mr. Bard demanded. The whole enterprise depended upon timing, you know – not just to serve the passengers, you see – but that the train should be the single one advancing upon a single track, without meeting another. At dreadful speed, you see ... a head-on collision between locomotives! That would be frightful, indeed. And would not do any good for the fortunes of the line..." Lolly blinked, as if she had just made the deepest insight, instead of the most banal. Minnie sighed again, and rose from her seat, giving her gloved hand to Major Chaffin in farewell.

"We have tickets for the first train east in the morning," she said. " I trust in Mrs. Bard's experience in judging these things, that this be our train. I am so happy for this chance meeting, Major Chaffin. I hope that we shall soon have another such happy encounter."

"You might count on that!" Major Chaffin rose likewise and bowed over her hand.

The arriving train was indeed the scheduled trail for Albany and points east. Minnie and Lolly Bard arrived in Boston three days later, to see the black crepe hung on the Brewer house, shredded by winter winds, for Annabelle's funeral was already done. Minnie sat in the Brewer carriage and wept into her hands. Too late, too late! Her sister of the heart was gone! She took some strength from Major Chaffin's words

– about duty, campaigns, and oaths. He would know about such things, being a soldier.

Minnie encountered him again; when the war was already begun, another ten years later. By then, the cause had been baptized in blood, and the two of them were alike sworn to serve.

Chapter 12 – Beneath the Starry Flag

November, 1852 – Boston, Massachusetts

"You could not have arrived in time," Sophia Brewer took Minnie's gloved hands in hers. Tears trembled on the younger woman's eyelashes. Annabelle's daughter was as fair as her mother had been, but with her father's honest grey eyes. Minnie had adored and cherished her niece, since the moment she had first laid eyes on her, a newborn infant in Annabelle's arms. Richard's coachman had delivered Lolly to her son's house and brought Minnie to the Brewer's house as the afternoon turned dark and snow began to fall again.

Now Minnie and her niece sat together on the ornate sofa in the Brewers' lavish and modern Back Bay townhouse. Richard himself stood with his back to the fire on the hearth, which had smoldered down to glowing cherry-red coals, banishing the winter chill from that cozy parlor. The songbirds which were Sophia's cherished pets cheeped sleepily in the tall cage which sat before the largest window. "We did not realize until that moment that Mama's condition was so uncertain. She had these spells of faints and weakness in her limbs for years and they always passed after a few days of rest. It's not your fault, Aunt Minnie. You must not blame yourself!"

"Still, I should have stayed closer," Minnie sniffed and dabbed at her eyes with the handkerchief that Sophia offered her. "And that I could not even be here for the funeral rites! We were delayed for hours, with ice covering the rails. I was beside myself! Poor Lolly! I'm afraid that I was unforgivably snappish with her, when I said that it would be faster if we got out and walked. We were so very miserable on the train, because of the cold and wind!"

Sophia giggled, in spite of her grief; so much like her mother, that Minnie was threatened with tears all over again. Because of the snow and ice on the rails, she and Lolly had arrived in Boston a whole day after the funeral service for Annabelle. Her coffin was already consigned to the ornate Vining family vault in the old burial ground, A constant stream of mourners had come to the Brewer house for the funeral meats, extend their condolences, and long departed.

"Auntie, if you could have willed it, I am certain that all the ice would have melted at your bidding! It is enough that you are here now, and that you came to us at once. Because your work in the cause ... it means so much. And honestly," Sophia added. "Dear Mama was wandering in her wits for most of those long hours. She barely recognized me! Not even Richie, and she loved him so much!"

Minnie felt the twist at her heart at that; Sophia and Richard's long-hoped-for living child after so many miscarriages. He was five years old now and would soon be six. They called him Richie, after Richard his father; he was adored by the family. He had grown into a handsome little boy, who had just put on proper manly breeches the year before. Annabelle had made every effort to spend time with him, to divert him by reading improving books to him, even to the point of getting down on the floor to play with him and his various toys – of which he had an ample number. Besides what had been in the nursery for Minnie and her brothers, and for Sophia as a child, Richard had added to those old nursery favorites without stint for the child that bore his name and would inherit all.

At that very moment, Richie appeared in the doorway of the parlor, his hand in that of Sally, Sophia, and Richard's maid-of-all-work.

"Mumma!" Richie launched himself from across the room and buried his face in Sophia's skirts. "I want Grammy! Where's Grammy! I want her to read to me now – where is she?"

"Your Grammy is dead, Richie. I explained it to you," Sophia's eyes were bright with unshed sudden tears. "She's in Heaven now, with all the lovely angels."

"Don't care!" Richie's voice was muffled by the folds of Sophia's black bombazine skirts. "I want Grammy! Make her come back!"

"We can't make your Grammy come back," Minnie reached out and stroked the light brown hair on the little head, buried in Sophia's skirts. Such fine and silken hair; it felt to her hand like feathers on a small chick. "Sweetheart, I will read to you, if you want."

"No!" Little Richie raised his flushed face from his mother's petticoats and skirt. "I want Grammy, not you! You're a horrid old woman and I hate you!"

Minnie felt as if a small and heretofore affectionate kitten had suddenly bared needle-sharp sharp fangs and sank them into her flesh. After that moment of shock, she reasoned with her own intellect: no, Richie couldn't possibly mean such a frightful thing, although his eyes were fierce and bright with that conviction.

"Don't fuss so, Richie," Minnie replied, her voice calm and steady. *How sharp the serpent's tooth* ... No, that was not something she could encompass with her intellect. Not the child of Sophia, the daughter of her dearest friend, closest in all the world, and Richard Brewer, her ally in the Cause, in all that mattered. "You can't possibly mean to say such a rude and awful thing. Your Grammy is gone into heaven, with all the lovely angels, and we miss her, awfully. It's what happens to everyone, when they get old, Richie. It's God's will."

"It's not fair!" Richie insisted, in a frantic scream. "I want Grammy – it's not fair!"

"Darling..." Sophia replied. "Don't fret, sweeting. I can't bring Grammy back for you, I really can't!"

To Minnie, it sounded like the same note of helplessness when Annabelle couldn't argue back.

"If you wanted to, you could!" Richie insisted. To Minnie's distress, he began kicking at Sophia's skirts and hers, along the edge of the sofa. "I don't want Grammy to go 'way!" Richie's lower lip stuck out, mutinously, "Make her come back, Papa! Make this ugly ol' woman go away!"

"Stop that!" Richard commanded forcefully. He strode across the small parlor and took his son by the ear. Richie began to cry. It was the end of a long, horrible day for them all, Minnie sensed; she, Richard and Sophia were at the end of their tolerance for a badly behaving child. "Behave like a young gentleman, Richie, or you'll get a good thrashing over my knee and be sent to bed without supper!"

"You're hurting him!" Sophia protested while Minnie and Richard exchanged glances of mutual exasperation.

"I'll hurt more of him than his ear, if he doesn't behave, my dear!"

Richard sounded exasperated, even as Sophia murmured, "All he hurt was his own toe, Richard – I doubt that the furniture has any feelings at all."

"It's an unmanly display of temper," Richard retorted, in lawyerly dispassion. "And Richie is sufficiently old enough to learn not to give way to them. He is supposed to be the man of the house while I am away, not a spoilt infant."

He led his wailing son out of the room with a purposeful step; within moments, the sounds of tearful juvenile tantrum diminished. Minnie felt as if her last few nerves were being drawn out as thin as strings on a harp. Sophia looked as if she was suffering from a migraine. Richie's bad behavior was the last straw on this fraught day; a day fraught and exhausting for both of them. Minnie felt as if she were a decade older than she had been before receiving Richard's telegram in Rochester, not four days before.

"We'll have supper soon," Sophia patted Minnie's hands. "Just a light supper. Only family; you and I and Richard. I would have allowed Richie to dine with us if he had only behaved better! You'll spend tonight with us, of course. I've had Betty turn out the guest room and make up the bed with fresh bedding. I'll tell Richard to have Briggs take you home in the morning, but for tonight you must stay with us."

"I don't think that I would be very good company," Minnie protested, just as a matter of form, but Sophia's expression lightened.

"You will, Aunt Minnie – you will! Tell us about your latest lecture excursion! And if you would ... I would take it so kindly if you would talk about yours and Mama's schooldays. Share with us your reminiscences about Mama, and your brothers, and the scrapes and adventures that you had, when you were young. That would divert us all, with tales of happier days and cherished memories – memories of so many of those are no longer here in this world. I would so much like to hear of happier times, after the sorrow of this day!"

"Of course," Minnie acquiesced. She loved Sophia as much as if the child had been of her own. She was exhausted from the journey. What better way to remember Annabelle than sharing a quiet meal in the Brewer dining room, being diverted by memories of happier days, before all those troubles and the blight of the 'peculiar institution' came to take over so much of her own life?

In the morning, Richard accompanied Minnie and her small traveling trunk to the house on Beacon Hill, where Mrs. Norris and her daughters had been alerted. The morning was bitter-cold, the early sunshine glittered off frost lining every railing and tree branch and painted pale golden light across the sweeps of snow in the Common. The carriage-ride was a short one, but in that duration, Richard unburdened himself.

"Aunt Minnie ... might I talk to you of a matter that concerns me, deeply?"

"Of course," Minnie replied. Of all the relatives left living in her family, Sophia and Richard were the closest, and the dearest loved. A matter of concern to them both was a matter of deepest import to her.

Richard hesitated, then plunged ahead. "Sophia worries about Richie; his tantrums are ungovernable, as you saw last night. Ungovernable, unless I am present to deal firmly with them. He is yet a boy, and I would not wish to break his spirit by harsh discipline, but he has such a strong will and fits of passionate anger. Sophia worries constantly, feeling herself not up to dealing with such a lad, while Mother Annabelle indulged his every whim. So mild and gentle is my wife, dear Aunt Minnie – a willful and stubborn young specimen as our son may be is naturally beyond her feeble energies."

"My brother Virgil would have advised that Richie ought to be whipped, every other morning," Minnie announced. "On general principals, for if you do not know the reason, he will!"

Richard sighed, in resignation. "I would not gotten yet to that old-fashioned extent, Aunt Minnie. It is irrational and unjust, to my way of thinking. I am hoping that when he begins school, that might kick some of the mad temper out of him, through the medium of sociability with his peers. We are social creatures, do you agree?"

"So we are," Minnie agreed, "You eventually plan on entering him in the South Grammar School. I think you wrote so in one of your letters. A dame school, even with the most formidable woman teaching him his letters wouldn't command his obedience! I agree that Richie demands a strong hand – a male hand in the form of schoolmasters. He has grown so very tall since I saw him last!"

"At least four inches, I think," Richard agreed, now in a much more cheerful mood. "And he got very brown over the summer from playing outside with his Brewer cousins in Newport. The boys are much older than Richie, but he does manage to hold his own with them, which is a good thing, with boys."

"It is," Minnie agreed. She knew that much, holding her own with her brothers and their friends, even in the earliest days. The Brewer carriage drew up before the Vining house;

Jeremiah Daley was sweeping snow off the steps and sidewalk. He set his twig broom aside to help Minnie down from the carriage and take her small trunk into his charge and welcoming her home. Minnie felt like weeping all over again, when Jeremiah told her that they had all gone to Annabelle's funeral.

"She was a fine lady," Jeremiah assured her, as he opened the door for her. "And we knew that likely you wouldn't return in time. Those winter storms are wicked powerful, ma'am, and this last one weren't any exception. We did our duty for the house, Mother Norris and I with my wife and Sister Jerusha. I knew you would have wanted that and then we helped out at the Brewers, with all the guests that came. So many of them, you would hardly believe. Mrs. Annabelle was a fine lady and very well thought of in Boston society. We were not all that surprised, though, knowing her as we did."

"Thank you, Jeremiah," Minnie passed into the familiar hall with a feeling of relief. Home again, for a few weeks as she could stay in it. Home, familiar and welcoming, the hallway floor of worn tile as swept clean as always, the woodwork dusted and polished with beeswax until it gleamed, and the faint smell of good cooking wafting up the service stairs from the basement kitchen.

So had Mrs. Norris always kept it, whether Minnie was there, or not. Mrs. Norris had worked in the house for so many years now that the house was her home as much as Minnie's.. Another trusty quality in Mrs. Norris and in Jeremiah; they were all resolute in their approval of her work. In their own way, they were as firmly against the institution of slavery as she herself was.

"After all, Miss Minnie," Mrs. Norris had said, wielding her rolling pin almost as a weapon, back when Minnie had first told them of her intentions to go on the lecture circuit. "Them black n—ger slaves, they would do the work of any of us, and where would be our wages, then? Heathens they are, the lot o' them, any roads.

Minnie had recalled at that point, what Pres Devereaux had said about maintaining slaves too old to work … and the obligation to care for them in old age.

"Not heathens, Mrs. Morris," she had said, then. "The enslaved folk that I met in Cousin Susan's house were as good as Christians as any I could name."

Mrs. Norris had sniffed, in a disparaging manner. "That may be as well as you say, Miss Minnie, but I daresay that they would work for less than a Christian wage, given the chance! And then where would we be?!"

For that, Minnie had no answer, not then or at any time later. For it was a fact indigestible; former slaves could find work at a living wage, if they had skills, but what if they had none? In either case, it was commonly assumed they would work for pennies, much less than other workers. At present, Minnie told herself that was a problem which could be dealt with later. One step at a time. First came the abolition of the vile, brutal institution.

She bent herself to correspondence and receiving a trickle of visitors who had known Annabelle and wished to mourn with her, on that day after her late return. It was only the following morning that Richard Brewer appeared, unannounced. Bertha showed him into the study.

"Miss Minnie, something quite dreadful has happened, and we have a favor to ask of you. A favor and a plea for refuge!"

"Why, what is the matter?" Minnie exclaimed. "Refuge for whom? Is there another escaped slave, throwing themselves on our hospitality and good will?"

"No," Richard appeared unsettled, even slightly revolted. "For Sophia's cage of songbirds. We need to remove them from the house, this very day. And it's winter outside, so we cannot merely let them go. They have been ... we need to find them shelter, Miss Minnie, this very day ... indeed, this hour!"

"Why do they need shelter?" Minnie blurted. Indeed, why? Sophia had cherished her tame songbirds for years, delighting in their antics and songs, even as a young girl, long before she married Richard; tame goldfinches, wrens, cardinals, and canaries. Many of Sophia's birds had formed pairs over the years. A fair number of her pets had hatched from eggs laid in the nests the parent birds had built, from twigs, and leaves, and scraps of yarn gathered from the garden and from Annabelle's and Sophia's mending baskets. That Sophia would give away her birds; something had gone hideously awry at the Brewer's house. Minnie knew that, even before Richard formulated his reply.

"Richie ... our son," Richard moistened his lips, and plunged ahead into explanation. "He was so very grieved at the loss of Mother Annabelle. And angry: It may be my fault, that he was so angry since he took the most horrendous manner of making his anger plain. This morning he ... he eluded the notice of Mary Ann, and Sophia, both. He went to the small parlor and opened the door of the bird's cage. The birds being so very tame and accustomed to being called ... Miss Minnie, he captured three or four, one by one and ... tormented them. Pulling out feathers, breaking the little bones of their feet. Ripped at least two of the poor birds limb from limb while living, and smashed their little bodies underfoot. The parlor carpet by their cage is marred with blood and their organs and feathers. It was a ghastly sight. Sophia collapsed in a dead faint when she saw it. And the worst part was that Richie was unrepentant over torturing those poor little birds! Sophia retired to our bedroom in hysterics. I can hardly blame her for that. I know how she treasured those dear little birds – her pets, and the focus of her maternal feelings..."

Minnie felt sick, down to her soul. She had always enjoyed Sophia's birds, their cheerful songs, and antics in the dead of winter, a promise of hope and spring. Their charming ways, the miracle of tiny eggs hatching, seeing the infant birds emerge from the shell, and the older fledglings venturing from the nest. Some of the birds – the very oldest, all of fifteen years – had lived out their lives in the vast silver cage, sheltered and cherished. This was monstrous, that a child should take out his rage and grief on those tiny, innocent, and trusting bodies!

"Of course, I will take them. Bring them at once," she replied, and Richard looked relieved. "I suppose it is only his grief at losing his grandmother, which impelled him to such a horrible act ..." she ventured, without much conviction. Richard needed comfort over the awful behavior of his son, the baby who had miraculously survived to the age of reason, who was expected to be all the best of his bloodline in intellect and character. "I expect that they will bring some cheer to this parlor," she added. "Have no fear for Sophia's birds. I will ask

Mrs. Norris if she will be their nurse if I am not present. She loves small and helpless things, and I am certain that they will be safe in her care, when I am absent in service to the great Cause. I have always loved Sophia's birds." She added. "I would have had a few myself before this, save Virgil claimed that the presence of feathers made him sneeze dreadfully. Bring the cage to my house – see, they will settle very well into this room, with a view through the parlor window, of the trees and the Common beyond."

"Of course," Richard already looked relieved. "I'll wrap up the cage in blankets and bring them this very day. As you may imagine, Sophia is deeply distressed, and so is Mary Ann. We can hardly imagine that a child of ours would be so ..."

"He loved his Granny Annabelle very much," Minnie replied. It was in her mind that she would have been much more shocked at news of this horrible cruelty by a child – if she had not seen the expression in his eyes, when Richie kicked at her and screamed, 'You're a horrid old woman and I hate you!'

The vast silver cage of songbirds was moved to the Beacon Hill house, although Minnie did notice that for some months thereafter, the birds were not much given to sing and frolic as they had before. Richie had been punished severely by his father over the massacre of the birds. Although Minnie did wonder if the child would become a horror, a kind of Gilles de Rias in juvenile form, that concern turned out to be fleeting. Her attention soon returned to the concerns of the Cause. But when spring returned to Boston and the north, the cage of songbirds was as tuneful and tame as ever they had been before.

One mild summer day, Sophia came to visit, and Minnie asked her if she wished to have the birds returned. now that Richie was in school for most of the day.

"No, Auntie – I can't countenance the risk to my poor little birds. Richie ..." Sophia hesitated, the sentence unfinished, until Minnie hinted gently,

"What, Sophia dear? Do you fear Richie might still harm your pets? Richard said that he thrashed the boy very soundly as punishment, until Richie promised that he would never do such a wicked thing again."

"I ... I do think so," Sophia confessed all in a rush. "Sometimes I think that I am imaging it, I tell myself that I am imagining it, but there are moments when I think Richie is being deliberately bad, and there is a devilish look in his eyes; a pure enjoyment of being wicked. Three days ago, I caught him teasing the stable cat by cruelly twisting it's tail, and I couldn't help thinking that Richie was relishing the cat's hurt. The other day, he was telling me that he and another little boy had gotten into a fight – oh, and my husband says that this is completely normal, that all boys ... but Richie dwelt on how the other boy's nose bled. Richard said it was only boys being boys, but I thought it was not natural ... and Richie had that look again in his eyes, as if he were enjoying causing pain to something or someone else. It frightens me, Aunt Minnie, and I have talked to my husband about it, but Richard says that I am seeing things that aren't there... truly, Aunt Minnie – was it like that with your brothers? Is it like that with boys?"

"I don't think so," Minnie replied, honestly baffled; her brothers had not gone in much for rough games and fisticuffs. As for taking pleasure in causing pain to helpless creatures, such a thing was outside of her experience, but not her knowledge. "I suppose that such creatures really exist, like devils and angels and witches and all that, but I have never seen such a thing myself."

"I suppose," Sophia confessed with a deep sigh, "That I must always be watchful, even if Richard says that I am imagining things. But my son worries me, Aunt Minnie. And you are the only one who credits me with having such worries. Take care of my birds, Aunt Minnie. Keep them safe."

"I will," Minnie promised. "And if I am not here, then Mrs. Norris will take up their care."

The birds remained at Minnie's house; in time, she nearly forgot the purpose for having them there in the first place, as Richie grew taller, advancing in intellect and good manners. Sophia never talked of her worries about him save on that one occasion, and eventually Minnie put it to the back of her mind ... for the matter of slavery and it's abolition took up more and more of her energy and attention.

***

Spring, 1860 – Boston, Massachusetts

"Auntie," Richard Brewer asked one afternoon, on a mild spring afternoon nearly eight years later, "There is a man I think that you would enjoy being introduced to. A Westerner, so you might not know of him, nor he be acquainted with you, but he is fierce regarding the limits of the slave system, and not allowing it in those proposed new states."

"I thought that I knew every prominent abolitionist that there is," Minnie fretted. She and Lolly were preparing for another lecture tour, this time to Illinois, where the fight against the vile institution was fierce and unrelenting – as fierce as it was in the Kansas and Missouri Territories, where the cause had already been baptized in blood – the blood of abolitionists and slavers alike. "But of course. When do you propose that we shall meet?"

"At our house, tomorrow evening for supper and a small gathering of like-minded among legal circles," Richard replied, with a grin. "And I'll have you know that he has expressed a desire to meet you, Auntie; the famed and impassioned lady lecturer."

"I suppose that my attendance has already been assured?" Minnie asked, concealing a small sigh. She had yet to pack for this latest circuit of lectures, although Lolly had already made most of the travel arrangements. Lolly was incredibly thorough about such matters; a miracle to anyone who had ever thought her one of the most feather-headed females imaginable.

"Of course," Richard assured her, with a bow over her hand. "I think you will enjoy Mr. Lincoln's company enormously; he is one of the most entertaining and companionable gentlemen I have ever had the pleasure of spending a number of hours with. I could have spent twice as many in his company, while laughing like a fool."

"Mr. Lincoln?" Lolly Bard exclaimed in delight. "Why yes – I know of him, and he is a delight, if your guest is that Mr. Lincoln who is the chief legal counsel for the Illinois Central Railroad! Mr. Bard was a shareholder in that company you know, and I still correspond with many of his old friends! They think the world of him, if that is indeed the same man!"

"It would be," Richard agreed, "For he has practiced as a lawyer for many years, and was elected to state office, and served representing Illinois in Washington for a term. The word is that he is a formidable man, for all that he looks the very picture of the ungainly country yokel, and never darkened the door of a schoolhouse after the age of about ten or so. They say he split rails and felled trees to earn a living, early on. You can imagine what our cultivated acquaintances will think of that!"

"Oh, my," Minnie exclaimed. She could just imagine what some of the other erudite, comfortably monied and well-raised Bostonians would think and say of Mr. Lincoln, the country-bred, self-educated westerner. "I have had occasion to meet many people, in my tours, Richard; many in ragged working-men's garb, who are more courteously mannered and considerate than ... then my brother Virgil," she added. Virgil, for all the wealth of Papa-the-Judge and the advantages of education, had often been waspish and rude – and not to put too fine a point on it, snobbish to a degree that would embarrass an English noble. "I would be honored to meet this prairie lawyer acquaintance of yours. If he is determined an abolitionist as you say, then he is already a man of whom I am inclined to think well!"

"I thought you would welcome the introduction," Richard said, "As you and Mrs. Bard are venturing into the near west, in the next weeks. It is my conviction that Mr. Lincoln will prove to be an important man on the national scene, soon enough. He has become a very notable voice in political circles. Reports of his speech at the Cooper Union in New York have made him a very notable voice in political circles, regarding the matter of abolition."

Minnie privately thought that Richard exaggerated; she had met all sorts when she was a girl, and Papa-the-Judge offered hospitality to a great many, either obscure or of note, but all interesting. She had met even more, as she had said to Richard, traveling from city and city, town to town, giving lectures on the iniquity of the slave system. But none of them were like Mr. Lincoln. Virgil would have said he was *sui generis*, one of a kind, when she was presented to him in Sophia's parlor; she and Lolly Bard and Mr. Lincoln were nearly the first arrivals. When Betty the maid opened the front door of the Brewer mansion, the sound of delighted laughter led Minnie and Lolly to the parlor almost at once, where Sophia and Richard sat with a tall, awkward gangle of a man clad in an ill-fitting suit, a man in intense conversation with Richie.

"... three boys," Mr. Lincoln was saying, "You'd be right in between Robert and Willie in age ... Ma'am!" he added, upon seeing Minnie in the doorway. He and Richard both rose hastily from where they sat, and Richard performed the introductions, barely concealing his own amusement, as Sophia took Richie by the hand and led him out of the room.

"I am mos' pleased to make your acquaintance, Miss Vining," Mr. Lincoln bowed over her hand; a very disjointed bow, like a badly-strung puppet, for he was very tall, towering over Minnie like a very tall tree; she who was barely taller than she had been at the age of thirteen. Rather to her surprise, his voice was thinner than she expected, a light tenor, like a boy whose voice hadn't broken yet. His hands were powerful, the hands of a working man who did more than just wield a pen; she sensed that he was particularly, purposefully gentle with her own hand, as she was in handling the birds, with their delicate bones, bones that could so readily be crushed without care taken. "I have read your articles in the *Liberator* with much interest, although I cannot honestly claim to be an absolutist when it comes to Abolition of the slave system."

"You are not a reformer, then?" Minnie replied, somewhat surprised.

Mr. Lincoln smiled; he had a rather homely face, with knobby features and a great beak of a nose. But the smile transformed his melancholy countenance, although the melancholy never really lifted from his eyes, deep-set as they were under a brow that the unkind would later liken to that of an ape.

"Of the Whiggish persuasion, Miss Vining. I would advocate for reformist measures in a slow and gradual manner, upon which most would agree."

"But your feelings on the matter of slavery," Minnie persisted.

"I would not be a slave," Mr. Lincoln replied, thoughtfully, "And I would not be a master of slaves, either. It is a great injustice to be the first, and an insupportable moral burden to be the other."

"That is exactly what was said to me, early on," Minnie replied earnestly. "By one who had good reason to know. But what is the principle with regard to the vile institution that you hold to, without reserve?"

"This one," Mr. Lincoln replied, with great earnestness. "That I would work to keep the institution from extending to those new territories of ours, which will become states, and very soon, I believe. They shall not have the stain of slavery marring them. And that is my governing principle, Miss Vining, although it may come about that I might be forced by circumstances to acquire others, as the situation suggests. Predicting the future developments in our world is a chancy thing, which would try the talents of a modern Nostradamus."

"Indeed," Minnie agreed, and Mr. Lincoln favored her with another one of those transforming smiles.

"Your late father, Judge Lycurgus Vining, was a notable jurist in his day, was he not? A number of his rulings and arguments before the superior courts were cited in several of my independent readings. Are you able to enlarge upon his reasonings in those matters? Mr. Brewer assures me that you were a student of your father's dealings in that regard!"

"At another time, perhaps," Richard Brewer intervened, as they heard Betty opening the front door to another guest. "We have invited all to a purely social gathering, Mr. Lincoln, not a meeting of the American Missionary Association."

"Still," Mr. Lincoln made a slight bow towards Minnie, and Lolly Bard. "I'd 'mire to meet with Miss Vining again, and speak with me, concerning her reminiscences of her father, and of her observances of the slave system."

"Of course," Minnie replied. Indeed, she had been charmed beyond words at meeting a man who might yet become an ally in the great cause – and who knew of and admired Papa-the-Judge.

Chapter 13 – Rally From the Hillside, Gather From the Plain

Spring, 1861 – Boston Massachusetts

"If I were a gambling man," Richard Brewer remarked on a windy Sunday morning in March, the week after Abraham Lincoln was sworn into office as the duly elected president, "I would calculate the odds on where the war will begin. Not if – but where." There was an unsettled, nervous mood in Boston. Richard and Sophia, with Richie, had gone to early church services, where the Reverend Slocomb still fulminated from the pulpit, having lived down the scandal of being named in the Forbes divorce. Meeting Minnie there, Sophia had impulsively invited her to join them for an early luncheon. "And if the weather clears," Richard added, with a glance upwards at the ragged gray clouds scudding across the sky. "A round of games in the garden – the snow has nearly melted, although it's still too soon for planting."

"A war?" Sophia hugged her mantel around herself. "Oh, surely not, Richard. Mr. Lincoln has been sworn into office, after winning the election, fair and square! Surely no one might object among our Southern brethren! Cannot we all go our separate ways, if they so strenuously object to Mr. Lincoln's principled stand against expansion of the vile practice?"

Minnie met Richard's eyes, across the coach which was taking them from the First Congregationalist Church to the Brewer home. There was a look of weary exasperation in Richard's eyes.

"Perhaps, my dear, if we all were genuinely intent on allowing each other to go our own way, in peace and with our best wishes. But I am afraid that it will not work out that way, at all." Richard sounded detached, clinical, as he continued with his analysis of the political situation. "How many Southern states have already seceded – furious at the election of a Free-State man, like Lincoln, and knowing that their preferences regarding the vile institution of slavery will no longer be indulged by the polity?"

"Seven, at last count," Minnie replied.

Richard nodded. "And likely more, as their legislatures and their secession conventions assemble to vote on the matter. Well, as much as I disagree with their preferences, as Voltaire noted; I might not agree with what you have to say, but I will support your right to say it. If those in the southern and border states wish to withdraw from the Union – if that is what their citizens truly wish, give them a kiss on the cheek and a pat on the bottom. Farewell, those who once were our fellow citizens! Forget that we were once one united people, in our marvelous experiment with rule by the polity. No kings, no nobles, only ourselves, judging what was best for ourselves and voting accordingly. And with the British government egging them on, in hopes of breaking up our Union and keeping our Southern brothers as cash-poor, or in debt, and downtrodden as are the unlucky residents of their many colonies, dependent on British mills to purchase their cotton crop, and their factories providing finished goods? I cannot see a future without a conflict, and that is the plain truth of the matter, my dears. It has gone too far, too many heated words and murderous deeds; grudges have a nasty way of abiding…"

"John Brown," Minnie said, sorrowfully acknowledging the wisdom of what Richard said. Richard Brewer was a brilliant lawyer, well-tuned to the vibrations which ran through the nation. "Brown might have been hanged and buried two years ago but he came out of Kansas, where there was already a bloody war fought between Free-Soil and slave-holding factions. There are already those willing to shed blood in our cause – the cause of abolition. I can't disagree that those Southern men are a proud and warlike breed, sensitive to their privilege and ready to respond to insult. What will be the flashpoint, Richard? The touchpaper to the trail of gunpowder?"

"Likely a federal arsenal or fort in the south, somewhere," Richard replied, with the cold-blooded analytical tone which marked his chief intellectual character. "The secessionists will demand that such a federal establishment will surrender to them – cannon, armory, and all. Those of our soldiers who see themselves as citizens of a state which has voted for secession – they likely will resign their Army commissions ... or if enlisted, desert their posts and go over to the secessionists."

"Where in the South do we have Federal troops in number?" Minnie ventured. She had never considered such matters of military interest until the present. The Army was so very small, although such local volunteer companies had begun to drill and hold marches and rallies everywhere, with more energy of late than they had displayed in years. She could bring herself to approve of such companies, as a true reflection of community concerns, but a federal army was a chancy thing, too likely to become the arm of oppression by a government.

Richard began ticking off locations of Federal arsenals and garrisons across the South. "There are substantial military forts at the mouth of the Mississippi, on Ship Island, mainly, which control the approaches to New Orleans, and thence to the length of the Mississippi River. The arsenal in Augusta, Georgia for another. There is also another large establishment in Savannah; I think it is called Fort Pulaski. Fort Sumter controls the harbor approaches to Charleston in the Carolinas. There are also small forts on key islands in Florida, I believe. Fort Pickens, near Pensacola, which is a notable harbor, and Fort Taylor in the isles of Key West. Then there exists a chain of forts along the Texas frontier to police the wild Indian tribes, with a headquarters at the old garrison fortress in San Antonio. That is a location well inland, and not readily supplied or reinforced by sea, as might some of the island forts intended to control approaches to ports. I assume that any attempt to resupply or reinforce any of those Federal establishments will be taken as a challenge by the secessionists. As a betting man, I would put my stake on Fort Sumter. Charleston is as full of secessionists as a stray dog is full of fleas, and the local militias have already laid siege to the island on which the fort stands. President Lincoln already ordered that Fort Sumter be resupplied and strengthened, and I assume that the locals will not be agreeable to that plan. In fact, it is my suspicion that President Lincoln intends goading them into taking the first shot. Then he will then be held blameless, or relatively blameless for the resulting war. And then the fat will be in the fire, my dear ladies, since our President will object to their cannonballs and lead shot with a call to arms of our own."

"You have made a study of this, have you not?" Minnie asked, and Richard grinned, entirely without mirth.

"My dear Aunt Minnie, it behooves a careful man who know from which direction and with what violence the next calamitous storm will arrive. To be prepared with knowledge is to be not taken with utter surprise and run around like a beheaded chicken. It is a wise and careful man who also takes heed of female intuition," Richard added. "Because of your judgement of Brown, I was wary of supporting him, although he was in every aspect but one, otherwise in sympathetic accord with my own views, and yours also, Auntie."

"A man of great courage, but little judgement," Minnie replied. "Who burned with zeal for the cause ... zeal and rage. Not a promising combination. Papa-the-Judge always quoted Napoleon's axiom, to the effect that anger should rise no higher than one's chin. Lolly Bard also advised against too close an association with him, when we met him ... what, three years since?"

"About that long," Richard nodded. "As you recall, Auntie, Mr. Douglass was also wary of Brown, as persuasive as he was."

"John Brown saw himself as a Moses, a new messiah, leading the enslaved out of bondage," Minnie replied. Her memory of meeting the legendary, and martyred John Brown were as vivid as that meeting with Mr. Lincoln, now President Lincoln. It was her honest judgement that Mr. Lincoln was a far more sensible and far-seeing man, feeling a way through the stark realities of the situation wavering on the brink of war. John Brown, tall, and rangy, a beard like one of the Old Testament prophets, with eyes that burned bright with what Papa-the-Judge would have called fanaticism; John Brown plunged ahead, regardless. Despite all who spoke well of his dedication to the sacred cause, Mr. Brown's presence awoke in her a sense of unease. John Brown lacked any real grasp of the realities, Minnie had decided immediately, upon meeting the man and hearing him speak. He was a man who would plunge ahead into disaster. That same unease also manifested in Lolly Bard.

Lolly had looked beyond the parlor windows of a gathering of Abolitionist supporters at residence of Doctor Samuel Gridley Howe and whispered, "Minnie, dear ... he is a perilous man. A perilous and violent man, although I am certain that his heart is in the right place. Our Cause has need of such, but not what he proposes and asks support for. Dear Mr. Bard never approved of vague plans and intentions based upon vaporous fancies. He preferred plans based on concrete realities and mathematical calculations."

"What do you think of Mr. Brown, though?" Minnie had asked on that occasion. Although Lolly still gave Minnie cause to think of her now and again to be the silliest woman of her acquaintance, Lolly more often proved herself to be more than randomly insightful. Lolly looked out of the parlor window, against which the rain was pelting. They were a little apart from the larger gathering, out of earshot of Mrs. Julia Howe, her eldest daughters, and the other guests – all men and women of devoted Abolitionist sympathies.

"I think that he has determined to be a martyr," Lolly blinked and replied apologetically. "If he cannot win through with his project, he will most certainly die in the effort. Die, and take the unwary with him. I am sorry to think so, since so many of those of our Cause think well of him – like Mr. Garrison. Mr.

Brown is also greatly inclined towards violence, if rumors regarding his actions in Kansas are true. Violence proposed as Mr. Brown has preached often enough may very well have a place in service to the Cause, when worst comes to worst and if the situation is insupportable as it was in Kansas during those years. But I do not relish it, Minnie. I would rather not encourage rash proposals such as Mr. Brown is promoting. There are situations where violence may be necessary, as dear Mr. Bard often observed – but best effectively wielded as a razor, rather than wildly as a cudgel. Mr. Brown is a cudgel, swinging in every direction without consideration of what may result. I think his plans will all end in tears, Minnie."

John Brown's plans indeed ended in tears and disaster, just as Lolly Bard feared. That grand plan involved taking the Federal arsenal at Harper's Ferry by violence, a plan not divulged at that time, least of all to the ladies present at that gathering.

Minnie had nodded, in apparent agreement with Lolly, and kept her own counsel. Papa-the-Judge had always been shockingly irreligious in private, distrusting what he termed excessive religiosity. Perhaps Minnie had inherited something of that dislike. Still, the others at that meeting at the Howes with Mr. Brown had been wildly enthusiastic and made no secret of their donations and support. Only Minnie had stood aside. When Richard had asked for her judgement on the matter, she had been as frank with him as she always had been. Richard had nodded somberly on hearing her thoughts, as well as Lolly Bard's. He had declined to contribute monetarily to what turned out to be a disastrous and quixotic plan, which spoke well of his judgement. Many of those in the Howe's parlor at that meeting had supported Mr. Brown's dangerous scheme with their monies and good name. Afterwards they spent nervous weeks and days, fearing that they would be implicated in the disaster at Harper's Ferry by supporting John Brown – but Brown died at the end of a hangman's rope, confessing nothing of the identities of those who had backed his plan. The taking of the arsenal was intended to set off a violent slave uprising across the south, but in the end the only result was that John Brown became a martyr, with most of his co-conspirators and followers dead. The slaveowners of the South were enraged anew, fearing a repeat of that brutal slave revolt in Haiti, so many decades before; a bloody revolt on their own home ground, revolt, treachery and murder, all cheered on by fanatical abolitionists, like Brown.

Within days, Richard's estimation was proved to be correct: secessionists in Charleston and the land-based forts around rained battery fire on the isle of Fort Sumter, after the Federal commander of the garrison quite rightly refused a demand to surrender the harbor fort to them. On the morning of Sunday, April 14th, Minnie was awakened just before sunrise by the sound of church bells tolling without cease, all across Boston. Alarmed, Minnie came downstairs in her wrapper, hearing that Mrs. Norris and her daughters were already busy in the kitchen, preparing breakfast. She had never before heard such a clamor. It seemed that every church tower in Boston was contributing to the dolorous symphony. She met Jeremiah Daley coming up from the kitchen by the back stairs.

"Oh, what is happening? Has someone died, someone important? A disaster come upon the city…"

In the shadows of the back staircase and the wavering flame of the lamp that he held before him, Jeremiah Daley's expression was grim.

"In a manner o' speaking, Miss Minnie. Fort Sumter surrendered yesterday, after holding out for a day and a half under heavy bombardment. The garrison has withdrawn, taking the flag with them. They say," Jeremiah added, "That only one poor soldier was killed, but I fear from the talk in town that he will be the first of many in the days to come."

When the Brewer carriage arrived at the Vining house to collect Minnie for early church services, Richard came around to help Minnie into it. He had something of the same grim humor in his expression.

"It is a good thing that I do not qualify to the practice of law in a courtroom," Minnie remarked. "I would lose every case, heard in opposition to you. Did you place any money with your friends on Fort Sumter being the crisis, and encouraging the secessionist traitors to fire the first shot?"

"Aunt Minnie, you well know I'm not a gambling man," Richard replied, hiding a smile which threatened to break out nevertheless. "Nor would I bet vile money on a matter of life and death. I have the decency of a gentleman as well as the dignity of an officer of our courts to uphold."

"Fiddlesticks," Minnie retorted, as Richard boosted her up the step into the carriage, where Sophia and Richie sat huddled together on one seat. "I know men; their tempers and their humor."

Richard's grin broke out into the open, as he climbed up into the carriage, slamming the door after him, and thumped his walking stick against the roof, as a signal to his coachman to move on.

"As I explained once before, Auntie," he replied patiently. "I want to know in advance from which direction and with what intensity the expected storm will break upon us. I prefer to be prepared."

"Papa, will there be a war for certain, now?" Young Richie asked with grave composure from where he sat, opposite Minnie and Richard. He was twelve now, a well-mannered and handsome youth, accounted very popular among his schoolfellows.

Richard nodded, somber and equally grave. "I'm afraid there will be a war, son. Too late to pray for peace," he added, with a significant glance towards Sophia. "But the matter on which the fight has been formed was building long time, since before you were born, and I'd rather that we get it over with, before you are recruited to fight in it."

"All right, Papa," Richie replied, having given every evidence of thinking soberly over that reply. After a moment, he ventured, "Will you go to fight in the war, then?"

"It is a matter of putting my body and heart where my beliefs have long since been," Richard replied, and Sophia drew in a deep, shocked breath. "It's what an honorable man must do," Richard added, upon noting his wife's reaction. "I won't be rash about it, my darling Sophia. I know – I have been a member of the militia company for years. It's a chowder and marching society, a jolly day out with my friends, playing at soldiering. But if Lincoln calls for volunteers for the various states to form regular regiments – and I soon believe that he will – I will volunteer as soon as I have set all my business

affairs in proper order. '*I could not love thee, Dear, so much,
Loved I not Honor more.*"

As Richard concluded, Minnie felt a chill at her heart. The
war was surely upon them now that Fort Sumter had
surrendered. Having long spoken for the Abolition cause ...
could she also now stand aside? What must she do, now that it
had come to open war, among countrymen and women,
between those who once had been friends and dear
companions?

It was a strained summer, those hectic months after the
surrender of Fort Sumter. There was feeling in the air as if a
powerful thunderstorm was building, lending the very air a
sullen greenish cast, while the skies hazed with heavy grey
clouds. The sounds of marching feet filled the streets, as militia
companies drilled on the Common, afire with enthusiasm.
Newly recruited volunteers assembled and marched away, clad
in civilian motley, but proudly led by the banner of their
company.

To Sophia's barely concealed horror, in mid-summer of
that restless, unsettling year, Richard was offered a commission
as a lieutenant in a Massachusetts regiment composed entirely
of Irishmen, recruited in Boston and vicinity, a commission
which he accepted with lively interest. He did as he said he
would do; volunteer in response to President Lincoln's call after
settling all his business obligations and tendering his
resignation to his partners in the practice of law.

"The company will be interesting, the music delightful and
the need for calm and resourceful leadership for these poor
working fellows is most necessary, if we are to win this war," he

repeated, on the day when he appeared in a blue uniform, shining brass buttons marching in a double row across his chest. Minnie and Sophia had spent several days sewing fine gold fringe to a scarlet silk sash, for him to wear under his sword belt. "Oh, my … really, Aunt Minnie? I cannot imagine a more useless bit of chivalric flummery, but I thank you in any case. The fellows will expect that I make a show. It's a bit like being an actor, I suppose. Like Edwin Booth, the Fiery Star … striding the boards and declaiming to the footlights…" Sophia burst into tears and Richard took her into his arms and kissed her soundly, several times. "My darling Sophia do not disfigure your face with tears. I am going no farther than Cambridge and Camp Day for the nonce. We may celebrate Christmas at home, I assure you. The chaps in the regiment will not be cleared for active service until they have been thoroughly trained. Since most of them are no more soldiers than I am, being laborers, farmers or ordinary working men, I may assure you that we will be months about training them to be proper soldiers."

This did not comfort Sophia in the least, while Minnie regarded Richard with a pang of mixed pride and dread. While the men of the Irish regiment might not at first be the stuff of which soldiers were made, Richard himself looked every inch a handsome and heroic martial figure.

Restless, and unsettled, Minnie confided her feelings to Lolly Bard, over tea in the front parlor. The summer breeze teased the light muslin curtains in the window overlooking the Common and brought to them the faint sound of marching feet – a sound which had become all too familiar for them both.

"I hardly have any interest in continuing my lecture tours," Minnie lamented. "With the whole of the North already ablaze with zeal to preserve the Union and secure freedom for all those enslaved, there seems not to be any real purpose. I feel useless, useless – Lolly, after having been a crusader for so many years. Now that Jerusalem has been conquered, then what is there for me to do now? Lay down my weapons and ... what?"

Lolly nodded, looking as wise as one of the goddess Minerva's owls. "Dear Mr. Bard used to say *'What was the future for a soldier after the war is won? Or for a worker, once the track is laid and completed,'* – he was so very wise, my husband. I suppose that once a campaign is done, one should search around for another, to engage one's sense of purpose. Did I told you, dear Minnie – that I have been accepted as one of the Boston agents for the Sanitary Commission? To see to the needs and welfare of our soldiers. There are so many of them now, I am told that the Army Department is quite overwhelmed."

"As they would be," Minnie replied, crisply. "For our own federal Army was very small, and so many of them departed service to take up arms for their states, when those states withdrew..."

"But the reality remains," Lolly blinked apologetically, "How are we to care for our soldiers, when they are wounded, sick or hungry. I cannot bear to think of our boys, sick and bleeding and hungry, without doing what we can for them. I believe that we must do our part, Minnie. Our sons and brothers ..."

"You mean, that we organize bazaars to sell needlecrafts and similar flummery to the patriotic public!" Minnie snorted in disgust. She looked at the tea tray; the fragile China-import porcelain cups and the silver Paul Revere-fashioned service all laid out so lovingly by Mrs. Norris. This very week, Jeremiah Daley had served his notice to Minnie, saying that he was volunteering to be a soldier, although he was not young. He was patriotic to a fault, and still quite fit, through having been a man of active work. His wife, her sister and their mother had seen him away with the other volunteers, with a bag packed full of comforts.

"You are quite right, Minnie dear," Lolly replied. "As it concerns yourself. Indeed, you have no patience with tedious details, and I confess that many of our lady acquaintances are exasperating ... it is not their fault, of course – it all lies in how most of us were raised with limited expectations as to our role in life."

"*Oh, that I were born a man,*" Minnie quoted, "*For I would eat his heart* – that is, the traitor Jeff Davis' – *in the marketplace!*"

"Indeed," Lolly's sweet, pretty face, framed in those fair and girlish curls which had been the fashion of three decades previous, took on a thoughtful expression. "I do believe that you could. Tho' it would be a teeny bit barbaric, considering. I think, dear – that some means of participating in the Great Cause will come to you. An opportunity, a new means of being of use to the Cause. You will know it when you see it, Minnie Dear."

Minnie snorted again, but just as Lolly had said – the opportunity presented itself within the week through the medium of a letter from her old school-fellow intimate, Mary Ashton Rice. Mary Rice had married a minister among the

Congregationalists named Livermore and moved with him to take up a congregation in the western city of Chicago.

My dear Minnie, Mary Livermore wrote, *I have a very dear friend here in Galesburg, Illinois, a respectable widow who has supported her family with a practice in botanic medicine since the death of her husband a year or two ago. Mrs. Bickerdyke is a most noble and public-spirited woman, who has undertaken to convey a sizable quantity of donations from this congregation and others to the aid of a field hospital established at Cairo on the confluence of the Ohio and Mississippi Rivers. She writes to me in much agitation, as the hospital is ill-organized, and the deprivation and suffering of those poor soldiers there is unspeakable, the sick and wounded alike, all in need of careful nursing, clean linen, and good nourishing food – but none to minister to their wants! She asks for aid and assistance in this most holy of missions. Stay at your hearth, my sisters, she says – prepare bandages and lint and all that is needful, and I will go to the wars and bind up their grievous wounds with mine own hands! She intends to depart for Cairo in a fortnight, accompanying all that has been collected and donated for the good of our soldiers at Fort Defiance. My heart is torn, but I cannot leave my family, my duties here to the congregation and to the Sanitary Commission, and my dearest Mr. Livermore. Mrs. Bickerdyke is a most determined and forceful woman, a tower of strength amongst our sex. But she is in dire need of assistance in her quest to bring comfort to our sick and wounded soldiers, and I fear that many might find fault with her blunt manner of address. She is not known outside the small circle of her friends in Galesburg, and it occurs to me that you, with your long experience of nursing your father and brothers, your considerable fame, and your notable powers of logical persuasion – that you may be perfectly situated to be of assistance to her in this time of dreadful need ..."*

Minnie sent a telegram in reply. *"On my way to Galesburg via Chicago. Will visit you soonest. Fond regards to Mrs. Bickerdyke and yourself."*

Chapter 14 - The Watch Fires of a Hundred Circling Camps

Summer, 1861 – Chicago and Cairo, Illinois

With a feeling of intense anticipation and relief, Minnie packed her small traveling trunk, left instructions to Mrs. Norris and her daughters to close the main part of the Beacon Street mansion, bid Sophia and Richie a fond but abstracted goodbye. and set off for Chicago and the west. At last, amid the tumult of events, she had a purpose and a goal, once more, would be of use in the grand crusade against the cruelty and evil that informed the slave system. The journey was no more or less comfortable than so many others she had made over the last fifteen years. The discomfort of this excursion was a little alleviated by a night spent in a very comfortable little compartment in a special car set up as a sleeping coach. It was, Minnie thought to herself, very much like a miniature stateroom on one of the more luxurious steamboats, all polished wood with pretty curtains to be drawn against the twilight, and a neat little bed made up with clean sheets and a feather comforter. The conductor informed her that this sleeping car was a special one, an experiment of sorts, and if it proved popular enough, soon most railway lines would offer such cars for the convenience of those traveling long distances. She slept extraordinarily well; the rocking motion of the coach going over the rails and the constant sound of the engine proved to be rather soothing. She arrived at the Galena & Chicago Union Station at mid-morning, refreshed from a good rest in the sleeping coach – so much an improvement on a comfortless night on a thinly-padded bench in the First-Class car! To her inexpressible joy, Mary Livermore met her on the platform.

"My dear Minnie, it seems an age!" Mary embraced her as if they had been apart for years. "There is so much going on these days, I hardly have time to think! When were you last in Chicago? I think you had gave a lecture at the Missionary Society Hall! Was it three years ago, or longer?"

"Two years, only two years," Minnie replied, returning the embrace. It was always startling to her to see Mary in her current incarnation, a stout middle-aged body, prim and earnest, afire with good works. She had been Mary Ashton Rice, back then; Minnie always thought of her as she was when first she and Annabelle met her at dame school in Boston. Mary remained always in Minnie's memory as the fearless and devout schoolgirl with her hair tightly woven into plaits on either side of her round face, earnest and serious, even when – especially when the light-hearted Annabelle teased her mercilessly.

"In any case, you are welcome as always," Mary took her arm, and they walked out to the street. "The train to Galesburg departs first thing in the morning, so of course you will spend the night with us ... are you wearied, Minnie dear? Are you up to a diversion, before I take you home; you must be exhausted!"

"Not a bit of it," Minnie replied, stoutly. "I had a good rest on the train, and nothing but time until tomorrow morning and the Galesburg train."

"Oh, good," Mary replied. "You see, we have a simply enormous bazaar today in Tremont House ballroom, to benefit the Sanitary Commission. So many of our good patriotic ladies have volunteered to make things, and to work in the booths, and I had such a large part in organizing it all that I simply have to make an appearance, even if Mrs. Armstrong does have all the volunteers so very well organized. I must introduce you to her, in any case. Feenie Armstrong is my good right hand, in Mr. Livermore's congregation. Her husband, Mr. Armstrong, is in finance, and both are such strong supporters of our efforts. A lovely young couple, they have three very charming and well-mannered children. You would like her, I think. I am kept so busy with writing and working for the Commission that I hardly have time to think. Dear Mr. Livermore has had to hire a housekeeper, so that I can keep up with all my obligations. I would mind it ever so much more, but he and the children are so understanding!"

Minnie groaned. "All the dear sweet ladies, selling bits of embroidery and fancywork to each other, and to the patriotic souls! Mary, I volunteered to go with your friend Mrs. Bickerdyke, just to escape this kind of feminine flummery. Embroidery. Sweet little paintings on china. Berlin wool-work slippers, and fancy samplers. Tatting ... did I ever tell you how much I despise tatting and other useless handiwork considered suitable for ladies?"

"No, you didn't," Mary patted Minnie's hand. "Not above a hundred times, beginning when you pricked your fingers and bled on your sampler, and said some very rude words in Latin which your brothers had taught you. Alas, I hated sewing as much as you did ... but I got better at it, eventually. So very helpful that Madame Dubois didn't understand Latin, but all the girls who did, were shocked to their souls," Mary smiled, impishly. "Ne'er mind, Minnie! We will not expect you to donate any goods for sale or expect you to mind a booth. I just want to introduce you around. This is a grand undertaking, and you should at least make yourself known to those dear ladies who will remain by their hearths and send up their prayers for you … and all our dear boys."

"I shall do my best to be cordial," Minnie relented, and Mary embraced her again, and took the small travel trunk from her.

"You will not regret it, Minnie dear," she promised. "It will do your heart good to know that Chicago is all for Union. I am certain that there are more for Abolition here in Chicago than there are in our old dear Boston!"

"I'll not argue that," Minnie said, as Mary showed her to a hansom cab, waiting among a crowd of other conveyances in the street outside the station, the single horse in harness pawing the dirt at his feet with weary interest, as if he had hoped to find a grain or two of corn in the filth, but wasn't really expecting such.

The Tremont House was the grandest of such in Chicago, Minnie already knew; the cynosure of all eyes, especially of the wealthy. The ballroom did not disappoint, especially not today, all hung with patriotic colors, and filled from pillar to pillar with tables and small booths ornamented with swags of bunting and fresh flowers, ribbon bows – and women, women everywhere, young, old, and in between. Their pleasant voices, and the rustle of their skirts filled the room, at least as much as their energy and good cheer, as well as the undernote of rustling paper money and the clink of coins, as all manner of home-made pretty things changed hands.

"We had a remarkable turnout for this fair," Mary remarked as they entered the ballroom. "Our dear Colonel

Ellsworth was of this city, you will remember. Our folk have taken his bloody murder at the hands of that vile Secessionist very hard. He and his Zouave company were much beloved, in Chicago."

"I know," Minnie replied. The handsome Colonel of volunteers was much admired throughout the North and had been a firm friend to President Lincoln. Indeed, Colonel Ellsworth had lain in state in the White House, his body lapped in bouquets of white lilies, or so Minnie had read in the newspapers. He had been shot by an innkeeper in Alexandria, across the Potomac from Washington – on a mission of taking down a taunting Confederate banner posted by the owner of the inn. A rash response to a taunt, but Minnie knew very well that men were like that. *Was this war a schoolyard taunt grown to continental proportions?* She wondered about that, now and again. The blood of a new martyr had focused all serious attention to the matter of war just this spring, electrifying the North after the Sumter surrender. It would not be over soon, or bloodlessly. First reckless words, then the surrender of Fort Sumter and the Federal garrison in Texas. Words and threats had been exchanged in broadsides in print and speeches, but the death of Colonel Ellsworth, even more than Fort Sumter meant that there would be bloodshed, and blood in quantity. Likely every woman in the Tremont ballroom on this morning knew it in her heart, even if she might not admit it publicly.

Now a younger woman at the nearest booth looked up, catching Mary Livermore's attention. She was pretty, still in the bloom of youth, clad in the most tasteful and subtly expensive of recent fashion; her brown hair, threaded with auburn highlights, was combed smoothly back from a widow's peak in her forehead and tidied away under a modish small bonnet. Minnie thought the woman looked familiar. Perhaps they had met when she herself was on the lecture circuit. One met so many others, and lamentably, only a handful of the most notable or eccentric really stood out in memory, sufficient to instantly attach a name. Three children stood at the woman's side; the eldest a pretty miss of twelve or so with curls of a brighter auburn shade, offering a basket of small nosegays tied with silk ribbons for sale. The younger lads – presumably her brothers – solemnly collected payment for the flowers and made change.

"I see you are putting the children to good work, Feenie," Mary Livermore remarked.

"My husband says that children are never too young to learn the meaning of work, or charity," Feenie Armstrong replied with a fond smile.

Mary Livermore chuckled. "So very correct Mr. Armstrong is in that! Never too young to be of good use in the world! Feenie, I would like to make you known to one of my oldest friends in the word; Miss Minnie Vining, this is Feenie – Mrs. Josephine Armstrong."

"So very pleased to make your acquaintance, Mrs. Armstrong," Minnie was still certain that she had met Mrs. Armstrong before. She recognized the younger woman's face; that distinctive heart-shape and grey eyes were familiar. Not from Boston, though; not the daughter of old friends or a distant relative. *And did she imagine the fleeting expression of … fear, fear and apprehension that crossed Mrs. Armstrong's countenance.*

"I have heard so very much about your work in the Cause," the younger woman replied, with every evidence of pleasure, after that first brief and inexplicable moment of dread. "I had often wished to attend one of your lectures, but never had the opportunity – for which I am very sorry."

"I share that regret," Minnie replied, "But I am certain that we have met before; you seem very familiar to me. Might we have encountered each other through friends and kin in Boston? Were you at school there? Are your parents someone that I knew?"

"No," Feenie Armstrong shook her head. "I don't believe so. I was an orphan from the age of ten, but I was blessed with an attentive guardian, who sent me to school in Philadelphia and supported me until I married Mr. Armstrong."

"Perhaps I recall someone who resembled your person," Minnie replied. At that moment she glanced at Mrs. Armstrong's daughter. In the space of a heartbeat, she realized, with a feeling like being struck by lightning, where she had first encountered Feenie.

She had first met Feenie Armstrong, or the woman who went by that name, in Richmond, the nearly white child named Josephine that she and Elizabeth Van Lew had purchased at the slave auction in the basement of the Old Fellows Hall in Richmond's Shockoe Bottom. A poor tearful child, frantic at being tossed in among the brutal slave system, rescued at the last minute, restored to freedom and the chance of happiness. It was all dreadfully clear in that one moment to Minnie.

Josephine was a woman now grown, settled in a prosperous life, and a happy marriage, content with happy and well-mannered children. But she must still live in dread, knowing that an unthoughtful or vicious word about how she had been bought in a slave auction in Richmond at the age of eleven years, just because her father died in debt and her mother had an ancestor of the Negro race and born in bondage. *Did anyone know of this, save Minnie herself, and the kindly Van Lew family, who had seen to Feenie's education and subsequent freedom into another life? Did Feenie Armstrong's husband even know of her past, although nothing of it was her fault in the least?*

No, she wouldn't say anything about what she knew of Mrs. Armstrong's past.

"Yes, I think that must be the case, now that I think upon it," Minnie declared, newly resolute, "I do not think that we have met, previously, Mrs. Armstrong. I am certain that I would have remembered very clearly such a charming person as yourself, and your dear children, too. I commonly meet so many people, that it is easy to become quite muddled over who I have met before, and someone who merely reminds me of someone I have met before. Let me wish you and Mrs. Livermore the very best of good luck with your benefit fair."

Armed with a letter of introduction from Mary Livermore, Minnie arrived in Galesburg the following day on the morning train. It was a glorious late summer morning; the farmers' fields alongside the railway were brilliant green and gold with corn and wheat, already grown tall, under faultless azure clouds, and woods of oak, chestnut, and elm, star-scattered with wild iris and sunflowers in the open places. She had donned a simple dark wool merino traveling dress, without hoops, a modest bonnet in the plain Quaker mode, and traveled with a single trunk, packed with clothing items of like simplicity.

Minnie was not there to make a show; she was there to serve, as best she could. The introductory letter from Mary crackled in her reticule, as she stepped from the Chicago, Burlington & Quincy train, and was directed by the hovering conductor to the Ladies' Waiting Room. For a relatively small and insignificant town, Galesburg was a very busy node on the western railways. The platform was crowded – mostly with men in blue uniforms or the motley of various militia units. The railyard itself echoed with the screeching of steel wheels on iron rails, the shriek of steam whistles, and men shouting orders and directions in voices which varied from the exasperated to the peevish. Minnie had long become accustomed to the convenience as well as the attendant discomforts of rail journeys, discomforts sometimes relieved by First Class travel and the attention paid to her as a notable personality of irreproachable character – how swift the transport, so much faster than by a horse-pulled coach, and how miserable such a journey could be, be it hot or cold, with the coal smoke spewing from the locomotive drifting in through the coach windows!

She straightened her bonnet and entered the Ladies' Waiting Room, her small trunk in hand. Just inside the doorway, she set the trunk down and surveyed the room within, and the women gathered in it. The quiet murmur of female voices, and the rustle of their skirts was a balm after the clamor outside. To her mild surprise, there was a good crowd of women already there, apparently seeing one of their number off on a long journey. Minnie's spirits rose; yes, she had been on time for the appointed hour. This must be the woman she was meant to assist in conveying comforts and organization to the sick and injured at the camp at Cairo, help in establishing a well-run hospital there, the woman that the others were gathered around, bidding her farewell with every evidence of affection and respect. That woman was a tall, sturdy female, formed in the classic Greek mode, who might have served as a model for one of the caryatids, or for a statue of Hebe or Athena herself. She had brown hair, lightly streaked with grey and combed back severely, under a plain cloth Shaker bonnet; a traveling costume every bit as plain and practical as Minnie's own. Minnie had already warmed to her on that regard, before the tall woman smiled at her friends and embraced them serially with every indication of fond respect – friends who were making their own reluctant and theatrically tear-sodden departure from the Ladies' waiting room. Minnie stood by the door, as most of them departed. Yes, this was Mary Livermore's good friend, the respectable widow of Galesburg. Who now came towards her, smiling slightly and holding out both hands in friendship.

"Miss Vining!" Mary Bickerdyke exclaimed, with every indication of welcome and pleasure. She had dark blue eyes – and topped Minnie by more than a head in height. *Well, of course – a modern goddess come to earth ought rightfully to be taller than mere mortals.* "Mary Livermore wrote to me, saying that you were on your way from Boston! I am so happy to see you, for it is a great work that I am bound to undertake!"

"Mary said that you needed assistance," Minnie replied. "So much necessary to take care of our soldiers…"

"Our boys," Mary Bickerdyke replied, earnestly. "Our sons and brothers, every one of them – our boys! Such awful disorganization, you know! Every woman I know simply emptied out their pantries of good things and sent them off packed higgeldy-piggily in among clothing and good books! The waste of it all, when the cars were delayed in the heat, and jars broke, and all those good things – fresh bread, fruit and vegetables decayed and spoiled through being delayed and roughly handled – and wrecked all the goods they were packed amongst! So I am traveling to the Army camp at Cairo with four boxcars packed full of goods for the benefit of our sick and suffering boys there. My personal supervision, to ensure that it all arrives where needed and is distributed accordingly! It was such a waste, all that first goodwill for our boys, spoiled in the heat and by misdirection! The good ladies of Galesburg and Mrs. Livermore don't want to see a repeat of such a disaster as that!"

"Why Cairo?" Minnie asked, "I know it is on the river, but why?"

"Because the Mississippi River is blockaded by the Confederates below Cairo," Mary Bickerdyke replied readily. "It is the impulse of the Army and all of our folk here in the West – to break that blockade, and free the River, that great central river, to free commerce. And that is our great intent," she looked seriously at Minnie around the edge of her somber Quaker bonnet, as they took seats on the plain wood benches of the Ladies' Waiting Room. "I read in the newspapers that in the East, the armies contend for Washington and Richmond ... well, good luck to them, we say. But the West is the heart of the country, and our generals will win it here, or else go home in shame, with their tails between their legs, like beaten hounds in a dogfight. Cairo is pointed like a dagger at the vile heart of the

Secessionists. It must be held, at all costs, but our boys must be cared for, when they fall to camp fever, or in battle, regardless!'"

Minnie nodded in agreement; it made sense, of course. Boston, New York, Philadelphia were all important places, but they were not the only important places. There was more than just the thread of settlements and colonies along the Atlantic seaboard as there had been in the day when Papa-the-Judge and Cousin Peter had shouldered their muskets and turned out with their volunteer militia companies to chase the British away.

"What shall we find when we arrive in Cairo?" she ventured, and Mary Bickerdyke sighed.

"I expect we shall find nothing so good and suitable as our boys would require," she explained. "For the Army has been quite overwhelmed. There are so many soldiers called to duty, the established camps are swamped and disorderly, and many of our poor boys endure hardships so rigorous as to make many of them fall ill. We received word from Miss Safford at Cairo that the hospital at Camp Defiance is quite overwhelmed – without even having fought a battle! Well, that will simply not do for our boys."

"I expect that we shall have to follow the example of Florence Nightingale," Minnie answered. "Not only nursing but organizing ... everything."

"Indeed, Miss Vining." Mary Bickerdyke nodded in agreement. "I do believe that we shall work well together, as you have an excellent grasp of the situation that may face us upon arrival at Camp Defiance."

The two women arrived in Cairo late in the afternoon — arrived in a chaos of dust and smoke; from the railyard and from a riverbank lined with armored steamboats, smoke which drifted from chimneys of more permanent establishments, and from fires dotting a ramshackle camp of shacks and tents appended on to a muddy brawling riverside town. The town and camp alike hunkered down behind high levees which protected a narrow 'v' of land on both sides. The heat and humidity was oppressive. Minnie could feel her shift sticking to her skin, unpleasantly damp with perspiration. She felt grubby from a day of travel. The noise of engines, of horses, the tramping of marching feet and the irritated shouting of drillmasters and work parties at labor, all threatened to overwhelm the two women, as they stepped from the passenger coach. There was not another woman in sight; a woman of the respectable sort, anyway. Mary Bickerdyke looked around, at a loss for the very first time that day.

"I was expecting to be met at the station," She commented. "I had telegraphed Miss Safford that we were on our way and would arrive today." Noting the query in Minnie's eyes, if not actually voiced, "Miss Safford is — or was a schoolteacher at a country school near Cairo. She came to Cairo to help in the camp hospital, only to find that the hospital is in a parlous state. She confessed that she and her few helpers are quite overwhelmed although those few city burgers of Cairo who are in sympathy to the Union are doing their best to aid her."

"We look around for a man clad in Army blue with gold or silver on his shoulders," Minnie said, sturdily. "That will be an officer and perhaps of high enough rank to have enough authority to order transportation for your goods from the railcars to the hospital."

"There is one," Mary Bickerdyke commented, with a note of relief in her voice, after she and Minnie had looked around the station platform. There was a tall, dark-haired man with silver oak leaves on the shoulders of his blue uniform coat. As he turned at the end of the platform and came about, Minnie saw with a thrill of pleasure and relief that the officer was someone she knew.

"Why I do believe it is Major – no, Colonel Chaffin! My dear Mrs. Bickerdyke, I am astounded beyond belief to see him here! He was a Carolina man, of an old plantation-owning family! I would have thought he would have gone to the South! I met him years ago when we stayed with kin in Richmond. I suppose they are all now for Secession," Minnie added with a touch of sorrow. She had been certain in her heart all this past year that Susan and Ambrose Edmonds, their daughters, and sons-in-law would have gone without hesitation for Secession with the greatest enthusiasm. They all probably cheered the fall of Fort Sumter, forgetting the certain inalienable rights – the rights to freedom and the pursuit of happiness that were the rights due to all, men and women, black and white alike.

Minnie and Mrs. Bickerdyke had no need to attract the interest and regard of Colonel Chaffin. He had noted their presence as they had noted his; the unlikely appearance of a pair of primly dressed ladies of a certain age, standing on the railway platform, and strode up the platform towards them.

"Miss Vining!" He exclaimed, upon recognizing her, and it touched Minnie that his countenance was alight with pleasure. He looked older, as was only to be expected, since it had been at least eight years since the chance meeting in the railway waiting room in Rochester. "What has brought you here, and what can be the purpose of this visit? Surely not to favor us with another talk on abolition of the slave trade! Such a talk would be superfluous in the extreme, given the current situation."

"Colonel Chaffin! You have been promoted!" Minnie replied, giving him her hand. "And so worthy an officer! I rejoice at seeing you again. No, I am not here to give a talk. Mrs. Bickerdyke and I are on a mission of mercy ... and it might be that you may aid us with it! We have come to organize the hospital at Camp Defiance! We have brought four boxcars of supplies for that purpose with us but have dire need of assistance in transporting all those necessary goods to where they are needed. May we call upon your assistance in this?" On noting Levi Chaffin's stern expression, Minnie added, "My dear colonel, this is for the good of the men ... for the sick and needy. Surely, you can find it within your authority to assist us?"

"Oh, of course," Colonel Chaffin released her hand. "But Colonel Prentiss, our commander, will want to know by whose authority you have come to Cairo."

"No other authority than that of our Almighty savior," Mrs. Bickerdyke replied, crisply.

Colonel Chaffin chuckled. "That authority certainly ranks over Colonel Prentiss. Consider your hospital established, ladies." With a brief gesture, Colonel Chaffin summoned another man to his side, this man also in blue uniform with a veritable zebra-array of yellow stripes on his sleeves.

"Sah!" The soldier snapped a smart salute to his officer, and a brief nod and tip of his black-billed cap in the direction of Minnie and Mrs. Bickerdyke. "Your orders, sah!"

"A work party, Sgt. Hand," Colonel Chaffin replied; his expression wry and humorous. "These ladies have appeared ... with sufficient goods to properly fit out the hospital for our lads in camp. Be so good as to organize a work party to unload all the traps and trash they have brought with them, bring it to the hospital tents, and then see to whatever else they require."

"Four boxcars full of goods," Mrs. Bickerdyke added. It seemed to Minnie that Sgt. Hand regarded her with a mixture of awe and respect.

"Excellent, ma'am!" The Irish came out in the sergeant's voice at full strength. "It shall be done as you order, sah! The lads sick in that hospital place – it's no good for them, as all can see! Especially as we need to thump the bloody slave-holding Sessesh, treat them a lesson – and for that, we will need every good Christian soul, present and with good heart and a bayonet fixed! Sah!" Sgt. Hand saluted again, as if to make certain of a good measure, wheeled on his heel and set off on his mission, as if it were his duty alone to bear the good news to Aix ... or at least, to the nearest party of idle soldiers.

"That's seen to," remarked Colonel Chaffin, and offered one arm to Mrs. Bickerdyke and the other to Minnie. "I shall conduct you to our camp myself. It is not far, a short walk, indeed. Hand is an old-school soldier. I think he must be on service to his third national flag. In any case, he is inhumanly efficient. I may ask his captain if he might be assigned to assist you in matters to do with the hospital."

"As for yourself," Minnie replied, mildly curious as to how Colonel Chaffin was at Cairo in the uniform of the Union, when she had wholly expected that he would have followed his fellow southerners into Confederate gray, as so many other officers from Southern states had done. "I am astounded and gratified to find you here, Colonel. You have defied the lure of the Confederacy and remained..."

"Ah," Levi Chaffin's mouth quirked in a wry smile. "Loyal. Loyal to an oath I took when I was a stripling youth. You would well ask, Miss Vining. Loyalty to a principle is not an easy or a simple thing. Were it so, many more would have remained true, I believe! I took to my heart the example of my commander in the Mexican War; General Scott. I took counsel with him, all these months ago, when he was still the commander of our armies."

"A man of Kentucky, I believe," observed Mrs. Bickerdyke with interest. Colonel Chaffin nodded in agreement.

"And many in the Confederacy spoke ill of him, in that he continued to serve as the commander in chief," Levi Chaffin's countenance reflected sorrow, a sorrow so deep that he vouchsafed no further word of it. "But when I asked – and General Scott was a man whom all who served with him held in reverence – he answered that in his life he had only ever taken one oath; an oath of loyalty to the United States. To him that subsumed any lesser regional loyalty. So I went to my quarters and considered long... and I came for the Union."

"I believe that it has cost you dear," Minnie observed with sympathy. She recalled well how Levi Chaffin appeared devoted to his kin and community, his friendship with his cousin, Pres Devereaux. Yet he had the largeness of spirit within him to regret the stain of the vile institution and to remain loyal to the Union and his oaths. She regretted that remark, noting the brief expression of anguish which crossed his face at that moment. "It <u>has</u> cost you, Colonel Chaffin, hasn't it? I am so sorry for the choice which was forced upon you. Loyalty is a hard mistress, indeed."

"It is," the colonel's jaw worked, as they walked with him, from the train station along the muddy streets of Cairo, streets crowded mostly with soldiers in blue. There were not so many ordinary citizens around; the various storefronts looked vaguely derelict. "My oldest sister wrote to me – a spiteful and angry letter, after reading the news in a Southern newspaper that I had declared my loyalty to the Union. She told me that the portrait of me in my father's house was taken down from the wall, dispatched to an attic, and that they would never again speak my name. Nor was I to think and advertise myself in the public spere as their brother and the son of my father ever again."

"It is a cruel thing they have done," Mrs. Bickerdyke remarked, and she covered the hand that he held upon her arm with her other hand. "To forsake and abjure kin! That is the cruelest thing that I can imagine! Can you find any comfort in the love and loyalty of a new fellowship, Colonel Chaffin? I would think of myself as your new sister in kinship from this moment ... as are all those who serve the Cause."

"I am so sorry," Minnie murmured. That was all that she could say in truth. For she could recall the golden afternoon of those days in Richmond, when all had been in amity among kin, kin who would never meet again, save on a battlefield.

"It is of no moment," Colonel Chaffin replied, at last. "I have no leisure to spend in regrets for the choice that I have made. It was the only choice which a man of honor could possibly make."

They walked on in silence, all lost in their own thoughts and considerations. Minnie had understood that Cairo was a river town, a port of significance on the mighty river. There was service by steamboat three times weekly to New Orleans – or there had been once. Now the landings which had once been crowded with tall-chimneyed steamboats, flat-bottomed scows and rafts of crude lumber floating to markets and mills downriver were all but abandoned. Not quite abandoned, though; tied up or moored in mid-river were a scattering of armored steamboats; all their fancy woodwork discarded in favor of heavy armor of thick planks and metal plate, the menacing muzzles of cannon poking out between. A vessel more unlike the noble oaken sailing battleships of old, with cannon lining two or three decks could scarcely be imagined. She could just barely see them over the rim of the levee which protected the town from being swept away entirely by the rivers in flood. They passed a ragged cluster of tents and shacks before they reached the main camp. Clotheslines hung heavy with flapping burdens ran every which way between them. Negro women labored over washboards and buckets in the open spaces and small children in brief garments or entirely naked ran and played among them.

"Might I ask, Colonel Chaffin; who are those people? Those women doing laundry. They look as if they are very busy at that trade." Mary Bickerdyke broke the brooding silence between them.

"Oh, them?" Colonel Chaffin looked toward the linen-hung camp. "Escaped slaves from the country down-river. They packed their traps and made their way overland, or cobbled rafts together, made themselves free with borrowed rowboats –

made themselves free indeed – and came to the Army to plead for safety and sanctuary. I'm told that some of their owners, knowing that they came here, showed up and demanded the return of their rightful property from Colonel Prentiss." He chuckled, dryly. "To which Colonel Prentiss replied, that valuable property of the Confederacy at open war with the Union – were rightfully seen as contraband which might enable them to continue at war – and we were fully within our rights to retain contraband property. I'm told that those owners went away, quite indignant..."

"As well they should be," Minnie replied, stout in agreement. "To hold another human soul in slave condition is immoral..."

"So we all know," Colonel Chaffin looked down at her with a brief, sideways grin. "For you have been saying so since we met at the very first. Now, the question remains; what shall we do with them? They have been held in bondage since birth – knowing trades and skills, but have come to throw themselves at the feet of someone who will tell them what to do. They have not yet not developed the skills inherent to free men. The eternal conundrum, Miss Vining – what to do with a people accustomed to a condition of slavery?"

"I do not imagine such to be as helpless as all that," Minnie replied, recalling the forceful intellect and ambition of Mr. Frederick Douglass, who had supported her at that momentous first lecture, all those years ago in Boston. "Indeed, I am certain that such held in bondage may have concealed such abilities and inclinations as a matter of preserving themselves!"

"Indeed," Mary Bickerdyke murmured. The other woman was regarding the contraband camp with an expression of consideration. Minnie had no doubt that the other woman was formulating a plan. "Tell me, Colonel – it seems as if they have hired out themselves to do laundry. Might they be willing to do such work for the camp hospital as the Sanitation Commission might pay for?"

"I suppose so," Colonel Chaffin shrugged. "They and their children must eat, and it does no one's moral character any good to depend on charity forever."

"Indeed," Mary Bickerdyke replied again; she remained silent as Colonel Chaffin escorted them past the pair of sentries at the entrance of Camp Defiance.

"Welcome to the salient of the Union," he said. "I'll take you to the hospital, ladies."

Chapter 15 - Our Jimmy Has Gone For to Live in a Tent

Minnie did not know what to expect of the hospital in an Army camp; she had no expectations at all of good order, cleanliness, and comfort, so she was spared any pangs of disappointment at what that establishment presented on that first day.

"The place was a brickyard," Colonel Chaffin explained briefly, as they walked into the main compound of Camp Defiance. "The largest open space within the town. The hospital tents are set up over here, as far from the parade ground as the terrain will permit. Colonel Prentiss has the men drilling, every morning when it is cool, and again at twilight when the thermometer falls. Can't be killing the men with heatstroke. We – that is, the old hands among us – have adamantly insisted upon the latrines being properly dug and their use regulated. We have only so many men in the force, you see. Having a third or half lost to disease because of unsanitary conditions would … at the very least, be an embarrassment." He cleared his throat, in a somewhat embarrassed fashion. "And at worst; losing the war before we have fairly begun. I will confess that all our established Army protocols and practices are overwhelmed by the sheer numbers called to our banner. But still, there are almost four hundred men down sick with the ague and fevers, so sick that they can't resist being carried to the hospital."

"The lives of every single one of our boys are precious to us," Mrs. Bickerdyke asserted. "Four or four hundred. Goodness, no wonder poor Miss Safford is overwhelmed! That they would be risked in battle – well, that is war, but there is no excuse for slackness and bad housekeeping. That they should not be cared for, before a battle and afterwards, as a mother would her own children? <u>That</u> is my mission, Colonel. The Almighty has given me this task, and I will carry it out to the best of my ability."

"I am certain that you will," Colonel Chaffin returned, although his countenance seemed haunted by dread and sorrow. "But know, this, Ma'am; many of your boys, as you call them – will suffer and die, regardless, as the cause of the Union demands. It is the way of war, bloody and cruel. You will not be able to succor and heal all."

"I know," Mary Bickerdyke nodded, in calm acquiescence. Minnie was reminded of a stern Roman mother. "But what I can do for them, I will. The Almighty commands me!"

"And the Sanitary Commission lends every aid," Minnie affirmed, stoutly in her voice, although she was apprehensive as Colonel Chaffin led them towards a series of tents set up along the farthest range of Camp Defiance. There was a cook-tent erected nearby, with a massive camp stove. A haphazard pile of empty hogshead barrels and broken crates lay behind and a little to one side of the cook-tent; obviously scrap wood intended for the cook-fire. Minnie sniffed at that. So very careless and messy, not a bit of what she expected from Army organization. The levee rose beyond them, a hill too regularly level at the crest and well-packed to be natural. A couple of rough timber staircases set in the landward side climbed the heights of the levee from the low-lying ground in between.

"Glad to hear it," Colonel Chaffin replied. "Ladies, I must leave you here. We drill in the early evening once the sun's heat begins to lessen. I will direct Sergeant Hand to perform any task that you require of him as soon as he and his work party deliver the Sanitary Commission cargo to the hospital. Likely he will relish the opportunity to be excused from drill, so please don't hesitate to ask anything of reason from him and the work party. I am afraid, Mrs. Bickerdyke, Miss Vining. that you have a great deal of labor set out in front of you, just as do we old Regulars, when it comes to training our army."

"We did not come here to take a holiday," Minnie replied. "Work is what we came to do."

"Indeed," Mary Bickerdyke nodded, magisterially. "We came here to see to the care of our boys. Thank you for your assistance, Colonel."

At the same instant that Colonel Chaffin bid them good evening, and took his departure, a very young woman in a calico dress which drooped hoop-less and looked by the hem of it to have been dragged through mud and other unclean matter, emerged from the nearest tent. Her apron was also similarly stained. She carried a bucket, which she set down as soon as she saw the other two women.

"Oh, merciful heavens, Mrs. Bickerdyke, you are here!" She was a very pretty, slender young woman, worn down to a thread and very near tears. "There is so much... and so many! I have done all that I can, and the contraband women and some ladies from Cairo are helping me, but there is only so much we can do with what little the Army can spare!"

"We are here now, Miss Vining and I," Mary Bickerdyke enfolded the younger woman in a comforting embrace. "And four boxcar-loads of supplies; linens, food, spare cots and blankets and much else as well, all of which are on their way this very minute from the railyard. Colonel Chaffin was good enough to put a trusty sergeant and a work party at our disposal. I do not wish to waste any time; show me the hospital, so that we may make plans to remedy the dire situation as soon as we are able. We may not be able to make improvements tonight," Mary Bickerdyke added, with particularly resolute determination, "But at least, we will have a notion of what needs to be done."

"Everything," Miss Safford sniffed, and rubbed her eyes. "Everything! The poor souls lie in their own filthy bedding for hours, for lack of anything clean! It is all that I can do to bring them beef tea and a concoction of willow bark, steeped in hot water, or Peruvian bark for those poor souls with the ague and chills."

"I have sufficient funds to hire laundresses," Mary Bickerdyke replied. "And I do suppose that the contrabands in the camp that we passed would be happy enough to be hired for that task. Now show me the hospital."

"All right," Miss Safford gulped back her tears with a commendable effort. "This way ... the convalescents are here, those who are still ill and not cleared by Surgeon-Major Frost to return to duty with their company. They help as much as they can, but they are hardly well themselves..."

The first tent was not so awful; filled with cots and bedrolls, most occupied by men, most in a state of dishevelment, or indeed, undress. At least half of them immediately dived for the cover of blankets or those garments they had set aside in the interests of comfort within the sweltering canvas roof, as the three women entered the tent.

"They are ... unclothed!" Minnie hissed in a startled undertone. It was not that she had been completely unaccustomed to the sight of naked or near-naked males. After all, when she was a girl, her brothers and their friends would swim in the Charles, when the summer heat was particularly oppressive.

"They are," Miss Safford acknowledged, in a welter of embarrassment and fanned her flushed face with her hand. "They are still recovering, and the heat is so pernicious. I try to think of them in the same manner as creatures in the barnyard."

"I was married to my husband Mr. Bickerdyke for twenty years, and have two sons," Mrs. Bickerdyke replied, serenely. "I'm not seeing a particle of anything that I didn't already know about."

Minnie felt the same flush of embarrassment rising in her face. Well, she would have to get used to this. It was one thing to minister to her brothers when they were ill, and when they were dying. It would be another matter entirely to see to the needs of strange men; boys, really. Perhaps she would do her best to consider them as infants and small boys, in need of sisterly or motherly care. Miss Safford, young and unmarried, seemed to have found a means of coping by thinking of their patients as horses and cows.

Conditions in the other tents were abominable. Hot, filled with the stench of vomit and feces, of unclean bodies and pungent male perspiration, stale air, and the indefinable odor of sickness. Minnie tried to hold her breath as much as possible. Mary Bickerdyke's expression remained stern and resolute, even as Miss Safford's expression reflected a degree of shamed embarrassment. But Mary Bickerdyke was unmoved, even serene.

"Rest easy, dear boys," she said several times, as she leaned over a cot or a bedroll, smoothing the ragged, stained covering over the shivering form underneath. "Rest easy, for in the morning, we will fix things. You will be cared for as tenderly as if you were home with your dear mother. Rest easy, boys."

It was fully evening when their tour of the hospital tents ended. The sun had gone down in the west, well below the edge of the levee, but the sky still retained the color of a bleached seashell in it, edged with pale apricot shreds of cloud. The distant sounds of drill and stamping feet echoed from the distant parade ground, a sound which had become so very familiar to Minnie, as familiar as the regular ticking of the old tall case clock in Papa-the-Judge's study, far away in Boston. Minnie took a deep breath of relatively fresher air. The compound of tents stretched away before the three women, many lit within by oil lamps, which gave the effect of a collection of Chinese paper lanterns. A scattering of campfires sent golden sparks up into the evening air, as ephemeral as golden fireflies. A bugle on the far side of camp sent a melancholy thread of music into the air. Minnie shivered a little, half in dread, half in anticipation. This would be her life for the foreseeable future, the regular tramp of marching feet, harsh male voices, the discordant music of drum and bugle.

In the open quadrant by the hospital tents a pile of crates and trunks steadily grew, as they were unloaded from Army wagons, under the profane direction of Sgt. Hand; profane until he noted the presence of the three women.

"God save the mark, Ma'am." He came to them, after bawling his last set of orders and commands over his shoulder to the half-dozen soldiers laboring to unload the last wagon.

"Here we have all of your traps and treasure brought from the railway. Was there anything more that you wish us to do?"

"There is," Mary Bickerdyke studied the stack of barrels and scrap-wood crates, piled next to the nearest cook tent. "Those hogshead barrels; I would like eight or ten of the soundest and least damaged to be sawn in half, and the bungs stopped with plugs. Can you do that for me by tomorrow."

"Of course, ma'am," Sgt. Hand appeared to be mildly nonplussed. After a short hesitation, he ventured a question. "May I ask, ma'am – for what purpose?"

Mary Bickerdyke looked up at him as if this were the most obvious thing in the world, although even Minnie and Miss Safford were puzzled. "For bathing the sick, of course. Those barrels will make admirable tubs. Cleanliness is essential for these poor lads and at present they are filthy-dirty. We'll start on the morrow, ladies," she added, with a look over her shoulder at the other two women. "Miss Safford, dear; have we a place to lay our heads down tonight, and perhaps have a bite of supper? Miss Vining and I are fatigued after a long day's journey, and tomorrow will be very busy for all of us."

"Oh, but of course," Miss Safford replied, somewhat relieved that the tour of the dreadful ward tents was completed. "Colonel Prentiss very kindly allotted me a tent to myself and Free Mary. She is one of the contrabands who has been assisting me. We have been issued some camp cots, and Free Mary is friends with the cook in the nearest camp kitchen. Besides, she brings me some good cornbread that her mother bakes ... she and her sister and mother all escaped together and took refuge with the Army. Free Mary will have brought us all something to eat, I am certain."

"Good," Minnie replied, mildly relieved that she and Mary Bickerdyke did have a place to sleep that night, as well as the prospect of a meal, although whether it would be edible or not was a matter of conjecture. She had a packet of food in the valise which she had brought with her from Galesburg; some slabs of bread and cheese, hardboiled eggs, and some cold fried chicken, in the event of the Army cook not being anywhere near as gifted as Mrs. Norris. She was as exhausted as she had ever been, after a long train journey, and contemplating the prospect of sorting out the hospital and it's suffering patients on the morrow. She was so tired that she thought she could have lain down and slept soundly on a bare pallet, just as the soldiers did. "Yourself, and Free Mary, and Mrs. Bickerdyke – all together, add one more Mary and we could sing the ballad of the *Queen's Four Maries*..." Minnie commented, and immediately wished that she hadn't, as it was a sad song, and boded ill for one of the Maries anyway. Still, Mary Bickerdyke smiled, a wry and amused smile.

The Widow Bickerdyke had an ironic sense of humor; at the clear evidence of this, Minnie thought again that they would work well together. Heartened by that thought, she was also heartened by the sight of the Army tent which was to be their shared quarters for as long as they were at Camp Defiance. It was one of those generously sized wall tents, about the size of her own bedroom at home in Boston, with a peaked roof which made it tall enough that both she and Mary Bickerdyke could stand at full height within. Most marvelously, it was fitted out with a wooden floor, and a narrow marquee canvas roof at the front, which provided a degree of shade for the small camp table and folding chairs which sat there. Within, it was fitted out with four folding cots made up in clean bedding and a field desk of the sort used by commanders on campaign in the field. A small screen took up a far corner of the tent, shielding a small washstand; there were already half a dozen tin buckets full of water standing beside it. Two lanterns hung from the peak of the tent, affording a degree of light within, now that the sun had slipped below the levee. Her travel trunk and that of Mrs. Bickerdyke already sat within, which sight Minnie regarded with gratitude. Sgt. Hand must have seen to that little detail. The tent which evidently was to be the female nurses' quarters now was simple enough, but homely; a vast improvement upon sleeping on the bare ground.

"Be warned," Miss Safford remarked, as she sat down upon the nearest cot with a sigh of relief, as she began to unbutton the sturdy flat-heeled boots that she wore, and strip off the dusty stockings that she had on underneath. She fished a pair of carpet slippers from underneath the cot and slid them onto her bare feet. "Now that it is dark, be sure to blow out the lantern when you are ready to put on your nightgown and go to bed. Our shadows may be plainly seen, against the canvas, with the light behind. Unless you wish to make a shadow-play of your person for the amusement of the soldiers." She flashed a weary smile in their direction, in response to Minnie's shocked expression. "They are young men, most of them, very far from home, and the shape of a woman they find to be of nostalgic interest. They are doing without, most of them so they will take what opportunity they can."

"Boys," Mary Bickerdyke pursed her lips. "They may grow in size, but they never really age. Well, most of them never do..."

At that moment a woman appeared in the tent opening; a young Negro woman, carrying an enormous, covered basket balanced on her hip. The stars in the evening sky were just beginning to wink into view, although the sulfurous glow from riverboat chimneystacks masked those closest to the horizon over the levee.

"Miz Safford, I brung you the clean laundry," the woman ventured, with a swift glance at the other two women. "Will you be wanting anything more today?"

"No, thank you, Mary," Miss Safford replied, correctly interpreting the questioning expression on the dark woman's face. She was a young woman, as nearly as Minnie was able to judge age. The woman's hair was covered with an immaculate white turban, neatly tucked and folded. "Mary, I must introduce you to Mrs. Bickerdyke and Miss Vining, who have come to Cairo to help with the nursing and setting the ward to rights. Ladies, this is Free Mary. She and her sister Seffie and their mother do laundry for me, as they can."

"Do you?" Mary Bickerdyke looked intensely thoughtful. "Indeed ... we might have use for several laundresses. And I have funds enough to pay for the work of at least five washerwomen for as long as the hospital needs them. For months, I expect. Especially if there is a battle in the offing."

"Ifn' they can come into camp freely, Miz Safford," Free Mary replied, almost at once. "A pass allowing them to come through the gate..."

"I can arrange that," Mary Bickerdyke nodded. She had made the decision. "We really must have a dedicated laundry for the hospital. Come to the camp gate tomorrow. I will meet you there and ensure that you have passes to come and go without hinderance."

"Thank you, Miz!" Free Mary smiled in relief, as if someone had just thrown her a lifeline to safety. "You won' regret it! Me an' Seffie an' Ol' Mama, we do good work. Ol' Massa had no complaint of us, evah! Fac' is, he came all the way to Cairo to ast the Army for us to be returned but the Big Officer said that we wuz contraband foah the Confederacy … and he wuldn't turn us back. No way, he say. We is free now!"

"Indeed, you are, Mary," Mary Bickerdyke replied. "Until tomorrow, then."

"Good night, Miz Safford an' all." Free Mary set down the basket of laundry just within the tent, and vanished around the edge of the tent, just as another two visitors appeared, the first an older soldier in his shirtsleeves with what looked like a bespattered butcher's apron tied around his relatively non-existent waist. He carried a covered pail in each hand and was followed by a very-much-younger soldier who carried a tray veiled in a napkin – a napkin not entirely clean. Obviously, the mess sergeant had not been availing himself of the laundry services offered by Free Mary and her fellow contrabands.

"Miss Safford, ma'am," said the older man with a courteous nod. "Ladies … I brung you supper. Good bully-beef stew an' fresh cornbread – sorry it ain't more fitten' for ladies an' officers, but it's all we got tonight,"

"I wouldn't presume to be eating better than the men," Mary Safford replied, with a smile that showed brief dimples. "Thank you, Sergeant Booker. May I introduce you to Mrs. Bickerdyke and Miss Vining? The ladies have come to help me with the hospital. This is Sergeant Booker and one of his helpers. They do the cooking for the officer's mess and for the hospital..." Miss Safford's voice trailed off, indecisively. It sounded as if Sergeant Booker only prepared ordinary soldier's fare for the hospital, and Minnie knew immediately that wasn't suitable. Heavy, indigestible, unappetizing ... no, that wouldn't do at all."

"I am certain that you are doing the very best that you can," Mary Bickerdyke, ventured. "But one of my tasks in organizing the hospital is to set up an invalid kitchen to cook nourishing, healthful things that the sick will relish. I am certain you can help me with this since you have taken the additional trouble with our meals."

Sergeant Booker was already shaking his head, even as the young soldier set out tin plates on the simple camp table and plain tin silverware on either side of the plates. "No, there's no room for specialty cooking. The lads have their issue and their own fires, it's all that I can do to set food in front of Colonel Prentiss and his staff, what with the poor vittles we get, and the camp stove that I have. Sorry, ma'am. I'd admire to help with that, but I was raised an honest Christian man, and I will not tell you any lies about my capabilities with this Army."

"Honesty is always refreshing," Mary Bickerdyke nodded. "I will see what I can do, regarding a proper stove. There is always a way, especially if I set my mind to it."

"Yes, ma'am!" Sergeant Booker and his helper withdrew. Minnie exchanged a glance with Miss Safford, as Mary Bickerdyke continued.

"A blessing on this meal, ladies. Tomorrow, we begin to set this place to rights."

To Mrs. Eulalia Bard, Boston, Massachusetts
From Minerva Vining, Camp Defiance, Cairo, Illinois
August 23, 1861

Dear Lolly – this is the first time that I have had a chance to write to you since I arrived here. Mrs. Bickerdyke and I have been extraordinarily busy, every moment of every day until this one, taken up with the matter of the hospital and our poor soldiers – our boys, Mrs. Bickerdyke calls them, as if every one of them were our brothers and sons. As indeed they are. I should tell you that at the very start, it seemed as if the labors of Hercules would pale beside what we faced in setting that awful place in proper order. But Mrs. Bickerdyke was determined, and infatigable. Upon touring the hospital tents on our arrival at Cairo, where our poor soldiers were lying in dirty linen and blankets, tormented by heat and filth, her very first command was to order that a number of large hogshead barrels should be sawn in half, converted to tubs, in which the sick should be bathed, clothed in clean nightshirts, and restored to rest in cots with clean linen and blankets, in tents which had been swept clean of all filth by freed slaves and convalescent patients, working under our direction. They did so with every display of eagerness. Such is the urgency of need yet lack of positive direction until we appeared.

Mrs. Bickerdyke's four boxcars of supplies included bounteous quantities of clean clothing, linen, blankets and folding cots, vinegar, soap, and all manner of excellent delicacies. Indeed – such a wealth of goods, intended for our sick and wounded soldier boys that we must, alas, keep careful custody of such! Many of the sutlers who are allowed to sell to the soldiers, and supply so much that is needful are a crooked, corrupt lot! The soldiers were suffering all this summer for the want of supplies. Great scarcity induced high prices in the locality. Milk was twenty-five cents a quart; eggs seventy-five a dozen, butter correspondingly high, and of such a quality as called forth the remark from the sergeant who tends to the nearest cook-tent that "He had heard of rank butter, but this butter outranked General Grant himself!" It is thought that many local merchants, if not actually in league with the Confederates are in sympathy with the rebels. Cairo was, after all, largely in sympathy with the South and might yet have joined the Confederacy but for the hasty dispatch of several regiments of our own soldiers by the Governor. Mrs. Bickerdyke was incensed just last week as one of our calico nightshirts was taken from the clothesline where it had been hung out to dry – and she saw it on the back of one of the officers, who felt that he had the right to make free with it, as a privilege of rank. Well, Mrs. Bickerdyke soon had him put straight, when she recognized that the shirt that he was wearing was one of ours. (Several of them were made of calico in a very distinctive pattern and color. The shirt in question was one of them; I believe an entire bolt of fabric was donated by a Galesburg merchant for the making of shirts, as it proved to be not popular when offered for sale.) She made him take the shirt off, right then and there, and return it to her, leaving a very embarrassed young man, as many of his men were witness to the scene. He has since been the butt of much coarse humor from his fellows and subordinates alike.

We have the promise from the Chicago branch of the Sanitary Commission of a continuing resupply, as well as any other goods which Mrs. Bickerdyke may request of them. She has already sent word, asking for a good iron kitchen stove, with which to set up our invalid kitchen, as well as laundry kettles, mangles, et cetera, as we must establish a functional laundry. We expect the arrival of these items momentarily.

For this enterprise, she has hired half a dozen former slaves from the camp outside the gates ... they are energetic in having chosen by their own endeavors to free themselves from the condition of slavery in which they were formerly held in the near locality. I believe this has happened wherever there is a large encampment of our Army, in localities adjacent to states where the vile practice was the custom. Those former slaves are jocularly referred to as 'contrabands' – as they are valuable property which if retained by their former owner, would aid the Southern Confederacy in their foul rebellion ... so explained the Army commander here, when slaveholders hied themselves to Cairo to demand return of their errant property. Those demands were fruitless and more escaped slaves appear every day. I honestly think well of them, for seizing the opportunity to claim for themselves the benefits as well as the responsibilities of free men and women.

Chief among those 'contrabands' whom Mrs. Bickerdyke has hired are a trio of women – Free Mary, who has proudly chosen to take the surname of Lincoln, in honor of our elected president. She was a trusted house servant in the home of a very wealthy planter on the Kentucky side of the Ohio River. She determined to leave the slave condition upon hearing that our Army camp had been established at Cairo and that the officers there were strong in abolition beliefs. She prevailed upon her sister Seffie, who was, as the Bible says of Mary,

Mother of Jesus, great with child. She persuaded Seffie's husband to leave with them, along with their aged mother who is nearly blind. They managed to build a raft in secret and float down the river to Cairo, where they sought refuge. I have often conversed with Free Mary and marveled at her courage and determination. Miss Safford, who was a schoolteacher formerly, is teaching her to read. I will send a letter to my niece Sophia, asking that she might send us some of the simple primers which her son has moved beyond needing. Might you ask any of your friends for baby linen and some small toys for Seffie's child, who will be born any day. Even just small things to clothe and amuse a tiny child would make that little family so happy. They had so little to begin with and left all but the clothing they stood up in behind when they fled their owner.

We have since been visited by General Grant, commander of the Army in Southeast Missouri, who has taken command here at Cairo, as it is such a strategic location at the joining of two great rivers. You may not know of him, for he is a westerner, and not a political general of any public note. From the camp rumors that we are privy to, the Army will soon begin advancing down the Mississippi River towards Memphis and beyond – all the way to New Orleans. I do not have much grasp of military strategy, but I can see that it would be logical – slice the Confederacy in two parts, breaking Texas off from the rest, and taking over one of their chief ports. Brigadier General Grant is a melancholy appearing fellow, a regular Army man, although you could not tell this from his appearance. Colonel Chaffin, who you will recall meeting in the train station in Rochester some seven *or eight years ago, served with him in the Mexico war, and thought very highly of him.*

Colonel Chaffin says that General Grant is a consummate horseman – and that he cares more for his horses than he does of his person, which is most usually shabbily-dressed. This I can confirm from personal observation. The general appeared alone and without fanfare one afternoon, as Mrs. Bickerdyke and I were tending to our patients. We assumed at a brief glance from his plain dress and diffident manner that he was one of Sergeant Hand's work detail of ordinary soldiers, detailed to assist us with the heaviest labor. When he asked, modestly, if there were anything that he might do for us, Mrs. Bickerdyke replied, "Oh, certainly – can you help us shift this poor boy, he is too heavy for us to lift, that we might put a clean sheet underneath."

It was only after he had assisted us that we noticed that he had a single silver star on each shoulder of his rumpled uniform coat! General Grant apologized very handsomely for the lack of proper introduction; his intent was to ask if there were anything that we needed for the hospital – if there were, it was within his authority to make it available to us. Mrs. Bickerdyke outlined our needs and resources, and the general smiled, very thinly, and said that we seemed to have everything in hand. He did warn us that the war would commence in earnest, very soon and that we would soon have more to cope with than those sickened by conditions in camp. I am disheartened, Lolly. It was always my understanding that military campaigns took place in the temperate months of the year, and retreated to a winter camp when frost burdened the trees and snow covered the ground. Then I recall that

Washington and his Army chose to attack the Hessian force on Christmas day, after battling across an icy river in the dark!

The war will continue without pause, Lolly. There is no admitting of weakness in the face of the slave power of the Confederacy. The front will be dictated by the River. To that end, our navy has gathered a substantial detachment here. In the middle of the continent, we have a naval command, mostly of armored steamboats, under the command of a curious Yankee sailor, whose enthusiasm for abolition and defeat of the Confederacy is nearly equal to his detestation of the demon rum. Somehow, I cannot think that he is terribly popular with his sailors, if I remember my father's stories ... but General Grant seems ready to pursue a war with whatever means he has to hand.

Please do not forget about the baby things. And they say that when winter comes, it will indeed be very cold. I will write to Sophia and ask her to tell Mrs. Norris to search out my warmest winter garments and post them to me soon.

With affection, your friend,
Minerva T. Vining

Chapter 16 - Soft Falls the Dew on the Face of the Dead

September 5, 1861

To Mrs. Sophia Brewer, Boston, Massachusetts

From Minerva Vining, Camp Defiance, Cairo, Illinois

My very dear Sophia — thank you indeed for the baby dresses and linen, and the school primers, which are all much appreciated, especially as Free Mary has learned the alphabet very well and has moved on to reading whole words and simple sentences. I received this very day, a trunk of my winter clothing and some warm blankets from Mrs. Norris, sent through the offices of Lolly Bard's office with the Sanitary Commission, so you need not take any more effort in that regard. I am very well set up now for winter, when it finally deigns to bless us with cooler temperatures.

Seffie's infant was born three weeks ago; a little boy, a fat healthy mite with dark eyes like raisins set in a face like a dear little brown biscuit. His parents are no end proud and happy, most of all because his mother recovered swiftly from the ordeal and the child was born into that condition of freedom which is the natural right of every human being. They have named him Benjamin Prentiss Lincoln, after the commander of Camp Defiance who first gave them refuge, and because his parents and aunt have taken the surname of Lincoln, in honor of our president. He came into the world very suddenly, at the very hour that Miss Safford and I were delivering the books and baby linen to the little shack where Free Mary's family has set up residence ...

Minnie chose not to elaborate in her letter, detailing how she and Miss Safford came to the Lincoln's shack in the contraband's camp on that afternoon; a shack which had been enlarged and reinforced, since Free Mary, Seffie, Seffie's husband Big Mose and the elderly and almost-blind Mammy Lincoln had been hired by Mary Bickerdyke to do laundry and assist in the hospital. Mammy Lincoln could do mending, and knitting, by touch. The hospital had a need of socks for their patients now that the weather was about to turn chilly. Big Mose sat outside the shack on that day, nervously smoking a pipe of rough tobacco. Above his head, the makeshift tin chimney stack puffed smoke in almost the same manner.

"You have a stove, now!" Minnie exclaimed, so very pleased that Free Mary's family were making a comfortable home out of the wages that they were paid. "And a glass window, too! Just in the nick of time, since you must keep the baby warm! We brought some baby things; dresses and blankets for the little one, sent from my friends in Boston."

"True 'nuff, Miss Minnie," Big Mose agreed. "Mammy Fee, she says the baby is coming so those things is mos' welcome! Jus' take them in to Mary an' Mammy, they'll be right glad to see them an' yourselves, too."

"Oh, my," Miss Safford remarked, "I suppose that Free Mary's reading lesson is off the schedule for today. We should go in and see if there is anything that we can do to help."

"Indeed," Minnie agreed, with misgivings that she was reluctant to voice. Miss Safford pushed open the simple door that made the entrance to the Lincoln shack. Minnie followed her in, and immediately wished that she were anywhere else.

The inside of the shack was immaculately clean, and tidy, as Mammy Fee was so nearly blind that everything must be kept to a place, and nothing on the swept scrap-plank floor that she might trip and fall over. A table and several benches, a single chair and the tiny iron stove took up most of the room inside – the two beds had been moved to the new room, which Big Mose had recently built onto the shack. But there was an indefinable odor in the place; not of filth, as Free Mary, Seffie and their mother kept the tiny place immaculately clean as befitted their calling as laundresses, but the coppery stink of blood, bodily fluids and sweat. Seffie stood in the middle of the room, clad only in a brief shift which clung to her body and her pregnant belly, propped up by her mother and sister on either side. Only that support kept her on her feet. Blood and something else stained the bottom of the shift, dripping onto the floor and running down Seffie's thighs and legs. Seffie moaned,

"Oh, Mammy – it hurts!"

"Take a deep breath and ride the pain!" Free Mary barked at her sister, and Minnie felt a buzzing in her ears and the world around her go a little grey. "Walk now!"

"We brought the baby things," Miss Safford said at once. "Can we help? Oh, Miss Vining! Whatever is the matter?"

"I do not feel well," Minnie quavered, her voice sounding very strange to her own ears. "Did you bring your smelling-salts?"

"I – oh, my!" Miss Safford exclaimed, and everything went even more grey in front of Minnie's eyes as the room seemed to spin around here. When she became fully aware again, she was sitting on Big Mose's bench, in the chilly out-of-doors, her head propped back against the shack wall while Miss Safford held the vial of smelling-salts under her nose. Minnie choked and gasped, waving away the solicitous hand.

"I'm quite recovered now, Mary – fine. I was just … overcome."

Beyond Mary Safford's concerned face, Big Mose loomed, plainly baffled, and concerned. "Miz Mary, you want I should fetch a doctor, or som'ting?"

"I'm quite well," Minnie insisted. "The atmosphere was so close! Just let me sit in the fresh air. I will be quite restored."

"I'll fix you a cup of tea," Mary Safford promised, just as an inarticulate cry came from inside the hut, followed in a few seconds by a thin infant wailing. "Oh, my! The baby has come! I'll just be a moment, Miss Vining – perhaps Free Mary needs help!"

The wall at her back shuddered as the roughly cobbled door to the shack closed on Big Mose and Miss Safford. Minnie leaned her head back again, glad for the momentary solitude, in which to compose herself.

Just those few moments in the shack; Seffie's moans, the sight of that swollen figure, the smell … all brought back those hideous memories of Annabelle in childbed, and the agony that she endured, so many years ago. Those fleeting moments also reminded Minnie of her own primal dread – that lingering terror in the back of her mind, a terror which she had resolutely squashed back into a tiny corner, never admitting to a single soul but Pres Devereaux. *I have never loved a man so much that I would willingly risk marrying and bearing a child to him, just so I told Pres Devereaux when he proposed marriage to me, and I said 'no'. Although I came close, so close. But my mother perished in bearing me, as did Papa-the-Judge's first wife, Leander's mother. I could not, not after hearing the stories that the servants whispered when I was a child, not after I witnessed how Annabelle suffered so horrifically in bearing Sophia... I just could not. All other fears in life for me pale beside that one fear.* Minnie sat with her eyes closed, warmed gradually by the thin autumnal sunshine, sheltered from the chill breeze off the river by the walls of the small dwellings around her, insulated from the bustle inside which she could dimly hear through the ramshackle walls and the single tiny window. Sometime later – she was never actually certain how long it was that she sat there alone, Miss Safford opened the door.

"Oh, Miss Vining, come and see! The baby is born, and he is so beautiful!"

"Of course," Minnie replied. Truly, she felt quite recovered from that momentary horror. Free Mary was a stalwart support to the hospital and Mrs. Bickerdyke, Seffie was a sweet young woman and Big Mose worked hard to support his family. He worked now for Mrs. Bickerdyke in the hospital laundry, cutting and hauling wood for the fires that heated the big boiling vats. Of course, she would go inside and admire the baby.

She stepped past the door held open for her, already noting that Miss Safford watched her carefully. In the tiny bedroom, Seffie lay propped up on several thin pillows, with the baby in her arms. She cuddled the baby close to her, beaming alternately between the child and Big Mose, who looked proud enough to burst the few buttons right off his threadbare shirt. Minnie half-dreaded that she would be taken by a faint again – but she wasn't. It must have been just the first ungoverned reaction to a situation that she had not expected, on this cool September day.

"Isn't he beautiful, Miss Vining?" Miss Safford cooed, and Minnie looked full and long at the tiny brown baby, swathed in one of the blankets that she had provided.

"He is," Minnie agreed. "Oh, he is a darling ... and so lively! He must naturally be very clever, to be alert so very young, not even an hour old. You must expect great things of him, I am certain! What are you going to name him, then?"

"Benjamin Prentiss," Seffie replied. "After the colonel ... but we'll jus' call him Benji, while he is so little."

"I am sure that he will grow up to honor Colonel Prentiss," Minnie replied. She touched one of the tiny hands, left free from the swaddling in the fine woolen blanket sent from Boston, and was enormously touched with that little pinky-brown starfish-shaped hand – those boneless fingers with their impossibly tiny and perfect fingernails closed around her own finger. The baby seemed to regard her with curiosity – and then he yawned, a tiny pink yawn like a kitten. "So handsome! He is tired, after all this fuss, the dear little babe," Minnie gently withdrew her finger. "And you must be, also. Have a nice long sleep, both of you. We'll go now and let you two rest."

Free Mary saw them out, vociferous in her thanks for Miss Safford's assistance, and for the gift of books and baby clothes and blankets. Minnie and her companion finally tore themselves free. The dim autumnal sun had finally slid down below the rim of the sheltering levee, putting the ramshackle contraband settlement into a shadowless twilight. Miss Safford spoke first,

"They say that it should properly be seen as a miracle ... a baby. A whole new creature, from out of some little bits of this and that."

"A dangerous miracle for all that," Minnie replied. "It often goes very ill with the mother and child both, as I very well know."

Miss Safford kicked the dust at her feet with her toe, for all the world like a sullen schoolgirl. "The ministers will say that it's a punishment for all, because of Eve having taken the apple and eaten it, but I cannot see why all womenkind ought to be punished for stupidly believing the word of a serpent! It's just not fair!" she added, with a sideways look at Minnie. "All right – then pushing something the size of a baby from between your legs ... yes, I can agree <u>that</u> would be uncomfortable, even painful. But it not ought to cost a woman their life, doing so! And it shouldn't cost the life of a baby, either! I can't see why it should, when we have seen such advances in medicine these last few years. Something ought to be done! Miss Vining, did you recall some terribly fatal experience, and that was why you were taken with such a fainting fit? I oughtn't to ask, really ... but you looked so awful, when you first came into that room."

"The atmosphere brought back some dreadful memories to me," Minnie replied, carefully, feeling just a little shocked at how cooly a well-bred and unmarried woman such as Miss Safford spoke of babies and childbirth. "Very suddenly, when I was not expecting such. Memories which I thought I had put behind me, long since. A weakness only temporary, I hope. We are nurses, Miss Safford; I expect that we will see much more gruesome sights, and very soon, if what Mrs. Bickerdyke tells us is the talk of General Grant's staff."

"So, it is true then," Miss Safford nodded in agreement. "The Army will move, and soon. Even if winter is coming soon. I've always thought that was not how a war was conducted. I have read many times in history books that armies went into a winter camp and waited to fight in the spring, after the snow melted. Was that not true, Miss Vining?"

"It may have been, in Roman times," Minnie agreed, thinking through all the history that she had ever read, or overheard her brothers and Cousin Peter discussing over the supper table. Being boys and Cousin Peter a veteran of the Colonial Army, the topic of war and campaigns was of surpassing interest to them. Perhaps Minnie had absorbed more knowledge of war, tactics, and the nature of generals than she had thought. "Or even during the medieval ages ... but this is America. Our own General Washington and his army attacked the Hessians at Trenton in the dead of winter... on Christmas Day even! General Grant is not a patient man. I think he wants to win this war and win it quickly, without waiting on the season, or anything else. As soon as the Army is ready to move, and the transports by boat are secured, I believe General Grant will give orders, orders to move against the Confederates at Fort Donelson, downriver."

Minnie proved right. Preparations for a Union offensive against the rebel army moving into southern Missouri were already in hand as the year drew to a close. The camp rumors brought to them by the reliable Sgt. Hand, now nick-named "Handy Andy", alluded to a strike along the Tennessee River, into Rebel-held Kentucky. When a steamboat outfitted at considerable effort as a kind of floating hospital by the governor of Illinois arrived at the Cairo waterfront, Mrs. Bickerdyke had already made her plans for the disposition of those volunteer hospital nurses at Cairo, with Minnie, Miss Safford and a new volunteer, Mrs. Porter, who was the wife of an army chaplain. Mrs. Porter arrived at mid-month, a gentle, soft-spoken woman, with dark hair and the pale complexion of an invalid herself. She had no children, and her husband was in the field with the Army.

"I decline to remain at home with my knitting, so I decided that I would make myself useful," Lydia Porter had announced on arriving. "Besides, I am accustomed to Army life – and my husband is in the field with the 11th Wisconsin."

"Miss Safford remains here, in charge of the hospital," Mary Bickerdyke consulted her notes. "The names of the nurses who will assist her are on this list. I anticipate there will be many poor boys sent here to recover, should they survive the battlefield and the journey. Miss Vining will have charge of those nurses on the steamboat chartered by the Sanitary Commission to serve as medical transport. I am given to understand that several Army surgeons are being sent to assist in that effort. Miss Vining, if you would select at least six women to accompany you – ladies that you feel are able and level-headed."

"And yourself, Mary?" Minnie asked.

"Mrs. Porter and I will go forward to the field. Where I am certain that we will be most needed, in the event of a battle being joined," Mrs. Bickerdyke announced. Her gaze went around the small circle of women. "My dear friends, we should armor ourselves with courage, and fortify our spirits with prayer, as I assure you that we shall face great challenges.

heretofore we have been nursing the sick; a situation which we have become accustomed to, if not in recent days here in Cairo, then when we were caring for our families at home. Very shortly we will be tasked with caring for those wounded in battle and we must steel ourselves against the most gruesome injuries and the most extreme suffering ... suffering which we may only be able to ease in some small way."

"We are called to serve," Mrs. Porter replied softly, after a long moment in which Minnie recalled how she had come over faint in the presence of a woman in childbed. She must steel herself against such weakness in the future. Lydia Porter continued. "Called to serve and endure as we must. *'I heard the voice of the Lord, saying, Whom shall I send, and who will go for us? Then said I, Here am I; send me.'* We will bear the burden, as long as we have hands to serve and prayers to utter."

"Hands and prayers may be very well," Minnie replied, with some asperity, "But what the Sanitary Commission sends to us in the ways of bandages, morphia, and blankets will be equally useful."

That brought a wry chuckle from Mrs. Bickerdyke. "All in service to the noble Cause," she added. "The spiritual and the material. I believe that the Army will move within weeks, so we must be ourselves prepared. Take little but a change of linen for yourselves, for we likely must travel with dispatch, and only carry with us what is absolutely necessary for decency."

April 20, 1862
To Mrs. Mary Livermore, Chicago, Illinois
From Minerva Vining, on the Hospital Steamboat City of Memphis, moored near Savannah on the Tennessee River

My dear Mary:

You would have read in the newspapers of that great battle fought near Pittsburgh Landing two weeks ago! To the Union our victory, as the Rebel Army has been driven decisively from Tennessee. But you cannot possibly imagine the suffering of those wounded over three or four days in miserable weather continues without let-up. This opportunity is the first that I have had to set my pen to paper on my own behalf. We have had so little leisure since the battle commenced, I simply cannot recall when I had more than three minutes to myself to eat, or sleep, or wash, so overwhelming are the labors of tending the sick and wounded, and not only of our own men, but those of the Secession left behind. I suppose that must be because the field is ours, so then falls to us the care of those poor fellows. I cannot really grudge the efforts, seeing of their misery. Every single one, even so piteously misguided as to defend the indefensible horror of slavery, is the son of a mother, whose poor heart must ache at the thought of her dear boy, so far away from the home hearth. They are only simple country folk, easily swayed by the persuasion and reckless rhetoric of those they assume to be their bettors.

I simply cannot confide my thoughts and experiences in letters to my dearest Sophia regarding the true travails of hospital life, as I know she will see her beloved husband in the form of every poor sufferer in Union blue. I cannot bring myself to add a morsel of additional worry to her lot, since the 28th Massachusetts, of which her husband is an officer, has been sent South to fortify an island off the coast of the Carolinas. Richard will be in the thick of it, I am certain – and if not now, then soon. I find that I simply must put down an account of my days, and by setting them in paper and ink, thereby unburden myself. You do not mind, dear Mary? As an agent of the Commission, you doubtless will be sympathetic, and will make careful note of whatever need I may inadvertently mention in my communications. Our immediate needs are so many! Of the most urgent of them is something not in your remit to supply – that being sleep and time! I am so wearied at this moment that I barely have strength to take up my pen and write to you – but I know that you will be concerned for both Mrs. Bickerdyke and myself, after reading the newspaper accounts of the battle here. Rest assured that we are both in good health and doing the work that we have been called to do.

Yours,
Minerva Templeton Vining.

Minnie set her pen away, and carefully recorked her ink bottle. There was still so much that she could not put on paper about being on the fringe of that battle, even now. She was safe on the broad reach of the river, the hospital transport *City of Memphis* steaming towards Cairo, decks packed with the wounded and dying, ranked closely like piles of cordwood in advance of winter. The wooden deck throbbed under her feet, with every powerful turn of the great wheels that propelled it. She did not have the words. For all the words that she had marshalled in the cause of abolishing the great wrong of slavery, there were none to properly set down what she had seen, beginning when Sergeant Hand appeared as dusk fell on

268

that momentous first day of the battle in the woodlands beyond Pittsburg Landing.

In accordance with Mrs. Bickerdyke's original plan, Minnie traveled with the party of Army surgeons on the *City of Memphis*, following a pair of timber-armored steam gunboats which commanded the river. The *City of Memphis* tied up at Pittsburg Landing. It had been understood that the various Union forces would assemble and camp in the fields and orchards inland from the landing before assembling to march on the city of Corinth, opening the way towards the rebel strongholds of Memphis and Vicksburg. Minnie, looking out in the early morning through the pearly fog rising from the water and obscuring the sky heard a curious rumble. Then came a distant popping sound, like the sound of bursting corn kernels; now louder, now fainter in the distance. No one needed to tell her that it was the distant sound of a skirmish.

Perhaps there had been a brief foray by a small party of rebel scouts, accidently blundering into the main Union camp inland ... but the rumble and the popping sounds went on and on, growing louder.

"It sounds so much like thunder," Minnie remarked to one of the Army doctor-surgeons standing at the rail of the upper deck with her, who merely grunted in reply, as he looked out at the tree-lined shore. The countryside was relatively flat upstream, broken here and there with stands of trees and small rivulets feeding into the river, splashing silver and clear between a scattering of cleared fields and orchards. To the west, above Pittsburg Landing rose a low wooded bluff, speckled with stones, obscuring the view beyond. The Landing and the stony bluff beyond were alive with blue-clad soldiers.

"It's not," the doctor-surgeon cocked his head, listening intently. "And look; there goes Grant's ship, the *Tigress*! Miss Vining, I do believe things are about to get hot."

The doctor-surgeon was correct; things were getting hot. Soon the landing was crowded with soldiers; not in orderly ranks, but a mob which to Minnie looked very close to being panic-stricken. A mob through which a scattering of horse-drawn ambulances forced their way to the riverside with great difficulty. Before the sun had even entirely cleared the tree line on the eastern bank of the river, Minnie found herself fully taken up with tending those wounded brought aboard on litters; cutting away blood-sodden garments from crushing wounds, standing at the surgeon's elbow with lint and bandages at the ready, while he probed with bloody hands and instruments for fragments of metal. She comforted the conscious with her presence and words, brought blankets and water for those who asked piteously for that succor, held their hands, promised them that they would be all right, and whispered prayers for the failing. She listened to men and boys alike begging for their mothers, secretly relieved every moment that she did not feel faint. All day long the artillery rumbled, now seeming distant, now close.

Sometime after sundown, Sgt. Hand appeared. Minnie was kneeling by the side of a frightened boy who was trying his best not to cry from the pain of his smashed left leg. It had begun to drizzle, adding another degree of misery and suffering.

"Beg pardon, Miss Vining," he said with a sad shake of his head, "But Herself sent word that she needs you at the hospital up on the bluff. Aye, and what you can bring with you of blankets and bandages, as well as your personal traps an' such.

I've an ambulance waiting with the other supplies that Herself asked for."

"How bad is it?" Minnie hoped that her voice wasn't quavering.

"I've seen worse," Sgt. Hand replied, and his certainty was reassuring. "General Grant is waiting noo for General Buell to grace us with his presence in the morning. All our troops were driven back by the dirty Rebs. Didn't expect them in force, y'see. Aye, we'll hold our own when the light comes in the morning. Meanwhile, the Navy is doin' their bit. Hear them, noo? That," and Sgt. Hand jerked his thumb towards a red streak arching across the twilight sky. "That will be the naval guns. Full 11-inches, they are and fall like one o 'Jove's thunderbolts."

Minnie gathered up her small carpet bag, and a much larger collection of remedies, and bandages. Sgt. Hand carried the larger bundle of supplies and a bale of blankets to an ambulance on the landing, where a pair of horses stood patiently in harness, a young soldier at the reins. He tossed them into the back of the ambulance and handed Minnie up to the seat next to the driver. "Away w' ye," he added. "Tell Herself I'll be along in a bit."

Minnie hugged her carpet bag to her, wondering how much more horrible conditions could be on the bluff than on the boat. Darkness mercifully hid the worst from her eyes, as the ambulance slowly worked along the track, the summer dust turned to churned mud by the passage of so many trampling feet, so many horses. The very worst was hidden from her until they reached the far side of the ridge. A small log house sat there, tucked just under the lee of the ridgetop, with a wide porch before it, which ordinarily would have offered a view of the lightly rolling countryside beyond to the west. Lanterns and torches hung from the porch posts and from the low branches of trees, illuminating a scene which Minnie could compare to the lurid imaginings of Dante's inferno, smoldering flames, blood, and tormented bodies. The doctor-surgeons were hard at work, their rough aprons splashed with gore, hands and arms bloodied to the elbow as they worked. Rough tables for surgical work had been set here and there under the shade of the porch, or in open tents hastily set up in the foreyard. There was a dreadful kind of low moaning, now and again broken by agonized cries, and sulfurous cursing. The trail of one of the naval guns sketched a red arc against the darkened sky. The muffled noise of the explosion it made upon landing, far towards the west was barely heard.

"Here, miss," the young soldier said. "Handy Andy told me to bring you here, where the surgeons have set up for doing their work. Miz Bickerdyke is inside."

"I see," Minnie replied, deeply shaken. This was so much worse than on the hospital steamship, down at the landing. "Thank you." She slid down, unaided from the ambulance, taking her bag in hand. She walked around a pile of bloody garments at the foot of the nearest table, trying her best to look away, but the horrors were on every side. A heap of severed arms and legs were piled up on the ground by the nearest table, a table where a surgeon labored over a soldier, the sleeves of his shirt rolled to his shoulders. The amputated limbs were as white as wax in the wavering lamplight – hands, arms, legs, and feet all muddled together like jackstraws; the dripping rain having washed the blood from them. The bodies of men lay all around, some on blankets, or piles of straw. The dead, the hideously mutilated but still living were all mixed promiscuously together. Even more wounded arrived every moment that Minnie stood there, men shuffling painfully, leaning on their rifles or on lengths of wood hastily pressed into service as a crutch, or carried by comrades. The door to the cabin stood open – no, it had been wrenched from the hinges entirely, likely to serve as a stretcher or table for the surgeon's grisly work. A woman stood in the doorway, a dark shadow against the dimly lit interior, a bucket and a tin cup in her hands, silver in the light: Mrs. Bickerdyke, her fine features drawn with exhaustion and grief.

"Thank you for coming, Miss Vining," she said, only. "We have such need of you here, rather than on the boat. This is so much worse than I expected."

Minnie looked around, momentarily staggered: where to begin? She wondered, and then she set down her carpetbag inside the doorway. *May as well begin with the nearest.* Poor, wretched scarecrows appeared in the wavering light of oil lamps and guttering torches, as they came off the surgeon's crude table.

Minnie bandaged wounds and stumps for what seemed like hours, murmuring a litany of soothing words, words which came without conscious thought on her part. All blurred together in her mind, the universe closed down to just a single point; the darkness, broken by the red streak of the naval guns, sketching a red arch across the sky, the constant drizzle of rain drumming against canvas and the cabin's crude shake roof, the moans and cries of the wounded, and the rasp of the surgeon's bone saws, as regular as a scythe cutting wheat ... save that this was a harvest of limbs and lives.

Sometime around midnight, she found herself sitting at the edge of the cabin porch. A man appeared out of the darkness, a man who limped painfully, but otherwise seemed to be unwounded. Minnie wondered if he was another casualty seeing medical attention ... but no. He removed his hat, seeing her, and she recognized General Grant, plain, unassuming and more shabbily clad than usual. It seemed that the day had not gone well for him, either.

"Evening, Miss Vining," he remarked, casually. "I was looking for a place to sleep out of the rain, and recollected seeing this cabin, early this morning ... but it looks as if it has been put to other uses."

"Indeed," Minnie replied, "I fear that it has. And tomorrow may bring even more of your soldiers here."

General Grant looked about, and in the flickering torchlight, his customarily melancholy expression seemed to deepen.

"I fear so, Miss Vining. I fear so. We had a bad turn today, no two ways about it. Billy Sherman is still smarting from being caught by surprise ... but I'll bet whatever you like, that will be the last time <u>that</u> will ever happen. But when Buell and his boys arrive ... well, then, we shall settle Johnny Reb's hash for good and all." He replaced his hat, nodded firmly towards Minnie – no one else seemed to notice or recognize the figure of the General, despite the single silver star winking on the shoulder straps of his blue tunic.

Minnie called after him. "Sir – you are limping! Are you hurt? I can find a place for you inside the house!"

General Grant turned and replied over his shoulder. "Nothing much. My horse slipped in the mud and fell, with my ankle under the saddle. Nothing to a horseman, Miss Vining. I'll find another place to rest. Good night, Miss Vining."

Chapter 17 – Say Goodbye to Goober Peas
1862 – 1863 – Along the Mississippi River

After taking the field at Pittsburg Landing, Grant's western armies moved with ponderous inexorability down the great river towards the South, the heart of the rebellion, all though that summer and autumn, into the winter. New Orleans was taken late in April by a Union naval armada, securing that strategic port on the Gulf Coast. The Union armies now held both ends of the Mississippi, but the Confederacy still had a tight grip on the length in between. Camp rumor had it that the next move by General Grant – whose initials "U. S." were now claimed to stand for 'unconditional surrender' – was aiming to invest and overwhelm the city of Vicksburg.

Minnie, Mary Bickerdyke and Mrs. Porter followed the endless columns of blue moving south, by river, rail and on foot, organizing temporary hospitals in the field in tents as the Army moved, and more permanent establishments in cities and towns. They moved in obedience to the requirements of the Army, ever southwards, deeper into what had been the stronghold of the Confederacy in the west. Mrs. Bickerdyke's hospital entourage now included a herd of milk cows, a flock of laying hens carried along in wicker cages by the hired contrabands, and a very cleverly designed bread oven, constructed of numbered bricks, which could be disassembled, packed into an Army wagon, and reassembled at a new location. Her original company of contrabands – escaped slaves – doubled and doubled again, especially after the turn of the year, when President Lincoln issued a great proclamation, ordering that all those held in slavery in a state which had seceded should be considered free.

"Which will do those poor folk no good at all," Mrs. Bickerdyke pointed out, as their heads bent over a page of *The Liberator*, which Lolly Bard had sent in the mail to Minnie. "A gesture only and no good at all, until our boys arrive to back up those fine words with steel."

Minnie shrugged. "A fine gesture it may be," she pointed out. "But the daring and spirited among the Southern slaves escape from their masters and run to our Army lines for refuge as we advance. I cannot help thinking this will at least inconvenience the rebels, since they no longer can enforce their will on their slaves. There is another aspect which is all to the good. Who now, among the European powers will think to ally themselves with the Confederacy, since Mr. Lincoln has tied the existence of the peculiar institution to them and made our own Union the champion of freedom for all, no matter of what color?"

"I had not considered that aspect," Mrs. Porter admitted. "But you bring up a good point, Miss Vining. Haven't we been lectured for years by ever-so-superior British and French men of letters over our American moral failing in permitting slavery to exist in our nation at all? Now, if they ally with the Confederacy, we might rightfully do the same; point the finger of scorn at them for tolerating such a horrid institution."

"Exactly," Minnie nodded. "Although there was a curious suggestion from the husband of my niece, in one of his letters to me this last year."

"The one who is an officer in a regiment of Irishmen?" Mrs. Porter asked, and Minnie nodded.

"Yes, that is the one. Many of his fellow officers as well as the men themselves have little reason to think well of the British government and many to think ill. Richard suggested that Her Majesty's government coldly and deliberately encouraged the rebellion; holding out the inducement of recognition as a legitimate national entity so that our nation would indeed break apart. With very little effort, Britian would scoop up another colony from out of our national wreckage. They certainly made an enormous fuss over the *Trent* affair."

"Because it was their ship," Mrs. Porter replied. "A matter of national honor and a point of international law – not out of particular fondness for the rebel envoys. But yes; the British would like to run with the hare and hunt with the hounds, as regards this war."

"Perfidious Albion, Richard said," Minnie continued. "He wrote that many of his fellows believe so. As he explained to me, it was like a troublemaker in a low saloon, egging on two other men to fight each other for his private amusement, without risking a punch in the mouth himself. I cannot see it myself, knowing how firmly the beliefs of Mr. Wilberforce and the Anti-Slavery Society became reverenced in Britain."

"Moral principles are one thing, I suppose, but profit and political advantage are another." Mrs. Porter replied. "My husband has often remarked that to nations, such advantage will always be considered before principles. A sad, sinful failing, but alas, only human."

The dreadful weakness fell upon Minnie with such soft feet that she did not feel particularly ill until early in the summer of 1863, when the Union Army was making final plans to invest and besiege Vicksburg,

"We shall then split the Confederacy in half, see if we will," one of the new nurses said merrily to Minnie, one evening as they prepared to move again. "And then dice them in quarters, see if we will!"

"Your words to the Almighty's ears," Minnie replied, and then everything around her went grey and soft and far away ... and when she woke up, she was lying on a cot in the nurses' quarters, with several frightened faces looking down at her, and the Army surgeon with her hand in his, as he timed her pulse. He was shaking his head in a doleful manner.

"My dear Miss Vining," he said, in sepulchral tones. "You are very worn down. You must go to your home, if the journey is not too much for your overtaxed system – and rest. Rest until you are restored to health, if that is possible after the rigors that have been placed upon yourself."

"Indeed," and that was Mrs. Bickerdyke, whose angular features were suffused with worry. "You must go home, Minnie – home to Boston. You have taxed your health to a degree which your constitution cannot bear. You must give over your duties to those who are stronger."

"I can't," Minnie replied, muzzy in her head from weakness and the shock. "The boys..."

"We will see to them," Mrs. Bickerdyke replied, firmly. "You have been laboring without rest for nearly two years. Miss Safford, who was with us from the first at the Brick Hospital in Cairo? Remember how her health so declined last summer from overwork that her brother sent her to an invalid asylum in Germany, to recover her health – and she was younger than either of us! Go home and rest. When you are fit again, come back to us. Even soldiers are permitted to furlough home. I am certain that the war will be with us for the foreseeable future," she added, with grim humor.

Minnie had no answer to that. For some days, she was unable to rise from her bed without the dizziness affecting her. When she was able to stand and walk across the room without feeling faint, she found that her small trunk was already packed. Mrs. Bickerdyke saw her off at the steamboat landing, along with another other volunteer nurse, Miss Lavinia Burford, also bound for her home in Chicago. They were accompanied by a party of convalescent soldiers on furlough and heading home to their families in Illinois, Ohio, and Wisconsin. Mrs. Bickerdyke entrusted both nurses with lists of items wanted for the hospital, and letters to be posted to families of those patients too ill to travel, or write letters themselves.

Many of the convalescents, pale and wan from confinement, and thin from fever and deprivation, had been her patients. If she had not been so worn down herself, she would have been amused at how assiduously the young soldiers – mere boys, really – attended herself and Miss Burford, especially the youngest amongst then, a thin and shy youth barely of an age to shave, who addressed Minnie reverently as 'Mother Vining'. He insisted on carrying her traveling rug and hers' and Miss Burford's trunks, seeing them settled in the tidy cabin of the steamship which would carry them up the river to Cairo.

"He seems to be very fond of you," Miss Burford remarked. She was a tall, rawboned young woman, very plain in feature, but strong and practical-minded, the daughter of a farmer who lived near Galesburg. When she smiled, the warmth of it changed and brightened her whole countenance.

"Billy – Private Mimms? Yes, he would be," Minnie sighed and settled back onto the narrow berth, which was what passed for luxury on the steamboat plying the Mississippi in wartime. Minnie had a soft spot for Billy Mimms, who had come to her ward nearly drained of blood through several ghastly wounds at the fighting around the Shiloh churchyard.

Lavina Burford settled the travel rug over Minnie's knees. "He told me that you saved his life, when all the doctors despaired and said that he wouldn't last through the night."

"Indeed. He was on the point of death," Minnie replied. "I shall always think of him, when I see a crock of pickles."

"Why is that?" Lavina settled onto her own bunk. She had come to the hospital from another, farther up the river, and so had not heard the story.

"He was in very bad condition, when he was brought to my ward," Minnie answered. "They were certain that he had only hours to live." Young Private Mimms had also suffered from pneumonia and a case of scurvy so bad that his mouth was a mass of sores. The military surgeon and the civilian doctor both despaired of saving him.

"The poor lad will not live through the night," the military surgeon had whispered to Minnie. He was a much-harried man, coping with a constant stream of casualties arriving every hour, day and night. "Make him comfortable in the time that he has left."

"Of course, I will," Minnie replied. Her heart was wrung. The dying soldier looked barely older than Richard and

Sophia's son, Richie. He was ghastly pale, the color of the sheet which covered him. Minnie was holding a cup of cool water to his lips, when he whispered,

"May I have a bit of pickle? I'd admire to have a taste of pickle..."

"Of course," Minnie had replied, thinking that it might very well be the last thing that the poor lad wanted before he died – and why not? She went to the invalid kitchen and found a crock of pickles. Taking out a small pickle, she set it on a small dish and cut it into tiny slips. Returning to the ward, she put a small sliver between the boy's cracked lips, watching carefully as he slowly chewed and swallowed that little morsel.

"Might I have another?" he whispered, and Minnie gave it to him, thinking still that the taste of pickle comforted the dying boy. *What harm could it do at this point?*

Before the boy fell asleep, he had eaten half the pickle and had not died, which gave Minnie hope. He was still among the living the following morning when he ate the other half of the pickle. After that, there was color in his thin face, and he gradually recovered over the next few weeks, much to the astonishment of the doctors. Now Private Billy Mimms was going home on a convalescent furlough, much as Minnie herself was going home.

She wondered now and again, throughout that long journey by steamboat and train, if she would find much changed. Not so much in Boston, she thought, Boston which was eternal and unchanging, much as the house on Beacon Hill had not changed since the days when Papa-the-Judge sat at the head of the table – but in herself. She was another woman entirely; completely impatient of cant and flummery, a woman accustomed to act decisively and on her own counsel even if she were a woman of a certain age and not a beauty.

Fatigued by the journey, although Lavina took every care that Minnie did not over-exert herself, she rested a week at Mary Livermore's house in Chicago, before traveling east. Mary would have fussed over her and insisted that Minnie stay longer, but the long hours she kept for the workings of the Sanitary Commission distracted her from overmuch hovering. As soon as Minnie felt herself able to face a journey on the railroad again, she set out. She sent a telegram from Rochester to Mrs. Norris and Jerusha, announcing her imminent arrival home, following on a previous telegram sent from Chicago when she arrived at Mary Livermore's house. Minnie was certain that the house would be ready to receive her, and that old friends in the Abolitionist circles would come to call, as soon as she arrived. She hoped that they would give her a week or so to recover from the journey. She feared that all the old verities about being 'at home' to callers would have been cast down, in spite of the present emergency.

It seemed, from the glaring headlines of a newspaper hawked on the platform of the Rochester station, that there had been riots over the proposed draft of soldiers to the Union Army in several northern cities, and another great battle in Virginia, at a place called Chancellorsville. General Lee's secessionist army had been thrown back after several days of bloody fighting and a high cost to both sides. She swiftly scanned the narrow columns, searching to see if any casualties had been reported among the officers of the 28th Massachusetts. There was no mention of Major Richard

Brewer, she saw with guarded relief. There was nothing in that issue about the fighting around Vicksburg.

It only stands to reason, Minnie thought, as she folded the pages together. *All the important newspapers were in the East. What happened there was of staggering import. What happened in the West was of small account.* She did note the familiar name of an old acquaintance. Colonel Levi Chaffin was promoted to the rank of general ... well. That was a fine reward for devotion to duty and loyalty to the Union. She made a note to herself – when she felt equal to the effort, to write a letter of congratulation to the now-General Chaffin.

Minnie rather regretted not staying in Chicago with Mary Livermore, long before reaching Boston on a hazy summer evening. She felt nearly as worn and ill upon being delivered by a hired hansom cab to the familiar door as she had that day when she first fell into a faint – the world seemed to be going grey and indistinct around her, just when Mrs. Norris opened the heavy front door.

"Miss Minnie!" Mrs. Norris cried, "Oh, Jeremiah – Miss Minnie is arrived ... sure now, and take her trunk ... is that all that you have with you, now, Miss Minnie?" The old woman hung on Minnie's arm, drawing her within the dearly familiar hallway, smelling of beeswax polish on old wood furniture, and lit by warm golden lamplight.

"It is, Mrs. Norris," Minnie replied – the dizzy feeling abated a little. "Oh, it is so good to be home, where nothing has changed! You did receive my telegrams ... I sent you twice..."

"We did indeed, Miss Minnie," The old housekeeper drew her under the light of the nearest lamp. "Oh, what have you done with your hair ... your complexion is quite ruined, and you look a perfect fright! What would your father or Mr. Virgil have said?"

"I am certain neither of them would have noticed, particularly," Minnie replied, riveted by the appearance of Jeremiah Daley, gaunt with hardship and with his left shirtsleeve pinned up to the shoulder. "Mr. Daley! Your arm! Sophia wrote to me saying that you had been injured, but not that you had lost a limb! I am so sorry!"

"I 'ain't, Miss Minnie," Jeremiah Daley replied, stoically. "For I'm done with the Army, an' I expect I will get a pension out of it. Don't fret about my arm, Miss; the right one was always jealous of it, and I can do as much work as I ever did ... just takes me a mite longer, that's all."

Minnie swayed a little, from exhaustion after the long journey; she was barely aware of Jeremiah Daley lifting her little traveling trunk, Mrs. Norris taking one arm, and Bertha the other.

"Now, you go straight up to your room, Miss Minnie! I won't hear another word! Bertha will bring you a good supper on a tray, Jeremiah will bring up hot water for a good wash, get all that nasty coal dust off you, and don't you even think of doing a single thing after you put a good supper inside of you but go straight to bed! You look like a puff of wind would blow you straight away."

"Yes, Mrs. Norris," Minnie agreed, feeling absurdly like she was nine years old again.

How luxurious her old bedroom felt! Although to a stern eye, the curtains shielding the window that looked out on the Common were much faded from the sun and the colors of the imported English flower-print wallpaper had all faded to indistinguishable shades of beige and gray. But the linen sheets were crisp and starched, exuding the odor of verbena sachets in which they had been packed away, and the feather bed beneath her aching bones was soft and yielding under Minnie's weary self. She fell asleep halfway through supper. She supposed that Mrs. Norris came and took the half-eaten supper away, before settling the bedcovers over herself and blowing out the single lamp.

June 10, 1863

To Mrs. Mary Livermore, Chicago, Illinois

From Minerva Vining, Boston, Massachusetts

Dear Mary:

Over the last few weeks I finally feel strong enough to come downstairs, sit at the old desk in Papa's study and write a lengthy letter to you. It seems that the condition of my health was such that I should have been well-advised to stay at your home when I first fell ill so many months ago. But I wanted so badly to be home in Boston that I carried on. I should have paid better heed to your counsel, for that last journey was almost beyond my strength. I lay upstairs for many weeks after arriving home, tended by dear faithful Mrs. Norris and her daughters, who chased away all but the most insistent of callers – in the person of my niece Sophia, whose husband is with the 28th Massachusetts. But I have been able to receive visitors, and pay calls over the last fortnight, although Niece Sophia does her best to ensure that I do not overtire myself.

There has been a great to-do in Boston in the last few months over a regiment of free Negros recruited for the Union – recruited in this very locality and trained at Camp Meigs. The officers for this regiment include the sons of families who have long been abolitionists. Two sons of Mr. Frederick Douglass are among those enlisted. You will recall that noble campaigner for his people honored me with friendship and support when I first began speaking publicly on the iniquity of the slave system. Their colonel is a fine young man from a good family, whom my brother Virgil tutored as a young lad. I recollect him very well and saw him often as a schoolboy. So terribly strange to think of young Robbie Shaw as a soldier, let alone as the colonel of a regiment! So many volunteers flocked to the banner of the 54th Massachusetts that they could pick and choose only the best and fittest recruits. There was great interest in Boston concerning the Negro regiment, as it is only fitting that free men should be permitted to take up arms and defend their own freedom. On the 28th of last month, the regiment assembled on the Common, and paraded through town, past the State House. They were to march down to the docks and take ship to South Carolina. The joy and encouragement from the crowds assembled along the sidewalks of Boston was such a thing to see; such a splendid, brave body of men ... but oh, the perils they will face, as I very well know! Not merely shot and shell, but that the vile secessionists have announced that any Negro soldier captured will be sold into slavery, and any officer of the 54th captured will be shot out of hand as insurrectionists. My heart aches doubly for this peril – yet knowing this, they were so stalwart and brave!

I do not know yet if my health – which is improving, now that I am at home and leisure – will permit me to return to the field, accompanying the noble Mrs. Bickerdyke. I long to do so and think on the situation of our poor wounded every hour ...

but I was so terribly run down by two years exertion. I spend most of my days, when not receiving a few visitors, writing an account of my experiences in the hospitals, and in letters to various offices on behalf of our nurses and our boys, outlining what is most needed. Such exhausts me rather rapidly on most days. I hope, however, to recover my former strength and energy soon, and return to work in the hospitals; if not in the west, then through Miss Dix. She writes to me of the need for careful nurses at the hospitals around Washington. I am considering paying a visit to her when I am more recovered to my former self.

Please write to me as your own duties allow,
Your dear friend, Minerva Templeton Vining.

July 23, 1863
To Mrs. Mary Bickerdyke, In the Field With the Army of the West
c/o Mrs. Mary Livermore, Chicago, Illinois
From Minerva Vining, Boston, Massachusetts
Dear Mary:
I hope that this letter finds you well – indeed, I hope that this letter finds you at all! I have sent this missive to you in care of our dear mutual friend, in the hopes that she may be able with her connections in the Commission to forward it to wherever you might be at present. I am still not yet recovered to full health and good spirits as of this writing – however, I am able to come downstairs, to apply myself to writing, and to receive visitors and well-wishers. Now and again, I feel well enough to walk a short distance into the Common, and to spend a few hours visiting my niece and her son.

We were concerned regarding the fate of her husband, who I have often mentioned to you – an officer in the 28th Massachusetts; a very fine man as dear to me as one of blood. We read in the first reports of the great battle at Gettysburg earlier this month that the 28th was present on the field of conflict. We were wracked with uncertainty for days, even to the point of taking the coach down to the offices of the Boston Evening Transcript on Washington Street so that we might immediately read all accounts of the battle, not wanting to wait upon delivery. Our fervent prayers were answered, in that his name did not appear upon any listing of the dead. My niece has since received a letter from him, which immediately dispelled all our fears for his safety. The battle was reported to have been bloody and protracted, fought in and around the hills and fields of that town, culminating in a great Charge of General Lee's army against a stoutly defended position. The invasion of our sacred and freedom-loving soil has been turned back, but at so heavy a cost! I note that the very same moment that General Lee was defeated, the citadel of Vicksburg on the Mississippi also fell to our forces under the command of the 'Unconditional Surrender' General Grant – but only a minor note was made of this victory in the West. The attentions of our scribbling clan and political chieftains is more usually bent upon the east, I fear. What happens westerly seems to be of secondary import – but that the lifeblood of commerce in the west now flows free, all the way from the great farmlands, cities and factories of the west, to the open sea! What a great deliverance is this! I can almost feel hope again, that our great experiment of a nation may be once again united. Do write when you can and tell me if

General G. is any less dyspeptic in his mood – or General Sherman any less peppery in temperament – upon the triumphant culmination of their campaign in the West.

I recover very slowly – but recover I will, although the doctors attending on me at the insistence of my niece say that it will be months until I regain anything like my former health and energy. Upon that day, I will return to nursing – knowing that such labors will be even more necessary before this fatal conflict is won.

Your devoted friend,

Minerva T. Vining

P.S. I believe that I wrote to you of the regiment of free Negros recruited from this locality, to much acclaim? We now hear to our great grief that Colonel Shaw, who was known to me as a boy, fell at the head of his noble regiment in an assault upon Fort Wagner, some three or four days ago. Boston is in mourning over this latest and most grievous loss.

August, 1863

To Miss Minnie Vining, Boston, Massachusetts

From Major Richard Brewer, in Camp at Morrisville, Virginia

Dear Aunt Minnie:

The regiment has taken a brief rest between muddy marches, sentry details, and policing up the field of conflict at this place, somewhat to the south and west of our capitol city. We badly needed to rest, and to refit our numbers, after the summer campaigns. Our General M. declined to pursue the Southern Paladin, General Lee upon the latter's hasty *withdrawal from Pennsylvania. I infer without being in General M.'s confidence, that this decision was made on the sensible notion that catching the wildcat would be as dangerous and wasteful of lives as pursuing it too assiduously. The regiment lost almost half of our number brought to the field at the Gettysburg fight, and nearly our colors, too! But for the cool head of Colonel Byrnes we might have lost them and more. I have hopes of being able to secure a furlough sometime this winter, and to come home to Boston; please embrace my dearest Wife and our Boy, upon receipt of this letter. I have written to them as well, but it is not unknown for missives to go astray. Assure them of my most tender affections and regard, dear Aunt Minnie!*

I was tasked with traveling to Washington last week, to assure Colonel Byrnes that our own wounded are being well-cared for. Colonel B., a regular officer although not Irish, is a most conscientious and painstaking man, with a praiseworthy attention to detail, and he tasked me with this duty. This involved a visit to every possible ward and hospital, upon searching the registry of patients for the names of men on our regimental roster. This was a not inconsiderable project, as I found that Washington is nearly ringed by camps and hospitals. Indeed, it seems as if uniforms and marching feet are the veritable heartbeat of the place.

I was tasked with searching out those of our men who had fallen wounded over this year's campaigning and if surviving, had been removed to the central hospitals in Washington; this to first assure Colonel B. of their satisfactory treatment, and second if possible, their eventual return to duty with the regiment, which is perilously short of men and may yet be disbanded, the remainder of our company allotted to other regiments. I will amuse you, Auntie, to know that I happened to encounter Mrs. Bard, upon several of these visits. She appeared in the ward, followed by a large male attendant bearing an enormous box. Going from bed to bed, she greeted each occupant and triumphantly produced this or that from the box – a pair of warm socks, a set of knitting needles, a packet of letter paper, a novel, some stamps – each item having been asked for by the invalid! She held a small notebook, and made a memorandum of what each asked for, in addition, before assuring each that she would return on the morrow or the day following with whatever small trifle had been requested.

Mrs. Bard greeted me most warmly, saying that she had received your letter of the 30th last month, but had not yet found the time to reply to it, as she was much involved with matters of the Sanitary Commission, and her regular visits to the hospital wards, procuring and distributing whatever small comforts have been requested by the men. 'It means so very much to them, you see," she told me, with such earnest regard. "Such small things, but so welcome, when our lads are suffering so much! I am only glad that I have the opportunity to undertake these small matters." She then asked most earnestly after yourself, thinking that I had received a more recent missive from the family, apologizing again for her tardiness in answering yours, and asked me to convey her best wishes to you, as well as hopes for your full restoration to health, saying that your work in the great Cause has been an inspiration and a guide for many, including herself.

Should you receive this communication before mine to dear Sophia, please assure her of my continued good health. I am reliably informed that when the regiment encamps for the winter that officers and men will be furloughed, for the purposes of rest, and to recruit anew.

With affection and respect,
Richard B.

Minnie's health revived as autumn cooled the fevers of summer. She took ever-longer walks along the margin of the Common in the mornings, feeling the blood pumping vigorously through her veins, as her former strength and energy returned. She walked to the shore, to the offices of the *Evening Transcript*, to the African Meeting House, towards the old North Church, to visit Sophia and Richie in the fine mansion with a large garden and a stable behind, which Richard Brewer had bought for them in the newer and wealthier side of Beacon Hill. Richie was fifteen now; a handsome youth grown more than a head taller than his mother. In the two years that Minnie had been away in the West, Richie had sprouted like a weed; magically from an ungainly boy with a spotty face and ankles and wrists forever sprouting from his too-short shirt cuffs and pants-legs into a handsome young man who looked very much like a younger edition of his father. Sophia had laughed at Minnie, the first time that Minnie remarked on this transformation, upon Richie's return from his boarding school.

"You have not laid eyes on him, all this time!" Sophia exclaimed. "No wonder you did not recognize him at first!"

"I would not have," Minnie agreed, thinking all the while with a twist of pain at her heart, that Richie looked old enough to be a soldier. In fact, he did appear much the same age as Billy Mimms, whose life she had saved by feeding him slivers of pickle.

She shivered at the thought. She might almost be well enough to go back to nursing soldiers, though.

After Richard comes home on leave, she decided. December. *I should be strong enough then.*

Chapter 18 - Treason Fled Before Us

December 1863 – Boston, Massachusetts

Reading war dispatches in the newspaper that the Union forces were besieged at Knoxville in Tennessee and that fighting had become intense around the city of Chattanooga solidified Minnie's conviction that she should return to nursing, now that her health was fully recovered. Her minds' eye and her memories filled in the bloody reality behind the black and white newsprint accounts of those battles. But the comfort of home, the quiet satisfaction of a settled routine – and the prospect of Richard Brewer having a furlough to spend almost a month with his family was a temptation too strong to resist.

Minnie wrote to Miss Dix, and to Mrs. Bickerdyke; her doctors in Boston had allowed that she would be fit and ready to return to nursing again in the new year. The replying letter from Mrs. Bickerdyke caught up with her, more than five months later and by then it was too late. Miss Dix's reply arrived much more promptly. Miss Dix would welcome her most warmly, in January, if she would be so good as to travel to Washington. There was a crying need, Dorothea Dix wrote, for hospital nurses there, as three years of war had glutted the ranks of sick and wounded, overflowing the hospitals. She would be most happy to make use of an experienced and trustworthy nurse. Moreover, as Minnie was of an age not to be tempted by an inappropriate romance, Miss Dix was certain that Minnie could be relied upon not to create a scandal or become the subject of embarrassing rumors. Miss Dix, who was chief of nurses hired by the Army in the east, was most particular on that requirement. This contrasted with Mrs. Bickerdyke, who cared only that the women who volunteered for her hospitals be strong and willing to work. That matter being settled – and knowing that she had decided upon a termination point to her holiday, Minnie applied herself to plan with Sophia for a series of splendid entertainments, excursions, and visits to enliven the Christmas holidays for Richard and Richie.

"I have so missed my husband," Sophia confessed over the teacups on one wintery November afternoon, when icy sleet lashed the windows of her parlor. The two women had spent a morning shopping for small gifts, until the inclement weather drove them back to the Brewer house. A warm fire burned brightly in the tiled fireplace, but there was a draft seeping in around the windows which the heavy curtains couldn't entirely banish. Minnie busied herself knitting another pair of warm wool socks for Richard, knowing very well exactly how hard that marching and the soldier's simple laundries were on socks. "Richie insists that he doesn't miss his father, but I believe that he does. He tries to sound so gruff and grownup now, saying that he is so proud that his father is a soldier. I wish ..." Sophia's words trailed off, and she gazed into the fire.

"What, dear?" Minnie prompted her, after a long moment had passed. Sophia started as if her thoughts had been very far away. When Sophia spoke again, it seemed at first that her words were irrelevant.

"I worry about Richie, Aunt Minnie. There have been times when I really wonder ... I wonder if he is possessed. I see something in ... how he looks and speaks... the expression in his eyes. And I wonder if he is really my son, or if the wicked fae took him away and left one of theirs in his cradle. That time that he tormented my poor little birds, Aunt – there was this gloating expression on his face, when we caught him in the act. He was only a little boy then, but I thought that he knew it was wrong to hurt helpless things. He didn't care – and I could tell myself that it was only because he was small and didn't know better. But..." Sophia hesitated until Minnie prompted her again.

"He has grown up, since then, Sophia dear. Surely, he has come to realize conduct like that is simply wrong, ungodly."

"I suppose that you are right, Auntie – but it worries me. Two of his teachers made mention of Richie bullying fellow students ... younger boys, they said. Boys who were not popular. They said that Richie encouraged other boys in bullying, and he seemed to find pleasure in their misery, and I recalled at that moment how he seemed to enjoy hurting my poor little birds. Mrs. Bradshaw – she lives opposite, in the house with the pretty gold-colored parlor curtains – she says that she saw Richie tormenting their stable cat by cutting it's poor tail and ears with his pocket-knife, and she simply had to tell me, as she could hardly believe it, but for the poor cat bleeding... this was three or four years past, Aunt Minnie, and of course Richie denied that he had ever done such a wicked thing ... but oh, I wish his father were still at home to put a stop to this horrible nonsense. Richie doesn't listen to me, but he will obey his father."

Because you do not <u>make</u> him obey, Minnie thought to herself, hating herself for seeing the situation with clarity, yet loving Sophia so dearly that she couldn't bring herself to be so cruel as to voice her own thoughts. *You only protest in the most feeble manner, and never lifted a hand to him when he was little and you could have made a punishment that would stick*

– and now he is taller than you, nearly grown ... and you are helpless. Annabelle was the same way – she spoiled him. Aloud, Minnie only said, "Boys will be rowdy and disobedient, Sophia. My brothers were sometimes very bad and disobedient – but they were good boys at heart. They meant well, just that they did not think, or consider the feelings of other people ... or beings."

"Perhaps I am imagining things," Sophia yielded with a sigh. "And you may be right, Auntie. Still, I will be so glad to have Richard home, home safe with us – especially," and she cast a glance towards the windows, now streaming with rain which the wind hurled with unrelenting fury against the glass, "... in weather like this. Was it horribly cold for your soldiers, out in the west in the bitter winter?"

"It was," Minnie agreed, relieved to be off the subject of Richie and Sophia's domestic woes. "But in the coldest weather, our soldier boys were quite resourceful at securing their little cabins against the cold ... and you must recall that many were accustomed to dreadful winters, being Westerners. Given enough time and wood, many of them created quite cosy little camps for themselves. They tell me that being in camp in the summer, the soldiers do plant little gardens, and make arbors of branches."

"So, a life in camp is not that awful," Sophia replied, her countenance brightening with relief. "That's good to know, Auntie."

"Yes, it would be, dear," Minnie replied. She had best not mention how the wounded after the Belmont fight had frozen to the ground in the harsh weather and suffered hideously until they were retrieved a day and a night later. Some of them had to be chopped from the frozen mud. *No, Sophia would not want to hear about that.* Sometimes Minnie wondered if people like Sophia and her Boston friends really wanted to know about what happened after battles ... the hideous wounds, the suffering; men, and boys in agony and begging for their mothers ... or if it would be too brutal to honestly tell them.

They had planned to meet Richard at Lowell Street Station when he arrived but had no very firm idea of what day to expect him. Sophia fretted, and Minnie finally consoled her,

"I think we can take our time and wait to hear from him when he is near to Boston. He would have had to make many connections on his way here, so the chances of him being on time will be very slight."

"Oh, I do hope that he has not been delayed," Sophia fretted. It was one of those cold, wet winter days, with an icy wind blowing off the Charles. "It will be so miserable, waiting on the train, when it is so cold!"

But out of the blue and without a word of warning, Richard appeared late one Friday afternoon, standing on the doorstep with a bulging carpetbag and a battered brass-bound trunk on the sidewalk at his feet. Sophia's housemaid answered a knock on the heavy front door, and cried out, "Tis the master himself! Ma'am, come quickly!"

At the same moment, Richie exclaimed from the stairs, "There's Papa!"

His cry brought Minnie and Sophia rushing from the parlor, scrambling in a flurry of skirts and crinoline. Minnie hesitated at the door. There was no place for her in these first moments of a family reunion, as Richard embraced his family; a quick and stoic embrace, for they were in public, after all.

With great relief, she thought at first that Richard Brewer was not much changed. She knew, from his and Sophia's occasional cheery letters to her that he had never sustained any wound more notable than a few cuts and bruises, and that he had escaped any serious bout of camp fever.

"Aunt Minnie!" Richard beamed with pleasure as he saw her for the first time, looking hesitantly around the half-opened door. "How marvelous! You look quite well, splendid, in fact! It's not truly a homecoming," he added, as he and Richie between them dragged his carpetbag and the trunk into the house, "Unless Aunt Minnie is there to welcome us! We have missed you, you know, all the while you were away in the West with the Sanitary Commission. They say quite the most interesting things about General Grant, and you have met him! What did you think ..."

"Must we talk about the war, dearest?" Sophia pleaded, "I don't want to hear another word about soldiering, and generals and battles, for the time that you are home with us! I don't even want to think about the regiment, or who replaces General MacClellan, or even if Mr. Lincoln should be re-elected or impeached ... not a single word! And come in, come in and get warm by the fire – dearest, your hands are like ice! Why you haven't caught your death of cold..."

Richard kissed her cheek. "My darling Sophia, your word is my command! I would like to put all of this behind me for the length of my furlough as well, but do recall, this is my business now."

"Let every man have amusement through his hobby," Minnie agreed, and they all laughed, although Richie looked as if he didn't agree.

Likely he would like to hear about battles, and such, Minnie thought. *Oh, perhaps when they are alone together, Richard and his son may speak of it. I hope that Richard will not encourage his son to volunteer – the only child of poor Sophia! I have written so many consoling letters to widowed mothers, whose cherished only son lay dying in my hospital! Selfish of me, I know, hoping for that cup to pass from us...*

Silent in the parlor, in a shadowy corner while Richie and Sophia chattered, Minnie studied Richard studying his face and bearing. In this second viewing, she knew that he had changed, he <u>must</u> have changed in becoming a soldier. He was browner in the face, weathered and roughed by service, just as his blue coat was a little frayed at the hems and faded at the creases. He seemed tired – as no doubt he would have been, traveling by train for several days and nights from the regiment's winter camp at Morrisville.

"So much has changed," Minnie observed abruptly, into the silence, when Sophia got up to see if supper was nearly ready. She had no idea why she had said that, but Richard smiled.

"Not anything that matters," he replied, as he stretched out his hands to the warm fire. "Will you be joining us for church service, on Sunday and for dinner afterwards?"

"Of course," Minnie answered. "It will be quite ... quite like it was before."

"Good," Richard replied. "I have missed our conversation, dear Aunt! Of all the hardships that this war has brought me, the most trying for me – after missing the company of my wife – is regular conversation with the most intelligent female of my acquaintance! I would enjoy hearing your opinion of the great

'Unconditional Surrender' general of the West. It's so good to be home, Aunt – isn't it?"''

"It is," Minnie agreed. As rough as the conditions in camp, following upon a battle were that she had endured, Richard must have experienced far worse. "I was so happy to be home. It will be so difficult to tear myself away again, when I return to tending the wounded and sick..."

"Then let us not think of it, dear Aunt, until we must," Richard assured her, just as a gust of icy rain splattered the parlor window. Sophia appeared in the parlor door, beaming on her family. "Supper will be ready in half an hour ... oh, my dear – it is so wonderful to have you home!"

The month passed in bitter cold, with trampled slush in the street gutters, and an icy gale blowing off the bay. It passed as if in a wonderful dream for Minnie; lightened by the holiday celebration. Papa-the-Judge in his lifetime had never embraced the English fashion for a Christmas tree adorned with garlands and ornaments, so Minnie only indulged in the custom of hanging garlands and wreaths of sweet-smelling cedar in that house, but Sophia and Richard had long taken up the ritual of decorating a Christmas tree. Since Richie had been born, the tree in the parlor had been ornamented to delight him, his friends, and the handful of child cousins. Sophia had a trunk full of delicate, blown-glass ornaments imported from Germany. Every year, Minnie, Sophia, and Annabelle strung garlands of cranberries, cut paper flowers and leaves to decorate the tree, and filled paper cones with sweets and raisins, all in secret as a surprise for Richie. Minnie knew from

Sophia's letters that she had carried on with the tree, even if it were only for herself, Richie, and the household servants.

"It will be so lovely to have the tree again," Sophia fairly glowed with happiness, as she, Minnie, and Sally, the Brewer housemaid, carefully hung the fragile blown-glass ornaments on the tree, on a morning, three days before Christmas. "Richie will love it, although I believe that he is beyond being surprised by it suddenly appearing in the parlor."

"That we are all in the parlor, with the door closed, and all others forbidden entry might be taken as a clue that something is up," Minnie observed, dryly. She threaded her needle with another length of red silk and continued stringing cranberries. A plain apron covered her day dress, against drops of juice staining it. "I fear Richie is likely too old to believe in Christmas magic, and a marvelous tree suddenly appearing in the parlor. He is nearly grown, dear."

"Well, perhaps there will be other children," Sophia, perched on top of a library stepstool, carefully hung several paper cones trimmed with gold lace from the upper branches. The cones were filled with candied fruit and other sweets. Minnie looked sharply at her niece; Sophia seemed to be flushed, and somehow ... elevated. *As if she hugged a delicious secret to herself.*

"When Richie marries, surely he and his wife will have children," Minnie replied. "Children to marvel at the wonderous tree..."

Sophia hung the last paper cone, and carefully came down the ladder. "And we will set up the Christmas tree, and pile the presents underneath it, and they will believe ... and my husband I will be old and bent and grey, and he will take the little ones on his knee and tell them stories ... and they will open their presents and play with them on the hearthrug ..."

"And they will all live happily ever after," Minnie giggled at Sophia's flight of fancy. She had so missed this kind of celebration, away in the west, for the last two years. A cozy warm parlor such as this, sheltered from the icy blast of winter. All the domestic joys had a richer savor to her now, after having done without for so many months.

"Of course," Sophia collected two more paper cones, and mounting up the ladder again, affixed them to a slightly lower branch. "How does that look, Auntie?"

"Perfect," Minnie replied. "I shall cherish the memory of this ... in coming years," she added hastily, recalling Sophia's stricture about mentioning the war, or anything to do with it. She had meant to say that she would think of this when she returned to the hospital service. It vaguely annoyed her that Sophia had forbidden any mention of 'war talk' while Richard was home. She herself would have liked to have shared how precious home comforts were, to all whom had served and were still serving. Richard was in and out of the house; he had recruiting for the regiment to attend, which necessitated long hours away from the Brewer mansion. It was almost like before the war, when Richard was in court, or consulting with clients during the day, but was there at the breakfast table, and for supper. Sophia was happiest of all, at those moments, having Richard safely at home, after all the battles that the 28th had seen and survived. Sophia was also made happy to show Richard to her friends – she was so proud of him, in the blue uniform of their country, fighting to expunge the scourge of the slave system.

Minnie finished helping with the tree and decided that she would walk home. All the more reason to enjoy the fresh air, now that the rains had blown themselves out. Clouds scudded across a pale blue sky, driven by a fresh wind. She plunged her mittened hands deeper into the depths of her muff and relished the feel of the chill breeze against her cheeks, a breeze unbroken by much of anything as it roared across the Common.

As she climbed the hill towards home, she saw that there was a dray parked before the door of the tall old house. The drayman, assisted by Jeremiah Daley holding the front door open for him, was lugging a small crate up the stairs. Richard Brewer stood on the stairs, supervising as befitted an officer. When he caught sight of Minnie, he waved.

"Hullo, Aunt Minnie! I brought you a Christmas present! It's too big to put under the tree, and I hate to think of putting you to the trouble of taking it home on Christmas morning ... so here it is. You don't mind that it's early, and ruins the surprise, do you?"

"No," Minnie hurried up the last bit of hill and climbed the stairs that ran from sidewalk to the front door. "I'm past being surprised by Christmas presents, Richard you should know that very well ... Good heavens, it's ... larger than I would have thought."

"It's just size of the crate, Aunt Minnie. I had your gift packed securely, since I didn't want it ruined. The finish is as fine as China silk."

Already intrigued, Minnie followed the men into the house, where Jeremiah Daley and the drayman were already breaking open the crate. Mrs. Norris hovered with a dustpan and a broom, falling on and sweeping up scraps of excelsior as they fell.

"Whatever my gift might be," Minnie took off her bonnet, and hung up her mantle and muff on the hallway stand. "I thank you for it, Richard – won't you come in and have some hot tea? Something to warm you up after being out in the cold?"

"Of course," Richard answered. "And besides, I want to see your face, when you behold your present."

"Of course," Minnie felt like giggling, giggling like a girl in pleasant anticipation. "Mrs. Norris, can you tell Bertha that Major Brewer and I will have tea in the parlor ... and if there are cakes just from the oven, we'll have some of them as well."

"Yes, Miss Minnie," Mrs. Norris replied, rather fretfully, pursuing yet another wisp of excelsior. The object in the crate was still wrapped in canvas. It appeared to be a small table. *If it was – where should she put it?* It must be something rather special if Richard took such much care in having it packed. Minne went into the parlor, a welcome refuge after a long walk from the Brewer mansion in blustery weather. Jeremiah had already built up the fire at mid-morning and brought in more wood against the chill of a winter day. She warmed her hands at the fire, and anticipated what her present might be.

She was rewarded when Richard brought it, attended by Jeremiah, who opened the parlor door for him. She could hear Mrs. Norris out in the hall, seeing the drayman out of the door and pursuing the last detritus from the crate.

"An early Merry Christmas for you, Auntie!" Richard announced, triumphantly. "I saw it in a cabinet-maker's shop of curiosities, and I knew at once that it would do justice for that marvelous chess set of yours!"

"Indeed, it does!" Minne was enthralled. Her present was a delicate small table, with elaborately carved ebony-wood legs, a pair of drawers for the chess pieces, and an intricately inlaid marquetry tabletop – not just the chess board itself, but the entire top and the drawer fronts as well. "Oh, Richard, it's gorgeous! Thank you! I do believe that is the loveliest chess board table that I have ever seen! Mr. Devereux would think..." Minnie was at a loss for what to say, then. It had been some years since she had said Pres Devereaux's name to anyone other than his cousin, Colonel Chaffin.

"He would think it worthy of his Chinese chess set, I believe," Richard replied. He shot a very shrewd look at Minnie before he continued. "He must have thought much of you, Auntie – to gift you with such a precious object."

"And I of him," Minnie replied. "For he was a very noble gentleman; I thought him quite worthy of marrying Cousin Susan's daughter, save for being favorably inclined towards the vile practice of slavery."

"They did make a handsome pair of lovebirds," Richard remarked, "Or so I observed, in that brief visit to Richmond, back then. Whatever has become of them, I wonder? I do not think that this war has been any kinder to the South than it has been for ourselves."

"I had seen a newspaper report," Minnie replied with a small sigh, "Early this summer, while I was still confined to my room. An English newspaper with an account of Southern gentleman blockade runners. Their writer did not give names directly, but his description of one such was sufficient for me to assume Mr. Devereaux was the person described." She paused, and then ticked off the clues on her fingers. "An old English surname, shared by the Great Queen Elizabeth's lover, that the gentleman was pleasing and gallant in his person and manners, a native of the Carolinas, with interests in shipping even before the War. I could not think it could be anyone other than Mr. Devereaux."

"It's a dangerous profession, running the blockade," Richard acknowledged, "But a glamorous one, considering – but for the boredom of weeks at sea, likely a good sport for a gambling man."

"From what I gathered from reading that account, it is very profitable, since our blockade of the Confederate states has bitten quite hard." Minnie forbore mentioning that blockade running was likely a safer occupation for a man in war than being an officer in an infantry regiment. "I would venture an opinion that old General Scott may have been correct in that the way to defeat the secessionists was to surround and squeeze them until the pips squeaked."

"Yes, and they made fun of him for all that, calling it the Anaconda Plan," Richard agreed. He settled into the nearest chair to the fire, a battered high-backed wing chair that had been Virgil's favorite. "All the new-minted generals laughed at his plan at the beginning. Not enough blood and glory for them, it appeared! And yet, it seems to have played out, exactly as the old man suggested at the very first. At least in the West it has, under General Grant. Which reminds me again, Aunt – since you have met him, what do you think of the man?"

"I thought much of him," Minnie settled into her own chair, casting her mind back to those scattered encounters. "He appears nothing like the great Fremont or MacClellan, all flash, and dash. Seeing him in camp, you would assume him to be an ordinary soldier, plain and humble to look at, like a simple teamster. Even a bit scruffy. A soldier in our camp at Cairo told me once that General Grant cares more for his horses than he does for his own person. But what he sets out to do ... he does, without sparing himself ... or anyone else, for that matter. I have great respect for him, as does Mrs. Bickerdyke. General Grant and General Sherman both repose great trust in her."

"Unconditional Surrender," Richard grinned like a boy. "And this General Sherman – another westerner? What did he do before the war?"

"He's an Ohio man," Minnie replied, "Red hair, what there is left of it. Terribly impatient of fools and brusque at best; he always looks rather grim. I think he was in the Army for a bit; a West Point man at first, but he managed a bank, mostly and dealt in real estate." She stared into the crackling fire for a long moment before she spoke again. "You know, Richard – I don't exactly feel eager about returning to nursing soldiers, but I simply feel that I must do something. Especially when I receive letters from Mary Livermore..."

At that moment, Bertha bustled in with a heavy-laden tray; a pot of tea and all the rest, served up in the brightly polished Revere silver service, with a covered plate of little cakes and thin bread sandwiches.

"Oh, my, Miss Vining," she exclaimed, upon seeing the new table. "How beautiful! Jeremiah said that it was your Christmas present – but Ma won't be pleased at yet another thing in the parlor to dust and polish!"

"It's all right, Bertha – thank you," Minnie replied. When the door closed on Bertha's back, Minnie thought again of how she would miss the quiet routine of life in this house. Mention of General Grant had brought back to her that hideous night on the bluff above the battlefield at Pittsburgh Landing, when the general himself came to the cabin on the bluff, looking for a place to sleep out of the rain, and went away again into the darkness, limping and leading his horse.

"The horrifying thing is how they all call for their mothers, *in extremis*," Minnie said suddenly, out of that memory. "All of them. Even the grown men. They beg for their mothers. Always. And the way that the land where a battle has just been fought ... just appears to seethe, at a distance. Like maggots writhing in a piece of rotten meat."

"Ah." Richard said only that, as he poured himself a cup of tea, adding sugar and cream to it. He stared into the fire for a long moment. "The fire from the Rebs ... there were times when it fell like hail on us. Leaden hail. Cutting down my men, just like a scythe slash through wheat stems. Clean and sharp. In windrows they lie, all those bodies in blue and I holding my damned sword like a fool, calling for those still alive to follow me, while the fog from gun powder rolls in on us like storm front. It's a damnable business, war. Sophia forbids any mention of it while I am home ... but in truth, I cannot tell her such things as what I have seen."

"Neither can I," Minnie admitted. "For it would be the worst cruelty, to tell all those trusting women who knit comforts for their men and send them jam and letter-paper. It would be obscene, to tell of their agonies when the surgeon cuts off a limb ... to describe honestly the blood and all of it."

She poured herself her own cup of tea, still immersed in those memories of Mrs. Bickerdyke and herself, going out with lanterns into a muddy field strewn with bodies, where dying horses screamed and thrashed, looking for those badly wounded men who might have been overlooked by stretcher parties. Richard also stared unseeing into the fire.

"Aye, Aunt Minnie – we have both seen the elephant now for certain, haven't we?" he remarked at last.

The holidays passed all too soon, in a comfortable and homey blur, a round of gatherings, social calls, celebratory parties with old friends. It hardly seemed any time at all to Minnie, until she and Richard met on the platform for the train which would take them away from Boston. All was done, and Richard's furlough was over. So was Minnie's period of recovery from the strain and overwork of field nursing in the West. She was bound for Washington and to nurse in one of the many hospitals there, Richard to rejoin his Irish regiment at their winter camp in the countryside some miles further on from Washington.

"I am reminded of how we set off for Richmond with Cousin Peter for the wedding," Minnie remarked with a sigh, as they waited to climb up into the carriage. She hugged her heaviest mantel about her shoulders, grateful for the muff in which Mrs. Norris had put a warmed half-brick. "Do you recall how the Irish porter made so much of Cousin Peter having been one of Washington's soldiers?"

"I do, indeed," Richard grinned, without much mirth to his expression. "Ah, well, Aunt – we are off to Richmond again, or at least I am. Richmond; so near, and yet so far! Ah, here we go – on time, at least." He handed Minnie up into the coach and carried her overstuffed carpetbag along with his own luggage, while Minnie reflected on how different this journey would be, so many sad years later.

Chapter 19 - Just Before the Battle, Mother

Summer, 1964 – Washington, D.C., Boston, Massachusetts

Minnie had visited Washington several times before the War – and on this arrival found it not much improved. It was a muddy place, now made even muddier by sullen rain, and the constant traffic in the unpaved streets. Many had been planned to be glorious avenues, as befitted the national capital. Washington was supposed to be adorned with imposing marble buildings and monuments, but as nearly as Minnie had ever seen, most of them were at best half-completed, and the rest was a warren of low boarding houses, saloons and worse. Washington wasn't anywhere as cultured as Boston, or as wealthy as New York, or even as pleasant as Newport. Still – it was now where the war had brought her. She had exchanged letters with Miss Dix, who had arranged a position and a small salary for her as an official Army nurse at one of the largest hospitals serving the wounded. The wards had been established in the halls and dormitories of a college on the edge of town, an establishment on a low hill at the edge of town, whose highest levels commanded a view of the Potomac River and the distant roofs of the city. Richard saw her to the front door of the Columbia College Hospital and bid her farewell.

"I will send you and your boys anything in the way of comforts that you want, within reason," Minnie promised. "Just write and let me know."

"I'll hold you to that promise," Richard kissed her gloved hands. "Goodbye, Auntie. Can I ask you to write to Sophia, as much as you can? I may not be able to send letters as often as I like, and I know my dearest wife will worry."

"Of course," Minnie replied.

"Look after her and the boy, as best you can," Richard took up his own carpetbag, and set his hat at a jaunty angle. "Especially if something happens to me – let them know."

"Nothing will happen to you," Minnie replied, suddenly alarmed, but Richard only laughed. With one final salute, he walked away. She watched from the steps of the Columbia College main building, until he was lost among the shifting crowd of blue uniforms. She only recalled much later, the old maritime superstition that it was bad luck to watch someone out of sight.

To Mrs. Sophia Brewer, Boston, Massachusetts

From Minerva Vining, Columbia College Hospital, Washington

March 2, 1864

My Dear "Little Wisdom" – The happy news contained in your last letter brightened every aspect of my existence! I would drop every duty that I have undertaken here and come home, but that I have seven patients whose weakened condition require constant vigilance on my part, and of course, your insistence that you are perfectly happy and well, in good spirits and lapped in every comfort and care imaginable renders my presence superfluous. Rest assured, dear heart, that I will return when the birth of the Little Stranger is imminent ... or upon word that your condition has changed. Otherwise, I do not have any desire to return to Boston, not when I can make myself useful here. I can't think of any other woman with whom I would exchange situations.

In spite of the primitivity of a soldier camp, or a hospital such as this, there is a charm which invests our poor soldier boys. Once he entrusts you with his affection and respect, then he makes a confident in you – and before you are quite aware, you have become mother, nurse, and dear friend – and such dear boys will heed reproof and instruction. In the afternoons, my ward is quite the little hive of industry, among those boys who are well enough to rise from their beds. The ward that is my charge is on an upper floor of the College building, and is favored with a generous bay window, in which I have put my workbox, and a nicely sized table, along with a number of potted plants to cheer the space and make it homelike. I am endeavoring to teach those of my recovering patients who are interested in the art of knitting... although I have one patient, whose left leg was amputated some months since, who is whittling his own artificial limb to replace it.

My work here is rather more of a predictable routine than when I was in the west. Patients arrive every day, woeful and wounded and depart cured and recovered for the most part. Most new arrivals have already been seen and treated in a cursory manner at the very least. Their names are taken down for the Hospital registry, and those possessions with them on arrival are carefully inventoried and stored, with a label of their name attached. They are bathed, their wounds carefully re-dressed and bandaged, and dispersed to a ward. As a general rule my patients are those recovering from wounds, for which I am grateful. Earlier this year, there was an epidemic of measles; all the sufferers were confined to a single ward, and the poor attendants and nurses were

314

quarantined – not allowed to go anywhere, and to have their meals brought to them.

Would you like an account of my daily schedule? It all begins before sunrise, when reveille sounds at 5 AM – all those patients who are able must get up, wash and make their beds up properly, so as to be ready at drum-call for breakfast. We nurses have our own breakfast an hour later, at 7. Our ward attendants – most usually fit convalescents or those unfit for field duty bring up breakfast for those who are not able to rise from bed. Following this, two fit and recovering boys wash up the dishes, two more sweep the floor, two wash the spittoons, while two hired contrabands take away the slops. Then we attend to the dressings on healing wounds and generally making the bedridden comfortable. Meanwhile, some of the boys are being helped to shave, or having their hair trimmed, while some are playing checkers or sitting in bed reading. I have attempted to teach the most promising boys the game of chess, as a diversion! At 8 sounds the fife-and-drum for surgeon's call – when all in the ward must be in apple-pie order. The orders for medicine, soap, crackers, et cetera are made at this time, as nothing is allowed in the ward without an order from the surgeon. Wounds are re-dressed following the surgeon's review, and blisters, plasters and medicines administered as directed. At 11, the prescribed medicines come up from the dispensary. At noon, the drumbeats for all who are able to go to the mess-room for dinner. Alas, company is usually in the ward at this time, and I must either forgo that meal, or eat it cold.

When dinner is done, there come several hours of leisure, such as it is. This is the time when our knitting and sewing circle meets in the corner by the bay window to mend socks. It is so amusing to see the pleasure the boys get from competing with each other to outdo each other with regard to knitting and mending! I have also taken to reading aloud from various books of light amusement that we have among us! My ward was diverted for many days by chapters from my beloved copy of Irvings' Tales from the Alhambra. The boys were much impressed that my copy was personally inscribed to me by Mr. Irving himself. (If you recall, this was a gift to me from my brother Virgil.)

At 5 PM, the drum calls for supper. After the meal is done, and trays brought to the bedridden, wounds are checked and redressed if called for, and the surgeon makes a round again – this is when sleeping powders, poultices and hot compresses are administered, if called for by the surgeon. At half-past the hour, the drum beats one last time, for all to be in bed. The bells ring, or taps is sounded at 9 – then lights are extinguished, and all conversation must give way to sleep. So ends my day, unless the condition of one of the boys demands my attendance. Mercifully, at most times I may then go to my own rest. As you can judge from this schedule, my day is measured by a strict routine.

One of my particular friends among the other nurses is Mrs. Rebecca Pomroy, a very respectable widow from Chelsea, near Boston, a gentle and sweet-faced person whose' pleasant and inoffensive aspect conceals a will of iron. Her father was a ship captain, who died in a dreadful accident on his own ship when she was but a girl. My father was acquainted with Captain Holliday and spoke well of him. Mrs. Pomroy, like Mrs. Bickerdyke, had long experience of nursing *invalids in her family – and so came to the attention of Miss Dix. Mrs. Pomroy's only son is serving in the field, an uncertain circumstance which she bears with considerable fortitude. Mrs. Pomroy was called to nurse the two sons of President Lincoln, when those poor lads fell ill last year and the eldest died, to his parents' abiding sorrow. Mrs. Pomroy was called again to tend Mrs. Lincoln herself when she was injured in a dreadful carriage accident. Hearing that I had made the acquaintance of Mr. Lincoln before the war, Mrs. Pomroy invited me to accompany her on a visit to the Lincoln family, with whom she is on the most friendly terms. What a sad, sad house the executive mansion is – the public rooms are not much more elegant than the basest kind of rooming house, bearing the evidence of many muddy boots and careless disposition of tobacco spittle. The private family quarters are not much better. You will be pleased to know that Mr. Lincoln recollected me at once, and of being warmly received at your house. He asked after yourself, your boy and Richard with the most tender concern. He seems most careworn, and so aged by the responsibilities of his office, as well as grief for his son, Willie. I think his sole consolation must be the antics of his youngest boy, Tad, who is very clever and bold, but allowed every indulgence by his parents and who can blame them in the least! A friend made Tad the gift of a box of child-sized carpenter's tools at Christmas, and from that moment on, nothing in the Presidential mansion was safe; planks sawn in half, nails driven through carpets and into the floor, doorknobs, locks, and latches disassembled, until those tools were taken away. Poor Mrs. Lincoln does not relish life in Washington, or the duties that her position requires.*

Trustworthy friends are few and far between among the circles in which she is expected to move. Mrs. Pomroy is one of those few friends. Mrs. Lincoln is often low in her spirits, and of course still mourns the boy that she lost.

Still, Mrs. P and I passed a very pleasant afternoon, and we were conveyed back to the hospital at the end of that visit, in a carriage especially called for, and laden with bouquets of fresh flowers from the greenhouse and every kind of delicacy for our patients. If you should happen to think on it, would you be so kind as to send me ten pair of knitting needles, for the use of my boys.

Your loving auntie,
Minnie

In the spring after Minnie took up a place at the College Hospital, the war moved with ponderous gravity to strangle Richmond. Under the command of Grant, the implacable "Unconditional Surrender" general, the Union army in the east marched through the Virginia countryside. The wards in the College Hospital filled to capacity and overflowed with wounded and sick. There were pallets laid out on the floor between the cots in the wards, and end-to-end in the hallways, after the second battle over Chancellorsville and action at the Spotsylvania Courthouse. A voluble corporal from the 28th Massachusetts turned up in Minnie's ward in late May, pierced through the left leg by a shell splinter, with news of Richard Brewer.

"Aye, our bhoys took a pasting," he reported to Minnie. "'Tis said that the commander of the division asked why we were not drawn up in company order afterwards ... an' the Major replied, "But this is all the company!" the corporal chuckled and then coughed. "Aye, but he is a game 'un, he is – an' lucky with it, too. There is no ball nor bullet made yet, wi' the name o' Major Brewer on it!"

But it seemed that there was indeed a bullet with Richard Brewer's name on it. Late in June, Minnie received a letter from Sophia – a letter blotched with what likely were dried tears – Richard Brewer was dead, felled between one moment and the next by a sniper's bullet, somewhere along the trench lines which ringed Petersburg. As was the sad custom for those officers of means, his remains were embalmed and transported to Boston, to the place of his residence for burial in the home churchyard. Minnie felt almost as if she had been struck by the same fatal bullet. In spite of those months spent nursing soldiers and knowing well the chances and mischances of a battlefield. in her own mind, she had always considered Richard indestructible. Like the corporal, she somehow believed against all logic and experience that there was no ball or bullet made with his name on it.

Telegram, 20 June 1864
From Miss Minerva Vining, Columbia College Hospital, Washington
To Mrs. Richard Brewer, Boston
REC'D YOUR LETTER OF THE 12TH. APPALLING NEWS. ALLOWED FURLOUGH. COMING HOME SOONEST.

"I must go," she said to Miss Dix. "I know – I do not want to leave my boys at this juncture – but his wife is my only close relative! Both of her parents are dead, and she is with child herself, now ... and she has endured so many past mischances in bearing a living child. I <u>must</u> go home to Boston."

"You are aware," Miss Dix frowned. "That once you depart from service to the Army that you will not be permitted a return – in spite of being one of my best and most experienced nurses?"

"A furlough," Minnie pleaded. "Only a furlough – that I may assure myself that my niece is comforted in her grief, and that her child may be safely delivered."

"When is the child due?" Miss Dix still appeared severe in her regard of Minnie.

"In ..." Minnie tallied up the months since December. "Late in August, possibly September. I would return as soon as my niece is safely delivered of the child – I promise."

"Two months, possibly three? I am not certain of being able to get along without you at the College Hospital for that long," Miss Dix sighed and tapped her fingers together. "I would have to assign another nurse there ... and such is the progress of the war, I know not where I could place you, upon your return. Very well," Miss Dix yielded, as Minnie hoped that she would. "I approve a furlough of that length, given the special circumstance and your own good character ... but upon your return, I may task you with duty at another location."

"Thank you," Minnie replied, much distracted, hardly hearing what Miss Dix had said, so wrenching was her grief for Richard and her worry over Sophia. "I will serve wherever I am needed, but at this moment, my niece needs me most desperately."

Minnie did feel some pangs of reluctance on leaving her ward – having taken such care tending to her patients there, but her concern for Sophia and the unborn child was sufficient to overwhelm them all. She packed her carpetbag and her travel trunk, donned the sturdiest of her plain dresses and her unadorned Quaker bonnet and set off on the long journey home. She was haunted by memories of that mid-winter dash from Rochester before the war, when she and Lolly Bard arrived too late for Annabelle in her last illness. At least it was not winter, but the bright sunshine of summer, the rich green leaves of the trees and colorful mounds of summer flowers did not make the funeral any less mournful.

Minnie stood with a solemn-faced Richie at the graveside, as the Reverend Slocomb pronounced the last words of the service for the burial of the dead. Sophia had fainted dead away at the church door, upon seeing the coffin in which Richard's body lay. Someone had thoughtfully brought a chair for her to the graveside, as she refused to leave. To Minnie's vague surprise, Sophia remained tearless and composed throughout the brief service, and silent on the return to the Brewer mansion, where a cold collation had been laid out in the dining room and in the parlor for the other mourners. Richie was playing host, as was entirely correct; he appeared to have matured nearly overnight. Sophia excused herself from the gathering of friends after a very short time. Minnie assumed that, pleading her delicate condition, Sophia had gone to her room to lie down. When Minnie went upstairs, thinking that she should really make certain that Sophia had recovered fully from her fainting spell, she found Sophia's room dark and empty.

"Ma'am is in Mr. Richard's study, I think – I saw her go in at about half past the hour," offered Sally, the Brewer's housemaid, when Minnie voiced her concern. "She must still be there. Do you want me to fetch her, Miss Minnie?"

"No, I'll go in myself," Minnie replied.

Nearly all the guests had departed. The little tray on the hall table overflowed with their calling cards. Minnie tapped on the door.

"Sophia, dear – may I come in?"

Sophia replied indistinctly from inside the study. Minnie took it as permission, and let herself in. The study was dim inside, as the curtains were drawn. The faint pleasant odor of old paper hung in the air, along with the faint remainder of pipe smoke. Sophia was curled up, child-like, in the depths of the comfortable old leather settle, her stocking feet drawn up under her black bombazine skirt. Her black slippers lay neatly, side by side on the worn rug by the settle.

"Are they all gone yet?" Sophia asked, sounding pathetically young. Minnie found her way to one of the chairs, set beside Richard's desk. Now she supposed that it would be Richie's desk, in time.

"Nearly all. Your son is doing very well, as your host. I suppose that he will be the head of the household, now. He seems so much older than his years." Minnie looked closely at Sophia; the younger woman's face and fair hair made a pale oval in the study's darkness, against the somber black of her dress. "Are you feeling well, dear? It was so very comforting, having so many people attending the service ... and coming to pay their respects afterwards. Richard had so many friends in Boston!"

"He did, indeed." Sophia sounded unnaturally detached. Minnie wondered if she should ask for a doctor to see her niece.

Sophia's eerie calm struck her as unnatural; even more unnatural as excessive grief would have been. "I am so happy that that so many of our friends came. Everyone has been so very kind, you see. The brave, noble officer at the head of his men ... so far away from Richie and me and Baby, too. I received a letter of condolence from Mr. Lincoln himself. Can you imagine that? I suppose that your friend Mrs. Pomroy informed him. Governor Andrew was in attendance today too – did you see him? So many people ... I should have spoken with them all but I wanted to sit in Richard's study, Auntie; I feel so very close to him, here. Closer than in our bed. His study smells still of his pipe tobacco. As if he had just left the room and would be back in a moment instead of lying cold in the ground. Never to lie in my arms again, never to embrace his son, bless the Baby. Glory and the Union! I will tell you something, Auntie. Something that I would never breathe to another living soul."

"What is it, Sophia dear," Minnie asked, tenderly. "You know I will keep your confidence. I always have."

Sophia laughed, a little, tinny laugh. "Just this, Auntie. You may depend on me to play the brave widow. Saying all the right, dutiful things – how it comforts me to know that my husband fell in the great cause of preserving the Union and abolishing the vile institution of slavery. That I will always honor his courage and devotion, that his life ... my Richard's life was a worthy sacrifice on the altar of freedom. I will do all those things, as I wear mourning for him; I will say all the right words, make all the gestures ... but know this, Auntie ... I care nothing, nothing for any of it." Sophia's quiet voice hardened, in some indefinable way, as if the words tasted bad in her mouth. "The sacred cause, the Union, Mr. Lincoln – John Brown and all of your abolitionist friends, Auntie – yes, and all the generals and their filthy flags and damnable cannon... they can all burn in hell for all that I care, and I will laugh and laugh at their torments, because they took my husband, my Richard from me!" Sophia's voice at the last sounded as if she would shriek those words, but she only whispered them fiercely, every syllable dripping with contempt and rage. "I care nothing for all of it ... but I will wear mourning, and lay flowers on their marble monuments, and speak the correct words, but underneath, I will go on hating them all, for taking Richard from me!"

"I understand, dear," Minnie finally brought herself to reply. *Could this be Sophia speaking, gentle affectionate Sophia, who was nearly as fierce in support for the Abolitionist cause as Richard himself has been?*

"No, you don't, Auntie!" Sophia hissed. "You don't – but never mind, I will never speak of this again."

Minnie opened her mouth to protest – she did understand the cost paid in lives and limbs for freedom, glory, and union; she who had seen a pile of bloody amputated arms and legs, piled by the surgeon's operating table on the edge of the Shiloh battleground, she who had seen the Elephant, as Richard had remarked. Before she could say a word of protest or pleading, Sophia uncoiled her legs, slid her feet into her flat slippers, and rose from the settle – awkwardly, because of the weight of the unborn child. "I'm going up to my room, Auntie. Convey my respects to anyone who still remain." And she was gone like a ghost, the whispering rustle of her dress as insubstantial as the faint scent of tobacco in Richard's empty study.

The balance of her mind is in disarray because of the intensity of her grief, Minnie told herself, by way of an explanation. In truth, she herself grieved over Richard, who was all but a younger brother or a son to her, just as Sophia sometimes seemed as much a daughter. Reminding herself that Richard had felt as strongly in the cause of abolition, and for the unbreakable ties of Union, accepting a commission as an officer ... it was very cold comfort indeed, next to the loss, the shadowed void in the world where Richard used to be. Minnie, after assuring herself that the Brewer household was in all ways secure for the night, took refuge for herself in her own house, and wondered why her eyes were quite dry – as if she had all but run out of tears.

Minnie divided her days of that grief-shadowed late summer between her own house and the Brewer mansion, alternating between mornings in her own parlor, penning letters to distant friends, and articles for various newspapers and bulletins, and afternoons with Sophia. She wished to assure herself of Sophia's continuing good health and ensure that the household ran as well as it ever did. Sally, who had come to the Brewers as a maid to look after the infant Richie had risen in authority to the position of housekeeper; a calm and competent woman who reassured Minnie almost at once.

"Naught for worry, Miss Minnie," Sally told her when Minnie first mentioned her concern. "Mr. Brewer, he has been gone away wi' the regiment for so many months, Miz Brewer, she has a good eye for the accounts and the management of the house. Even young Richie ..." Sally hesitated. "He is a good help to the ma'am. No doubt. Still – I wisht that the ma'am would have a dog in the house. A dog is a good creature to have, you know. If the house was afire, or some bad 'un trying to break in ... I suggested it to Ma'am once, when me brother's fine watchdog whelped puppies, but she said no, no, for the mess 'an bother the critter 'ud be."

"Perhaps I might suggest it," Minnie assured her, but when she did, Sophia shook her head. No, they were safe enough, and when Minnie pressed the issue, Sophia became agitated, and so Minnie thought it was safer to drop the subject.

Minnie wrote to Mary Livermore in Chicago; one of the few with whom she could voice such fears.

I endeavor to remain close at hand and watch carefully without seeming to do so. Our dear Little Wisdom suffered so many disappointments before bringing their son into the world. She is past the danger of an early miscarriage now but I take no comfort in recalling how she and her mother alike suffered agonies in childbed, and given our family ill-luck in that regard. I am only indifferently devout, much as my dear father was, but my nightly prayers for my niece are unrelenting...

As it turned out, there was little need for worry. The baby came early – in the last week in July. Minnie thought she ought to spend nights at the Brewer house, in order to be close at hand for Sophia. Minnie came down to breakfast one morning to find Richie alone in the dining room. She helped herself from the covered dishes laid out on the sideboard, before asking about Sophia.

"Mama's in her room," Richie reported, oddly cheerful. "She thinks the baby is on the way. Sally has sent for Dr. Hubbel, but he sent word that he is out attending on another patient, and he will come as soon as he can. Mama is not worried – she thinks that it will be hours yet."

"I must go to her ..." Minnie rose from her seat, and Richie grinned.

"Mama thought you would say so," he helped himself to more dry toast and some more bacon. "She really did say it would be hours yet. Finish your breakfast, Auntie. Mama is not worried."

Nonetheless, Minnie hurried through what she had served for herself, before going up the stairs and tapping on the bedroom door.

"Come in, Auntie!" Sophia called from within, sounding quite composed, even cheerful. "Did you bring your knitting? Baby and I will be a while, I think."

"Little Wisdom!" Minnie exclaimed, simultaneously comforted and concerned. "Shouldn't you be resting!"

Her niece was sitting in the window seat, looking out at the garden below – the garden that she cherished – at the height of summer, an oasis of flower plantings which nearly rivaled Cousin Susan's garden in Richmond, so many summers ago. Sophia had her wrapper on, over her thin cotton shift. The loose wrapper barely closed across her belly.

"I'm perfectly fine," Sophia replied. "I feel better, walking, when the pains come. Really, Auntie. I have no worries. Baby will be safe, and I will be all right." A brief grimace – and Sophia gasped, but continued after a moment, in a perfectly normal tone of voice. "I feel certain that Baby is a girl. I just have that feeling. And Sally said since I was carrying high, that meant a girl. Although Doctor Hubbel harrumphed and said it was complete nonsense, an old-wives tale. But it doesn't change anything. Richard also thought Baby was a girl." Sophia smiled, a sad smile, although her eyes didn't fill with tears, as Minnie had expected. "He wrote me so, in his last letter to me. He thought that it was very careless of us not to be specific."

"Had you picked out a name for Baby, yet?" Minnie asked, carefully, relieved that Sophia did not seem about to fall into hysterical tears at this moment.

"Of course. Richard insisted on it. Sophia Minerva Louise; Sophia for me, Louise for Richard's mother." Now Sophia looked most keenly at Minnie, although her expression of confidence otherwise didn't change. "And Minerva for you, Auntie. Because ... you will promise to look after her, won't you? In case anything happens to me."

"Nothing will happen to you," Minnie replied. "Be assured of it; I will look after f your children as if they were mine. Since I do not have any of my own, it leaves me the leisure to do so."

"Leisure," Sophia essayed another smile, dimmed briefly by a flicker of pain. "Auntie, dear, I don't believe you have spent a moment of leisure in your life. Even when you sit down, you have a bit of needlework or knitting in your hands, if not a pen and a quire of letter-paper."

"None the less," Minnie promised. "I will look after Baby Sophia, to the best of my ability. I promise."

"Thank you, Auntie," Sophia's head tilted at the indistinct thump of the front door opening and closing again, and voices in the hallway on the ground floor. "It sounds like Dr. Hubbel is here, Auntie – are you going to stay with me?"

"Of course, I will," Minnie promised, although she did fear that she might be taken in a faint, as she was at the first, when

Seffie's infant was born, in that shack in Cairo. "Of course, I will."

She didn't faint. To her surprise and relief, the infant Sophia came easily, without any fuss and only the usual quantity of blood and other fluids; plump and pale, damp little tendrils of light brown hair curling all over her pink skull. She looked around with the unseeing blue eyes of a very new baby, vaguely baffled at having been translated from the warm dark shelter of the womb into a cold, light-filled world. Minnie wrapped her in warmed towels after Dr. Hubbel snipped through the livid birth-cord and attended to examining the afterbirth for any missing portions.

Minnie put the bundled Sophia into her mother's longing arms. "Here is your daughter," she whispered. "And she is beautiful."

Chapter 20 – Hurrah, Hurrah, The Flag That Makes You Free
April, 1865, Virginia

The last Confederate armies were dissolving, as they fell back from Petersburg, falling back west into gently folded hills, wet with April rain. Everyone said that the war was nearly over, at least in the East. Richmond had fallen at long last, came the word among the teamsters. The traitor Jeff Davis had fled, no one knew where he and his fellow secessionists had gone to earth. The last Rebel troops had fired Richmond before they fell back into the countryside, or so rumor had it. The Negro contrabands who did the hard labor of setting up a hospital in the muddy fields did so with a cheerful air that day. Still, Minnie heard the distant crackle of rifle fire, as she and the other volunteer nurses set up the wards for a hospital near a small town at the crossroads, west of Petersburg. There was no particular reason to set up the hospital tents in this place, save that a half-wrecked barn appeared to have served as a shelter and surgery for the retreating Confederates. Most of those injured left behind still clung to life, although verminous, half-starving, and very, very ill – from wound fever, malaria, semi-starvation, and camp-fever or perhaps all four in combination.

Minnie had returned to nursing since Sophia Brewer seemed to have no need of constant attendance after recovering from giving birth and her grief over Richard. Baby Sophie thrived, plump and sweet-tempered, and Richie looked to be settling into a comfortable place as head of the family, even though he was not yet sixteen years old. Miss Dix, when notified by letter, sent Minnie to an Army hospital attached to General Sheridan's Army of the Potomac, a consideration for which Minnie was grateful. All that she wished for now was that the war should be done. Now it looked as if it was winding down, like a tall clock with a slackened spring in the works.

There had been a stack of putrid amputated arms, legs and blood-soaked garments left in a pile seething with flies on the far side of the barn. Minnie, holding folds of her apron over her nose and mouth, had instructed the orderlies to start a bonfire – and if the wood was too wet to burn, to dig out a trench and bury the reeking pile.

The war had dissolved into a series of sporadic running skirmishes, as the last of General Lee's Army of Northern Virginia fell back towards the west, towards the high green ridges that ran like a spine down the length of Virginia. Those men who fancied themselves tacticians said that General Lee was trying to break south, to join up the General Johnstons' force in Tennessee, but that 'Little Phil' Sheridan kept leapfrogging ahead of him, blocking escape of what was left of the largest Confederate army. Looking out from the cluster of cream-colored canvas Army tents and pavilions which made up the hospital, she could see the wet countryside, the muddy and rutted road over which an army had lately passed, see where planks had been laid down in those spots where the mud was deepest. Rumors flew that General Lee was on the point of surrendering, but rumors always flew thick and fast, among the marching armies.

"Dr. McNelly says that we are not all that far away from Richmond," she remarked to her fellow nurse, Lavinia Dillard, as the two women stood under the shelter of a large wall tent, the front flaps turned back to admit light and air, "I visited there, years ago, to visit close kin. Alas, we parted ways over the matter of abolition. My cousins' folk were all for slave power, and I could not countenance remaining silent. I suppose that the war will be over soon. I wonder if I should venture a visit there, now."

Increasingly of late, Minnie wondered how the war had treated Susan and Ambrose and the husbands of Susan's daughters. All would have been expected to join the Confederate brigades, even though Ambrose might have been exempt as an ordained minister. From what Minnie had read, the Southern draft had fallen on every free male from the age of sixteen, all the way to men of fifty. She counted back the twenty years since that momentous visit, enshrined in her memory like an insect preserved amber. Yes, Lydia and Charlotte's first-born sons would have been old enough to serve as soldiers; if not when Fort Sumter was fired on, then at least in the last few years. Maybe one of those sons lay on a cot in her hospital at this very moment, wounded and sick nearly to death.

"I don't suppose that you would be received with any more courtesy," Lavinia replied. She fidgeted with a corner of the apron tied over her work-dress. "After all the blood and the misery, and the hatred ... it will be almost impossible to put it out of mind and go back to being one country again."

Minnie nodded in agreement. "We're doing at least something to make up for it, in tending their wounded." She resolved at that moment, that she and the nurses would do everything possible to see that no more soldiers died under their care, not with the end of the war so close at hand.

Certain word of General Lee's surrender came at mid-morning more than a week later. As if in acknowledging that miracle, the sun came out from behind the lowering grey clouds. The trees around had put out fresh green leaves and even the bare-shorn fields where the hospital had been set up were furred with new growth. Minnie went to find Surgeon Major McNelly, the chief of the hospital and senior surgeon. She had worked with Surgeon McNelly for some months and liked him very much for his grasp of practicalities, his wry intelligence in conversation and that he was a very good surgeon; adept and above all, swift with his bone saw and his needles. He was an older man, somewhat fat, who had served in the regular Army medical service, well before the war began. He had a wife living in Baltimore. She knew that because he received occasional letters from her. He also had two sons; one in the Army, Surgeon McNelly said, vaguely, the other still in school, engaged also in learning the practice of medicine, intending to follow in his father's footsteps.

She found him in the main ward; a pair of big wall tents joined together, with both ends open for the fresh air that it admitted. Forty cots were sheltered within, twenty to a side and all of them occupied by patients. At least half of them were those who had been left behind by the ragged retreating Army of Northern Virginia, too sick or unconscious to be moved. Surgeon-Major McNelly sat on a folding camp stool next to the one nearest the open end, placidly puffing on his pipe. Suddenly concerned, Minnie touched the back of her hand on the patient's forehead and turned back the covers on him. This was a Confederate soldier with his left arm gone below the elbow, in a hurried surgery which had every indication of having gone in a bad way. The survivors of that crude Confederate hospital way-station had been found laid on fouled coverings, or none at all, in the dirty straw of the wrecked barn. They'd been put into clean cots and fresh dressings, in a properly-organized hospital. With relief, Minnie saw that the black horsehair stitches over the stump where a lower arm and hand had once been for this poor young man were no longer oozing; no blood, no evidence of putrid discharge. But still, that the doctor surgeon sat by the cot ...

"Doctor, is there something wrong with this patient?" Minnie demanded.

Surgeon-Major McNelly took out his pipe from his mouth and replied, "No. He is merely one of those whom I am glad to see that rough surgery and neglect didn't carry off, in spite of every invitation to do so. His appearance just reminds me of my son."

"Your son?" Minnie replaced the coverings on the unconscious patient, noting that his temperature was normal – the hectic flush of a high fever was gone. He was a tall young man, gaunt with deprivation and hardship, but almost too tall for the standard hospital cot. Fair lank hair fell across his pale forehead. There was a scar across one cheek and brow of that slack and unconscious face, pulling one eyebrow upwards – an otherwise pleasant and even handsome countenance. "The lad who is presently in school?"

"No," Surgeon-Major McNelly replied, with an indefinable expression of sorrow. "My older son. Edward. He would have been twenty-six this year. But we received word last year that he was killed during the Gettysburg fight. With the First

Marylanders in Steuart's brigade, attacking our positions on Culp Hill. He was a believer in the rights of states to determine their own, you see. He went with the Confederacy when it all began. His choice, although it grieved his mother and me no end, almost more than hearing that he had died in the slaughter there."

"I am so sorry," Minnie replied, shocked down to the soles of her feet in sensible boots. "I didn't know ... although I can see now..."

Surgeon-Major McNelly sighed. "The things that this war has done to us. Rending brother from brother, father from son – family against family, just as it was with your Richmond kinfolk. I had always believed – as I think that you also believe, Miss Vining – that the peculiar institution was a poisonous boil, one which might eventually have caused the death of the nation, just as such a boil would have proved fatal to one of our patients. That boil would have to be lanced and drained of pustulent matter, for healing to truly begin, however painful that process might be. I still wonder if we had any notion of how awful a slaughter that it turned out to be, and five years of it, from here to the Mississippi and beyond! Would we all have gone to war so eagerly, as if it were all a game for boys ... boys like this one, like Edward, my son? What difference might it have made, if any at all."

"All over a quarrel that should have been resolved sensibly." Minnie replied, stoutly.

Surgeon-Major McNelly shook his head, somberly. "No. The matter was not one which could have been resolved peaceably, not when there was no intention of either side to compromise on a single iota. Not after so many poisonous words said, so many vile accusations thrown at each other. Was it all worth it, I wonder? Will it have made any difference in the end? *Scarcely are they planted, scarcely sown, scarcely has their stem taken root in the earth, when He blows upon them and they wither, and the tempest carries them off like stubble..."*

Rather shaken, Minnie considered the quandary that Surgeon-Major McNelly suggested. Was a victory worth all the lives that the war had cost? Above all, the life of Richard Brewer, leaving Sophia a widow in deepest mourning, Richie and baby Sophie orphaned, the dead and dying in windrows of blue and gray, swept by a scythe of lead shot falling like hail had cut them down without mercy between one moment and the next. She recalled the dreadful night in the field hospital above the field of Shiloh, where General Grant had come, looking for a place to sleep out of the rain, while the cries of the wounded and dying haunted that bluff. No wonder that the general looked so sad, bearing the dreadful burden of knowing that his orders led to all that. There must be millions of bereaved widows and children. Dying was cruel and brief, for the most part, but for those who had loved their soldiers, the living in grief would go on for years.

She looked out beyond the trampled meadow, to a stream running close to the edge of the wood where the hospital laundry was set up. Great cauldrons had been brought out from the wagons, to hang over fires to soak soiled bedding and clothes in hot cleansing water, and when scoured clean, to be hung from lines strung between trees. The camp-followers and laundresses, the men cutting and hauling wood to feed the fires – all of them Negros – and all now free men and women. Free

336

to work where they wished, to marry whom they wanted, and now assured that their children, their husbands, wives, and parents would never be torn away from them, sold to another owner, never to see their loved ones again. She remembered what Miss Van Lew had said, after Pres Devereaux had successfully bid for the club-footed girl with her infant boy– what was her name? Lizetta, and the other little girl, who was all but white and now living the life of a respectable wife in Illinois, burying her slave past as if it had never happened. *'It is little enough, in the face of the numbers … but this little means everything in the world to Lizetta and Josephine.'*

"So much to us," Minnie replied at last, looking across at the laundresses hard at work. "But it will mean ever so much more to them."

Surgeon-Major McNelly grunted, cynically. "A great price we paid for their freedom," he said. "I hope they're grateful for it." He looked down at the sleeping patient, the Confederate soldier who reminded him of his dead son. "It's cost this lad his hand and half an arm. I wonder if he will grudge that price?"

Minnie looked at the tall, fair young soldier, now maimed for the rest of his natural life, be it a long or a short one. "Might he be one of your sons' comrades, do you think?"

"I doubt it," Surgeon-Major McNelly replied. "One of the other lads says they were about the last left of Hood's 4th Texas Infantry."

At that moment, there was a sudden murmuration in the camp, a murmur like a disturbed beehive, punctuated by shouts and grief-stricken wailing. Something was wrong, something had happened.

"He's dead!" a voice cried from the margin of the trampled road. "Father Abraham is dead! Murdered!" There was a crowd gathered by a lathered horse. A courier had come and gone, leaving consternation in his wake, spreading like ripples in a pond into which a heavy stone had been thrown. Surgeon-Major McNelly sprang to his feet, moving faster than one might have thought an older, fatter man capable of moving.

Minnie followed the surgeon, running in an attempt to keep up with him. The center of a weeping crowd of black and white, soldiers and civilians, women, and men, lamenting together. Surgeon-Major McNelly reached the crowd well ahead of Minnie, spoke to a sergeant with many stripes on his blue sleeve, a man with tears running down his grizzled cheeks. It was bad news, Minnie knew, as if she had been there. When she caught up, gasping from her own haste, Surgeon-Major McNelly turned toward her, his own countenance already grief-stricken.

"The president is dead," he said, plainly. "He was attacked two nights ago by an assassin and passed away the next morning."

Minnie gasped in horror, grief piercing her heart. This was even worse than when Richard Brewer died before Petersburg not even a year ago. Dear Mr. Lincoln, his bony countenance alive with humor that never quite erased the somber look in his eyes, who had been so kind to her soldier-patients at the College Hospital and sent a letter of condolence to Sophia after Richard died. And poor tragic Mrs. Lincoln, doubtless still grieving the death of hers and Mr. Lincoln's little boy. This new loss would have devastated her. Minnie hoped that Mrs.

338

Pomroy was still in Washington, and able to console the new widow.

It was almost too much to take in. Minnie went to the edge of the meadow where they had set up the camp laundry, and walked a little beyond, into the leafy green wood. She sat on a fallen log and thought about what she should do. It seemed that the war was now all but over. The Union was whole again, or nearly so, and the malign institution of slavery all but ended.

"Perhaps I should go to Spain, and see the Alhambra for myself," she said out loud, and a squirrel in the branches overhead chattered indignantly, annoyed at human intrusion. "Although maybe I ought to go to Richmond, first. I know Susan was angry at me, after that first lecture at the Freeman's meeting hall... but she and her family are kin. For Cousin Peter's sake, I should see if there is anything that I might do for them, since the rebels have suffered so. Surely, they will receive me if they are still living on Church Hill..."

Three weeks later, in the middle of May, Minnie was in Richmond. She and Lavina Dillard were on their way to Washington. Miss Dix had sent for them; the Armies of the East and West alike were going to parade in triumph down Pennsylvania Avenue, before the great dome with the statue of Freedom crowning it. Minnie and Lavina traveled in an Army ambulance, escorted by a small detachment of soldiers charged with seeing to their safe journey through a ruined city, under the authority of a young captain of cavalry.

Captain Dawson was an Ohio man. He frankly confessed that he didn't know anything about Richmond, but he was agreeable to spending a day there, once he had seen his soldiers to a safe billet in the nearby Union camp, squiring Minnie and Lavina Dillard to where she wished to go.

"Matters hereabouts were a bit lively when the Secesh folks pulled out," he confessed with a jaunty air, "But it's all settled down now. Even the President and his Missus came for a tour of the place, not even a week after the surrender."

Still, Minnie's heart sank upon seeing the ruins of the Tredegar works and the Armory, the rows of ruined buildings along the river bottom, jagged like broken teeth, and the pilings of the shattered Mayo Bridge, dropped like stones in the river. The air still smelled of smoke and ashes, although the fires which burned Richmond city had been quenched weeks since. They had already passed by places where the railroads had been torn up, iron rails heated over a bonfire and bent like horseshoes around the trunks of sturdy trees.

"It looks like pictures of the Roman forum, in medieval times," she observed to Lavina. The state capitol building still seemed to float serenely above, white classical columns seemingly untouched by the hand of war.

"The Rebs set fires themselves, before they fell back to Danville," Captain Dawson explained. "Exploded the powder magazines, the armory, the Tredegar machine-works, and burnt the bridges. The fire got away from them that were left ... but to good fortune, it didn't get all that far beyond the basin and the Bottom..."

"The Shockoe Bottom," Minnie elucidated.

"You know it, ma'am?" Captain Dawson was surprised, and Minnie shook her head.

"Knew of it as disreputable sort of place. My relatives lived on Church Hill. Her husband was the head of a girl's school nearby."

"I don't think the fire reached that far," Captain Dawson assured her. "But you should be prepared, Miss Vining ... there's been a lot of hard feeling 'bout us Yankees, hereabouts. I wouldn't let you go about town by yourself, it ain't at all safe for anyone in blue, or any who are friends of theirs. I'll wait in the street when you talk to your kinfolk ... if they are still in town."

"Thank you, Captain – but I am certain I will be safe enough," Minnie replied. Captain Dawson clicked his tongue, and slapped the reins over the back of the two horses drawing the ambulance in which they rode. Up the hill, away from the burned district, away from the odor of burning, and the deathly silence, broken only by the distant cawing of crows.

Minnie was afraid that she would not recognize Susan's house, or that it might have been destroyed in the fires that raged uncontrolled after the Confederate government abandoned the city. It had been so long since that amber-tinted summer of leisure in the lavish garden on Church Hill. Five years of war, culminating in defeat and occupation must have taken a toll on even the well-to-do neighborhoods of Richmond. This she observed, as they drove up Broad Street, the avenue which climbed the long hill towards the steeple of St. John's, pointing a slender white finger at the sky; the houses and mansions standing in their gardens, once immaculate and well-tended, now appeared worn and seedy with peeling or sun-faded paint, gardens unkempt and overgrown, fences ramshackle. Windows gaped, empty of glass. Once broken, a few windows had been repaired with brown paper at best, or boarded over entirely ... at worst, left unrepaired and open to the elements.

"When the Armory and the powder stores were fired," Captain Dawson explained, "The blast broke every window around."

Those houses which had once been painted or white-washed were peeling and decrepit. Brick walks and terraces once swept clean of every twig and leaf were littered with what looked like several seasons of moldering debris. A few trees seemed to have been damaged by that blast. But many more, even damaged by fire or the need to cut wood for fuel were out in new green leaves, and the four-petaled dogwood trees that Minnie remembered from her visit before were out in full bloom.

Susan and Ambrose's house appeared in better condition than most in the neighborhood. Curtains hung in the upper windows, a light breeze stirring them like gauzy ghosts. She could see the top of the summerhouse pavilion over the top of the hedge that surrounded the garden, a hedge now overgrown and spindly. Children played in the garden; she could hear their excited voices.

"Let me out here," Minnie asked. "I'll be but a moment, if no one is home."

She walked up to the front door, noting that at least the walkway was swept, but the paint on the door, and porch was faded and cracked. The brass doorknob and the knocker bore evidence of someone having polished it recently, which did give her some hope. She let the knocker fall several times, hearing the faint echo of it within the house. No one came to the door, though. Minnie didn't want to leave without at least speaking to someone in the house. She considered leaving a note, but she could hear the voices of children, children playing in the garden. There must be someone in the house.

She walked around the front of the house, towards the gate into the garden, the garden with the summerhouse, and the green clipped lawn, where Susan and her daughters had met with friends. Where Pres Devereaux had proposed to her. Her skirts brushed through deep grass, grown tall and lank. But yes, there were children in the garden, three girls in short gowns of calico much mended and faded through washing. The girls sat on the steps to the summerhouse, playing with dolls while a pair of little boys, romped with a ball. Two women sat in the summerhouse in the patchy shade: a white woman with a basket of mending at her side, and a Negro woman shelling spring peas.

As Minnie hesitated at the garden gate, the white woman raised her eyes from her mending, and looked straight at her. She looked like a very much younger version of Susan. It took Minnie a long moment before she recognized Charlotte, Charlotte who had married Pres Devereaux; the girl who had been all of sixteen and begged Minnie to teach her how to play chess and divert the man who was going to be her husband. The Negro woman was Hepzibah, Susan's housekeeper from that time before the war. Minnie opened her mouth to call to them both. At that moment, Charlotte looked up and saw Minnie; looked directly at her for a long moment, standing hesitant by the garden gate. Charlotte's face turned venomously angry, contemptuous. She rose from her seat, said something to Hepzibah, and called to the children.

"Go into the house!" Charlotte commanded. "This moment!" Charlotte came down the two steps of the summerhouse, shooing the children before her, without another word or glance at Minnie. Minnie saw that Charlotte's stomach bulged under the apron tied over her faded calico dress with the hem turned up; she was hugely pregnant. In the space of a moment, women and children vanished into the house, the door slamming behind them, as if in emphasis. Minnie stood there, momentarily shocked. *No,* she told herself. *I should have expected a reception like this.* No need to remain; she might as well resume her journey towards Washington. Disturbed and saddened, she retraced her steps towards the front of the house and the street where Captain Dawson waited.

A great pity. I would like to have known how Susan's family all fared in the war. I suppose I can put some flowers on Cousin Peter's grave. I expect that he's buried at St. John's. If we go to the church, perhaps we can find someone to tell us which is his grave.

"Miz Minnie!" Someone called her name; Hepzibah, pulling a light shawl around her elbows, as she quietly closed the front door after herself. "I thought it might be you, come to see Miz Susan!" Hepzibah's dark face was alight with pleasure, but she kept her voice low, and drew Minnie out towards the street, beyond the hearing of anyone inside the house.

"I thought that I might see how the family all fared," Minnie replied. "Since Miss Susan's father was so very dear to us in Boston. I know that he would have wanted me to do so, even with all that happened between us. The war ... and everything before."

"Oh, Miz Minnie," Hepzibah's pleasure dimmed. "I know dat. But they won't see you. Miz Susan, Miz Lydia, Miz Charlotte ... none of them. Miz Charlotte, she was so angry when she saw you! She'll be angry that I came after, spoke to you, but I don't care none. You were always civil, respectful ... you and Miz Annabelle, both."

"What can you tell me of how they all fared," Minnie asked. "That is the reason that I came to Richmond. What can you tell me?"

Hepzibah was shaking her head, sadly. "Nothing much of good, Miz Minnie. All them menfolk in the household, they all done volunteered for the war. Mr. Ambrose took sick after Malvern Hill, two year gone it is now. He's dying. Miz Susan, she's none too well herself, and they all be as poor as dirt, what with the school closing an' Tredegar's burnt an' gone. Young Mr. Chaffin who married Miz Lydia, his place all burnt to the groun', all the hands done run off when Gen'ral Sherman came through last year. Young Mr. Chaffin got killed in the first year o' the fighting, an' her oldest boy died in camp ... cholera, they told her. Miz Lydia, she came home with her younger chirren, as she had no other place to go. Miz Amy's husband got hisself killed in Kentucky with Morgan, they told her. Cavalryman, he wuz. Miz Amy thought the sun rose an' set on his word. She ain't been herself, since. Shuts herself in her room, most days." Hepzibah shook her head in pity. "Poor chile; all the life drained right out of her, when she heard."

"What of Mr. Devereaux, Miss Charlotte's husband?"

"Him?" Hepzibah folded her arms. "He was one o' dem blockade-runners out of Wilmington, being that his fambly was in the shipping trade. He was last here with Miz Charlotte, 'round about las' August. I recollect, as it was Miss Charlotte's birthday, an' he told her he wuz gonna bring her a silk shawl from Paris, an' he did, too. She ain't heard a word in months. Rumor be that his ship was sunk by Federals, tryin' to sneak into Nassau, but no one heard anything definite. Miz Charlotte, she tells the chillum that he's away; China 'r Indee, somewhere in them foreign parts. An' I'se the only one of Miz Susan an' Mr. Ambrose' people left, me an' my daughter Reeny, to take care o' the house an' Mr. Ambrose an' all." Hepzibah briefly looked tired, and every year of her age. "Ain't none o' the folk stayed – Miz Susan, she cain't pay no wages. Sampson an' everyone else, they would of stayed, if they was paid. Miz Susan, Mr. Ambrose – they are good folk. High-class folk."

"You remain, though," Minnie pointed out, too shaken by Hepzibah's report to be anything but frank. "Even if you aren't paid. You know, you don't have to stay. You aren't slaves any longer. You can go where you want, work for what your work is worth!"

Hepzibah's shoulders squared, and she looked proudly at Minnie.

"I know 'dat, Miz Minnie. But Miz Susan an' all – they are my folk! I cain't walk away an' leave them, not in the sad way they are now. No more than you could walk away from your Miz Annabelle, were she sick an' poor. I'll be all right." She lowered her voice, as if conspiring. "I got me some money saved – gold, an' good Union greenback money from before. Reeny an' me, we'll be all right." Hepzibah looked over her shoulder at the house – someone calling her name from within. "I gotta go, Miz Minnie. You gwine talk to Miz Lizzie, Miz Lizzie Van Lew. You recollect her? Jus' aroun' de corner, in Grace Street, big fancy house on the corner. You talk to Miz Lizze, she tell you all about what you wanna know. You cain't miss dat Van Lew house," Hepzibah added, over her shoulder. "Gotta big ol' Union flag hangin' over de door." The front door of the Edmunds house closed on her back, leaving Minnie considerably baffled.

"What did they tell you?" Lavina was all a twitter with curiosity when Minnie returned to the waiting party. "I saw you talking for the longest time with that darkie woman! Did she tell you about your kin?"

"She did, and all of it sad," Minnie felt heartsick. "They won't receive me, and I honestly cannot blame them. All their menfolk are dead – or dying, or missing. I expect it's because of the war, and they blame my abolitionist sympathies for having a part in causing it."

Lavina made a wordless, indistinct sound of sympathy, and Minnie continued. "Their old housekeeper, Hepzibah – that was Hepzibah that I was talking with. She said I should speak with Miss Van Lew, whom I was acquainted with, once. She and her mother were in sympathy with the abolitionist cause; very rich and respectable, so no one held it against them. The Van Lew family lived just around this corner – Grace Street. I think she will receive my card, for the sympathies that we shared, once."

"Likely Miss Van Lew will," Captain Dawson had been listening with interest to this exchange. "For General Grant paid her a visit and she served him tea – she was always loyal for the Union and many of our folk held in Libby Prison sang praises to her, for aiding them in their miserable captivity."

"I am not surprised, knowing how the general values loyalty," Minnie remarked, as Captain Dawson slapped the reins on the backs of his horse team. The captain sent her a sideways look.

"Camp rumor has it that she was more than just loyal," he said. "That she was a spy, and regularly sent messages to our side, reporting on what the Secessionists were up to at the highest level."

"That was ..." Minnie shuddered, suddenly chilled with horror. "Very dangerous for her! She might have been shot! They can do that to spies!"

"Well," Captain Dawson looked thoughtful. "I suspect that Southern chivalry regarding a woman from a respectable family had a lot to do with her getting away with it all this time. To their mind, a silly little maiden lady couldn't possibly be doing anything so unladylike as to be a dirty old spy."

"Of course, that was the case," Lizzie Van Lew agreed serenely, some twenty minutes later when Minnie asked. "Everyone was quite accustomed to mine and Mama's eccentricities. We did collect some very dark looks, and many of our neighbors were quite indignant when we visited the prisoners in that awful Libby place, but I don't think anyone ever suspected for an instant that I was sending coded messages across the lines."

"That was very fortunate for you," Minnie replied.

She should have expected that, recalling Miss Van Lew's steely resolve in the matter of that long-ago visit to the Shockoe Bottom slave markets. Of course Lizzie Van Lew would risk so much to aid the Union, in the face of all danger.

Accompanied by Lavina and Captain Dawson, Minnie had presented her calling card at the front door of the Van Lew mansion. Just as Hepzibah had said, a Union flag hung over the front door, the red, white, and blue folds stirring in the fitful spring breeze. A Negro maid in a neat black dress with an apron tied over it answered the door.

"Miss Vining, and some friends, to see Miss Van Lew," Minnie presented her card to the maid, just as a familiar voice from within the house called,

"Who is it, Mary?"

Upon the answer, Miss Van New appeared, holding out both her hands, and smiling warmly. "My dear Miss Vining! Do come in! Would you like some tea and refreshments? I have thought so much about you since we last met!"

"And I often thought of you," Minnie replied, although she hadn't, really. She introduced Captain Dawson and Lavina Dillard, as Lizzie Van Lew led them all to the parlor, and saw them settled in comfortable chairs. She was a little changed from the woman Minnie had met in Susan's parlor. Her hair was paler, fading from the yellow that it had been, and now drawn severely back from a face in which her beak of a nose was even more prominent.

"I have not received so many visitors, of late," Lizzie explained, with a touch of wry humor. "This house is no longer held to be respectable among Richmond society, you see."

"But some very important ones from our side," Captain Dawson remarked, and Lizzie smiled.

"But of course! I even sent General Grant flowers from my garden, on occasion. We were quite in the way of old friends, even before he came calling. There wasn't a development in Mr. Davis's government that I wasn't able to find out about, through my ring of informants. There were so many free men and women who owed my family a debt of gratitude! Gathering information was a simple matter," she added, with a touch of pride.

"You were very brave, Miss Van Lew," Lavina was frank in her admiration, and Lizzie brushed it off, as if it were nothing.

"It was all that I could do for the Union," she replied. At that moment, Mary appeared with a tray, and set it down on a low table. Miss Van Lew dismissed her with a nod and began pouring tea. Conversation turned polite and general for some minutes; Lavina and Captain Dawson waxed effusively in their gratitude for the refreshment and hospitality. After refusing another slice of dark plum cake, Minnie broached the matter of the Edmons family.

"I wanted to pay a visit and assure myself that they had not suffered more than anyone else – and if they had, if I could do something for them," she explained. "We were once fond friends, until the matter of slavery came between us ... Mrs. Edmonds refused communication with me. When the war began, we were cut off entirely. They would not receive me today," Minnie confessed. "And I know they are suffering terrible hardships now. Mrs. Edmond's housekeeper, Hepzibah, spoke with me, though. Mr. Edmonds is near to death; the family is impoverished. They were once dear to me, and I would not see them suffer so much more than they have already. If I leave you with some money, can you discreetly convey it to Hepzibah? She still has charge of the household, and she has always been trusted without question. I believe that Hepzibah would be able make use of funds to better their situation without revealing that they came from me."

It sounded like such a silly plan, a child's stratagem, but Lizzie nodded thoughtfully. "I think that it can be done, Miss Vining. Mary is friends with Hepzibah, and I trust her implicitly. It speaks well that you should offer Christian aid to folk who have treated you so badly. I would do it for no other family in Richmond and only because it is you who ask."

"They are kin," Minnie replied, "And blood is thicker than water." Her heart still ached for Susan and her daughters, knowing that tragedy and uncertainty had struck such a terrible blow. Perhaps the passage of time would ease the sense of loss and erase that terrible anger that she had seen on Charlotte's face. Maybe. In any case, Minnie knew that she could sleep at night, by stealthily sending money to support Susan's household and grandchildren.

"There are so many!" Lolly Bard exclaimed, as she, Minnie and Lavina watched the Grand Review from a window of the Willard Hotel. Twenty abreast marched the Army of the West, a river, a veritable torrent of blue, passing along Pennsylvania Avenue. The army from the east had marched the day before – today it was the turn of Sherman, and the men who had taken Vicksburg, Chattanooga, New Orleans, and Atlanta. The streets were hung with banners in the patriotic colors, and flower arches – now and again a black crepe garland for mourning the slain Abraham Lincoln. It seemed as if the music played by the various military bands never stopped – nor did the cheering from spectators as the soldiers marched past, so perfectly in step that each of a thousand marching feet struck the ground as one. The sidewalks along Pennsylvania avenue were thick with standing spectators – every window and roof-edge likewise, waving small flags, and cheering until they were hoarse. Daring boys had climbed high into the branches of trees, and perched on lampposts, to watch the triumph. Spectators had been pouring into Washington for days, until every hotel and boarding house was crammed to bursting. Even the owners of private houses were renting out their parlors, porches, and spare bedrooms. Minnie counted herself fortunate that Lolly Bard had shared the hospitality of her own lodgings, and that another friend had secured a place to view the parade from a window at the Willard. In all the history of the Republic, in peace and war, there had never been an event like this. It even made the inauguration of presidents seem staid and tame. Now the noise of the crowd sounded to Minnie like the roar of the surf at the seaside.

"They do look rather ragged, dear," Lolly Bard commented. "It's a pity that they couldn't have been supplied with something to better show them off."

That was true. Many of the marching soldiers in blue wore coats and trousers that were faded, almost ragged, patched and repaired, stained with the battle smoke and mud from four years of hard campaigning. They were rough and ragged, many with beards and uncut hair, some even without hats. But each man had a blanket-roll slung over his right shoulder – and their weapons and every bit of metal and leather about their person was polished until it gleamed. The bayonets affixed to their long rifles shone like splinters of ice in the fitful sunshine. They strode along, every one of them as if they owned the world.

"I thought so, too," Minnie replied. "And I said so, when I encountered Sgt. Hand ... he was the sergeant who aided Mary Bickerdyke and I when we first came to Cairo ... he told me that the boys all thought that if their uniforms were good enough to wear to Washington, they were good enough to parade in. 'We're the fighting Army,' he said, 'no' a bunch o' candy-box mannikins.' He also told me that General Sherman thought that the good folk of the east should see his regiments on the march just as the Rebels saw them … bummers, contrabands, and all."

The appreciative roar of the crowd crashed like a heavy wave, as another brigade appeared, led by their mounted officers … and a single woman, a woman in a plain calico dress and unadorned bonnet, her back as straight as a cavalry-trooper.

"There she is," Minnie leaned a little farther out of the tall window. "Mary – Mrs. Bickerdyke. Sgt. Hand told me that General Sherman wished to honor her most particularly – that she should be part of the review, as she did so much to aid his soldiers. She didn't want to, but the General insisted, saying there was no higher honor that he could award her."

"All of you nurses should have been honored likewise!" Lolly was firm in that insistence.

"The gratitude of our soldier boys was thanks enough for me," Minnie replied. "And now that the war is done … they'll all be mustered out. They may all go home, home to their families, to their farms and businesses."

Left unsaid was Minnie's thought; if there still was a home for them and if, having once seen the elephant, they could pick up their old life again, return to the routine of an ordinary life and work. The dead would still lie buried in their graves, their mothers, fathers, and wives, like Sophia Brewer, would go on grieving them. But after today, there would be no more dying in in job-lots in fields and trenches, men in blue and grey alike, struck down in windrows like a scythe sweeping through a stand of wheat. Now was the time to mourn the dead and meditate upon what the great victory had cost. *Would the families and once-friends who had been wrenched apart over the question of union and slavery, ever be able to reconcile, once the banners and regimental colors were put away, to fade and accumulate dust?*

The music of the brigade's band faded with distance; the cadence of marching feet and the joyful roar of the crowd below, opposite, and above filled the avenue.

"And will we go home, likewise?" Lolly asked. "Sit in our parlors, receive callers and do needlework?"

It was an unexpectedly pertinent question although Minnie had long known Lolly to be strangely perceptive. And in that moment, Minnie came to a decision.

"Oh, no – I could never do that. Never really wanted a conventional existence and now I know that I am not fit for such. My father saw to that, indeed he did. I'll take up some other cause, I think. Aid for crippled soldiers, perhaps ... maybe greater rights for women, or secure sanctuaries for poor orphans. I'll know it when I am called. But for now, I'd like to rest for a bit. And when I am not so tired, I think I will go traveling. I've always wanted to see the glories of Europe. I have long dreamed of seeing the Alhambra, in Spain, about which Mr. Irving wrote so magically. Rome for certain, and the wonders of the Holy Land. I had always longed to see those places. And now I can! Lolly, would you like to come with me, as my companion? You are so very good at making arrangements for travel when I was on the lecture tours! Do you think that your sons can spare you?"

Lolly giggled, almost girlishly.

"Their wives certainly will say so!" she answered. "Likely they will help me pack my trunks."

"Then let us make plans," Minnie replied.

And when I am rested, and I have refreshed my soul by walking in those places that I have only dreamed of ... then I will return and see what there is yet to be done.

Notes

Like the story told in my previous series of books, *The Adelsverein Trilogy,* a lot of the background to this story was new to me. I wasn't raised in the South, and the ancestors of my one American-born grandparent was a fire-eating abolitionist. Frankly, all I knew about the chattel slavery in the South was what there was contained in generalist history books pertaining to the Civil War and articles in my mothers' issues of *American Heritage.* There was nothing much in my store of knowledge about the nuts and bolts of actual practice, as it was in the time in which the first half of this book takes place, so a deep dive into contemporary accounts of travels in the South were required.

Richmond, Virginia, was the second-largest wholesale and retail market in the South: I have tried to describe what Minnie would have seen and experienced in that visit to Shockoe Bottom and create conversations that she would have had with Southerners like Pres Devereaux and Levi Chaffin, Susan Edmonds and with slaves like Hepzibah – all of whom would in real life in that period would have said something like the dialog which I wrote for them. There is a word for readers who will assume that such words are my own thoughts on the matter of chattel slavery, as they are very much counter to contemporary mores. That word is "idiot." That term also extends to writers who bolt conventional contemporary attitudes onto characters set in another place and time. It is a disservice to readers who honestly want to explore other places, times, and situations, and a grim transgression against the art of building a story, in that it basically puts 21st century characters in unconvincing costumes.

Details are taken from contemporary accounts. Minnie would not have witnessed a slave auction first-hand; so far, all the accounts and pictures that I have found have only men attending the auctions. For most Southerners, a slave was a luxury good. A first-rate young field hand was worth $1,500-2,000; something on the order of $25,000 to $30,000 in today's dollars. A slave trained in a particular skill might command an even higher price.

The escape by rail travel of Miss Bonnie Beauchamp and her servant/husband was based on a similar occurrence; that of William and Ellen Craft from Macon, Georgia in 1848. Ellen Craft, who appeared sufficiently white to pass as such, dressed in male clothing, bandages, and spectacles, claiming that injuries prevented her from signing hotel registries and deafness as an excuse to not chat with fellow passengers. They posed a wealthy young planter and his manservant, and gained safety in Philadelphia, Boston and eventually England, after many close calls and fraught moments.

Boston was practically the epicenter of the American abolitionist movement, a movement which roiled the political world in the U.S. for more than two decades, finally culminating in open war. Whether it was slavery, or economics which served as the touchpaper to war is a matter still disputed by historians, but to the real-life contemporaries of Minne Vining, there was no question at all: slavery was the issue.

The existing pre-Civil War US Army was a small one as national armies of the times counted, with a correspondingly tiny medical corp. All of that went out the window when the fighting began. Congress authorized the creation of the Sanitary Commission in June, 1861. The Sanitary Commission served the Union Army much as the combined military medical commands, the Morale, Recreation and Welfare offices and the Red Cross serve our armed forces today.

Although the national leadership of the Commission at the upper levels were male, women made up an extraordinarily large number of mid-level workers, fund-raisers, administrators, nurses, and general support personnel. Being also proud of their contribution, many of those women contributed memoirs written after the war. Those accounts make for stirring reading and I have depended on several of them, especially a memoir left by Rebecca Pomroy to fill out Minnie's experiences. The account of Minnie's daily routine at the Columbia College Hospital was taken from Mrs. Pomroy's memoir. There was a lot of overlap between abolitionists, temperance activists and women's rights advocates during that period. Many of the best-known women volunteers were active on all three fronts, as well as being friends with each other. Minnie's friend, Mary Ashton Livermore was one in real life. She also served as reporter and editor for a newspaper which her Universalist minister husband owned.

As related, Mary Jane Bickerdyke was an early volunteer nurse in the western theater. Perhaps we do not realize today how much of a woman's domestic duties then involved caring for the sick and invalid, before sanitation, sterile surgery, and vaccination for common childhood diseases. Both Mary Bickerdyke and Rebecca Pomroy had cared for invalid husbands for years; they and other volunteer nurses had already done a lot of practical nursing, without the benefit of formal medical training. General Grant endorsed her presence and actions as Union forces advanced down the Mississippi. It was the peppery-tempered General Sherman who responded one of his subordinates complaining about her, demanding that he do something about that 'damned bossy woman' by saying, *"I can't – she ranks me."* Mary Bickerdyke was, for all intents and purposes, the head of the Western Army's medical command. She participated in Grand Review of the Armies in Washington, DC, at General Sherman's express request.

Mary Jane Safford, the nurse at the Cairo Army hospital when Mrs. Bickerdyke and Minnie arrived, was a real person also – who later studied medicine herself and became a one of the very first female gynecologists to practice in the United States, and a professor of gynecology at the Boston University School of Medicine.

Elizabeth Van Lew of Richmond, Virginia, was indeed a spy for the Union all throughout the war, and upon defeat of the Confederacy, was the first in Richmond to hang the US flag from her house. It has been claimed that one member of her spy ring, Mary Elizabeth Bowser, a former slave freed by her family, was placed in the household of Confederate President Jefferson Davis. Her spying and philanthropic activities eventually drained her family fortune, and in later life she was supported by the families of former POWs held in Libby Prison during the war.

The character of Colonel Levi Chaffin is based on the experience of General George Henry Thomas, known as "The Rock of Chickamauga" – born in Virginia to a plantation-owning, slave-holding family, but married to a woman from upstate New York. Like Grant and Sherman, he was a graduate of West Point and a veteran of the Mexican War ... and he broke with his family in remaining with the Union. His family never forgave him for that disloyalty to his native state. They burned all of his letters, never mentioned his name again, and did not attend his funeral when he died prematurely of a stroke, barely five years after the end of the war. A modest and competent man, he may have been the only Civil War general on either side who never wrote a post-war memoir and burned his private papers.

Finally – this account of the experiences of a 19th century American woman who was not all that unusual as an activist and campaigner for all kinds of causes – fills in or provides a background to certain stories and characters in my other historical novels. Minnie's deceased younger brother Horace, husband to her dear friend Annabelle, is the bigamous husband of Margaret Becker, of *Daughter of Texas* and *Deep In the Heart*. Unknown to Minnie, the unconscious Confederate soldier in her field hospital in the final chapter is Horace Vining's youngest son, Peter Vining. In the opening chapter of *Adelsverein: The Harvesting*, Peter Vining returns alone and on foot to his family home in Texas, after the defeat of the Confederacy, and tries to figure out a new life for himself. An octogenarian Minnie herself appears in the first chapters of *Sunset and Steel Rails*, belatedly providing her grandniece, Sophie Brewer, with the means of escaping Boston and the machinations of her lamentably sociopathic brother. And finally, Minnie's experiences after the battle at Shiloh are briefly referred to in *My Dear Cousin*, with Sophie Brewer's granddaughter Vennie Stoneman as an Army nurse in WWII.